SPLENDOR OF THE DAWN

BHARAT M ROCHLIN

HERE & NOW DREAM PUBLISHING.

TIRUVANNAMALAI, INDIA

This Edition Published in India by
Here And Now Dream Publishing.
Tiruvannamalai, India
www.ombharat.com

Cover Design By Dream Designs
Cover Illustration By Bharat
Designed And Typeset By Dream Designs
India Library Cataloguing in Publication data available
Library Of Congress Cataloguing in Publication data
Available

ISBN 978-81-906273-3-7

To that, which cannot be touched

PART ONE

Pronouncation of Names

Kareae -   Ka-ray
Fritaye -   Fra-tay
Janeac -   Jan-noc
Zolade -   Zo-la-de
Susea   -   Su-see-a

PROLOGUE

I looked out from the edge of a rock cliff into the soft morning mist, and dove quickly into the river Goma, surrendering wholly within its swift turbulent currents. The river carried me in its grip until my arms thrashed out and my legs kicked back to take charge and I splashed to the surface. The moment filled me with timeless wonder.

My name is Kareae. I am without an I. It has always been that way.

On the quay in the distance, Hanu, Kanparu Temple's head guard, was urgently waving for me to return.

"Kareae," he called out when I swam closer, "come, your father has summoned you."

Hanu with his strong arms helped me easily out of the water and handed me a towel.

"Thank you," I smiled, giving him the Raian hug of briefly touching foreheads.

"Yes, it is time," I continued, "I've been feeling it all morning. Walk with me for awhile up to my quarters and after my meeting I will look for you at the front gate."

Hanu silently agreed with a nod of head and we began our walk through the vast temple complex.

Kanparu was commonly known as the Temple of Love. Every Raian in their time came for blessings for their marriage and children. Nevertheless, Kanparu was much more than that. It was the foremost center of learning and exploration into Higher Consciousness, and was the spiritual heart of the entire kingdom. At any one time, over 500 monks lived there and were engaged into discovering the higher mysteries.

Hanu and I passed by many orchards and fields full of crops to reach the main areas where the numerous buildings, halls, temples and living quarters were located.

At the center square, Hanu left to resume his post and I returned to my quarters behind the main temple, which was adjacent to where my parents, the High Priest Ashara and the High Priestess Leila lived.

I was just finishing dressing when there was a knock on my door. My beautiful and serene mother - the powerful high priestess, Leila, entered accompanied not only by the scent of her perfume but also by the overwhelming fragrance of her pure heart and mind. Indeed, Raians from every corner of the kingdom flocked to experience her divine presence.

"Kareae," she said after sitting on a sofa, "lets us go to the meeting together. But first, I want to simply be with you in this moment before we discuss and decide what to do. I don't think our lives will be the same after today."

Giving Leila a formal bow I sat next to her and replied, "Yes, I was just discussing with Hanu that I felt a shift in the collective energy field, almost deliberately by some conscious effort. Have you had any insight into what this might be?"

The high priestess frowned with a look of concern.

"We may know and that is why your father has called a meeting. I want to give you a blessing now before the meeting and your soon final initiation into masterhood. Come here my son."

I stood and kneeled before her placing my head on her lap. In the silence of the moment, when she placed her hands on my head, I felt a rush of power entering within me and I dissolved in blissful unity with all the forces my mother commanded.

After some moments my mother said almost with tears in her eyes, "Yes, my son, you are ready, this I know. After your final initiation, I will no longer consider you my son but a fully initiated Master. Now come, let us go and not keep your father waiting much longer."

*****

We found Ashara sitting with some students by the lotus pond. He looked up with warmth in his eyes when we approached. He dismissed his students and he bade us to follow him back to his study.

My father was the astute high priest of the entire Rai kingdom in name and form, but as well, in his mastery of the powers that ruled the world and the powers of the mysteries. To achieve this virtuosity both my mother and father surrendered their personal identities to the greater forces that controlled their destinies. Soon it will be my turn, I thought.

Romdev, that ancient giant of man who was a dear friend and teacher to both my parents and me, was sitting in the study examining a small exquisite statue of a female deity. "Beautiful," he commented, "I've never seen such a style before."

"Yes, isn't it," Ashara reflected as he approached, "It comes from Pi. A gift from one of our pupils."

Ashara's study reflected the intelligence and power of the man. The walls aligned with many bookcases, were filled with ancient and modern tomes on all subjects. The room itself was exquisitely styled with artistic crafted pieces of furniture and a huge array of artworks. Within this, it was a comfortable room catering to the needs and comfort of whomever used it.

A novice monk served refreshments and discreetly left. Once everyone was settled Ashara began, "I called you together today at Romdev's urgent request. He recently uncovered what seems to be an attempt to permanently alter the collective energy field matrix. Perhaps you have felt that shift today?"

Leila and I both nodded in agreement.

"Romdev, why don't you tell us what you found."

Romdev stood up and gravely moved to the center of the study wrapped in his famous blanket and shining shaved head. His massive body was almost filling the room.

"I didn't think it was possible," he began, 'but someone has learned to penetrate the core of the energy matrix and today was successful to shift it a small degree. Fortunately, the force of the penetration was weak and did not cause damage. I felt that it was only a test probe but I have serious concerns about what might come."

"Did you attempt to deflect the penetration, Romdev?" I asked.

"I tried Kareae, but there was nothing I could do to prevent it. I sensed that even if we tried to block it collectively, it would not be effective. It seems that the level of awareness of the penetrator is beyond the scope of our powers and there is nothing we can do to prevent it."

Romdev continued, "I feel that the only person who could accomplish such feat is Kalo."

"What!" exclaimed Ashara, standing up, "Kalo disappeared at the time my grandfather was high priest. How is it possible?"

"Yes, he disappeared then but was not gone." Romdev answered. "Once in a very long while I had a subtle awareness of his presence."

"I remember hearing about Kalo as a child but I thought it was just a children's story." I said. "He was experimenting with inter-dimensional travel or something like that."

"Yes, that's right, and he was making great progress until he began to change progressively after each journey." Romdev replied. "At first, we hardly noticed but then it became obvious that Kalo was becoming increasingly angry and antisocial. He became very critical of the policies of Kanparu to raise human consciousness. Finally we had to restrain him but we were not successful. Shortly, he escaped into another dimension and we have never been able to locate him even with collective probing. It is too bad because Kalo was such a gifted person. He was in training to become a high priest together with your great grandfather Alo."

Leila, who had been sitting silently during the discussion asked Romdev, "What is it, Romdev, that you think Kalo can bring about?"

Romdev turned to Leila in a most solemn fashion. "Having the ability to manipulate the matrix, Kalo will be able to reprogram all the mental and emotional fields. His wish will become our wish. His hope will become our hope. Indeed, most likely we would not even notice a difference."

"In the end he will permanently subjugate the entire Rai Kingdom if not the planet to his own will."

We sat with the seriousness of the implications of his statement; the air seemed heavy and thick, the world disappearing in our reflections.

Finally Romdev said, "Let us meet tonight when the moon is at its high point in the main temple sanctuary and open our minds together. I have an idea that might work but before I tell you about it, I need to test it out and see if there is any possibility."

"Good," Ashara said standing and signaling for his attendant, "I will go now and inform the senior monks to remain focused during our experiment. This is certainly crucial news and the greatest threat our kingdom has ever received. We must do everything possible to prevent it."

*****

In the moonlight, my body seemed almost as translucent as my mind. Thoughts and images floated pass me like a raft floating on the sea. From where I could observe them seemed like a huge distance and yet, I was focused perfectly on whatever was happening around me, completely grounded in the present moment.

My parents were waiting at the front entrance of the main temple with hands joined facing each other. Even though they were standing separately, I had difficulty to discern where one body began and the other ended.

"Kareae," Ashara said when I approached, "Romdev is inside preparing the altar. He will call us in when the moon is at its zenith."

We stood in silent communion until we heard the bell signaling us to enter. Within the candlelit and incense filled temple, we walked through the structural maze starting clockwise from the outer perimeter until we reached the center inner sanctum.

Romdev instructed Ashara to sit across from him with Leila on his right and myself on his left side.

At the sound of the next bell, we opened our minds together. I felt myself rising upwards out of the body, then merging and mixing into each other as it normally happened when we opened our minds together. In the past, I always retained a sense of myself within the merging. However, this time, after I felt an unusual jolt of energy, we completely dissolved into a new entity of consciousness without a trace left of my former self. I cannot say how long we remained like this.

At first, my sense of self seemed very far away like a distant point on the horizon but slowly it became nearer and stronger until we all could let go and enter into our individual bodies once again.

"Yes, it is possible," Romdev proclaimed after we recovered and returned to the Ashara's study. After a moment of reflection again gazing at the small female statue he said, "Yes, I think we can do it and it's probably the only solution. We need to raise the consciousness of the entire kingdom to a new level where Kalo's powers will be ineffective. Unless we can achieve this, we will be powerless to stop him. Tonight was the first time I could successfully merge our individual consciousness into a collective consciousness. I tried it before unsuccessfully, as you know Leila and Ashara, but never with Kareae. I feel he is pivotal in facilitating this merging. Kareae, without you it cannot be done. But, I must warn you that you will be at great risk, more so than all of us if Kalo gets wind of your powers."

All eyes turned to me. I stood and approached Romdev placing a hand on his shoulder. "My teacher, I am ready to do whatever is necessary. I am not concerned about the risk. What is your plan?"

"My plan," Romdev sighed, " is a long shot. We need to raise the consciousness of the entire realm. I do not know if it is possible yet. I would say in fifty years as the population evolves, it would be conceivable but now... I am not sure. Our only chance is to accelerate the evolution of the kingdom. We would need to have around five percent of the population at the new level before we could cross the threshold for the entire kingdom. Right now, I think it is safe to say that about two percent of the population is living at this level. So, we need to enlighten around 3,000 people within two years. That's a very arduous task."

"Kareae, I want to move up your final initiation for the next new moon. That is if your parents agree."

"Yes, Kareae is ready," Leila injected. I checked him before we came here tonight."

Ashara added in, " I still need to do some additional work with Kareae but yes, I think we can be ready by that time."

"Very good, and afterwards we can send Kareae to make his worldly quest as we have all done except this time with a very special purpose," Romdev replied.

*****

I wrapped my cloak tightly around me in the cool night air. All was quiet, silent, just before the first signs of the dawn's light that would be calling upon the birds to announce its coming. The majestic ancient built arch that stood at the front gate reached out to remind me of the highest that man could achieve.

Hanu was coming out of the guardhouse when I arrived. Looking at him, I could only see power. What he actually looked like seemed inconsequential. He was not tall or short, big or small but every part of him emanated strength and intelligence.

"Come Kareae, lets sit by river and watch the sunrise. It has been a busy night; Romdev and your father have been very active calling impromptu meetings with the senior and the more advanced monks. Even your mother has been unusually joining the groups speaking privately to individuals. I can't remember a night so high and poignant - Leila's presence seemed to fill the room with inexhaustible radiance."

At the cliff's edge with the naked sun just above the horizon Hanu shared, "Romdev opened his mind to me earlier. It's hard to believe that one man could have such power over us. But seeing his earnestness, I know it must be true. I could sense when Romdev opened his mind that he was not hopeful that we could achieve our goal."

"Hanu, what do you know of Kalo?"

"Not much really, I was a small boy at that time. I

do remember he always wore a long black cloak with a large red dragon embroidered on the breast. The same dragon relief that is carved into the arch that you always bothered me about when you were younger."

"Ah Hanu, don't remind me that you still have not told me what the dragon means and I know you know..."

Hanu laughed but then said in a low tone, "In your time of need, the meaning of the dragon will be revealed to you. All I can say and you know this, is that the arch and the dragon are ancient remnants from the last civilization before the great wars."

"Okay, I surrender to your mysteries," I said lightly as I stood up and started to disrobe. With laughter in my eyes, I walked to the edge and dove into the Goma.

Soon to follow, Hanu jumped out like the warrior he was and together we swam the width and breath of the river in abandoned ease.

Chapter 1

THE JOURNEY BEGINS

(Fritaye speaking)

Every morning for years I, known as Fritaye, enjoyed sitting near the well in the courtyard polishing the goblets for my restaurant. It gave me time to reflect about my family and the business of the inn. With my breath still slightly visible from the chill of the spring dawn, I watched a young traveler walk in from the King's Road. As the inn was set half a league from the thoroughfare in quiet surroundings, I had the opportunity to observe him. Hmm, something is different about this man, I reflected as the traveler approached. He is dressed well like a merchant but his youth and demeanor suggest something else.

The bright and graceful traveler entered the courtyard and stopped near the well to shake the dust off his clothes. He sang out to me, "Dear sir, please draw me some water to quench my thirst, and I will satisfy your curiosity about me."

I was a little startled by the traveler's familiarity, as

if he knew me. I answered, standing up with a hand on my stiff back, "Yes sir, I am more than happy to bring you refreshment and later food if you so desire."

I was unlike most Raians, who were tall and slender. My wife would describe me as more on the squat side with a nice round belly but with a face ready to smile and serve.

I scratched my head for a hesitant moment, then said, "But yes, after your are finished eating and taking rest, I would like to have a moment with you, if you would be so kind."

"Yes, of course," the man said, his heartfelt smile having a relaxing effect on me.

The sun finally rose above the trees, casting its warm rays upon squinting eyes, brought relief from the chill of the night.

Under an enormous spreading oak tree, close to the well, were several tables for customers to dine when the weather was suitable. The traveler sat there, placing his small backpack beside him.

Hmm, he is traveling light, I first thought. But, when I picked up the backpack to clean the table, its heavy weight aroused my curiosity.

As if he knew what I was thinking, the traveler said without looking up, "The bag contains special stones. I'm taking them to Rai for placement in a temple."

"Oh, is that so?" I replied, a little puzzled but feeling especially drawn to the man. I noticed that even the animals around the inn seemed to be attracted to him. I often enjoyed watching the dogs dash and frolic around the inn in the morning. On this day they remained silent, sitting under his table after the traveler pet and said a few words to them.

The inn was particularly full because it was festival time. As the morning danced along, the sounds of breakfast being served and guests being helped on their way filled the air. A few lodgers came outside and sat close by the traveler, exchanging the usual morning greetings.

Although I was fully occupied, I couldn't help sneaking a look at the traveler when I had a chance. I saw my wife noticing my unusual behavior by her puzzled looks and I was relieved she was too busy to inquire about it.

Finally, when most of the guests were taken care of and it was quieter, the traveler caught my attention and signaled me to come over. Why am I so pleased to meet him? I thought as I joined my mysterious guest.

With friendly eyes the traveler said, "Please sit down with me." When I complied, resisting the impulse to sit too close, he continued with a gentle voice, 'Thank you sir, for this wonderful food and drink and for providing such a cheerful place for us weary travelers. Please tell me your name."

I could not help but smile and said, "My name is Fritaye, and it is my pleasure to serve and provide comfort to travelers. My family has been running this inn for many generations. As my father before me, I was born here and most likely will pass away here. Hopefully my son will take over when I am gone and then his son."

"Look," I said pointing to the main inn, "we have just finished renovating the central building, and over there, towards your left, you can see our new barn we built far enough away so as not to disturb the guests." After reflecting thoughtfully for a moment I said, "I cannot imagine not running an inn. I guess it is in our blood to help and serve."

"Yes," returned the traveler, "I know your heart is pure, and this is reflected in the wonderful atmosphere of this inn." He spread his arms out gazing over the entire complex saying, "It is a delight to be here."

I lowered my head to accept the compliment, but when I looked up the traveler turned directly to me and continued in a totally different way. With a clear face looking intently into my eyes, he said, "Please Fritaye, don't worry about your daughter, she will find a good husband and your son will take over when he is ready. Give him space and he will come by himself. Your wife's illness is serious; she needs rest, but most of all, she needs more attention from you. Make it your business to spend more time with her and less on guests."

I felt my head spin and almost lost my balance. But then, bracing myself, I said almost in a whisper, "By Rai, how can you know this about me? It is as if you have known me for years. Who are you?"

"My dear Fritaye," the man said placing his hand on my shoulder to steady me, "I am you in the deeper sense. I am the trees, the sky and the dog that sits here. I am not attached to any definition of myself as an individual person. That is why I can look and see into you. I have felt the pure flow of your heart, and I know you are ready to receive."

Having said this, the traveler stood and touched my forehead. In complete surprise, I felt a strong power enter me, filling my whole body with a new tingling sense of joy. A humming began in my head that became louder and louder. And then, when the sound totally filled my head, I felt myself rising upward, traveling somewhere new and unknown, losing awareness of my body. I found myself floating in a void where nothing could be defined.

After a few minutes in this eternity, I returned and looked into the eyes of the traveler. I saw the vastness of my own self without separation between the world and me.

"It is so simple," I exclaimed, "why have I not seen this before?"

"Now, please don't talk," the traveler said, his voice soothing, "allow yourself to experience what has happened. Please continue with your duties as if nothing has occurred; the understanding will reveal itself to you in time. We can talk again when I return this way."

The traveler reached for his backpack, took something out and said, "Please accept this small stone. When you have the need, hold it and you will feel me."

I asked softly, "Oh special one, please tell me your name and something about you that I can take into my heart?"

"Yes, my name is Kareae. I grew up not far from here in the temple you know as "The Temple of Love." My parents are the high priest and priestess of the Kanparu Temple. I am pleased to meet you on my travels to the capital city Rai."

"Ah yes," I said, "I have visited that temple on many occasions to receive blessings for my marriage and children. It is a very inspiring place."

Then looking at Kareae I said, "My home is your

home. Come anytime, and you shall be received, ask for anything I can provide and I will give."

Kareae assented with a nod and again a flow of energy and a sense of understanding was present between us.

Gathering his backpack Kareae said, "I continue my journey now with the warmness of the sun on my face. You have no obligations towards me. I am delivering only what is yours. The purity of your heart bought me here. I will return, but only as a friend."

With that Kareae left the inn and was gone.

I watched Kareae leave, remaining spellbound on the spot. Finally my wife, Clarae, came over and asked, "Are you not feeling well, dear?"

Slowly I regained my presence of mind. I looked at my still handsome wife with new eyes of acceptance and said, "I had the most incredible meeting with that man who just left. In only a few minutes he changed my life by showing me who I truly am." With this I gave out a loud "Hurrah!" grabbed Clarae, took off her apron, and started dancing with her around the courtyard.

"My dear, what has gotten into you?" Clarae questioned at first but then started laughing, caught into my excitement.

Afterwards, when we were both exhausted and out of breath, she said, "My husband, it has been a long time since we have danced like this; I am not used to it anymore. And still there is work to be done!"

"Ah, my wife, let the work wait for us, I want to sit and hold you for a while," taking her to our favorite place near the oak tree.

"Are you sure you don't have a fever?"

I just silently smiled, gathering her in my arms. " Oh well", she said relaxing in my embrace, "Give me a kiss."

*****

For days I experienced the sweet presence of the traveler everywhere in the inn, even when I slept. The rest of the family gave puzzled looks to each other when they found me doing unusual things like sitting and just staring into open space. They were very curious about what had transpired.

I wanted to share with my wife and children what had happened, and how I was forever changed, but it was not possible at first. I needed time to absorb the experience and make some sense out of it. My family finally relaxed their attitude when they realized how soft and accepting I had become even if they didn't understand my new behavior.

Almost immediately, I could tell that the guests at the inn sensed the more loving and caring atmosphere. In the next months the inn became an even more popular place to break a journey. Visitors told me how pleased they were to be here. And when they left, they always seemed to have a sense of solace, feeling rested and ready to continue their travels.

Chapter 2

SIKTU

Several days after my meeting with Fritaye at the inn, I was walking along the King's Road on one of the thickly forested stretches between villages. My long slender but solid figure glided effortlessly over the many leagues I covered. I stopped to take in the silence of the forest. The wind passing in the trees, the fresh earth smells and the call of the birds captivated me. Never in Kanparu had I experienced such a pristine silence.

A flower growing from an outcrop of rocks caught my eye. I went over to observe it and for a few minutes, there was no separation between the flower and me.

******

Later that day while continuing with my travels, I thought of Romdev's last visit. He came to my room minutes before leaving Kanparu entering with the quick smooth grace of a dancer. His energy was in such a swirl that a cat sleeping on a soft chair rose and left the room.

He handed me a package and said, "Kareae, inside is

a map to a temple I recently built in the forest. It contains landmarks to show you how to find it."

Before I could react, he continued with a gleam in his eyes, "I came across this unique location some years ago and had a vision of building a temple there. Two years ago, when there was some time between projects, I began. I kept my mind closed about my plans and I enlisted the aid of several trusted monks who were very discreet. This is why you are surprised to hear about it. Fortunately, the work went quickly and we were able to finish some months ago. I want you to go there to open and establish the temple. It will be very useful in our work to stop Kalo."

"Yes, of course," I replied as I unfolded the map on the table and gave it a quick look. "Hmm, it seems simple and clear."

Very good," Romdev said softly, giving me the short Raian embrace of quickly touching foreheads. After a few minutes of loving silence Romdev said, "Now I will take my leave and bid you farewell until we meet again."

"Until then," I called out, watching Romdev disappear into the night.

After he left, I took another few minutes to study Romdev's map. It was a comprehensive map of Rai that clearly delineated how the kingdom was uniquely bordered on all sides with high ghats, or mountain passes. This afforded it natural protection from foreign invasion and helped to create a moderate climate with abundant rainfall and many windy days. The Raians had long ago taken advantage of the wind to develop efficient airstream stations for their power needs.

The map showed that the mid-central area of the Rai kingdom was blessed with long stretches of primary forest virtually uninhabited except for a few isolated villages. The populated areas were noted in the western and eastern central sectors. Rai, the capital city, was prominently situated in the eastern central portion directly on the Sigma River.

Included in the map was the extensive roadway system made possible by the numerous public projects the King of Rai initiated some years ago to rebuild and maintain the roadways and other infrastructures. The well-built and maintained King's Road ran from the Western Ghats to the capital city. The roads beyond the city to the Eastern Ghats were smaller but equally well maintained.

******

I was scanning King's Road for the first landmarks to direct me to Romdev's temple but I had yet to find any clues. The sun was chasing the horizon in the late afternoon when I noticed a small natural opening into the forest. I entered hoping to find a good place to spend the night.

Soon afterwards, I was surprised to perceive the presence of someone of a high caliber with a pure heart almost as a fragrance that overwhelmed my senses. It was this awareness that directed me to the innkeeper.

I began to follow the scent.

This area of the virgin forest consisted primarily of a tall straight-growing type of conifer tree with a scattering of twisted oaks and an occasional birch. The many slippery pine needles covering the ground gave it a richly carpeted look but compelled me to walk slowly and carefully. The smell of the slightly damp earth intoxicated my senses. Several times I stopped to take deep breaths just to draw in more of the luxurious scent. Spread intermittently were many huge boulders and rocks, some with natural overhangs that offered protection from the rain if needed. Where the forest thinned, many fern plants grew in abundance, adding to the magnificence. The sunrays filtering through the trees imparted a primeval sense of beauty while the music of the birds and natural inhabitants made the forest sing out in aliveness.

I finally came to a stream by a natural circular meadow bathed in direct sunlight. In the middle of the circle sat a woman. The soft gurgling sound of the stream and the sunlight on her face, in the midst of the deep forest, imparted a mystical impression, as if I were seeing an angel.

I stood transfixed, watching her sitting crossed-legged, with a blanket encased around her and her long black hair covering most of her face. She appeared to be in a deep trance state. Nevertheless, even though I walked towards her silently without thoughts, she immediately opened her eyes and in that moment our beings met like a waterfall rushing to meet the ground. Without words I heard a sermon recited. Without sound a sacred song was sung. In that moment I knew I met a kindred soul that recognized the absolute source of oneness.

I sat in front of her and discovered we could communicate in the ancient way of telepathy. With our minds open, we were able to merge and reveal the deepest realms of our beings. Only after a long silent interval did

I hear within me the woman say, "I have traveled far and wide. I have met many different kinds of people. But now I see the reason for my obsession to wander has been only to find you. My search is over and I have no need to travel further."

"My name is Siktu, dear one of the mysteries."

"And I am called Kareae," I said bowing my head.

I continued facing Siktu and within moments we entered again into a deep togetherness, our consciousnesses merging as one. We remained connected this way until nightfall, when I rose to make a fire for the night.

The animals sensed our high vibration and came to meet us with absolutely no fear of us or the other creatures of the forest. Towards the middle of the night, several wolves appeared from the darkness and sat beside the fire as if they were domesticated dogs.

In the chill of the morning, we took a ritual bath and washed our clothes. Later, we shared Siktu's blanket and food from my pack by the fire. I explained I was on my way to a small temple my teacher had built. As soon as I said this, it was silently understood that we would travel together to the temple and Siktu would become the priestess there.

We walked back to the stream to gather our clothes and spied a young deer watching us. Feeling no fear, the animal returned to quench her thirst. Siktu picked up a branch from the ground, then turned to me and said, "I have been wandering for some moons unable to stay in one place for more than a day. I don't know what drew me to the forest. When I came to this spot, I sat down after washing my face and quenching my thirst thinking I would not stay long. But somehow I kept on sitting. For three days I've sat here, and then you arrived. I didn't know I was waiting for someone until you were standing in front of me. You seemed to float into my vision like a feather on the wind. When I opened my eyes, at first I thought I was dreaming. I didn't know it was possible such a person as you could exist. I thought you were only a hope. I am so grateful to be allowed to take care of your teacher's temple."

I listened quietly, unattached, and yet in full empathy. I answered, "Yes, I see how our destinies have crossed. I see how this temple is for you to take care of and know as your own eternal home. I see you helping many beings who will find their way there."

I paused but then continued tenderly, "It is we who will feel grateful to you."

"When you're ready, let us depart and begin our journey together."

Chapter 3

FOREST TEMPLE

We spent the next day moving quickly on King's Road. By the afternoon, we spotted one of the first landmarks Romdev had described on his map. Once again we entered the forest and were immersed into an even more magical cathedral type atmosphere. I looked at Siktu in that background and could not help myself from embracing her. With our energies instantly merging, we remained in ecstatic bliss.

At last I said, "Siktu, do you feel it? I sense a power but it seems far in the distance."

"No, I don't sense anything, Kareae. What is it?"

"It seems to be a natural vibration but not coming from a human source. Romdev mentioned it and instructed that I should follow it to its source. Come, if you are ready, let us find it."

We tracked the vibration with the sagacity of a homing device. For two days we wandered easily in the enchantment of the forest, communing with the animals and sleeping under the huge overhanging rocks. On the third morning, we arrived at the temple area.

The place was amazing. The temple complex was built in a perfect location close to the southern ghats with a small waterfall and water pool nearby. The sheer walls of the ghats defined its southern boundary and the forest surrounded the rest of it. The nearby terrain was so ingeniously landscaped to protect the temple that I would have had trouble to find it without Romdev's instructions.

Siktu rushed up to me, laughingly took my hand and we both began to run joyously through the complex. We discovered that the grounds contained a temple and several small structures built around overhanging rock formations.

"By Rai Kareae, this place is incredible," Siktu said while taking off her clothes and jumping into the small pool adjacent to the temple. "Come, the water is delicious."

I stood spellbound in front of the temple. Never has a building touched me so profoundly though Kanparu is full of many beautiful temples.

Following Siktu's advice, I jumped in as well into the cool pool that gave me goosebumps. We were like two children enjoying the refreshing fun of the water, splashing, laughing and jumping up and down.

Later I watch Siktu emerge naked from the pool, her firm and young body glistening in the sunlight. She appeared as a goddess. Siktu stood before me, unpretentious in her nakedness, and invited me to come to her and again we merged gloriously into oneness.

Afterwards we stood before the temple. The flowing rectangle shape of the temple, with its rounded edges and a pyramid shaped dome rising from the middle, gave it an uniquely harmonious look as if the temple rose from the earth and stood forever.

We entered its inner sanctum where I placed a few of the stones I brought from Kanparu. Then we performed several ceremonies to energize the different idols.

Exploring further we found on the other side of the pool, a cave perfect for meditation.

The main house was our next visit. It contained a living space with adjacent several bedrooms. Next door was an adjoining kitchen. Behind the kitchen was another building containing a large storeroom. We were delighted to find it contained supplies and equipment.

Everything we needed to establish the temple seemed to be available. Even some of the forestland was cleared already and readied for planting. We found seeds for many vegetables including hemp seeds to be later utilized to make clothes.

"Kareae," Siktu said, " I so much love it here. I am so grateful. It a miracle how complete everything is almost down to the last detail."

"Yes, and at some point I'm thinking to make a trip to the nearest farm to bring several cows and chickens to provide milk and eggs," I replied. "You will have everything you need to stay here after I leave. Come, let's see about bedding and opening the kitchen for our first meal."

Thus began our life at the temple. Every morning after prayers and exercises, we worked in the fields: planting, then maintaining and watering the crops. I was inspired to built an irrigation system similar to that employed in Kanparu.

Once the work on the fields was finished, we spent days making the grounds and the cave area more suitable. Often we sat together exploring the deeper realms of awareness that were easier to access in the quietness of the forest. Very few words were spoken, as we knew each other's mind. We worked and lived together in complete synchronicity. We felt complete within ourselves, yet sharing in ease.

The days flew by. Within one month, we were able to harvest the first vegetables. By the span of three months, it seemed like the temple had always been there.

Siktu came over one warm day while I was working bare-chested in the fields and wrapped her arms around me. "Kareae," she said with a little naughtiness in her eyes, I just enjoy watching you working in the fields or sitting at the temple studying the designs. You move with the grace of a mountain lion."

I lifted and carried her to a nearby tree. Setting her down we embraced fully, every pore of our bodies touching in wild ecstasy. We did not move for hours.

Later, I confessed to her, "Beside the fact that you look like a goddess, your strength and presence captivates me. I never get tired to look at you."

Siktu stood up. "Well, my beautiful prince, you can watch me as I walk to the kitchen. Tonight we having our usual staple of rice and beans but with a new batch of fresh cheese and wild mushrooms I found in the forest this morning."

"Hmm, that's divine, let's take a quick jump in the pond and then I will come and help you prepare dinner."

"Sounds good to me."

******

I loved taking long walks in the forest. It gave me a sense of freedom I never knew before in the confines of Kanparu. Every step I made refreshed my contact with the world. The moist smell of the earth came to me like an exotic perfume capturing my senses. I allowed my ears to open to all the sounds that sometimes exploded like music within me. I delighted in opening my mind to nature and animals during these frequent walks. Often I was so in tune that a creature was surprised by my presence.

On one recent wandering, I was sitting by a campfire, enjoying the heat of the flames and the aroma of the burning wood. I sensed the presence of an animal that seemed to possess a certain amount of power. The next morning I soon discovered the fresh footprints of a wolf. I took off that day and followed the animal's vibration, trekking into an even deeper area of the forest that was rarely inhabited. As the evening drew near, I found the animal's den in an outcrop of large boulders. From the vibrational strength, I knew that the animal was within the den but I decided not to enter. Instead, I continued on to a nearby area and set up camp. Late that night with the fire fading out, a female wolf cautiously entered the camp area, eventually coming near me sitting by the fire. I didn't move even when her nose touched me. I was very surprised to sense a primitive form of thinking within the animal. The wolf herself, it seems, was puzzled why she was not feeling danger but some sort of attraction. I remained motionless until the animal left.

The next night I was sitting by the fire with open

eyes when the she-wolf arrived. I felt her thinking but this time I allowed my mind to enter into the wolf. I was astonished at her level of awareness.

When I was a young boy, an old monk at Kanparu, who took care of many of the livestock, taught me how to send my mind into the animals to soothe them if they were hurt or in a rage. Sometimes I would enter the mind of a small creature for fun, but soon I lost interest when I realized how milky dull their awareness was. This wolf, however, was different. She had an expanded level of intelligence far greater than normal. My mind was able to enter into her and I was able to experience what it was like to be a wolf, to look out of her eyes and run through the forest in a wolf's body. Unfortunately, I also discovered that her rudimentary awareness was not sufficient for her to escape primitive emotional and physical pains. I realized that when the wolf was not in physical distress she was suffering often from strong emotional discomfort. Remembering some of the techniques the monk had taught me, I was able to relieve her of a great deal of anguish.

Upon my return, Siktu said, "What have you done to your jaw? I've never seen it so tense."

"I had an incredible experience of meeting an intelligent wolf. I was able to enter and experience her reality. Unfortunately, eighty percent of her consciousness is centered in her mouth. I must have picked something up from her."

"I see. Come and lie down and let me massage you."

After only a few minutes my jaw relaxed but Siktu continued, enjoying our physical contact.

Several nights later an unusual sound brought me outside to find the female wolf sitting by the fire area. Some of the other animals grew excited, but I quickly calmed them, and then went over to welcome her. Siktu came out and quickly bonded with the animal. In the middle of the night the wolf left, probably to hunt for food, but returned shortly. Gradually the wolf became a regular visitor to the temple.

*****

The area in front of the cave had a natural overhead that provided a convenient sitting and storage area with a fireplace. The cave itself consisted of two rooms, one larger space and a smaller space that was perfect for two to three to sit comfortably, though it was not possible to stand upright as in the first room. On the far side of the second room, there was a small tunnel not big enough to crawl through, but that reached far into the cliff. The cave had fresh air so the tunnel must come to the surface at some point.

The first time I entered the cave, I recognized that the power I initially felt when I entered the forest, was mysteriously emitting its primordial force from inside the cliff. I remarked to Siktu, "I subtly sense something very ancient has occurred here like a fragrance of what once was but still is. It is almost like a portal to another age, to another time."

In complete darkness with the cave entrance closed, I heard the eternal sound of existence become as loud as a roaring ocean, transporting me deeply to a primordial source I never found before. Afterwards, I felt reborn, as fresh as baby.

One day we sat together in the cave, relaxed without any intentions. We both felt our consciousness rise out of our bodies and merge to form a new entity, similar to what occurred with Romdev in Kanparu. The fusion lasted for some hours until we separated and returned to our bodies.

Afterwards in an soft embrace, I said, "We have merged and have reached the highest in love with each other."

Siktu kissed my cheek and silently nodded in agreement.

We walked to our favorite place on a ledge above the cave that gave a greater view of the forest area. I took Siktu's hand and said, "I will be leaving in several days to continue my journey. I'm very happy. I could stay here forever with you but I must continue with the work I set out to do. I would ask you to join me but I know you want to remain here in the forest."

Siktu lovingly touched my head running her fingers through my hair. She answered, "Yes, I know the time is coming for you to leave. I have been feeling it for days as well. There is no need to mention it but we are two souls as one. Where you go, I go. Always our hearts will beat together."

In the silence that followed we embraced, our physical bodies also becoming alive. We entered into physical oneness with the purity of no passion nor desire, just a melting of love. For the next days until I departed, we slept together, sharing in physical and spiritual love.

We spent the last night in the temple performing rituals and sitting silently. When I left the next day, my happiness was even deeper than before.

*****

Every so often Siktu left for one of the nearest villages to buy supplies with money provided by Romdev. The villagers sensed her purity and love but were also aware of her strength. They saw a slender twenty-year-old woman, with dark long hair, beautiful and embodying a power and presence that few could resist.

Her origins appeared to be mysterious. In truth, she came from a distant temple family similar to Kareae's. Her parents were not the high priest and priestess but were sufficiently placed so that Siktu received the full education afforded to the children of the high priest. Early on, Siktu was recognized as special and was given extra training. Until she departed because of her restlessness, everyone thought that eventually she would become the high priestess. Indeed, her family waited with great expectations that she would return and take her place as the high priestess.

The villagers respected her enough not to follow her back to the forest after her visits. They were not unfamiliar with someone like Siktu, as often there were wandering monks. But Siktu was exceptional and they were very pleased to see her, as she was always as natural and simple as they were. Their nature was not to be jealous and they had no need to gossip about her. Indeed, Raians, whether living in the villages or the city, were quite spiritually advanced and intuitive.

Siktu accepted life as it was with no desire to change it. She was not interested in being worshipped; being a recluse suited her nature. Occasionally someone came and she shared her being with the visitor, but mostly she enjoyed her aloneness. Any lingering longing for the external was fulfilled once she met Kareae.

At that point her search was over.

Chapter 4

THE CARAVAN

Several moons after Kareae's visit, a caravan of eight wagons arrived at Fritaye's inn. They entered slowly through the small grove of oak and walnut trees onto the picturesque cathedral-like drive lined with overhanging willows. This led to the cobblestone courtyard, where the old well stood near the rustic barn stood. Further on were the new animal shelter and a camping area for the many wagons passing though.

The clip clop of the carriages crossing the cobblestones bought Fritaye into the courtyard to greet his guests. The smell of sweaty horses hit his senses, confessing to the end of a day's journey.

He helped the travelers disembark.

"Greetings. Well, by Rai! Welcome Jacki. It's good to see you again."

"Thank you. I'm glad you remember me. Let me introduce my son Arjin and my daughter Susea. As you can see, we are part of the pilgrimage to the annual Empowerment Festival."

"Ah yes," Fritaye said, nodding to Arjin and Susea, "I

assumed so by the size of your caravan. Look," pointing to the camping area, "our new facilities are just behind the barn there. When you are settled, please come to the office and register. How long do you plan to stay?"

"Well, I was thinking to stay overnight, but seeing your delightful inn again makes me want to stay a day longer. There is still enough time to reach the festival before the commencing on the full moon."

"Ah, we were there last year," Fritaye said. "What a joyous and solemn occasion to pay homage to our most sacred site. And the landscape... so different from here, so completely dry and arid but breathtaking. Okay, I take your leave now and wait for you at the reception."

Back at the inn, his wife Clarae inquired about the new arrivals.

"Oh, that's Jacki, a rich landowner from the south central. He was here a few years ago while you were visiting your family. A nice man really and well respected. He's in charge of his local temple and functions as their priest-counselor. Well, between us only, I've heard that sometimes Jacki uses his temple position to influence others for his own interest. Poor man, though, his wife died early on, leaving him to raise both a son and a daughter.

You will see them when they register. The older one Arjin is built like his father, strong and muscular. I tell you, they are very alike. The last time he was here Jacki confided in me he was training Arjin to take over his responsibilities. Anyway, he shared how much they enjoyed being together, which I guess makes a perfect arrangement.

"And the daughter?" Clarae asked.

"Susea, the younger one. Well, Jacki admitted over drinks late one night, that as a child she was often left to herself. He insisted, though, that she was never neglected. He said this helped her to develop her independent nature and still retain the same purity of heart as her mother. As far as I could tell, a very pleasant young lady."

*****

Once they had pitched camp, Jacki said to the delight of Arjin and Susea, "Let's take advantage of the inn and book rooms for the night and maybe spend another day here. This might be the last time we will see an inn until we return from the festival."

"Come", he said, jokingly looking around to see if anyone was near, "we can sneak off and leave the rest of the caravan to look after themselves."

"Oh father, we can't do that," Susea laughed. "Go on, I will inform a few of the pilgrims so they don't worry."

"Thanks, sister," Arjin said taking his father around his arms and heading off to the inn, "Let us meet in the restaurant, I'm starving."

Hmm, Jacki thought as they walked away, my daughter is growing up. Not only is she becoming physically beautiful but also her inner grace, how she cares for the others, is just like her mother. He noticed her long dark hair, big eyes and rounded face with full lips, and her small but shapely body. By Rai, he thought, she reminds me so much of my wife. Well, even after all these years I miss her. If only I can find a suitor that Susea approves of._

Fritaye was at the door to welcome and register

them into a suite of adjoining rooms with a central sitting parlor.

"Will you be eating tonight in the dining room?" Fritaye asked as he was handing them the keys.

"Yes, it is always such a pleasure to stay at your inn. When my daughter comes, can you direct her to our table?"

"Yes, of course," the innkeeper replied but then taking them aside, he said, "Tonight I recommend our specialty of the day. Actually my wife, Clarae, prepared it for the family using vegetables straight from the garden. But, there is enough to go around, and it would be a pleasure to share it with you."

"Yes, thank you, thank you very much; that is very considerate of you," Jacki replied. "Indeed, I can't wait."

When Susea joined them at the table, the men were already sharing a glass of wine. Jacki looked up and said, "I don't know what it is but there is something different about the inn and the innkeeper. Well, before it was a enjoyable place, but now it is more relaxed and cared for than ever before."

"Yes, I feel what you mean Father. When I just met with the innkeeper, he was greeting me as if I was his daughter."

"I agree, that's it, they treat us as their loving family," Arjin said, swirling his glass around, "and the wine is excellent I must say. Ah, but here comes the food."

For the next thirty minutes there was not a word spoken between them as they feasted upon the steamed herbed trout with lightly sautéed vegetables and baked potatoes.

During the dessert of fresh fruit and cheese, the robust Clarae came over, and they exchanged pleasant words with great praises for the food and wine.

When Jacki mentioned about the changes he felt, Clarae with an inner knowing sigh said, "Yes, a wonderful miracle happened some months back that changed my husband forever and transformed him into such a sweet man. We are still wondering how it all came about? He said a stranger came one morning and touched his head."

"Touched his head?" Jacki said.

"Yes, touched his head, and we have never been the same. Well, it is a mystery, but between us, I tell you our life at the inn has become a real joy. Every day is just full of amazement." A few tears slowly escaped her eyes while she said, "We are so, so grateful."

"And you say a stranger came and touched his head?"

"Yes."

"Well, by Rai, that is a handful." Jacki said slowly rising from the table taking Clarae's hand to thank her for her hospitality. "We surely appreciate it. Now, if you so please, we will be off to our rooms for a welcome rest. Come you kids, let's go. Lets give them a chance to clean up."

"Thank you; good night and rest well," the innkeeper's wife replied, signaling her helpers to clear the table.

Chapter 5

SUSEA

(Susea speaking)

After we slept in real beds and delighted in the innkeeper and Clarae's great cooking, there was no question of spending another day at the inn. Finally on the next day, father gathered the caravan and we moved happily onwards to the next big camping halt, a long three-days journey. My father took the lead; Arjin drove the second wagon, while I commanded the third vehicle. At the end of the second day, we stopped at a small camping site just near the side of the road.

"Susea," my father called, " Why don't you tend to the horses while Arjin and myself look for firewood. An early dinner and then we should sleep to get a good start tomorrow."

"Okay, I said, " please just unharness the horses and I will take care of the rest."

That night I spent a long time brushing my hair in the wagon while watching the many stars in the sky. My mind was full with thoughts about my boyfriend. I just couldn't decide whether I should accept his proposal of love. However, the following morning was leisurely pleasant. I waited until the hazy mist of dawn lifted and sun began to smile before I began dowsing the breakfast fire.

At this moment I first saw him for the first time.

He seemed to appear out of nowhere. I had the impression of seeing someone solid, but at the same time, his boundaries gave the sense of changing and shifting like the shoreline of a roving sea. He walked directly over but it seemed like his appearance before me was instant. The man bowed in greeting and then with direct eye contact, said something so astonishing that I almost lost my breath. I examined him with great earnestness.

"How could you know what I was dreaming?" I said a moment later. "And yes, I was watching the stars last night. I was thinking of what I should do about my friend's offer of love." Then with a frown I said, "So you think I am not ready?"

"If I may give you some advice, if you have to think about it, then you are not ready. Does someone think first about running out of a room on fire?"

"Hmm," I said, unable to stop looking into his eyes, "I guess you are right."

By now everyone in the caravan was aware of the stranger. Arjin came running over to check. He must have noticed my attraction because with a perplexed look on his face he inquired, "Do you know each other? You seem like friends."

After a moment Kareae turned to Arjin with an open expression and said, "As well as I know you, dear sir. For example, your back on the right side has been troubling you ever since you fell off a horse a while ago."

"By Rai man, have you been following us?"

"No, I just know by looking at you. It is something I've always been able to do."

Just at this moment Jacki arrived. Kareae formally introduced himself, lightly touching Jackie's forehead with his, "Sir, my name is Kareae from the Kanparu Temple. I am traveling to Rai. I became curious about your caravan and was feeling the need to rest."

After a moment of reflection Jacki relaxed into a smile, "Yes, you are welcome. Come to my wagon Kareae and refresh yourself. There is still some hot tea brewing."

Kareae bowed to Arjin then turned to me and said, "I take your leave now, but let's talk later."

Arjin and I were both a little breathless from our meeting with Kareae. It seemed our bodies tingled with aliveness. The world around me appeared as clear as a mountain stream and colorful as never before. Arjin was not the type to trust someone right away, but in Kareae's benevolent presence his heart seemed softer. I was simply left in awe of his power, his mystery and most of all, from a sense of something fantastic happening in my life.

Arjin left saying, "I'll go get the horses ready."

I hardly heard him, as I was bemused by Kareae's magic spell.

*****

"Drawn like a magnet I soon joined them. Kareae and my father were examining his wagon.

"I'm impressed by the design of your wagons, Jacki," Kareae said, sipping on his hot drink.

"Yes, this is the new design coming from the land of Mi. These wagons," he said proudly," are made with a special lightweight and very durable material formulated also in Mi. The wagon design is aerodynamic while the suspension and wheels are built in such a way as to give an optimally smooth ride. I say, traveling in these wagons is a dream,"

Putting his hand on Kareae's shoulder he continued, "I feel so drawn to you as an old friend. If it is okay with Susea, I would be pleased if you join our caravan and come to the empowerment with us. We will turn off King's Road soon on the next crossroad and head north. In two days time we will arrive at the festival grounds."

"Yes, I would like that," Kareae replied.

"What do you say Susea, is it okay? "

"I guess so," I stuttered

"Good, then Kareae can ride with you."

Just then, I saw three birds on the wind flying north, gliding on the slight breeze in the air, and the sun in its steady climb danced with the small clouds floating by. We stood there transfixed for some moments by some unusual feelings of stillness.

We walked back together to my wagon. I started fumbling about trying to finish packing. I became flustered, dropped a crate and blushed in the rush of excitement of being near him.

"Is it really okay that I come with you?"

"Yes, you... you are welcomed to join me," I said. "I will appreciate your help. Can you handle horses?"

"Yes, since I was a child."

"Oh, very good," I said fiddling with a box I picked

up.

"Here, let me help you." He took the box from me and carried it to the wagon. "There is something, if I may, that I want to tell you. That is, you are the reason I'm here and joining this caravan. I want to present to you what you have always been longing for."

"What did you say?" I exclaimed. "You are certainly very direct and don't waste any time in what you do or say. You continue to shock me yet ... I feel your kindness and certainly your strength."

I took a step closer to him , "I don't know why I'm saying this and I must be crazy because we have just met, but yes, I am ready to receive from you."

"Yes, I know," Kareae replied.

We continued to stand by the wagon in a timeless moment, as if the world had stopped and nothing else existed. We remained this way until the sound of Jacki's voice announcing our departure bought us back.

Without saying another word we climbed into the wagon and departed; our vehicle was again the third wagon after Jacki and Arjin.

For hours we traveled in silence, yet a friendship was transpiring between us. We passed through a beautiful colorful section of the road surrounded by a forest on both sides. So many different shades of green and brown. Slightly rising hills gave a wide vista of the countryside especially at the higher elevations. We drove through a few small villages but did not stop, preferring to make our breaks only at isolated areas. I loved seeing the cute little thatched-roof farmhouses.

Finally, I could not contain the tingling sensation

throughout my body. I said, "I have never felt this way before and yet it is so familiar. In your presence there is no doubt and everything just is."

Kareae turned to me. "Yes, it is because of your pure heart that you can understand me."

Tears filled my eyes and I felt my whole body relax. From this whispered space I said, "I am complete as if finally I have come home."

Just then, the wagons up ahead stopped. Jacki dismounted and walked back from the lead wagon. He said looking around, "Lets take a break now while we are still in this picturesque forest area. Soon we will come to the crossroads and turn north. Afterwards, the countryside is not as rich."

Knowing my father's looks, I was amused that he was considering if Kareae was a suitable man for me. From Kareae's light smile, I had the impression he seemed to know it as well.

Jacki directed the caravan to a spot off the road where we could take our lunch. Nearby was a small running stream with clear water and a soothing sound. "Make sure to fill your water tanks before leaving because it will be some distance before we see water again."

I unhitched the horses and led them to the stream to drink.

Stepping into the stream, I allowed the bottom of my dress to get wet, enjoying the gentle caress of the brook and took some of the cool water in my hand and wet my lips, tasting a hint of the fresh earth.

Afterwards, I let the horses wander on the small meadow on other side of the stream. I saw a snake but relaxed when I realized it was of a harmless garden variety.

I returned to find Kareae and Arjin sitting together in earnest conversation. They became quiet when they saw me coming. I overheard Kareae say they would finish their discussion later.

After some time Jacki joined us, and we ate our meal in quiet harmony.

"Let us rest for an hour or so and then get ready to continue," Jacki said as he lay down in a shady spot under a tree.

In just over an hour everyone was ready to leave.

On the road again, gently at the reins, I asked Kareae about his conversation with Arjin.

"I said something that will take some time for Arjin to understand and accept about himself. It made him uncomfortable."

"Oh," I replied but thought I knew what Kareae meant.

Kareae grinned, "Yes, you are almost correct in what you think."

For the second time, I was taken back by his uncanny ability to know my thoughts. I ran a hand over my head.

"I see you can read my mind. Is that something you can teach me?"

"Yes. Until recently I thought everyone could. My parents are able to tune into a person's mind frequency as I am. I find it to be just natural. Everyone has the potential so you can also develop this ability. First, begin to understand that your mind is not only yours but part of the universal consciousness. Our minds are just one segment of an eternal flow of life force, the same stream is passing though all of us. When you open to this idea, it becomes easier to tune into someone's frequency. If you practice, within three months you will be able, on your own level, to read my thoughts. That is, if I let you."

We reached the crossroads in an hour's time. Meanwhile, the air became drier and the landscape more sparse.

The narrower road north was well maintained, as were all the roads in the kingdom. When a vehicle came from the opposite direction, one or both of the wagons had to partially get off the road so they could pass each other. Still, the ride in the wagons was smooth and easy.

The travel for the rest of the day was pleasantly uneventful. Kareae and I enjoyed feeling the power and viewing the stark beauty of the land. In the distance were small hills sometimes consisting of large round boulders that appeared to be placed there by some giant hand. On both sides of the road were fields growing rice and every once in a while a small village appeared. The more north we traveled, the more unpopulated the land became with only a few scattered houses in the distance.

The caravan took a short rest in the late afternoon and traveled onwards almost until sunset around nine o'clock. The sun sinking into the western sky was breathtaking that evening. At last Jacki led the caravan to a beautiful campsite he knew from his other trips to the festival. Several other wagons were already camped but luckily the site Jacki preferred was still free. After getting settled, Jacki left to dine with the other pilgrims and did not return until late.

The three of us prepared dinner together on an open fire. The food was simple but had a good taste. Nothing was said about the discussion Kareae had with Arjin.

Kareae went for a walk afterwards under the almost full moon. He was sitting on a huge rock when I approached him.

While Kareae helped me onto the boulder, I looked into his eyes and felt a warm flow enter around my belly area. My entire body started to vibrate spontaneously and shake so strongly that Kareae had to hold me. Then, he gently placed me down on the stone.

I became quiet and opened my eyes, but felt as if I was swimming in soft deep pools. I sighed in joy and bliss. "My god, what is this? What do you do to me?" I said, as I rose into his arms.

"It is nothing I do," he replied. The purity of our hearts touched each other. Your innocence brought me to you."

I lightly touched Kareae's cheek. In the distance I heard the sound of a dog barking and could see the lights of the different caravan fires. A single tree stood close by, in contrast to the barren landscape, looked alive in the moonlight. I noticed how silent the place felt and how still my heart was. "Kareae, I am ready to go with you, to wherever you want to bring me. My life has been a shadow until meeting you today."

Kareae simply nodded his head. He touched my shoulders with both hands in a confirming way. Afterwards, we walked back to the campsite.

Arjin seemed surprised again by our obvious intimacy when we joined him by the fire. We were debating whether to put on a last log when Jacki returned saying, "Better to get some sleep. Tomorrow will be a long day over rough terrain. If all goes smoothly, we will reach the sacred festival site by nightfall tomorrow."

The Raian custom was to position the wagons in a semi-circle so that our heads were facing east and our feet west during sleep. The fireplace was situated in the center. Kareae placed his mat near the fire, as the nights were still a bit chilly.

After breakfast, the wagons were readied for the day's journey.

As the caravan proceeded north, the terrain became increasingly rugged while the vegetation became even sparser. The raw earth colors of the hills were beautiful and the earth pulsated with power. Everyone was filled with vitality.

By this time, the many caravans on the road gave a festive flavor to the air.

Chapter 6

FULL MOON CELEBRATION

The annual Empowerment Ceremony provided Raians with the optimal opportunity to affirm and renew their relationship with life. They achieved this by realigning with the natural life forces all Raians intuitively felt. The empowerment was so potent, it not only benefited everyone who attended but most of the Raian population as well. Initiated by the ancients, the empowerment was perhaps the oldest known ceremony in Rai..

When children reached the age of ten they attended their first initiation. Beforehand, the children underwent a special process of cleansing and fasting. This aided and protected them from the profound nature of the first alignment. After the empowerment, a new knowledge and maturity arose from the experience. From then on, they were no longer considered children. Surprisingly, though, their innocence and purity remained intact.

At the main sacred site, amidst the vast but barren landscape stood a natural stone idol perhaps two hundred and fifty hands high. This idol was positioned perfectly with the movements of the planets and the moon.

During this particular full moon, the stone was in direct alignment with the sun, the moon and several planets including Jupiter and Pluto. The Raians considered this a very auspicious moment.

Many Raians wanted to attend the festival but because of a rotation system they were able to attend only once every four years. This afforded each person the possibility to undergo the renewal without feeling rushed or crowded.

The campground was tingling with anticipatory excitement. Many participants were rushing about, meeting old friends and making new ones. Individual campsites flowed with colorful banners. Each person wore his or her finest costume to commemorate the occasion. It was as if they were collectively being married to the whole existence.

Jacki was assigned to one of the choicer campsite near the idol. After the camp was pitched, Arjin and Jacki left to mingle with the throngs, attired in colorful costumes designed by Susea.

Jacki was found later sitting with his friends next to the main community tent, where tables and benches had been set up to serve refreshments. He was keen to tell his associates about the mysterious man who joined his caravan a few days before and the story of the innkeeper.

"I think he is the same man," Jacki concluded after his animated conversation.

"Well then, who is he? Where does he come from?" one of his friends piqued.

"Hmm, by Rai, I don't know, it never crossed my mind to ask. It's strange, but when you are around him, it feels so comfortable you never think even to ask. All we know is he is on his way to Rai for some purpose."

Another of his friends said, "I noticed him immediately when your caravan arrived. I was half thinking that maybe Susea found herself a man. I was thinking that, hey, that's a nice looking man for her."

"By Rai, I had the same thoughts about him at first but after being with him for a few days, I had the feeling he is not interested in marriage and children. He seems to be on some sort of mission. Sometimes he mentions the work he is doing, but I can't figure out what that is as yet.

"Pardon me, my dear fellows," a voice called out from the next table. "I could not help but overhear you. This man you're talking about interests me, what is his name?"

The men looked up to see an unusual looking gentleman. He was solidly built, wrapped in a dark cape with a red dragon embossed on the breast. Instinctively, the men slightly withdrew when he came near. They had the uncomfortable sense that their boundaries became less solid.

He must be a priest or monk, perhaps from Kanparu, Jacki thought.

"His name is Kareae, dear sir. He is the son of the high priest of Kanparu." Jacki said unable to stop himself from speaking in the stranger's presence and not knowing how he knew he was the son of the high priest.

"Ah, I thought so. Then the moment has finally come." The man said almost to himself.

Jacki quickly said, "But come, lads, it's time. Let's

take our place by the idol while there is still some room. Good day to you sir."

"Aye, let's go," they said in unison, finishing their mugs and almost jumping up to follow Jacki.

"Who was that man?" one of the men asked.

"I don't know but I'm glad to be away from him." Jacki replied. "I felt drawn into his power. He must be some sort of priest. It's strange. He gave me an ominous feeling."

"Yes, I agree." His friend shuddered.

*****

Towards the afternoon Susea and I finally had some moments to be alone together, sitting mostly silently enjoying each other's company. I recalled that when I left the forest temple and returned to King's Road, I immediately sensed Susea's presence, like a sweet fragrance lighting up my senses. Even though I had to backtrack towards Fritaye's inn, I set out to find her. Closer I came, the more I realized what an immense purity Susea possessed.

Suddenly, my train of thought was interrupted when my body began to vibrate and I felt like a heavy weight pressing on head.

Susea looked up, "Kareae, what's wrong?

I said after a few minutes slightly perplexed, "I feel a man of power is near but when I probed, my energy was not only deflected but pushed back. It was very unusual, almost hostile."

I shook my head for a second and that seemed to clear my mind.

I said, "Susea, after the opening ceremony, after you

have made the seven prostrations and circumnavigations around the idol, let us meet before I leave tomorrow."

"Yes," replied Susea, only able to look briefly at Kareae, "I would very much like that."

"Good, now I will climb that hill yonder and sit there for the ceremony."

*****

Susea watched Kareae walk away feeling her heart fluttering. Never in her life had she felt this way. She gently touched and picked up the mat he had been sitting on. She brought it close to her face taking in his presence. The love and compassion and acceptance she felt was overwhelming. And yet, there was no urge to take possession of him in a physical way even though he was especially pleasing to gaze at. She thought about his long slim but solid figure, imagining running her hands through his shoulder length black wavy hair. But what she loved most of all, was his eyes - they seemed to ooze light and kindness.

*****

Arjin joined his friends listening to their tales and stories without mentioning Kareae. His thoughts, though, frequently turned to him, uncomfortably remembering what Kareae said about his overriding self-interests. How can this man know so much about me? he pondered. Hmm, if I didn't see that Kareae was a good man and had those kind eyes, I might have started something with him. But I can't even think about getting angry. What is that?

*****

The ceremony began at sunset, when the moon was rising and the sun was setting at the same moment. Most participants, like Jacki, gathered around the idol hours before. There was very little conversation; almost all were silent and vigilant. At the start of the ceremony, over 5,000 people were present, and not a sound was heard. Nobody wanted to disturb the potency of the auspicious event.

At the appropriate moment preceding the rising of the moon, Jacki heard the sounding of the sacred bell to commence the ceremony. He became more still with less thoughts. He sensed that the participants around him became quieter; almost he forgot them. Everyone experienced a surge of synchronicity within the gathering. By the end of the third ringing, Jacki was without thoughts and any sense he was somebody, as if he was in a bubble above his body.

A different sounding bell announced the beginning of the chanting of the ancient prayers every Raian learnt as a child. All Jacki's concentration was needed to recite the complex and long chants performed in several stages. This lasted for several hours until the moon was directly overhead..

The single-pointed intent of the singing created a life-energy field that reverberated over all of Rai and even beyond.

The sacred bell was sounded three times again to signal the end of the prayer ceremony. Jacki prostrated and in unison with the group began to circumnavigate the idol. He repeated this seven times. No one was aware of the passing of hours or having any sense of a separate identity. It was as if they had all merged into a timeless state of being.

The stone of the idol itself contained several minerals that changed color in response to different lights. In the full moon light, the icon emitted a luminous blue-green glow. When this glow reached its full luminosity, it signaled the most favorable peak of the intunement and the chanting changed to its final stages.

At this stage everyone was transported into complete egoless unity. One aspect of this healing state was the absence of barriers that prevented the flow of life and caused many problems and diseases. This was one of the reasons why everyone felt empowered. The ego returned after the ceremony, but slowly, sometimes only after days or weeks..

The effect of the empowerment was: to affirm their relationship with the universe, to align their individual life energy field with the universal field, to dissipate old thought patterns both positive and negative from the collective unconscious and finally to create a most peaceful and nourishing atmosphere for all that came into their collective power field.

******

From the advantage point of the hill, I could watch the entire ceremony. Towards the end I realized that I was not alone. I turned to my left and there I saw from the shadows a tall man approaching completely cloaked in a dark cape. I noticed the symbol of the dragon brightly stitched in red on the breast of his wrap.

"Greetings, grandson of Alo, son of Ashara" he said in a strong deep voice, "You are becoming quite a powerful man."

" Yes, thank you, man of the night who keeps his mind

so tightly closed. How do you know my grandfather's name and how shall I call you?"

"You can call me Kalo for now. Let us say I was a colleague of your grandfather. I have been following with interest your father and now you. Only recently I've become aware of your conspiracy with Romdev and your father to alter the consciousness of Rai. Romdev has been very clever to discover my intentions. Did you know that the original idea came from your grandfather?

"No, that is news to me. Tell me Kalo, what does the dragon represent on your cape? I've been wanting to know its meaning for a long time."

"Ah, my young one. This dragon has a great secret but I will only tell you the secret lies in what a dragon can do. But I didn't come here to have friendly discussions but to warn you not to continue with your plans or suffer the consequences. I never expected Romdev would be successful so quickly to create someone like you. I warn you son of Ashara, that if you continue with your plans you will suffer dire consequences.

"Why are you doing this?'

"I could say I am recreating the balance of the universe or perhaps I could say to settle a score or perhaps I represent another order that has their own reasons. Or, perhaps for no reason at all. Perhaps for all those reasons or some or none of them. Nor does it matter for you cannot prevent me but I can prevent you.

"How is that?"

"Ah, my usurper, you are not the only one with powers. I will scatter you to the corners of the universe if you proceed. You have been warned."

I watched Kalo fade into the shadows absorbing his warning and yet I was not concerned. But after meeting Susea, I must communicate with Romdev, I thought.

*****

The night was almost over when Susea and I met again on the hill facing the idol. I saw golden light radiating from Susea as she approached and said, "My beautiful Susea, I see your work is finished. There is nothing left for me to do. We meet as one, your feelings of separation will never return. Only now your real life work can begin."

"My real work? What do you mean?" But then Susea said, "Hmm, I sense where you are pointing. In this wholeness I have become, it will direct me to where my work lies and it is only now that I can be effective."

"Yes, your wisdom is deep for such a young age,"

Susea wrapped her arms around Kareae. She laughed and said, "Well, I can say the same to you."

The sun could just be seen rising on the horizon. They watched the colors of the landscape change from the luminosity of the moonlight to the brightness of the sun. Some birds were seen flying in the cloudless distance. The campsite was silent, still, as most people were resting in their wagons. Actually very few could sleep; they remained quiet, immersed further in the experience of the ceremony.

After a while Susea said, "Please promise me I will see your physical form again."

I acknowledged her with a gentle look and said reassuringly, "There is no doubt we will meet again. But let us return now to the camp for some food and rest. I still want to speak to your father before he sleeps."

Susea shared as they were walking closely together, "Kareae, I just can not find the words to describe the inexpressible state of walking together with you. There is no sense of a you or me, and it feels so natural. We are like two beings acting as one, yet in separate bodies. This is such an unique experience for me."

Jacki was awake sitting by the campfire listening to the music of the flames. He looked up when we arrived and after a moment said, "What miracle have you performed on my daughter? I feel as if I am looking at a goddess," Jackie said standing up and embracing his daughter.

I smiled with a slight twinkle in my eye and said, "It is not I who have done this. The whole existence can be blamed. Let us rejoice in this miracle of transformation. Jacki, I wanted to tell you that your daughter is no longer the person you raised, but I see you are aware already of her transformation. May I request only that you take care of her as if she is the goddess and honor her in that fashion. Please drop any plans for her to live in the normal way as a wife with a husband and children. Arjin can continue your bloodline."

Turning to Susea I said, "Susea, when the time comes, you will know what to do. Follow the wisdom that comes from deep inside you; it will be correct.

"Yes, you are right."

Jacki looked at his daughter who was no longer his daughter still in awe and amazement.

He said, raising his hands to the sky, "This pilgrimage is certainly the most transforming one I have experienced.

I laughed and said, "but now I want to take my rest

and in the afternoon I will depart."

"Why not stay the rest of the day and leave in the morning?" Jacki inquired.

" Hmm, perhaps you are correct, I will do as you say."

" Fantastic, this will give me some time to prepare some provisions for your journey. If I don't see you again, I wish you now good travels and give you my blessings, I love you as my own son."

With this, they embraced in deep acceptance. Kareae then bowed to Susea and wandered off to rest.

Susea turned to Jacki and said, "Father, you will always be my father no matter what becomes of me and where destiny leads me. Never forget that even though there might come some time when that is challenged."

"My dear, you will always be my daughter." He said gently, " Come, I am tired, let us get some sleep."

"Hmm, yes, Father."

That evening with the moon bright overhead, I came to Susea's tent and embraced her. She woke up looking into my eyes and we exchanged our love in silence.

Until dawn, we remained in a warm embrace of love, looking into each other eyes in a unity of silence and wonder.

I finally rose to prepare for my journey. I wrote a farewell letter to Jacki, including a Kanparu crystal. I left a message for Arjin, bidding him farewell with promises to meet and spend more time at our next meeting.

Susea, from her timeless space could only watch me move around. After a while I returned to lie once again at her side.

When I rose again, Susea sat up. She watched me pick

up my backpack and walk out onto to the road. Finally, I disappeared in the distance and I could hear her mind say, until the next time my sweet teacher and soul friend, I will miss your presence.

Chapter 7

THE POWER OF THREE

I felt fresh, full of energy and life, ready for whatever would come. Traveling once again on the road, free to be in nature unfettered to embrace the sounds and smells that surrounded me.

Jacki's family, the festival and Kalo were behind me now. They left no imprint even though the family's presence was deep in my heart. Even the story with Kalo didn't seem to affect me at my core.

After I left Susea yesterday, I walked into the distance and sat on a flat rock with two acacia trees adjacent to it. I opened my mind and concentrated on an image of Romdev. Almost immediately, I could see Romdev in Kanparu as he could see me. I waited while Romdev absorbed the images of my mind.

He said, "This is serious. How he found out so quickly about our plans is distressing. There's nothing to do but continue and hope to beat him in the race. Against Kalo's powers I feel helpless. Take care Kareae, keep your guard up even though there is not much you can do if he attacks you."

"I agree Let us continue as we don't have the power

to stop Kalo. It's our only hope.

*****

The dry cracked parched earth in mosaic swirls gave beauty to the harshness of the land. A wonder any of the sparse vegetation could exist and even bloom with flowers in this arid climate. After a few days of walking and camping, I reached the main road. Again the forest welcomed me with its aliveness and beauty. I saw deer, and the quick scampering of small animals like squirrels made me laugh. The beautiful music of the birds and the insects buzzing around me was like a symphony. I picked up some moist earth and thrilled in the smell, the rich aroma only the forest could give.

On King's Road, I headed west towards the capital. Several hours later I came to an inn and decided to spend the rest of the day there. The luxury of having a wonderful hot bath and sleeping in comfort on a soft bed was irresistible.

This inn was smaller than Fritaye's establishment, but the proprietor Jon and his staff were just as friendly and helpful. In a large pleasant sunny room facing the forest, I could see the hills in the distant from his window. Jon explained he specially chose the location of the inn because it had a slightly higher elevation that afforded a scenic view. "I spent many moons searching for such a spot to build this inn and I am very pleased about it," Jon said.

At sunset after a stroll, I entered the dining room feeling famished and ready to feast. I noticed sitting at a table by a window, two men and a woman engaged in lively conversation. I smiled and bowed in greeting while passing their table. They looked up to return my salutation. Afterwards, they sat for a moment, a little bewildered by me. Being polite they returned soon to their conversation.

I did not need to read their minds to know they were having troubles. With a little psychic focusing, I learnt the details of their story and it quite amused me. Lovingly, I thought of a way to solve their problem. But first things first, I dived into a very hardy stew Jon's wife prepared, loaded with fresh vegetables. I even drank a glass of their homemade wine the innkeeper was so proud of. I noticed the curiosity and eyes of the other diners but I felt relaxed and at ease, enjoying the fire that had been lit a short time ago.

Just as I was finishing the meal, one of the men from the trio strolled over to introduce himself and asked if I would like to join them for a final glass of wine at their table. With a bright face I immediately agreed. After introductions to the others, we settled down with our last drink.

From their accounts and from what I could see psychically, their story unfolded. The three of them came from the large village Do near Fritaye's inn. The young pretty woman's name was Rosea and the men were known as Stepen and Sternan. Both men looked remarkably similar: tall, slender with black wavy hair and handsome in the Raian way. Stepen was the one who invited me to their table. He was the more lively and talkative of the two. Sternan was more reserved and was known as a deep and sincere man. Both men, I knew, were good honest men in the Raian tradition.

Rosea and Sternan were childhood friends. He lived on a farm close by hers. Often as children, Sternan sat on his fence teasing Rosea on her way to school. One day Sternan yelled out something that so angered Rosea, she pushed him off the fence and they fought. Afterwards, they became close friends, and when they got older they eventually became lovers.

Stepen was a recent addition. He met Rosea in Do at his business establishment. Love bit him at first sight. Finally one day, as he was helping her to carry her packages home, they stopped to sit near the river bridge and it was there on a lovely warm afternoon watching the gentle river roll by that Rosea fell in love with him as well. Rosea felt she had no choice in the matter. When she confessed her love for both men later, each one demanded she make a choice. A choice she could not make. This led to her escaping Do and coming to Jon's inn to sort it all out.

Rosea was as beautiful as her namesake. She exuded a sweet aura any man would find attractive. She was young but alas, not very wise about using her beauty. Now Rosea had the dilemma of sitting here with two men in love with her without knowing what to do. She loved both of them and did not have a preference. Rosea tried to escape but both men on their own accord followed her and arrived at the inn nearly at the same time. Each one immediately declared their undying love for her. Now they sat together in hopelessness and frustration as young people could be.

I pretended to ignore my compassion for them, keeping the conversation light and amusing. The trio listened to some of my entertaining stories and began to relax and forget about their problem. They were just about to say good night when I said, "I know how to solve your problem but you must agree first to accept the outcome regardless."

"What!" said Stepen. "How can you know our problem and yet solve it? Excuse me, but I think the wine has gotten to your head."

"I know," I began, "that you are both in love with Rosea, she loves both of you and cannot decide which man to be with."

"By Rai, is it that obvious?" said Sternan placing his hand on his forehead and then brushing it over his head.

Rosea gasped at my words and broke down sobbing. Both men jumped up, colliding with each other, falling down in their attempt to soothe her.

I helped the men up. When they were all seated again, and after Rosea stopped crying enough to listen, I asked them, "Are you ready to solve this dilemma? I will have you both perform a test, and the winner will marry Rosea. Sleep it over and if you all agree, come to my room to sign a agreement, and receive instructions of how to proceed."

"I retire to my room now. Have a pleasant sleep, relax and allow your decision to arise without worry or thinking if possible."

"Yes," Rosea said, "we will discuss what you say and give you our decision in the morning. I don't know why but we all trust you as a old friend even though we just met."

"Good, then good night."

"Good night."

I left feeling very light and a bit tipsy from the wine. I shall have a good sleep tonight, I thought as I prepared for bed.

I left the window open for the night. In the morning I woke from a deep sleep to the calls of the birds. The morning air filled my lungs when I looked out the window and welcomed the new day. A slight mist and chill grabbed me, for the sun had yet to penetrate through the curtain of trees. I dressed quickly and went out for a brisk walk. The morning felt fresh and alive like the quiet mind before it gets busy with the thoughts of the day.

I hiked deep into the woods and then found an inviting spot to sit, under a tree facing directly east. I closed my eyes and did not open them until I heard someone walking towards me. When I looked up I saw Rosea standing in front of me.

"Ah," I said, "I am glad you came; I was just feeling about you."

"I hope you don't mind and I hope I am not disturbing you, but when I saw you leaving the inn, I just had to come and see you, I don't know why."

With a slight wave of my hand I said, "Come, please sit with me for awhile and then we will talk."

Rosea nodded and sat close to me, leaning against the next tree.

With eyes closed, in a few moments she felt a movement rising somewhere inside her, like a light current pulsing through out her body. It made her tingle and at same time she felt herself relaxing. She noticed her heart started to move and shift. Her mind became absolutely quiet and still. We sat together in silence until I opened my eyes and gently said, "Take your time to adjust but let us go soon for your friends will be worried. How are you feeling?"

Back in the visual world, gazing as a small child, she hit her arms lightly to feel her body again. Rosea said, "There is a definite shift in my heart. Before this moment I was incomplete, always feeling a gap. Now it is gone. I am whole. I can hardly imagine what I was so worried about. Now I understand my love is such it can love more than one. There is no need to choose one over the other." Rosea came and touched my face with both hands. She said, "My god, who are you and what have you done to me? How can I ever thank you for giving my heart back?

I closed my eyes to her touch then opened them with a faraway look. "It is my joy and my purpose to meet and show you what has always been but has been covered with doubts and fears. Now you know your own pure essential nature and it will never be covered up with doubts and confusion. Come, let us go to your men and share what you found here today."

Rosea bowed her head, "Yes."

Stepen and Sternan were pacing up and down on the lawn in front of the inn. They looked upset and angry as if they had been in an argument. When we returned, both the men felt a jolt of shock in their hearts. They dropped their worry and ran to her but could only stare speechless. The change in Rosea was so profound they did not know how to reach out.

"My dear friends," I said approaching close to them, "come, let us go to my room and be together. We can have our breakfast there."

Rosea took their hands and we went inside.

By the time we entered the room, Stepen and Sternan were feeling their hearts shifting inside as well.

Stepen was about to say something when I lifted my finger to his mouth, "Please be quiet for now; we will talk later. I go now to arrange breakfast and will return shortly."

Both men were bewildered but had the sense something vital was happening even though it was so new and in a way confusing. Now when they looked at Rosea, their heart and their minds deepen. Gone was the need to possess her.

By the time I returned, the atmosphere was thick with love.

We remained quiet until there was a soft knock on the door. The innkeeper brought the food personally because he sensed something was going on but had not expected to experience such deep loving silence when he entered the room. He almost dropped his tray and would have if I had not been quick enough to catch him.

Everyone laughed while the innkeeper apologized and quickly left the room saying, "Please call me if there is anything you need."

"Yes, we will, thank you, you are so kind," I replied.

I served the guests and without a word breakfast was eaten.

Not until I had removed the breakfast trays outside the door did I speak. "Thank you, for understanding so quickly and being open to allow the healing of your hearts. I don't think there is need of a test now. No longer will you long for the other, since what you search is already present inside you. Your relationships will arise from a deep sharing rather than a need to fill a hole inside you. In this sharing of love and openness will come the solution of how the three of you will be together or not. Now join hands and make this agreement in your hearts and mind."

Rosea stood, embraced both of them separately then together, and after that the men held each other. They joined hands, and each one made a silent vow of agreement.

Sternan and Stepen both came to Kareae with a short Raian embrace.

After a potent moment Sternan said, "We know now what is true in our hearts and we cannot help but to live its truth. You have brought such peace and joy to us. Our home will always be yours and I speak for all of us that we will always be in gratitude and ready to help you if there is any need."

Kareae nodded in thanks, "Yes, perhaps I will visit you and will need some assistance. And if you need me, just think of my presence and something will happen."

The four of them spent the rest of the day together exploring the area around the inn. They enjoyed the majesty of the forest and the life that lived within it. Kareae so much loved the power of the forest that gave such strength to the earth. They found a small meadow with high grass and decided to take some rest before making the return trek to the inn. Each one was left alone in the high grass to feel the elements of the earth, air, fire and water and sense their connection with it.

Sternan shared later, "I have walked in the forest all my life but always as an observer, separate. Now, it is like the nature is part of me and I am part of the nature. Such love I've never known,"

Jon watched the party of guests return to the inn from their outing. He could not keep his mind off what he experienced before in Kareae's room. Now as they entered the lobby, he felt all of sudden refreshed like he had just came out of a cold stream after swimming.

Unable to restrain himself, he knocked on Kareae's door later in the evening before the dinner hour.

"Please excuse me sir, may I come in and talk to you?

"Yes, please, come in," replied Kareae. "I had the feeling you would come. It makes me happy your heart is so sensitive as well. It seems that innkeepers are very advanced. I had a wonderful meeting with the innkeeper near Do."

"Is that so? Actually I don't know why I am here but I could not stop myself from coming," he confessed.

"The mind does not know but your heart does. Now please sit down, close your eyes and listen to the sound of the wind in the trees."

In the late afternoon there was a slight wind singing its way through the forest.

Afterwards, Jon opened his eyes with tears of joy and gratitude. There was no need to talk for a long while.

Finally I gently reminded Jon that the dinner hour was approaching and he was needed. "Now," I said, "your work will not be work but a sharing of love and joy with everyone who comes under your roof."

That evening in the dining room was a night that

impressed all the guests as something very special even though nothing unusual seemed to be occurring. There was a synchronicity felt by all. The trio sat together quietly with me in deep awe. I took it all in my stride, perfectly comfortable in my role of teacher who restores wholeness. The innkeeper came over more than usual to fill our glasses and share in the harmony. It was an unforgettable night.

When they returned to Do, Rosea wrote

Dear Mother,

You can't believe that just when I was ready to pull my hair out in frustration of my love for both Stephan and Sternan, a marvelous event occurred that has filled me with deep love for my men and the world. Oh, mother, I can't wait to meet you in person and give you a big hug. Please tell dad not to worry, the poor man, I know so much he cares for me.

I've had a long talk with both of my darlings and we decided if we cannot all get married together then we would live together according to common law. Please, mother don't be shocked by this, it is the only solution. Stephan and Sternan both love each other and are not jealous. Yes, believe it or not, they both have had such a stunning transformation

We owe it all to a man we met at the inn while having dinner. I never met someone quite like him before, but he seemed to know all about us and how to solve our dilemma. Actually he didn't really do anything but being around him, our hearts melted and our doubts disappeared. I really hope someday you can meet him.

Well, I've got to go, please don't get too excited about my news. I will try to visit next week. I miss the farm and all the animals.

Your loving daughter,

Rosea

Chapter 8

THE WARRIOR RECLUSE

I departed with the morning's dawn, embracing as a young lover the quietude of the thick woodland, the last great forest before approaching the countryside of the capital. On my second day of discovery, while engrossed in watching a pair of hawks circling on the wind, I picked up the scent of a faint vibration coming from deep within the forest. The unusual nature of this vibration intrigued me, urging me to find its source. I felt as well, a strong pull to commune more deeply in this exquisite forest environment.

The woods were packed solid but I found a small opening. Entering the forest was like stepping into a magnificent temple. I bowed my head to its divine beauty. The passing of light through the tree branches created many tones of subdued colors, imparting a green luminescence. In the vaulted silence, the absolute beauty of the light and trees and earth were sublimely accented. With no wind, everything was absolutely still, not even a small animal was running about. My breathing was the only sound I heard.

I walked half a day following the direction of the vibrational scent. At last, I rested next to a small stream. Towards the afternoon I began to hear a steady sound that became louder and louder as I walked. I recognized finally, the sound of a waterfall. In addition, the vibration I was following became strong. I approached an opening in the forest and spied within a rushing stream, a fairly large pool of water and a small waterfall. The cascading water fell only for a few feet but the arrangement of the stones and the natural pool made it unique and beautiful.

I stepped into the spraying mist of the rushing stream, allowing it to surround me in freshness. Invigorated by its soft coolness, I quickly disrobed and entered the pool. The freezing water kissed every cell of my body. When I jumped out, I was tingling with the sparkle of life, renewed after my long day's journey.

I sensed someone was present but sat quietly by the pool with my eyes closed. However, I was surprised when a hand gently touched my shoulder. I looked up to see a huge man towering above me. A smile came naturally when I said, "I am happy to meet you. My name is Kareae."

"Are you not afraid to see me as most people?" the man said

"How can I be afraid of my own self?" I answered,

"Hmm, a man of my own heart," the big one said, then he lifted and embraced me in a mighty bear hug.

"My name is Janeac (Jan-noc), I come from the kingdom of Mi, and I belong to the clan of Mians that have always been warriors."

"You're a long way from home and have come to a place where warriors are no longer needed."

"Yes, that is exactly the point. I am at the end of a traditional line of warriors. I want this tradition to end with me." He took off his clothes and jumped into the pool. "Come, let us swim."

I watched Janeac dive in and swim to the waterfall, then disappear behind it. After several minutes, he returned saying, "Please come, you will enjoy this."

I followed his command this time: disrobing and jumping into the pool, then swimming behind the waterfall. Inside there was a small cavern perhaps large enough to accommodate two. At the back of the cavern was a smaller gentle waterfall. I sat under it allowing the pleasant water to cascade over me. Afterwards outside the pool, Janeac was already drying himself in the sun. We laid together without speaking, each in our own way in tune with the nature.

In the late afternoon with the sun hiding behind the clouds, Janeac gathered his clothes and said "Now my friend, come with me to my campsite before it gets dark. We can share some food. I found a small cave not so far from here that is perfect to stay in. And as you can see, the nature here is magnificent."

"Thank you."

We walked alongside the river. Although there was not a real path, the way was easy enough, as the elevation of the rocks rose like steps. We took a turn inwards and in several minutes came to Janeac's campsite.

Janeac's body seemed to pulsate power and life. In contrast, a gentleness about him could almost be missed because of the power he emitted.

Under a massive overlapping boulder that sat on top of another huge rock was Janeac's campsite. This afforded complete shelter from the elements. Janeac constructed walls on both sides of the outcropping with small branches and bush so that the area was enclosed on three sides. The front opened out to the east receiving the early morning sun. Just in front of the cave, Janeac had his campfire and did his cooking when he felt like eating.

He built a fire to boil water that also provided warmth for the still chilly nights. After simmering herbs in the heated water, he handed me a cup.

"This is a drink from wild herbs I've found here in the forest," he said.

"Mmm, quite good," I commented. "Tell me, how long have you been here?"

"It's two moons since I arrived. For one moon I searched before I found this place. As I mentioned before, I am the last in the line of a great warrior lineage having received all the powers and strengths of my ancestors. But I found, as I grew older, that my outlook and vision was radically different from that of my elders. I no longer saw the need to fight or use violence to achieve peace and prosperity. I experienced on many occasions I could achieve this end just with my intelligence and insight into the situation."

"When I reached twenty-one and had to undergo my last rites of manhood, I felt the need to come to terms with my powers. To do this at home seemed difficult. I decided to retreat to the forest until it became clear whether to follow the traditions or trust my own intelligence and create a new custom."

"This is the first time in my life that I'm alone. What I have discovered is that I really enjoy this freedom. There have been a few incidents when someone wandered close by, but I put on my most ferocious face and scared them away. I was about to commence that with you, but as I got closer, I felt you were different and I had an instant liking to you."

"And me to you," I admitted lightly. "But please, show me this ferocious face I missed."

Janeac rose, walked to the edge of the campsite, put on his ferocious face and came charging at me screaming, not stopping until he was almost on top of me. Indeed, he did fall over me in great laughter.

"Yes, that would scare anyone and anything away." I said, bursting with hilarity.

Janeac started to prepare by the fire some wild roots, mushrooms and green leaves he gathered earlier to make a soup. "My food is simple but good. Sometimes I catch a fish, but since being in the forest I discovered that I can nourish myself with the power of the sun."

"That is amazing," I said , "you are the first person I met, other than my teachers, who utilizes the power of the sun. Tomorrow morning let's sit together."

I enjoyed watching the mesmerizing movement of Janeac preparing the meal. His body was huge, but he moved like a dancer, gracefully and full of purpose.

We sat by the fire after the meal, happy in the presence of each other. Sometimes we heard an animal moving in the forest but none ventured towards the fire.

Janeac said, "I have seen huge stags and deer and there is evidence of wild boar, but I have yet to see one. Let us rest now. Tomorrow I want to hear about you and what brings you to the forest."

"I can answer you quite easily. I came into the forest to meet you. But, yes, I agree. Let us wait until the morning for a full a explanation."

*****

I rose before Janeac. I loved this time of morning before the sun appeared. By the time the bursting beams of sunlight hit the campsite, Janeac was up and signaled me to follow him. By the river we washed, and then Janeac took me to a high boulder where we sat and caught the sun's rays directly.

"The method I learned from my teachers is to raise the eyes upwards and look slightly above the sun," I explained, as Janeac followed my instructions. In this way the whites of the eyes receive the sun's rays. I find the sun will turn black at some point. That's right, keep looking until you feel it is enough, then close your eyes, rub your palms together and place them over your eyes. Repeat this twice, then lie on your back for a short time to allow the absorbed rays of the sun to penetrate deeper."

Janeac said afterwards, "Yes, that is basically what I've been doing except I've been looking directly at the sun."

The rest of the morning we spent by the pool swimming and sitting under the waterfall, enjoying the warmth of the day.

"Are you interested," Janeac said, "to follow the river higher up? I want to show you a place where you can see the forest until the horizon."

"Yes, I would like that," I said, jumping up to follow Janeac who already was walking up the path. I was again impressed how gracefully Janeac moved.

After climbing a series of ascending boulders, some of them tricky to navigate, we reached the highest point just when the sun was at its height. The stone area was completely bare of any vegetation. Before us, the majesty of the forest unfolded elegantly, spreading its emerald cape as far as the eye could see. "What a sight." I said

"Yes, it's marvelous" Janeac said, "but now I want you to explain how you came to the forest to meet me. How could you know that I was here in this remote area?"

I gave him a direct gaze and considered him for a moment. Finally I said, "It might be difficult to understand, but I am sensitive to vibrations. When I tune in, I can feel the power of others around me. I know very easily how a person is and if I want I can hear even his thoughts. When someone has a pure heart, the power is very strong. Your vibration is strong. I felt it faraway on the King's Road to Rai. It was easy for me to enter into the forest and follow the vibration to its source, which is you."

"I never met a man like you before, Kareae. You have amazed me since we met. I have trouble to keep my eyes off you and that has never happened before even with a beautiful woman. I feel as if we are brothers. But tell me, why did you travel all this way to meet me?"

"I am here to give you what you are searching for. I am here to show you your truth so that you can fulfill your destiny and yet remain true to yourself."

Before Janeac could react, I jumped up and placed

both my hands on Janeac's head. The power passing through me was so strong that within a few moments Janeac passed out. He remained unconscious for most of the afternoon until at last he started to regain wakefulness, and finally sat up.

Janeac could not speak; the experience was so overpowering. When he could walk, we took a long time to return to the campsite. Janeac was like a little child seeing life for the first time, stopping every few moments to look at the world. He spent a long time just watching some ants crawling in and out of an anthill. Indeed, finally I had to pull him away.

Janeac remained quiet for the rest of the day. For long periods he laid in trance, only able to open his eyes for short moments. I stayed close by to make sure he had everything he needed. Periodically I forced Janeac to drink, so he stayed hydrated.

I felt humbled but exhilarated by the happening myself. I did not plan to touch Janeac's head. It was not premeditated but a spontaneous outpouring. The intensity of the power was like never before - a merging of two primordial forces.

The next morning Janeac spoke about his experience.

"I was lying above my body the entire night. I wasn't sure if I would come back or even if I wanted to. When you touched my head, I sensed a vibration like a sound inside that kept getting louder and louder until I dissolved into it. I don't know where I went, but I was no longer in my body or in this world for that matter. After some time, I noticed I was sitting within a circle of men and women. At first their forms were indistinct and their voices hardly audible, but as my focus became more concentrated, they became clear and distinct. All the members of the circle were dressed in unusual tight fitting robes made of a material that seemed to be a cross between metal and cloth. Other than that, there was nothing unusual about them. What was strange was that even though they were sitting, there seemed to be no chairs underneath them.

I don't think they noticed me at first but slowly I came into focus for them as well. They stopped their conversation and stared at me. I never felt so looked at as in those moments. Finally one of the men spoke. "We have been waiting forever for you, but we are very surprised you have come now. We were not expecting you to evolve enough spiritually to arrive here for at least a few more lives. Someone must have assisted you to enter. In any case, you are ready because you are here."

"'Let us begin," he announced to the other members.

"An ageless looking woman stood and ceremoniously came in front of me. There was something familiar about her but I couldn't quite place it. She announced, 'I am Ki, the Mother of Mothers, the Protector of the Protector of the Mian warrior clan. I pledge myself to you, Janeac, now that you are of age.'

"Then to my great astonishment, she rose and walked inside me and became part of me.

"Next was a smaller woman of a gentler nature. She explained she was Mati, the Mother of my mothers. Mati showed me in my mind's eye all my births starting from a one-cell organism to what I am now. This occurred so fast I could hardly take it in. Then in detail, she flashed several of my past lives in front of me. It was a revelation to see my roots and my development. I've been everything: the king, the pauper, the murderer, the murdered, the good and the bad. When she finished, she pledged herself to me like Ki, then stood and entered inside to become part of me."

"Actually 'me' at this point was not the 'I' as I knew myself but I could not say who I was."

"Next to stand before me, wearing a small golden headdress was a slender man called Pai, the Protector of all the Mian clans past, present and future. After he made his pledge, he removed his headdress and placed it on my head declaring that from now I am the Protector in the three worlds. Then bowing before me, he entered inside of me."

"All the remaining members of the circle came in front of me, each one representing a different aspect of life. After they announced who they were and gave me their knowledge, they made their vow and stepped inside me to become part of a bigger me. At last, the first man who spoke appeared before me. His light was so strong almost I could not look at him. He declared, 'I am Mi, the Lord of lords, the highest protector of the Mian realms.'

"We began a conversation in earnest that answered all my questions and doubts. I experienced I was in a everlasting stream of communicating knowledge. I don't know how it is possible but I can't remember the details of what we spoke, but I know we discussed my life and my destiny and the destiny of the world and I know the knowledge is inside me.

"At last, he stood up and entered into me in a fusion of light and sound. When the synthesis was finished, I felt something I used to call myself returning to the body and the world. Finally I opened my eyes. The Janeac who was present before I am aware of but now I am something more: I am the consciousness of all that I've heard and seen and all those that entered me."

"I know now for the first time who I was, am and will be for all eternity. Absolutely, I am not this body nor this mind nor who I thought I was. My quest and retreat are now complete, I can return to my homeland and take my position in life."

We sat silently for a while drinking a herbal tea I made.

"My friend, I am so grateful for what you have done for me. How can I ever repay you?"

"There is nothing to repay; I was only the vehicle. And in this instance, it was happening to me as to you, the intensity of the transfer was beyond anything I've ever experienced. I feel also the changes you feel. We should allow our transformation to land and settle. Let's spend at least half a moon here before traveling again."

"Yes," Janeac said, "you're right and I want to spend this time with you. Who knows when we will get a chance like this again?"

"We will meet again and for sure the circumstances will be different. Yes, let us enjoy this special time together."

We spent the next days having long conversations. We explored the nearby forest and especially enjoyed the excitement of climbing several of the steep cliffs without ropes. At the evening , Janeac spoke often about the kingdom of Mi, the influence of his family and what would be expected of him when he returned. He discussed the different policies and projects he would implement when he returned to be the leader.

"I have several ideas but I must see how they accepted. I know the Mians are not as advanced as the Raians spiritually. We are a people of the earth, more solid and physical. There has always been a class system and the warrior clan of which I represent, is the leading force of Mi. Our merchant class has produced great achievements in technology, as you probably know. Many products were developed first in Mi. We are blessed with a vast kingdom with plentiful resources and our potential seems boundless. Unfortunately we have always been in the shadow of Rai, as is the western kingdom of Sol. Probably, if not for the difficult ghats, our armies would have invaded more often. Mians, especially the warrior class, love to fight. And we are over thirty percent of the population. The winds of change are coming to Mi, but I know the work will not be easy. I am not worried about any challenges to my power, as I am the strongest man in Mi. Nobody can defeat me in a duel. Now, with the incorporation of the wisdom of my ancestral spirits within my soul, I am in full power to raise Mi to new heights of understanding and achievement."

We spent many hours sitting, exploring the inner worlds of our new awareness. For me it was natural to live and function without an ego. For Janeac, it was like being reborn. He needed time and guidance for his body was still used to the habits of twenty-one years. I tried telepathic communication with Janeac but he was not that sensitive. His huge body was earthy and remained that way, on the ground. However, he possessed powers of strength and willpower that I could not equal.

Towards the end of our time together, I suggested to Janeac that he visit the forest temple to meet Siktu, the priestess. "She will initiate you into the secret ways she learnt during her priesthood training."

"Yes, I am ready to learn."

"Good, the temple is hidden deep in the forest near the southern ghats. It is difficult to find so I will have Siktu meet you on the King's Road. I will be in communication with her. Siktu will teach you the ways of many practices and teachings."

Several mornings later, we broke camp. We traveled together until the King's Road.

"In several days travel, you will come to a nice inn near Do. Please stop and spend a day there if you like; Fritaye the innkeeper is a good friend and quite a devoted person. Tell him I sent you, he will be happy."

"Yes, I will stop there; a good inn will be a welcome sight after all this time in the forest. My dear friend, you are deep in my heart, always present."

"Yes," I replied as we embraced and then gazed at each other in loving friendship. "Don't worry about finding Siktu, she will find you."

Janeac nodded, picked up his pack and took his leave.

I watched Janeac disappear down the road, then I picked up my backpack to continue the journey to the capital.

Chapter 9

BROKEN WHEEL

Everyday brought me closer to Rai. I walked swiftly and steadily, without interruptions through the remaining forest. Isolated houses in the distance came into view, and the forest gradually became thinner. Continuing farther west, farm and grazing land began to appear, along with the sounds and smells of domesticated animals.

Traffic on the road was surprisingly light, but towards the middle of my third day of traveling, it began to pick up. I saw several well-built coaches parked up ahead along the side of the road. When I drew nearer, I observed that one of the coaches had a broken wheel. A cluster of men who looked to be the drivers and coachmen were fixing it. On a field nearby, gazed a team of very beautiful fine and healthy horses, almost fifteen hands high and in prime condition.

Under a bright canopy engraved with the royal crescent, set up with a table and chairs, was a lively group of travelers. They were enjoying a midday meal and carefree discussions. Everyone was excitedly speaking;

it seemed, at the same moment. Dressed in the current style of the court, the men with loose breeches, half boots and flowing long blouses, and the women in flowing full dresses with tapered bodices, made it obvious the party belonged to the court of the King.

Just as I was passing amidst the eating, laughter and conversations and barking dogs, a man came on the road and called out to me, "Excuse me, I say, sir, I hope I do not disturb you, but would you like to join us for refreshment and rest from the hot sun before you continue your journey?" He directed me to the group with his hands.

I acknowledged the earthy looking man possessing intelligent eyes, with a friendly warm nod. I looked at the rest of the party and said, "Yes, thank you, I would very much appreciate a cool drink and some rest from the sun."

Meanwhile at the table everyone stopped to watch me.

"Let me introduce myself," the man said as we approached the group. "I am Prince Zolade and that beautiful woman at the far end of the table standing up now, is my sister, Princess Sabna. I must confess, she asked me to stop and invite you."

Kareae bowed in the formal Raian way saying, "It is my pleasure to meet you both and I thank you for your invitation. My name is Kareae. I am on my way to the capital, but I come from the temple Kanparu. My parents are the high priest and priestess."

Princess Sabna returned the formal bow looking directly at me with the same intelligent eyes as her brother. She smiled politely, "It is my honor to meet you.

I have heard about your parents, their fame is well known in the capital. Before I marry, I will visit the temple for their blessings." I noted that Sabna's perfect features complemented her sharp mind and regal bearing.

Zolade introduced me to the others, and then he requested I sit next to Sabna.

Once again the air became festive with everyone talking at once. I joined in, and in a short time I felt like I was part of the family.

In the course of the table conversation with Sabna, I asked how she was related to the King? She was surprised by my question but explained, "My mother's sister is married to the king's brother's son. Our position is far enough away from the throne to give us the freedom to go about our business but close enough to enjoy being part of the court."

"We were returning to Rai after a visit to one of my cousins when the wheel broke down. I don't know why but as soon as I saw you walking down the road, I just had to meet you."

"Thank you, it's good you stopped me. It would have been a shame to pass by without meeting."

Debating whether to follow her impulse, Princess Sabna finally decided while Kareae was silent and said, "Sir, would you mind having a walk with me? There is something I want to discuss with you. I feel you might be able to help me."

"Yes, of course, let's go."

Sabna stood and announced to everyone's surprise that she was going for a short stroll with me. She took my hand and quickly we were off onto the road.

"Don't go too far, as I can see that the wheel is almost fixed," her brother called out.

When the princess was sure she could not be overheard, she said, "I will come right to the point as we don't have much time. There is something I would like your advice about. Seeing that you come from the temple, I feel I can trust you."

I waited, giving her my full attention.

Sabna hesitated, it seemed, a little afraid to begin but then she confessed, "I've become involved with someone, a boy really, coming from a good family. We are in love, and he wants me to run away with him, to leave Rai and live somewhere near the border at one of his family's estates. I love him and yet... there is some reluctance."

I answered quickly, "If you run off with this boy, you will regret it for the rest of your life. You will not be happy and you will not be fulfilling your ambitions and your destiny. Stay in Rai and allow your fate to unfold. It will satisfy both your heart and your mind."

"How do I know my destiny?"

"When both your mind and heart say yes. In your case it will be so apparent there will be no doubt."

"You speak as if you know."

"Yes, I can see. It is something I have always had. Someday, when it is appropriate, I will tell you, but until then, please trust me. I know your mind is strong and clever, so try to see it as a test of discipline."

Sabna said, feeling perplexed "How can you know me so well when we have just met? Well then, okay, I will try."

"Good." I said softly. "Look Princess Sabna, the coach is ready; let us return."

"My dear sir," Sabna flashed, "why not finish your journey to the capital with us? We have plenty of room."

"Yes, that would be perfect," I replied, looking down at my worn sandals with almost broken heels.

Meanwhile back at the wagons, the horses were being hitched up while the rest of the livery took down the canopy, storing it away with the table and chairs. Everyone was eager to depart and again there were looks of surprise when Sabna announced that I would travel with them.

Sabna invited me to sit in the coach with her, Prince Zolade and Sabna's young niece, Tia. The rest of the group piled into the other coaches.

The well-built coaches were comfortable and afforded a smooth and easy ride, especially on the excellent King's Road. Everyone was relaxed, enjoying the drive through the countryside.

The forest was behind us now. Only small tree groves remained between the land used for farming and grazing. More houses appeared, and the traffic increased as we moved forward.

"We could reach Rai in five or six hours, but as it is late in the afternoon, we will stop once more. I know a very beautiful spot to make our camp," Prince Zolade informed them. "I want the horses to be fully rested when we reach Rai."

"I always appreciate how well my brother loves and cares for his horses – although I think sometimes he cares more for them than for people." Sabna said

Zolade smiled, folding his arms together. "Yes, there is some truth to that. Animals are genuine, there are no pretensions; they love you and are loyal to you. People, on the other hand, are much more complex, loyalties are divided; you never know what their true feelings are. I prefer to be with my animals."

"Yes," I said, "I see the simplicity of your heart, Prince Zolade. You are right, people are much more complex. They never fulfill your expectations as everyone has their own personal agenda. If you want them to be loyal like your animals, then your heart will always be troubled. I see also your heart is distressed. When you stop having expectations of others, your pain will disappear."

Prince Zolade gave me a hard look. Few people had ever spoken to him in this way, so direct to the point, so correct.

"My dear sir, your words pierce me like an arrow, yet I feel your good intent. I will think about what you say. I have never considered this before. May I come to you sometime to discuss this matter further?

"Yes, let me get settled in Rai and then I will come to visit you. We have important issues to discuss, and I want to see your estate and your stocks of animals.

"Okay, I look forward to your visit, you are always welcome."

For most of the remaining time I spent playing with Tia.

I taught her a word game I learnt as a child. Tia caught on quickly. This impressed both Sabna and Zolade with her understanding. Sabna commented, "I didn't realize she was so bright, you seem to bring out the best in her. Hmm, I am impressed how you seem to adjust to people and yet at the same time you appear aloof and independent. How unusual in a man."

"It is interesting how you see me, I never give it much thought," I responded.

Sabna and Zolade watched the countryside rolled by. I could sense they were taking the time to reflect upon my observations.

At the campsite later that night, Sabna joined me where I was sitting. "May I talk to you for a moment? I'm sorry to disturb you."

"Of course you may, I'm never disturbed by you," I replied. "I'm just gazing at this beautiful clear night sky. So many stars, each one a mystery."

"Yes, they are beautiful," she answered after making the effort to look at them. "I've been so much thinking about what you told me that I've hardly noticed the stars."

"Ah," I murmured.

"I've come to the conclusion you're correct. Running away would not be the best course. I feel such a relief. I want to show my thanks by giving you this gold ring. It has several brilliant small clear stones from some faraway land, and look here, there are sacred symbols engraved into the gold. I don't know what they mean but are beautiful."

"It is truly a marvelous gift, thank you, I will cherish it." And I'm glad you made the correct choice. When a decision brings such relief, rest assured it is right."

"Tell me, how can you know so much, be so sure, when really you are no more than a boy coming into adulthood?"

"Princess Sabna, please don't be fooled by the age of my body. I am much more than what you see. I am eternal with infinite knowledge. My body will come and go but I will always remain. Does this make sense to you?"

"Not really. If I hit you, you will feel pain, is that not so?

"The body will feel pain but not I."

"This really makes no sense to me, but I cannot deny your sense of authority and wisdom. Can you teach me to see as you see?

"In due time, my dear Princess Sabna, in due time."

"I've taken up enough of your time. I will leave you to your stars. Get some rest, tomorrow promises to be a full day."

Sabna demurely came close, her perfume deliciously surrounding us, rewarded me with a quick kiss, then lightly stole away.

PART TWO

Chapter 10

RAI

The wind caressing my face and the slight swaying of the carriage imparted a sense of deep reflection. I turned from gazing out at the Raian countryside and watched Tia and Kareae playing and laughing. They seemed so at home, enjoying the same word game over and over again.

Zolade, I thought, my brother, you seem to be in the same reflective space as me. You have hardly spoken all morning.

Passing a particular beautiful lake area full with overhanging willow trees, I suddenly snapped out of my thoughtful state. I turned to Kareae and said, "Kareae, where will you stay in Rai? Why not come with me? I would be honored if you stay at my residence until you find something on your own. There's more than enough room. What do you say?"

"Yes, I would like that. Indeed, it would be a great help for me. My father gave me several addresses, but still, it would take time to find them."

"Marvelous. Zolade will drop us off and continue onto his estate, which is still a full day's ride ahead. Tia lives near to him."

"That's perfect," said Zolade, "I can't imagine you leaving us now that we have met."

The countryside near Rai changed slightly from larger farm acreage with livestock scattered about, to smaller stretches of meadows intermingled with small woods. Tina was thrilled to see herds of cows roaming about. Residential houses started to appear; some of which could be considered large estate size.

Rai was a beautiful city, with rolling hills, graceful meadows, surrounding forests, canals and rivers. Almost all of the houses appeared to be constructed with style and love, built with an awareness that they did not oppose each other.

Centrally located in the kingdom with the majestic river Signa gracefully flowing through it, Rai flourished with numerous natural river tributaries that were expanded into canals. Upon these canals were beautiful stone-constructed bridges found throughout the city.

Numerous temples, large estates and the King's palace were built on the rolling hills. This gave a very airy and regal feeling to the city. There was one long winding main road that threaded the city. However, city planning had kept congestion at a minimum with alternate parallel thoroughfares throughout the capital.

Raians prided themselves in keeping the city clean. Even the animal droppings, whether of horses or cows, were picked up regularly by the city's sanitation department.

Situated on the highest rise on the eastern side of the city where the forest began and the Signa protected its southern border, the palace took its place as the cultural center. Residential houses and estates existed on the northern border and on the western side, not far from the palace, stood an old fortress wall with a huge gate.

A small natural harbor with quays to moor boats gave Rai a strategic point on the river. River transportation was only within the kingdom because of the steep ghats. Barges were loaded and cruised to the ghats. From there, the goods were transferred and transported overland beyond the kingdom.

One of the great engineering marvels of Rai was the construction of roads on both the eastern and western borders traversing the ghats. The roads connected Rai with Sol on the east and Mi on the west. Even after many years, both passages remained a tourist attraction.

As the kingdom was surrounded by high mountain passes, the Signa flowed into huge lakes many leagues long and wide. These lakes were very popular. The King had his summer palace on one of the many tributaries.

A walk along the farming fields around the capital during the growing season gave good evidence of the richness of the deep dark fertile soil. During the rainy season, the river overflowed and deposited minerals and soil for the crops and numerous orchards. Many canals with extensive drainage systems were built to contain the overflow of the river during this time. Now it was rare for the city to flood.

There were about 100,000 inhabitants living in the capital and probably another 300,000 throughout the rest of the kingdom. The population was naturally small as the Raians did not favor large families, and the King did not encourage it because he wanted to keep the ecology in balance.

Raians as a whole were tall and slender but solidly built compared to the people of other kingdoms. The women liked to wear flowing clothes while the men were more comfortable in simple garments. No matter what they wore, Raians were stylish, taking care of how they looked even in the rural areas.

In essence, Raians were a down-to-earth, intelligent people, possessing a very good intuitive sense that felt the subtle vibrations of natural forces controlling their destiny. They were comfortable with who they were but were not arrogant. This trait was beaten out of them in the ancient wars. In this regard, Raians were considered evolved and advanced compared to the other kingdoms.

The style and cleanness of the city reflected this. It was difficult to find an area in Rai that was not well kept and cultivated in such a way so as not to lose the natural feeling of the land.

Raian farming techniques, even though non-motorized, were quite efficient, not requiring many workers. Wind power was fully harnessed for irrigation. A perpetual-motion system had been developed, enabling the turbines of the windmill to move with the slightest wind and then accelerating itself with its own generated energy. With wind often coming off the ghats, it made the system the best for generating power.

The crops were grown on a collective basis. When labor was needed, the townspeople were always available.

Indeed, it was a joy for them to help during harvests, a very festive time for Raians.

Long ago, the industry of Rai evolved to produce only goods that were absolutely necessary and could not be produced elsewhere. The Raians sense of style prohibited the building of industrial areas that stripped the nature of its beauty. Luckily, Rai was a rich fertile land and the Raians had enough intelligence to circumvent the destruction of the natural resources.

*****

A Raian man entered one of the temples that flourished in and around the city.

The Raians came with great respect to the temples to tune in with the natural forces of life and existence rather than worshiping a deity in human form.

The man bowed and placed both hands on the idol.

Usually contained inside a Raian temple sanctum was a polished stone perhaps six hands high with rounded ends, quarried from an area close to where the full moon festival was held. This stone possessed an unusual mineral composition that changed color when exposed to different wavelengths of light. The Raians greatly revered this stone.

After his prayers, the man circumvented the shrine to complete his attunement just when Zolade's coach passed by. Kareae watched with interest and expressed his admiration not only for the temple's unique pyramid style but for Rai itself. "Sabna, I heard about the splendor of Rai, but never did I imagine it would be this beautiful,"

I gave a soft knowing look, proud of my city. I watched Kareae look out with childlike enthusiasm, wondering, How can this man exist? What a marvel! I am fortunate he comes to stay with me. I wonder what it is he sees about me? Too bad I promised not to pursue it. Perhaps he will reveal it soon as he promised. Oh well, we shall see.

During a recent break to rest the horses, Zolade shared with me his bewilderment. "How can this mysterious man who seems to know everything still look at the world like a small innocent child? How do I place this man in my mind?" Not receiving an answer, Zolade remained quiet for most of the trip.

The carriage turned into a winding side road and followed a tree-lined street for several streets until it stopped before the gate of a walled-in estate.

"We have arrived." I said to Kareae "Welcome."

While the luggage was being unloaded, fond farewells were exchanged with Zolade and Tina. Prince Zolade extended Kareae a standing invitation to visit his estate. Tina was so taken with Kareae that she had to be coaxed with the promise of a visit in the near future to let go of him.

My house sat amidst a well-cared-for and established garden full of colorful flowers and unusual trees. In several areas were small ponds connected by tiny streams and mini waterfalls. Just at the entrance was a small wooden arched bridge that imparted the feeling of crossing into a magical world.

I introduced Kareae to the house and housekeepers and showed him his room.

"We are just north of the palace. Quite a few influential families have their homes here. I love my house; it suits my needs. The garden... what can I say? It is my joy and passion. I try to spend as much time as I can taking care of it.

"Yes, your garden is superb."

"Please feel that this is your home. Unfortunately, tomorrow morning I must leave for my brother's estate to help oversee the transplantation of some saplings that have arrived recently. I would prefer to spend this time with you but this work must be completed now. I am sorry but I will be gone for perhaps seven days. Let us have a light quiet dinner later; there will be plenty of time to meet my circle of friends and influential people. Oh, and I can give you the address of a friend of mine who deals in houses. I am sure he can find you a suitable home. You will like him, he's quite an interesting man."

Kareae took my hand, "I appreciate all your help and this house is so fine."

When Kareae looked at me, I saw myself go into a timeless space. I felt the joy of innocent children playing in a garden without a care or trouble for the world. I felt the relief of not having an intellect always analyzing and making judgments. I felt the freedom from my mind that always tries to control my enjoyment.

I lost my balance and fell into his arms. In only a few moments, though, I regained control and opened my eyes, softly seeing outwardly as if in a dream, completely relaxed.

"Ah, excellent," Kareae said. "After a few more minutes you will be perfectly able to function again. Please let's sit for awhile."

I nodded, still held by Kareae. Undeniably, I wanted

that he would hold me forever.

"I don't know what just happened but I am delighted, as light as a child without worries. Sweet Rai, what have you done to me?

"It's nothing really. You will notice its effects for some days. When you return from Zolade's estate we can explore this further. It's good you are so open."

I looked at Kareae in silence absorbing his words but now unable to respond other than with a nod.

"Why not have a bath, relax and then we'll meet later at dinner." Kareae said.

Still unable to speak, I smiled and left the room.

Chapter 11

FIRST DAYS IN RAI

After Sabna left, I had a chance to explore Rai. The city gently unraveled before me in colors and contrasts of natural and created beauty, the elements blending in harmony. The stark white of the architecture stood proudly against the green hush of the surrounding meadows and woods. Immersed in this backdrop, the Raians seemed sharp and awake, without pretensions.

Rai, it appeared to me, sat on a strong power-spot that caused life to vibrate higher and faster. Perhaps, I reflected, the direct alignment with the earth's axis, the power of the river, the surrounding forests and the distant ghats are all combining to create this special effect. It is almost like someone is gathering energy and spreading it throughout the city.

Further into exploring on a beckoning morning, I traveled to an address of a man my father Ashara had insisted on me visiting. His name was Rusai, a man of deep mystery. Not even Romdev spoke about him. All I knew was that he lived with his wife on the southwest side of Rai across the Signa in a sparsely populated rural area.

I was sitting on the banks of the Signa wondering how to cross when I finally spotted a man in a small boat paddling towards me.

"Dear sir," I called when the man approached, "would you be so kind to take me across to the other side?"

"Aye," said the puzzled boatman " but I don't know why, there's nothing over there but empty barren farmland."

"It seems a friend of my father lives somewhere nearby." I replied.

"Well, get in, I can take ya."

The gentle downstream current of the Signa effortlessly carried the boat to the other side. We both were drawn to each other in some mysterious way but we remained silent until we reached the shore.

"Pretty isolated place out here. Would ya like me to wait, sir?"

"Yes, please."

The walk to Rusai's house took around thirty minutes through empty farmland.

Ashara had described the house's uniqueness so I had little trouble recognizing it. And, all the more so, because the house was the only one in the area. This house, similar to the forest temple, appeared to have risen from the earth organically. I was once again impressed by the use of sacred geometry.

As soon as I entered the gate, a round and bearded

Rusai came out of the house to greet me saying in a fine voice, "Ah, a visitor. This must be a special day because no one comes to visit here. I can see from your clothes young man that you are not from Rai but most likely coming from somewhere west. Indeed, I can say you are coming from Kanparu and that in all likelihood you are the son of Ashara and Leila."

I bowed my head in the formal way and handed him a letter from my parents.

Rusai continued with a gleam in his eye, "I was wondering when you would come to see me? I began to feel your presence several days ago. Well, come inside, meet my wife and after we have a cup of tea, we can get down to some serious business."

Being in the presence of Rusai was not something I had expected. The force field around him was immeasurable, greater than anything or anyone I ever met even in Kanparu. I was left speechless unable even to say his name. Rusai literally had to take my hand and bring me inside the house. His wife, Evane, in contrast, appeared very normal and natural bringing tea and cakes and then leaving quietly. The quality of love between them, though, was easy to see in their eyes.

When I was able to function again we both began laughing. This laughter was contained in such a whirlwind that I could hardly tolerate it. As Rusai's body shook and vibrated with his laughter, we seemed to expand and rise until we were sitting in another reality and then another.

When finally I could speak I said, "Respected sir, my father gave me no warning about you. He told me simply to come and deliver this letter. It is only now that I see the importance of meeting you."

"I see." Rusai said nodding his head, "then I will tell you right off... I am one of the Keepers of Creation." His eyes pregnant with expression, he spread his arms out wide, "Without me none of this world would exist in the way that it does. In simple terms, one of the reasons Rai is a blessed land is because of my maintenance of the purity of the creation. This leaves Rai to develop without interference on many levels you would be surprised existed."

Rusai continued, "You have not realized it yet but people who pass by won't even see this house or me. For them it is invisible. That you were able to see and then walk through the gate is a great event and feat. We were wondering if you would be capable of even finding the house. I am sure your father will be astonished to hear you made it so easily. This is the reason why Ashara did not tell you more. He made the journey here long ago but was only able to find the house with my help. You, Kareae are your father's son and much more. If I did not see it, I would not have believed it possible. Romdev has not come here yet even though he knows of my presence. I am hoping one day he will find his way to me."

"The fact we can meet shows you are ready to facilitate the coming uplifting. When the time comes, I will do everything in my power to help you. Indeed, don't be surprised if soon you experience yourself going beyond your normal capabilities."

Rusai stood signaling for me to rise, "It is not good for you to be here much longer. Finish your tea and then you should go, but rest assured that I and the power of creation are behind you."

I rose and bowed again in the formal way, paid my respects to his wife and left.

On my return to the river, I looked back at the house, but to my surprise it was no longer there - only empty farmland with a scattering of a few trees on the edges of the fields.

The boatman was astounded to see me, " By Rai, it was like ya disappeared in front of me from one second to the next and now ya reappear in the same way. What's going on?" I did not comment but asked him about the house. "What house?" the boatman answered, looking at me even more strangely, having no idea what I was talking about.

I could sense that the boatman was wondering about me, this stranger with the warm gentle eyes crossing the river in a deserted area. And, he had been puzzled by why he felt so drawn to take his boat to this deserted part of the Signa for really no reason.

"Well, ya might as well get in sir, and I take ya to the other side before the weather changes," he said. In his mind I heard him was promising himself that he wouldn't do this again.

*****

Princess Sabna returned from her brother's estate to find me, my face smeared with earth, tending her garden. "It's funny. I was thinking all morning about the garden, whether it was tended to, and here you are taking care of it."

"It is also my pleasure to work with plants. Just a little caring and they give so much."

"That's true, I never looked at it that way before. Kareae, after lunch, lets visit Baleae, the dealer of houses. I heard from some friends a very good house has just come on the market.

*****

Baleae, a jolly little man with many children was happy to show us the house.

The just vacated house imparted the feeling of being welcome like old friends meeting after a long time, something so familiar and inviting and yet new and different. Standing on its magnificent terrace, Baleae pointed to the palace in the south. Princess Sabna was impressed with the flourishing garden and the panoramic view from the terrace. The house was small but had a guest cottage that I liked.

Between the guesthouse was open space that I immediately had the vision of a small temple I would design and built.

Baleae explained, "The owner is a rich merchant whose family became too big and has built a larger house."

Without hesitation I said to the dealer, "I will buy the house."

"Dear sir," he began, "There is one stipulation the owner is insisting upon. An older woman has been the caretaker of this house for many years. The new house is too big for her to take care of. The owner would have taken her and used additional help, but she insisted on remaining with the house. The owner will agree to the sale only if this woman is allowed to stay and be taken care of. He is very concerned because the woman has been with his family for many years. What do you say?

Can you agree to this?"

I took a few moments to absorb this information and answered, "Yes, of course, I am sure we will get along just fine. Please have her join us here at the closing so we can meet."

The move into the house one moon later was quick and easy. Some furniture was left over, particularly two huge bed frames that were too cumbersome to move. Sabna and I spent several days shopping, choosing bedding and curtains. Kitchen utensils were purchased in addition to the equipment Sabna donated, as her own kitchen was over equipped.

"Kareae, you continuously surprise me. I never expected you would enjoy looking for curtains."

"There is nothing that prevents me. I can tend gardens, build temples or buy fixtures for bathrooms. I love to see the different textures and colors of the curtains and beddings."

*****

A reminiscence of something long ago but not forgotten; like a whisked away fragrance whose imprint could still be scented, surrounded Regina and me. We sat in the garden facing the golden night lights of the palace.

Somewhere in her middle forties, with grey showing through her black hair, the housekeeper emitted a caring gentleness. Her intelligent eyes were filled with tears. She formally bowed and said, "I have been waiting so long to meet you but I always knew you would come. You came to me in a dream many years ago that had such a profound influence and changed my life. I saw us being together in this house and great changes happening in the world. I arranged to work here, so I could wait for you. I know who you are and I am here to serve you."

They sat quietly together, holding hands. Finally I stood and embraced her. "Yes Regina, let us fulfill our destiny together."

Later Sabna asked, "Kareae, why was Regina waiting so many years for you? Actually, you were only a boy when she had her dream."

"She made a vow in a previous life that has to be fulfilled," I replied. "Regina is very sensitive even though she chooses to be a housekeeper. It is perfect to have her here."

Chapter 12

CONNECTIONS

The Hot Springs of Rai were renowned for their unique rejuvenating qualities. Bathers traveled even from kingdoms as far away as Pa to soak and experience the healing effects of its magical waters. The most famous and popular of the several bathhouses, Seven Springs, was located not far from my residence and close to the palace. The palace contained its own bathhouse but many of the King's ministers and well-placed persons preferred Seven Springs. Many important meetings and decisions were made at the springs while enjoying the healing waters. Often, members took advantage of its relaxing qualities to help sooth their clients when negotiating contracts.

I received from Princess Sabna, a gift bathhouse membership, when I first moved into the house almost two moons ago, but I still had not used it. That morning, during breakfast on the terrace, an image of someone at the baths soaking in the hot waters appeared in my mind. Responding to the vision, I announced to Regina while she was clearing the breakfast table, "Regina, I like to go to the baths today, do I need to bring anything?"

"No, sir, all is provided but don't forget your membership card."

"Yes, of course, thank you."

"Shall I prepare lunch for you?"

"Hmm, I don't think so. I probably will be occupied. I will send a message beforehand if I do return for lunch."

"Very good, sir."

The stunning Seven Springs was constructed as a complex of seven small pyramid shaped buildings connected to a large central building. Each small unit contained a hot pool ranging from pleasantly warm to scorching hot. Right beside each pool was a cold-water plunge. Cozy lounging and resting areas surrounded both pools. The large central building contained the reception, main lounge and dressing rooms.

I stopped to inhale the warm rich moistness upon entering the baths. I marveled at the mixture of topical plants in contrast to the rich texture of the exposed wood structural beams. A hostess immediately welcomed and offered me a hot beverage, then assisted me to register.

With a map in my hand, I was directed to the changing rooms. The morning was quiet; only a few bathers were presently enjoying the benefits of the magical waters.

The hottest pool was so scorching hot that even the slightest movement send ripples of burning heat to the body. I entered one very slowly and was careful to remain as motionless as possible. When I could not stand it any longer, I left as slowly and jumped into the cold plunge. Afterwards, I wrapped my body completely in a robe and towels and then lay supine allowing the process to go deeper. The experience of the hot and cold plunge was quite dramatic: every cell in my body tingled in the ecstasy of calmness. I repeated this process thrice, each time for a longer interval in the water.

The moderate pools were bigger and could accommodate more bathers. I was relaxing in one of them when a distinguished elderly man with silver hair and a broad smile entered.

From the gentleman's body language, it was obvious he wanted to make contact with me. After an exchange of greetings, a conversation commenced between us.

"Excuse me young man, are you new here? I have not seen you before."

"Yes, that's correct, I answered. I arrived in Rai perhaps three moons ago. My pleasure to meet you, sir. My name is Kareae."

The elderly man instinctively moved slightly closer to me, "Ah, yes", he said with a warm look of recognition. "My name is Janan. I try to come to the baths everyday for a break from the pressures of work. I am a businessman, but I take joy in solitude and contemplation. Hmm, you look to be an interesting and intelligent person. Do you mind if I ask you your opinion about a long standing question I've been contemplating?"

"Please, go ahead, of course."

"Alright. Which is more important, the Realized Man or the Teachings?"

I gave a second glance to Janan. I was impressed by his deep and bright question yet saw that the question itself was a clever test. I allowed the moment to build and then answered, "I am!"

I could tell that Janan was stunned. He never expected such a profound answer from a young man, showing such insight and at the same time communicating to him that I was aware the question was a trick.

I took advantage of Janan's shock by touching his third eye (spot between the eyebrows) with my forehead. I locked our heads together, holding the back of Janan's head with my hands. I could sense that Janan immediately exploded into an "I am-ness", a direct experience of himself without the filters of the mind and ego. The sense of Janan disappeared and what was left from "I am Janan" was "I am." Our heads remained locked together until I was certain Janan had received the teachings. I gently let go of him and said, "Come, let us get out of the pool and rest." Several bathers had tried to enter the pool earlier but left when they felt the solemnity of their meeting.

When Janan could speak, he shared, "This question was always on my mind. You are the first person to correctly answer it by showing me the true answer. My gratitude and respect to you. Please, you must come with me now to my house for lunch and meet my wife. It is a great day. I feel I have met my teacher and found a son."

I answered, "Yes, I would very much like to join you. I see you have received the answer, the teachings and the realized one at the same time. It is certainly a day to celebrate."

A brisk wind met us outside the baths; our eyes squinted in the brightness of the cloudless noonday sun. We walked swiftly but several times we stopped to greet walkers on the street. Obviously, Janan was a well-known and respected man. I felt his pure heart earlier, at my home in the morning. Nevertheless, I appreciated Janan's compassion with people who were obviously of need of him.

Besides the King's palace, Janan's estate was probably the most impressive in Rai.

The grounds were extensive. It took somewhere over an hour to walk around the perimeter of the property. The main house stood on a rise with several smaller buildings built at slightly different levels. Covered walkways paved with many uniquely shaped stones connected the buildings. On both sides of the sidewalk were a variety of exotic plants, flowers and trees, each walkway having a specific theme. Along one footpath was found only rare bamboo at different stages of growth. Another aisle was filled with flowers like roses and lilies mixed with ferns. Further along the pathway, there could be found delightful small ponds inundated with lotus flowers. And, among the exotic vegetation were works of art, woodcarvings and statues. Benches or large stones were placed at special places for people to sit.

Close to the outer perimeter of the estate was a small but substantial lake with a wooden boathouse and dock. Janan took me there for a short tour so that I could have a good view of the house and then we returned to the main entrance.

At the head of a stairway leading to the main house gracefully waited a slender elegant woman to welcome us. I noticed that her radiant inner beauty more than matched her outer loveliness.

"Please let me make the introductions. Kareae, this is Divea, my wife. My dear, this bright young fellow is

Kareae, whom I met at the baths and invited to join us for lunch."

We both bowed in the formal greeting while looking into each other eyes. Divea seemed almost to faint, placed her hand on a surprised Janan for a moment but then said, "Kareae, you are most welcome in our house. I see you are not from Rai."

"Yes, that is correct, I said calmly but with my heart exploding. "I grew up in the temple Kanparu; my parents are the high priest and priestess. Perhaps you heard of them?"

"Yes, of course, we had their blessing when we were married. Are you here on business, Kareae?"

"Sort of in a way," I said with amused eyes, "but I plan to settle here. I purchased a house only a short time ago."

"Oh," Divea said softly.

Eventually she suggested moving to the terrace for lunch.

Divea escorted them through the house to reach the terrace. I commented, "I have never seen such a beautiful, light and spacious interior full of plants and artworks. Your furniture seems to have been poured out of the earth and is perfectly molded to the house. This house gives me a feeling of completeness. I feel at home and relaxed."

"Thank you." Divea said, "It is most kind of you."

We sat on the terrace before lunch, gazing out at the lake and the incredible gardens. "Romdev, a great architect, teacher and master, designed the house and grounds." Janan explained, "The house is built along the lines of sacred geometry. That is why you feel so at home here."

"Hmm," Kareae reflected, "I know Romdev since I can remember. He is my teacher and long time friend and member of our family. He designed many of the buildings in Kanparu. I was aware he designed and built a few private residences in Rai. This house is magnificent, like entering into a temple. You are very fortunate to have such a home."

"Yes, we are grateful to have been blessed with such wealth. My family has been in the shipping business for many generations. Most of the ships you see on the Signa are owned by Thor shipping, our family company. I took over from my father when he died ten years ago. The whole operation runs smoothly. We have some very good managers, and I give my heart into overseeing the company. Employees are paid well and have many benefits. Plus we are in the process of initiating new policies to incorporate employees to take more responsibility by offering partial ownership and profit sharing. Because of this, we get the crème of the crop to work for us. This gives me the added blessing of free non-worry time to pursue other interests." Janan paused to reflect, then said, "Romdev has become a member of our family as well. We first met when I contracted him to design and built this house. Since that time he has become my spiritual advisor and friend. When he comes to Rai, he prefers to stay with us rather than the palace. Indeed, we expect Romdev to visit at any time these days."

"Excellent," I replied, "I would very much like to meet him here in Rai."

Janan's house workers elegantly served lunch in

a whisper-like fashion. We dined quietly as was the custom of Raians. For the main course, we had garden fresh salad, natural mushrooms sautéed in crème sauce with wild natural rice and assorted fruit slices for desert. After lunch we enjoyed a small glass of a light pleasant wine coming from Sol, the kingdom east of Rai.

We were all aware of the natural harmony between us. I shared how much I was reminded of being in the presence my parents. Spontaneously in a silent circle of friendship, we joined hands.

Unusual for that time of day, several birds on the wind landed on a high branch near the house. Their singing created a moment that seemed to stop time forever in a magical world of everlasting joy. At last I said softly, "What a amazing thing to find you both. I thought only in temples exalted ones like you exist. What a benefit that you are in such a position to give your love and your wisdom to help so many people."

I continued, "I must confess, Janan, that this morning I sensed your vibration and could see you in my mind's eye sitting at the baths. I went there to meet you."

"Ah by Rai, so that's it!" Janan exclaimed not even questioning my vision. "I was so drawn, I almost felt compelled to come to the baths this morning, and I did not know why. Normally I go more towards the evening. I must confess to you, as well, I knew from Romdev you were coming to Rai to live and do your work, but I was not aware when. I was wondering how to meet you and how to know when you arrived? That it has happened so easily and our connection is so harmonious gives me great joy." Turning to Divea he said, "I am sure Divea feels the same way."

"Yes, it is so," she said quietly.

"Our daughter is away at the moment," continued Janan, "but when she returns you must meet her."

"Yes, I would be honored,"

"Now, I must leave you and show myself in the office. You are always welcome here, my son."

"Thank you," I said rising with Janan and Divea to leave.

I turned to Divea at the door, took both of her hands, gave her a silent look and left.

*****

Janan lovingly put his arm around Divea while walking slowly back to the garden. "Divea, I've never seen you so quiet and smitten by someone."

"Yes darling, Kareae makes me speechless and breathless. It is as if there are no boundaries, no resistance only oneness, love and surrender. I feel a tingling and excitement inside like something unknown and exquisite is about to happen."

"Yes, I feel it as well. Kareae is as Romdev said, the herald of the new man in full natural consciousness. My dear, feel free to explore with Kareae as you wish, you always have my love and support."

"I know," she said with love and gratefulness, "I am relieved to hear your words as I would be afraid with these new feelings, of hurting you and that would be the last thing I would ever want."

"Please don't worry, my love for you is unconditional. You know it has been a long time since our relationship moved beyond possessiveness, beyond attachment. We are blessed with a natural love that is just love with no address of me or you."

With tears in her eyes, Divea embraced Janan and bowed her head in profound respect.

*****

I took a leisurely way in the general direction of my house, stopping at one of the many quiet nature spots in and about Rai. This one was situated next to a canal having a grassy meadow. The many geese and ducks roaming about made it not such a quiet spot but still delightful. Once in a while a private boat passed on its way to the main river.

I sat absorbed within myself. In this state, even meeting Divea, which sent my heart spinning, was left behind. When I opened my eyes again, I set off to visit a contractor Sabna recommended. I found Patai at home and was welcomed into his abode. I liked the feeling of spaciousness in his house. Each room openly ran into each other to create space and yet was placed at an angle to preserve its integrity and privacy. High ceilings added to the spacious feeling.

The house was built with wood and natural stone, as were most Raian houses. Since Raians took such an active role designing their houses and making sure their house was in proper alignment with the natural lay lines of the earth, it was rare to find a house close by that had the same look.

Raians had a custom to place a small stone idol in the center of their home, symbolizing the inner spiritual core from which all arises.

Patai had two children, which was typical of most

couples. If a couple chose to have more, usually it was only much later. Raians believed in spending a large proportion of their time raising and educating their children. All Raian children were schooled at home. It was only when they specialized in a field of learning did they go to a formal school, and even those were kept small usually on a one-to-one basis or two at the most.

Raians were not aggressive. They taught their children early on the necessary social skills of non-violence, and how important it was not to hurt others. Mostly, it came naturally to them. In this regard, tension did not exist in the community. The richness and wealth of the land afforded the people to be tolerant and respect the rights of others to be and to live.

For one moon in summer, Raian children attended different camps on the eastern lakes for fun and games. Both the parents and the children enjoyed a carefree time. Sometimes even the King put in an appearance.

At the drawing board in Patai's office, after explaining my vision, I laid out the plans and specifications of the temple for Patai to study. Patai looked up when he finished his examination enthusiastic, "Yes, I am very pleased with the design. I would be honored to build this temple. Did you create it?"

"Yes, but I was inspired by a temple my teacher built in the forest. Perhaps some day I can take you there, I'm sure you would to like to see it and I feel there is something there for you to learn."

" Hmm, perhaps you are right," he said, bringing his hand to cover his mouth in a pondering gesture.

"If you can quickly draw up a contract, I can return

tomorrow to sign and arrange to transfer the necessary funds to you."

"Of course, I can immediately draw up a simple contract and we can begin construction within days. After we sign tomorrow, I would like to come with you to see the site, if it is possible.

"Then plan to have lunch with me and we can sign the contract then. I will leave you directions to the house."

"It's not needed; I know the house."

"Good then, until tomorrow."

Chapter 13

EARLY KANPARU YEARS

On my way home I stopped along one of the more beautiful canals to admire some of the picturesque arch stone bridges. The subdued afternoon light created a soft backdrop to view the boats, the vehicles with their traffic, the people and the many birds landing and searching for food. A group of children ran pass me with loud voices enjoying the day as only children could. Just as I was crossing one of the bridges, I received telepathically, a message from Regina that Princess Sabna was at the house waiting for me.

I had been training Regina to communicate with telepathy. I found initially that she was an open sensitive channel but her abilities were never developed.

For her first lesson, to sharpen her concentration, I bought her into a room illuminated only by a single candle and instructed her to stare at it without blinking for as long as she could. I was pleased Regina could stare for twenty-three minutes but instructed her to continue this exercise daily until she reached sixty minutes.

When she was able to stare for a full hour, to help

focus her mind's eye, I gave her simple phrases to repeat continuously out loud and at the same time told her to hold a mental image of the words and see them in her mind's eye. In addition, I instructed her to unfocus while looking at the lit candle, and see what is there at the edge of the vision. Regina was able to see almost immediately once she knew what to do. This opened up for her a whole world existing just on the edge of normal awareness.

And last and very important, I would communicate telepathically with her to facilitate opening her pathway more each day. At first, Regina could only hear a word, then sentences, until finally whole images would appear in her mind's eye. Once this was established, it was easy for Regina to project her thoughts outward.

I was pleased today she could so quickly project her thoughts over such a distance.

Sabna was surprised and touched with the wild flowers I picked for her. "You never cease to amaze me," she said. A little speechless she continued, "I have a message for you from Prince Zolade. He requests your presence at his estate for the full moon celebration not on the next full moon but the one after. That is in forty-five days."

I readily agreed but then excused myself to bath and change for dinner.

We enjoyed a quiet evening in each other's company as if old friends. Sabna told then, the story of meeting her former boyfriend announcing her intentions not to marry.

"After the initial shock, Jain felt relief as well. He was not ready to leave his friends and his nice life in Rai, but he was under pressure from the family to marry. I am glad we could remain as friends. It was the families that created quite a stir. There were so many discussions imploring us to do the sensible thing that my ears began to hurt. I guess many business arrangements had already been initiated between the families. Indeed, Jain found himself defending my decision."

"I really do like him but as you know my destiny seems to lie elsewhere," she said giving me a probing look, but I remained silent.

"Well, hopefully by the time of the full moon celebration it will have all died down."

"Come," I said rising from the table, "let's go to my office; I want to show you the plans for a temple I will be soon building. The site is just over there," I pointed, "by the side of the house where I plan to construct it."

While I was explaining the design, Sabna remained near to me all of the time. At some point she even inadvertently ran her fingers through my hair.

Sabna said later, "Kareae, you are amazing. Where did you learn to be a designer and architect?"

"I'm very fortunate to have, since I can remember, the architect Romdev as my teacher and advisor. My temple design is inspired by another temple Romdev built. He will be amused and happy to know I am building one on my own because I never showed much interest in architecture when I was a boy.

They returned to the starlit terrace to find that Regina had prepared hot drinks and snacks. Sabna said, "Tell me Kareae more about your childhood; it seems so fascinating."

"Well, yes, okay. As you know I grew up in the temple of Kanparu. I am a descendent from a long line of priests; my father Ashara is the high priest as was his father before him. However, it is not my destiny to be the high priest of the temple. Someone else will take over after him to create a new lineage."

"Kanparu is not just a temple but a huge complex containing many buildings and land with many orchards. There is a beautiful river Goma that flows on the western border of the temple grounds."

"Within the complex, there are perhaps several hundred priests and monks living and dedicating their lives to obtain higher consciousness for themselves and for the earth. Many experiments are carried out to invoke higher vibrations and to send them throughout the kingdom."

"My parents met during my father's travels when he was young. In truth, his journey was to find a woman he could marry and become the high priestess. It is a very beautiful story how they met, and perhaps I will tell you at some other time."

"Kanparu was my world until I left to come to Rai. I spent many joyful days in the orchards and by the river. I have many friends among the monks and priests. I especially love the head monk guard, Hanu, an amazing, powerful man whose presence is enough to scare anyone but is so gentle and kind. Often I could be found with Hanu at the front gate of the temple checking the incoming visitors. Recently I met a man in the forest who reminds me much of him but that is another story."

"My training and education was intense and strict. I

had to undergo many tests and initiations throughout my childhood even at the age of three and four. I was never treated as a child because my intelligence and level of awareness demanded I be treated as an equal."

"I'm sorry to interrupt but what type of test can you give to a three year old?"

"Well," Kareae replied, "every day past the age of five, I was woken up at 4 a.m. and brought to a well to take a cold bath. Sometimes in the winter, the water was icy cold. It was a shock, but this gave strength to my body. I never get sick, and it eliminated any sleepiness I might have had. When I wake from sleep I am instantly fully awake."

"I was given many mental tests like having to remember how many objects I just seen passing by a room or exactly how a certain object was placed. I never knew when they would test me so I had always to be aware. I was given many exercises to focus the mind to keep its awareness in the present moment - like repeating complex sentences while doing intricate physical movements. The complexity of these exercises would increase with my age."

"Frequently, I was instructed to sit or stand for long periods without moving. And I always had to be ready if one of the instructors all of the sudden commanded me to stop whatever I was doing and be still. That was quite something."

"For me none of this was a hardship, I loved the training and the exercises and everyone acted with utmost love and caring even if they were very strict."

"I've always been naturally aware of who I am on the

deepest level. I feel completely one with my parents, with my teacher Romdev and with everyone and everything else for that matter."

"Because my parents were often busy with functions of the temple, Romdev directed much of my formal training and education. Kanparu is one of the most important centers for the development of Higher Consciousness, following the principles of Tantrism. Tantrism employs the utilization of natural forces to obtain higher consciousness. Both my parents are Tantric Masters. In this regard they worked with me directly through rituals and practices to transmit this knowledge to me. Recently I was fully initiated as a Tantric Master as well."

"I have a loose plan to organize a small school of Tantrism here in Rai. Perhaps you will be one of my first students?"

"Yes, I would be very interested in furthering my development and perhaps at some point you can explain in more detail what I can expect to learn. But please tell me, when you say you are conscious of who you are, what do you mean?"

"Ah, I'm glad you ask. Knowing who you are is the fundamental existential awareness of one's true self without the distortions of the mind with its ideas and concepts of who we think we are. It is pure awareness, aware of itself when there is no observer and observed."

I rose from where I was sitting with Sabna and touched her forehead. Sabna instantly entered into a silent state similar to her first meeting with me. Some minutes passed before she could open her eyes. Overwhelmed but yet calm, she said, "Oh, I now know what you mean.

What your words don't express is how blissful this is."

Silently Regina came to refill their tea and offered additional small cakes she baked. She was swimming in the love as they were. Sabna looked at her as if for the first time, understanding why she was with Kareae. She took Regina's hand in communion together. The three of them sat in pristine harmony listening to the night.

"When the time comes, Sabna, you will permanently be rooted in this. Your mind still needs to function in the old way just for a little while longer. Don't be upset tomorrow if the purity of tonight's knowledge becomes cloudy again."

"Yes, I understand although I wish I could have it all now. I am aware on my own accord that my destiny awaits me."

We remained sitting quietly on the terrace for the rest of the time. The night was clear with the moon rising very late. Regina brought blankets to stem the chill in the air. Towards dawn, Sabna took her leave, but I remained sitting longer.

I took advantage of this time to open my mind to Romdev. When he opened his mind, I received the information that the king had offered him a commission to build a temple on the palace ground and he would accept, if only to throw Kalo a little bit off guard. Again, he warned me to be careful; I could be in great danger especially when our plans progress. Better now to converse in person when I arrive in Rai. With that Romdev closed his mind and I returned to sitting until the sun was strong.

During breakfast, I said, "Regina, the construction of

the temple would begin shortly in a few days. Today, the contractor comes. We will sign the contact and then look at the building site. Afterwards, I invited him for lunch, if that is okay with you?"

"Yes, I will prepare something special to celebrate the signing."

"Thank you, Regina. In the afternoon I am planning to meet Janan at the baths, so don't expect me home until late."

Chapter 14

JANAN

A blast of the hot wet air enveloped Janan when he opened the door to enter the steam room. He quickly closed the entrance and after a minute standing in the saturated foggy mist, he could barely recognize me sitting on the far end. Even in this hot environment we enjoyed each other. But soon, as the time ticked slowly away, the heat became almost unbearable. Janan was thankful for the buckets of cold water available to pour over him. Nevertheless, he left after only a short stay. Later, I found him lounging by the tea area. Anyone watching us would think we were father and son enjoying a day together.

"I'm glad we can talk before our massages, Janan, I want to speak to you about Divea. I am …"

Janan raised his hand interrupting him, "My son, you do not have to be concerned.

"Thirty years ago would have been different. Divea is a very attractive woman. Many men were not only attracted but made overt gestures to seduce her even after we were married. I often experienced jealousy and possessiveness. Indeed, there was a period when I could not stand for her be out and about. But Divea is a pure hearted soul. Each time I had an attack of possessiveness, she would soothe me, calm me down and show me it was not real."

"It all came to a finale when a distant relative of the king came to Rai to attend a wedding. They met at the celebration and were dancing together when I went into a rage, directly accosting the poor man on the dance floor and knocking him down in front of the entire court. I was embarrassed and felt remorse to my core. Divea once again that night, sitting together until dawn on the palace grounds, showed me my jealousy was not real. Now since that time, it hardly ever bothers me. Kareae, if you were less of a person that I am convinced you are, perhaps there would be some reaction. But from our experience of 'I am', I fully trust you even with my life."

"I am totally aware of the impact and consequences of your meeting with Divea. I am open for whatever needs to happen. Divea is a very evolved, mature, independent being in her own right. I learnt I do not possess her, even if she is my wife and mother of my child. I know only the highest will happen between her and you."

"I am concerned about my daughter, though. I don't feel she is ready for this yet, so please be discreet when she returns."

I nodded in agreement sitting up to look at Janan. "I bow my head to you sir. I sensed your advanced state of wisdom, but to hear it directly from you gives me great satisfaction.

"Thank you, Kareae."

"I think that after we leave here, we should go to

my offices on the river quay. We can take our dinner there, and I can show you the new ships with some very innovative designs. Plus, I would like you to meet a few of my staff."

*****

We arrived at the river quay after a brisk walk during the busiest time of day. Several ships were bustling with workers loading or unloading their cargoes while others ships were waiting their turn to be processed. I had never been in a place with so much activity and exotic smells. Regardless of the crowds of passengers and porters, our presence was immediately noticed by many of the dockworkers. A few of the foremen and some of the workers came to pay their respects, to ask advice or just to say hello. Janan was on a first name basis with many of them. He was known to treat each one with respect, going out of his way not to offend anyone even if they were upset or angry. His presence could usually calm the most agitated man although a worker getting agitated was rare.

Raians were a hard-working, naturally intelligent people having a sense of community- even among the quay workers class distinction was not a factor.

Poverty was eliminated long ago in Rai. The advanced level of their intelligence and the unique richness of their natural resources was certainly a factor. More over, the natural protection of the ghats freed their wealth from spending on building armies to eliminating poverty. Fortunately, their leaders were not interested in conquest or building monuments to their egos. Kosa, the current king of Rai, was more interested in increasing the spiritual awareness of his people rather than increasing the size of his kingdom and wealth.

Many generations have passed since it was decided that the advantages of a motorized industrial society were small compared to the cost of the quality of life and balance of nature. Fortunately, the harnessing of wind and solar power was so advanced there was no need for the more polluting ways to generate power. Transportation was kept deliberately non-motorized except in special cases as with the ships and barrages. Raians simply realized the futility of speeding life up even if the vehicles were non-polluting.

The ships belonging to the Thor Shipping Company utilized a combination of steam, solar and wind power. In some unusual instances, horses were still used to pull the boats upriver.

The windmill was so highly developed as a self-perpetuating engine that the smallest amount of wind generated enough power to start the windmill turbines turning, which then accelerated itself in a unique way to generate and operate on its own power. When there was absolutely no wind, steam was used based on the same high efficiency principles. Solar power, although efficient, was the third choice because of the need of industrialization to produce the casing for the needed batteries. Interestingly, photosensitive microorganisms were discovered, which could store and even generate electricity very efficiently.

The new ships Janan showed me were of the same aerodynamic design as Jacki's wagons. In addition, the ships were constructed in such a manner that they became more buoyant as their weight increased. In this way, the heaviest loaded ship floated and moved as easily as an unloaded ship. Janan was very happy about this amazing breakthrough.

I asked, "Janan, how is this possible?"

Janan replied, "I don't quite understand the physics completely but the hull of the ship is so designed that when weight is applied to it, it triggers the same weight in terms of water pressure to be equally applied upwards onto the hull. The result is that the buoyancy remains the same. I heard there is a fellow by the name of Patri in Mi who is the inventor of this hull and was instrumental also in the development of the self-perpetuating engine. If ever I go to Mi I want to meet this man."

"Yes," I reflected, "so would I."

The Thor offices and storerooms were clean, light and efficient. Janan's office was very comfortable with warm colored sitting areas created with rugs and works of art. After they had taken food, I was introduced at a staff meeting to a few of the managers and employees. Again I could not help but notice the respect of Janan's employees, not only to him but for each other as well.

One of the managers took a long time to explain how the company operated on a communal basis with shared responsibility and profits. "We are the first company in Rai to initiate these programs, and we are very proud how successful we are," he said in conclusion.

Walking along the quay in the soft afternoon light with the smell of the river in the air and the singing of the birds coming to roost, Janan explained to me that he tried first to promote the sense of love of one's work, and second the service to community they provided and then third, generation of wealth for themselves and the community.

"I try to instill a sense of balance by never hurting anyone with harsh language or actions, even if they have made a huge costly error. It is the company policy not to blame others but always to seek solutions. I will not let a person remain as a manager if he is not able to follow this policy. Over the years, we are fortunate that all of the staff have taken to this faultless vision and our efficiency and profit have greatly increased."

"Janan, it is truly brilliant what you have accomplished with Thor Shipping. I'm sure your father would be proud of how you use your wealth and power to promote compassion and fairness in the marketplace."

"Yes, I think you are right although at first he probably would have raised the roof when I handled over control of Thor Shipping." Janan laughed. "And now I have more profits than ever and a new business of teaching high-level managers and owners how to make this transition."

"Ah, I love this part of the river where it becomes quiet again and the willow trees branches are hanging over the water."

"I want to tell you, interestingly enough, I overheard at our last seminar the other day, people talking about you. Do you know that your presence in the city is already being noticed? And the talk is that you have been seen several times with Princess Sabna."

"Oh yes," a soft smile lighting my face at the mention of her name. "Sabna. I met the princess on my journey to Rai. We have become close friends; I stayed at her house until mine was ready. But don't worry Janan," noticing his unease, "we are only friends. Now tell me, what is your concern?"

"Hmm, well, yes, we would like you to meet our daughter Neelu; there has been discussion with Divea and even Romdev. You see, our daughter is very special and we want the best for her."

Kareae took a moment to reflect what Janan just said and came out with a light laugh, "Oh is that so, Romdev is involved." He nodded his head in amusement. "Yes then, when Romdev arrives we will discuss my meeting Neelu, but for now, please don't worry my dear friend."

In that moment, Kareae looked across the river and saw Kalo sitting on bench with a knowing grin on his face. He felt Kalo's power come into him stirring up his inner space, making him feel dizzy and confused and powerless to prevent him. Kareae said nothing to Janan, who continued speaking.

"Yes, thank you, you are right, I don't why I am this overly concerned when it comes to my daughter, I know it's not rational," .

Just at that moment Janan's train of thoughts was interrupted by a strong breeze that seemed to rise up from nowhere rattling the leaves in the trees and causing of a flock of ducks to quack loudly and fly off.

"But let us go before the weather turns," Janan said seeing some dark clouds in the horizon.

As the sun began its great descent to kiss once again the earth, the two men embraced before returning to the offices and then bid each other farewell until the next time.

Chapter 15

DIVEA

On an auspicious morning a few days later, a groundbreaking ceremony took place for the temple. With only Regina and Patai present, I chanted prayers and invocations and blessed the site with holy water from the river Gama. In my mind I could feel the form of the temple already creating a vibrational energy field. Instead of the usual pyramid shape, I decided on the pentagon shape. This represented the four elements and that, which was beyond. The apex of the pentagon, the inner sanctum, looked to the east while the entrance faced west to optimize alignment with the natural forces. Inside the temple, a maze led to different areas and finally to the inner sanctum. Each area would be energized to promote particular vibrations that I will use in my work with people.

I was giving instructions to one of the workers later that day when someone arrived with a message from Divea asking me to visit her today. I stopped my work and immediately went to her. A housekeeper let me in and directed me to one of the small meditation rooms off the main living area where I found her sitting silently.

I took a place behind her becoming in tune with her. It astonished me how immense was the fullness of her being that pulled me into a vortex of ecstasy. I placed my hands on her shoulders. She opened her eyes and immediately her eyes rolled up into her head. An avalanche of bliss overcame her and she lost control of her body. She fell back into my arms, and we remained together in this way for quite a long time. The silence was broken when we both started laughing like children. Divea opened her eyes to find me beaming at her with the most exquisite white light. She was overwhelmed again and lost control. This time I picked her up and carried her to her sleeping chamber. I removed her clothes and placed her on the bed. Even though she was in her middle years, her body was still beautiful, retaining its youthful look. Her breasts were firm and full while the rest of her body still had the delightful curves to excite any man. I removed my clothes and lay next to her. When she regained control, I sat her up then sitting facing her, entered into her. Our state of oneness became even more complete, any residual separation of him or her, any feeling of a personal body dissolved into a wonderfully steady continuous and calm orgasmic ecstasy. This remained for some hours before the feeling of having a body returned.

Afterwards when I was leaving, Divea spoke the first words between us, "Kareae, my dear soul of my soul, please return tonight for dinner with us." We embraced and kissed, then I bowed my head in love and surrender and left without saying a word.

*****

When Janan returned later that day and saw his wife, he immediately knew something had happened. When they embraced, the joy and peace emitting from Divea entered Janan and he joined in the oneness.

"Kareae comes tonight for dinner, and we can talk together then," Divea said after they embraced but were still holding each other.

"Yes, let us talk together; I want to but there is also no need my love, I do not feel separate from your experience today either with you or Kareae."

"My husband, you are truly an amazing man; your actions follow your words. My meeting in oneness with Kareae was beyond anything personal, but I still felt some concern for you."

"Thank you." Then separating from Divea he said thoughtfully, "My only unease is for Neelu. I feel we have to be discreet with her until we are sure about her relationship with Kareae."

"Kareae knows about our interest in their meeting. When I mentioned that Romdev was involved, it seemed to affect him particularly, as if a mystery had been revealed. I've asked him to be discreet although I know there was no need, I trust Kareae with my life. Now, my dear, I want to go to the baths to soak these bones and be refreshed for our meeting tonight. Perhaps you would like to join me?"

"Yes, what an excellent and delightful idea. Give me twenty minutes to get ready and give instructions to the cook."

*****

Regina noticed immediately my beaming state when I returned but did not say anything. She quietly prepared my bath and meal but still was wondering what had happened.

In the evening, after giving instructions to the foreman for tomorrow's work, I joined Regina on the terrace, "I see that you are wondering what has happened to me; you notice a change in me. Yes, there has been a transformation today. I had a meeting with a woman - not an ordinary woman but one whose depth and connection to the source is infinite. We met in oneness. I experienced myself going beyond and deeper than ever before."

I gently embraced Regina, transmitting the silence, the love to her. "This love is not my love, this silence is not my silence," I said, "I am only the cup to drink from the universal well."

Regina blissfully opened her eyes and laughed. "But what a cup you are. I've been waiting my whole life to serve you; you are my destiny and now it is complete."

"I am the instrument to complete many people's destiny. We are just beginning, and you are a great help to me."

"My dear employer," bowing her head, "I will serve you forever and as you wish."

Even the workers leaving for the day could feel the lovingness. The foreman had to actually tell them to go home, but he was just as enthralled watching us on the terrace. The spell broke when Regina separated to return to the house. I walked to one of my sitting areas and remained still for hours.

*****

The dinner that night was light. There was not much talk, only sharing and embracing. Oneness was one and not two and they were swimming in it. Janan was particularly happy; his connection with Divea was as close as it has ever been. Divea felt immense relief and joy to finally give the milk of her soul freely. She told me that somewhere along the line there was a connection between her family and your mother's family.

"Now that you that you mention it, I do see a similarity between my mother and you."

We had risen from the dinner table and were strolling along the lake. Just a slight ripple of wave was heard. At the boathouse we sat, looking over the lake. The lights of the palace were twinkling in the distance and overhead the sky was clear with many stars. Once in awhile a shooting star was spotted, and we all became excited.

I explained I was a Tantric Master, as was my parents. "Before I left on my journey to Rai, I received the full initiation into Tantrism from the high priest and priestess, my parents. It was a secret initiation lasting seven days. I will not tell you the details of this initiation but in the last ceremony, I achieved oneness with a tantrika (female tantric) who had undergone the same long prayers, chanting and fasting for the seven days as I did. When we entered into oneness, the tantrika was no longer a person but the goddess, the female power. I was no longer Kareae but the male principle. I tell you this because being with you today Divea, I experienced the same quality of godliness as with the tantrika. I'm always in awe that transformation is ever a possibility no matter how transformed we are."

With deep empathy for Kareae, Divea answered, "We are so honored you tell us this secret of your initiation. We have been to Kanparu for blessings when we were married as most couples do. We saw your parents, they had just become the high priest and priestess, but we didn't really meet. I remember I had a strong sense of recognition when I was briefly in front of your mother and we looked into each other's eyes. For some days I had a special sense around me but I was young thinking about other things to pursue it."

Janan took the hand of Divea while she was talking. For a while afterwards, nothing was said, they sat together in unity. I rose and embraced both of them. The circle of harmony became an ecstatic current, which seemed to pulsate around us and beyond, almost touching the universe. Janan cried out in joy and wonder while Divea felt herself become even a deeper channel than this afternoon. When I separated from them, we all collapsed into our chairs.

Much later a house worker came with hot refreshments and small cakes. "This is the first time I really taste the food or see this beautiful sky," Janan said in awe.

I shared with Janan that the experience of ecstasy was what was missing from him. Now the last step has been taken, and his work is finished.

"My dear son, you have brought joy into my life," Janan said, "and I will always be thankful and ready to help you."

"Yes, I know. There may come a time when I will

need your help, but it might not be easy for you."

Janan rose, put his hands on my shoulders and in earnest said, "Whatever it is, I am ready." He embraced me.

Afterwards he said, "Let us go back to the house; it is getting late and there are still a few things I must do."

Chapter 16

ZOLADE'S ESTATE

The journey to Prince Zolade's estate could be completed in one day, but Kareae and Princess Sabna decided to stay overnight at a cousin's house, and then arrived at her brother's estate mid-morning the next day. The explosion of reds, yellows and browns in the late fall filled their eyes with beauty throughout the drive, impelling them to halt several times to just view the incredible outpour of colors, sometimes leaving the carriage and running like elves through the fallen leaves.

After they settled in their rooms, Kareae and Sabna found Zolade down by the horse stable supervising the preparation of a stallion to mate with one of his mares. The stallion's tension and enthusiasm to mount the mare gave an electric atmosphere to the corral especially when the mare was led out of the stable into the corral close to the stallion. After much hassling about, the stallion was released. He quickly mounted the mare, and it was soon over and everyone could relax.

Obviously satisfied with his morning work, Prince Zolade embraced his sister and gave his hand and a Raian embrace of briefly touching foreheads to Kareae welcoming him to the estate.

"Let us return to the house," Zolade said. "I'm sure there is food prepared for us and then afterwards Kareae, if you are open to it, we can take out the horses and tour the land. That is," he said in a lighter tone, "if I can break Sabna away from you. What do you say?

"Marvelous, I've been looking forward to explore the land with you." Turning to Sabna, he teased, "But let's see if Sabna allows me to take her leave?"

"My dear brothers," Sabna laughed, "I will be brave and suffer the moments without the both of you. Anyhow, I need to attend to the preparation of the full moon festival tomorrow. I must go over the guest list and make sure there are enough accommodations. I heard my brother invited some very important guests."

"Yes, I did. But I'm sure it will be an quite an interesting time for all us," Zolade said walking away. "I will join you after I wash and change."

Zolade's house was built in a style familiar with Raians: a central big space containing the kitchen, dinning and living areas with the bedrooms and studies extending outwards either separately or joined by walkways to ensure privacy. This allowed the social activity in the central area to go on as pleased. The house had wonderful wooden floors and a fireplace exquisitely designed to be both functional and beautiful to gaze at.

Many of the same people from the road trip were

present at lunch. Although it was the Raian custom to eat meals in silence, as it was a special occasion, there were lots of noisy conversations and laughter. Almost all Raians were vegetarians even though they drank milk and ate dairy and eggs. With the abundance of vegetables and grains, it never seemed appropriate to kill an animal for food, but sometimes fish was eaten for health reasons. The menu consisted of assorted steamed veggies from the garden, three different types of salads, and several types of cheese, breads and at least three different types of sauces. Raians loved to drown their veggies in sauce. For dessert, fruit and simple cakes were served.

Little Tia sat on Kareae's lap throughout most the meal. Ever since Tia met Kareae there had been a noticeable change in her although nobody could quite get what it was. Kareae knew that her ego, the sense that I am somebody, which was starting to form before he met her, dissolved. Kareae was pleased to see it was still so.

Sabna sat across from Kareae engrossed in a conversation with her cousin Julen, Tia's mother. Sabna was so engrossed watching Kareae with Tia that Julen had to repeat twice her questions to her.

"What is going on with you cousin?" Julen asked.

"Oh, I just can't keep my eyes off Kareae sitting with Tia – such gentle and carefreeness between them.

"Hmm, Now that you mention it, I see what you mean."

Julen was a few years older than her, but somehow Sabna was always the more mature one until Julen got married. Now, Julen seemed the more mature one. Since Tia returned from her trip with Sabna, Julen began to notice the change in Tia: She seemed more complete in herself, contented to play with friends or be on her own. Sometimes Julen was a little shocked and amazed at the clarity of some of her comments. As she watched Tia with Kareae, Julen suspected Kareae had something to do with it. She called out across the table, "Kareae, I love seeing Tia together with you. You know, she has not been the same since she met you. What is your secret with her?"

Kareae looked to Julen for some moments in a silence exchange then said looking at Tia, "I treat Tia as an equal and not as a child. Your daughter's soul is very wise and this part woke up when we met."

"Yes, that is true, lately I've been impressed how clear her statements are."

"I see that you give her this freedom. Good, please continue to encourage her"

"I will, thank you," Julen said softly, feeling his strong gentle sensitivity.

"Kareae," interrupted Zolade standing up to leave, "please meet me by the stables in twenty minutes. I have a wonderful mare for you to ride that you will not be disappointed with. I left some riding clothes in your room that should fit."

"Yes, thank you," replied Kareae looking up at Zolade. "I will come as soon as I can tear myself away from Tia." He stood placing Tia back on the chair with a hug, bid everyone a farewell with a funny formal bow and left.

A general wave of goodbye ensued from the table as they watched in appreciation Kareae leave.

*****

"This mare is magnificent. Indeed, I see that all your

horses are very fine specimens."

"Yes, I take pride in my horses, they give me much pleasure."

Zolade and Kareae had been riding hard for some time through rough terrain. They allowed the horses to get up a good sweat before they slowed down to rest and walk them and have conversation. They were so focused riding that Kareae didn't even notice the landscape.

"I'm impressed with your riding, Kareae. I took you through some difficult terrain."

"Yes, I know but I loved it. To experience being one with this animal riding in this vibrant forest with you, makes me feel so incredibly alive."

"Funny, I don't know why I thought you were not the outdoor type"

The area through which they were riding was densely covered with natural and undeveloped forest. The terrain was mostly flat with increment scatterings of hilly areas. The estate itself was huge, comprising thousands of eagles of land.

"Our family decided generations ago to keep the land as untouched as possible. We have some cattle and sheep to graze the land and the breeding of horses to support the estate. We sometimes receive huge prices for our best horses. The stallion you saw today is worth a small fortune. A colt from that horse will quickly sell and for a high price. We maintain our livelihood this way and yet keep the ecology in balance and as untouched as possible. We do some logging but only to thin and maintain the forests from over-forestation. This helps to control forest fires and the spread of diseases among the trees. Once the horses are rested, I will take you to the only high point where we can get a good view of the property."

The uphill ride to the point, through narrow passages strewn with low branches and many fallen trees, sometimes required challenging high jumps. But, they enjoyed the thrill of it and being together. Zolade spurred his horse faster, choosing the most difficult jumps yet Kareae stayed right beside him. Zolade gave out a loud scream of triumph to express the exhilaration he felt.

They reached the top with the horses in full sweat, foaming at the mouth. Both of them fell onto the ground totally exhausted, out of breath but full of laughter.

Zolade and Kareae embraced in deep brotherhood.

"The view from here is amazing." Zolade said, "On a clear day you can see to the great lakes. All this land from east to west belongs to our estate. Further north begins lands belonging to the king. To the south we own a vast majority of it."

Zolade continued, "I want to thank you for your earlier advice. It was hard for me to hear. Over the next few weeks I noticed in spite of myself that it was true: I was getting disappointed with people because of my expectations. I've been practicing not to expect anything and when I can do it, I notice my relations with people are much smoother."

Kareae nodded. "Yes, if you continue with your practice; you will become more rooted in it and it will become automatic without effort."

Zolade rose to the horses. "Let's go, we need to

return soon, I invited one of the sons of the king and he should be arriving shortly. It would be bad manners not to be there when he arrives."

*****

Sabna was surprised to see the name of Torent on the guest list. She was just a small child the last time they met; Torent was five years older than her. She personally went to the room assigned to him to make sure his accommodations were up to the standards of a king's son.

Sabna was still in his room when she heard Zolade and Kareae return. Seeing their friendliness from the window gave her goose bumps, and she felt a surge of happiness. She ran out to greet them and they embraced in laughter.

"Now, let us get serious; the king's son will be arriving soon," Zolade said, watching the stable hand take the horses and petting some of the dogs that came running on their return.

"Yes, I saw from the guest list that Torent is coming. How long has it been since you've seen him?" Sabna asked, self-consciously pulling back her hair and not looking directly at Kareae.

"I met him for the first time in years last month in Rai. He recently returned from the travels every son of the king makes before taking on the responsibility of governing. He has grown into a man. We shall see what type of man he is."

"Yes, but meanwhile, come, I left food for your return. You both must be starving?"

"Hmm Sabna, yes, we worked up a good appetite, I'm

famished"

They returned to the main hall after bathing and putting on fresh clothes. They found many of the lunch people were still around having conversations or reading. Julen approached Kareae for a second, gave him a grateful thank you and then left. Tia was asleep near the fireplace so Kareae could eat in peace.

The main topic of conversation was Torent. Everyone was excited to see how he looked since his return from his travels. One man was overheard saying the gossip was that of the three sons, the king favored Torent to become the next king. Already there was talk about finding a suitable wife for him.

Zolade welcomed the approaching evening by starting a blazing fire for those who wanted to sit and watch the flames dancing within the wood and be caressed by its warmth.

*****

The almost full moon was high in the sky when Zolade went out to greet Torent. Surprisingly, he arrived alone on horseback. Torent was tall and slender with easy movements, taking after his mother side rather than the well built muscular shape of his father. He kept his chestnut hair longer than what was the current Raian style. For the son of a king, his look was unpretentious and sensitive but his royal upbringing was clearly noticeable in his manner of dress and speech.

On the way to the house Torent explained, "During my journeys I became accustomed to traveling alone. I discovered how much I enjoyed it. Now I welcome an opportunity to travel this way because I know once I take up my position in government it will not be possible for me to do so."

"There is a carriage following behind that should be here in a few hours. Some of my cousins are very keen to come to the full moon celebration."

Sabna and Kareae still were sitting near the fireplace gazing at the fire in conversation. A nice burning wood aroma plus the numerous lit candles, gave the room a rustic, romantic atmosphere.

Torent was introduced to Sabna and Kareae in the formal way. He said to Sabna, "The last time we met you were a small child. Sabna smiled in recognition, "Yes, I remember, you were one those big older boys. But look, now I've grown into a woman, and you are a man."

"Yes, I see." Torent laughed but eyeing her from head to foot, "How life is always changing. Who will we be the next time we meet?"

Torent turned to Kareae, "I met Janan the other day. He told me you would be here, and I should make sure to meet with you. Now that I see you, I can understand why. Let us speak together sometime."

"Except for early mornings I am always available, please come at your convenience," Kareae smiled. "We have much to discuss."

"Now, Prince Torent let me show you where you will be staying," Sabna said as she took his arm. "If you are hungry I can have food sent to your room."

"Yes, I am tired from my journey, but please do send food; I will retire after I wash. Until the morning then."

Zolade and Kareae remained by the fire each absorbed in their own reflections.

Zolade said, "Torent seems to have developed a maturity I have not seen before. I'm glad to see that."

"And," Kareae added, "I can imagine that he will develop even more maturity to fulfill his destiny. Ah, Zolade," he reflected for a moment, "I can tell you this: your destiny is closely related to his, so keep an eye on what Torent does."

"Yes, I feel you are right, I will take your words to my heart." Then laughing and patting Kareae on the shoulder Zolade said, "I do really like your mysterious advice, it always makes me more alert. Well, tomorrow will be a very busy day; most of the guests should arrive early. I need to get my rest now while I have the chance. I left word with the night watchmen to wake me when Torent's carriage arrives."

"I am not tired. I can welcome the cousins. Please get your sleep."

"Thank you, I will take up your offer; peace my brother, until morning."

Kareae walked out into the night passed the horse stable towards a small forest grove he noticed before. He found a place to sit and remained silent until he heard the sounds of a carriage and horses. At the gate, he welcomed the rather exhausted cousins. He showed them to their rooms and then took his leave. He met Sabna waiting for him by his room looking very soft and beautiful.

"I wanted to say good-night to you. I just left Torent; we had a pleasant conversation. He has much insight for a young man. I had some reservations about having the king's son here but I am glad he came." Well, my silent friend, good night. Sleep well."

"Yes, my lovely Sabna, sleep well."

Whether it was the full moon or the meeting with Kareae and Torent, Sabna was not able to sleep. She spent the night gazing out of the window at the moonlight, not troubled but unable to close her eyes. She thought of Kareae, whom she loves and would not resist if he showed romantic interest in her. She closed her eyes imagining what it would be like if she made love with him but she could feel only the love that she already had with him. She thought of Torent, whom she felt was nice, but after all he was the king's son.

Kareae was resting but sitting silently in state of wakeful sleep. Tonight he was not projecting himself outward but staying in a neutral field.

In fact, the only person asleep was Zolade. Torent was awake, thinking about his meeting with Sabna. By Rai, I felt an immediate attraction towards her. Hmm, What a beauty. When we were sitting together earlier, it was difficult for me not to touch her. Too bad, she seemed not to notice me physically at all even though I must say she was very friendly and open.

For a king's son, Torent was not arrogant but rather on the humble and gentler side. He played the role of the king's son but was often not comfortable with it. The years away from Rai were great periods of freedom for him, something he would always cherish. Now he had returned, and must assume the role that destiny had given him. One of the main reasons he came to this festival was to speak with Kareae. Meeting Sabna was a delightful added surprise; he spent the rest of the night feeling a warm glow.

*****

Next morning early, Kareae rode off on the mare alone.

Sabna felt refreshed even though she hardly slept. Together with Zolade, they were busy all day welcoming the guests and making sure their needs were being looked after. When the performers and musicians for the night's celebration arrived, Sabna got lost in a chaotic but joyful madness to get them settled and ready for the evening.

Torent spent the morning quietly inside with his cousins but towards the afternoon he came out to mingle. Many people wanted to meet and connect with the king's son. Every time he glimpsed Sabna greeting guests, showing them to their rooms or where their tents were, he felt his heart stirring. At the midday meal, he spoke briefly to her but they were interrupted constantly.

By late afternoon, his longing for her had grown so that he had his horse saddled and rode out to settle his mind and feelings.

The ride through the forest was a relief. He could relax from his new obsession, be himself, and not worry about being the king's son. When he was just about to turn back after a brisk ride, he heard the approach of another horse. He turned and saw it was Kareae. For a moment, Torent was sure he saw Kareae and the horse as one, merged into each other immersed in a radiant white light. Then Kareae was beside him with an amazing look on his face as if it the greatest event in the world to meet him. This look was hard for Torent to resist. He felt himself relaxing and becoming peaceful.

Kareae said, "Don't discount what you just saw, those

moments can be more real than the so called normal reality."

Torent could only look at him speechless.

Kareae continued, "Let's ride a short way; I noticed a beautiful spot where we can sit."

They rode to a small clearing where the sun was still shining. "Let us sit here while the light is with us." Kareae said.

Almost in a daze Torent sat.

"Now, where is the king's son?" Kareae asked, placing himself in front of Torent.

"What do you mean? I am the king's son! That is my problem - I have to be the king's son rather than just be me."

"And who is 'me'?"

"By Rai, what a strange question, "I am ... hmm," he stayed silent for a moment then said, "Actually I don't know."

"Good, now stay with the 'I don't know' without trying to define yourself."

After several minutes Kareae inquired, "How are you now?"

Torent replied, "I feel relaxed, at ease, alive, complete."

"Where is the king's son now?"

"He is not here," he said with great surprise, touching his forehead in perplexity.

"And Torent? Where is he?"

"I don't believe it but he is also not here."

"Then, are you any different?"

Torent reflected for some moments and said, "No, I

am the same no matter what."

"Yes, Torent, this 'I am what is the same' is more the real you. Make this your home when you can. Being Torent or the king's son is just a role you take on. Accept these roles, you must, but always know the real you. Do this and your life will be much more harmonious. I leave you now; please remain and reflect upon what I just showed you."

Kareae rose and mounted his horse, pulling on the reins he said, "Torent, you are blessed."

Left alone, Torent pondered over his new realization. He tested being the king's son, then taking it off. Then being Torent and taking it off. And then being no one in particular. Yes, he thought, Kareae is right, I can be all these roles, and I can be nothing. It is so simple, why didn't I see it before? With an immense relief, Torent mounted his horse to return.

Both Zolade and Sabna watched Kareae ride out of the forest. For a fleeting moment, they had the same vision as Torent. They saw Kareae merged as one with his horse immersed in a radiant white light. They felt for a brief moment as if they were entering into some fairyland tale. They greeted Kareae at the stable and Zolade asked if he has seen Torent? "We saw him ride away some time ago and we are wondering where he is?"

Kareae explained with a twinkle in his eyes that he just left him in the forest, "There is no need to worry about him."

They both laughed, knowing if Kareae was up to his usual business, Torent was more than okay.

At that moment, Torent rode out of the forest and

came directly to the stable. He dismounted with a lightness in his face that nobody missed. With only a grateful smile without saying a word, he excused himself to get ready for the evening's activities. Zolade, Sabna and Kareae walked together back to the house to prepare as well; the full moon would be rising in only a few hours.

*****

When the moon rose and the sun was setting simultaneously, the hundred or so guests gathered in a circle at a small temple near the main house. The stone idol of the temple was bought out and placed in the center of the circle. Chanting began for the intunement with the great natural forces. When the sun fully set, with the atmosphere charged by the chanting, a great fire was lit that would burn all night. Everyone rose and circled the fire seven times while continuing to chant, as was the Raian custom. Once completed, everyone sat again and remained silent, absorbing the charged flow until a bell rung three times to signal the end of the initial ceremony. At this point the empowerment was achieved: everyone's energy field was perfectly balanced and tuned to synchronize with the natural earth forces and with each other.

Prince Zolade stood and welcomed everyone to his estate. "After food is served, the band will play, and we can dance until the sun rises if you wish. When the moon is at its highest point, I will call you again as a group to chant and honor the night. Until then, please enjoy yourself."

The crowd slowly meandered to the food area, many coming to Zolade and Sabna to thank them. Kareae wandered off to the edge of the activities. Torent came over and they sat together watching the festivities. "How is it possible," Torent asked, turning to Kareae, that a few words can have such a profound effect upon me? You have cleared up a life-long problem in a matter of seconds. You must come to the palace and meet my father."

"Yes, soon your father will send for me," Kareae replied. "Look there she is," pointing at Sabna. Torent blushed, his eyes showed a shock of recognition of his feelings he thought he had hid so well. "Is it that obvious?"

"Only with me."

The moonlight floated its way through the tree branches near them, reached the stones and gave them a luminescence look as if they were alive. Kareae reached over and gently touched one of them as if it was a lover, then looked at Torent with such benevolence that Torent began to weep.

"Torent, allow these tears of love to wash you away; these are the tears of your open heart. Go, the music begins and be with the one who can hold these tears."

Torent nodded and they embraced in spiritual love.

The power of the full moon made Kareae feel so overflowing that he could hardly move. The strength of his being was so poignant that it was almost as if another presence was merged with him. He remained this way until he heard the bell signaling the beginning of the next ceremony. Having no sense of where he began and ended, he moved into the crowd, finding himself surrounded by all his dear new friends. The love was so present, so thick and touching, he dissolved even more, entering into the soul of everyone. The crowd became one, fused into a new consciousness. Nobody could talk; indeed, people were falling down unable to remain standing. Raians were naturally intuitive and often experienced their sense of ego being overwhelmed. However this evening, a quantum leap into the unknown was experienced by everyone. The planned ceremony was forgotten, the instruments lay on the ground next to the musicians, even the horses in the corral were quiet and not one dog was howling to the full moon. For years later, this evening would still be talked about as the first time the new consciousness was experienced as a collective event.

Sabna was dancing the traditional Raian dance, alone and yet performed together with the group when she saw Kareae enter the dance floor. She spontaneously took Kareae's hand at the same time Zolade took the other. They started rotating round and round until the world disappeared and she entered into a void, dissolving and merging together into oneness. Any thought of time dissolved and it was not until the moon began its final descent and the first rays of the sun tickled the sky that any sense of self and time reappeared. People rose and slowly made their way to their rooms and tents to rest and digest fully the beauty they had just been part of.

Torent was dancing close to Sabna when Kareae made his appearance but was unable to make direct contact with her. He as everyone else got caught up in the happening, forgetting his purpose. They met the next day but the exchange remained brief and casual; the experience of last evening's event left everyone feeling inward and unable to relate much with others.

Chapter 17

THE KING'S COURT

Although Rai was a city, the nature was never far away. If left to her own means, the abounding mother earth would regain her throne in only a short while. Fortunately, the local people were diligent and caring to maintain the beautiful gardens, the tree lined boulevards and waterways.

Commercial activity was limited to the river area near Thor Shipping. This kept the residential areas free from most of the traffic and noise. Each local area had its own central square, some with fabulous fountains, where shops and cafes thrived. Raians often met to chat and drink the local teas. Senior citizens could be seen for hours playing the local board games and watching life go by.

I loved to walk around the city. Today on impulse, I sat at one of the cafes. While enjoying a cool mint tea, a well-dressed middle-aged woman with short brown hair and a lively look approached. "Excuse me sir, May I speak to you for a moment."

With an inviting look as if I had known her for years,

I answered, "Yes, please sit down, I've been waiting for you."

"Would you like a drink?" I said, calling over the waiter.

"Yes, please but tell me how could you be waiting, when only this minute I decided to speak with you?"

After the waiter took her order, I continued, "I know more than that. A very close friend of yours died some months ago. Someone you were lovers with and still you have not completely made closure. You feel guilty about his death because of a quarrel you had just before his accident. I can help you to heal, but you must come to my house in the evening two days from now when there is no moon. We will perform a healing ceremony together."

"I heard from friends who attended the full moon celebration that you were exceptional, but what you say leaves me breathless. I will come in two days; I know where your house is. Until then, I don't want to take up more of your time."

She began to rise but I stopped her and said, "It is no bother, but please tell me your name."

"Rea. My name is Rea."

"Rea, when you arrive at my house you will be greeted by my housekeeper. Please follow her instructions even if they seem unusual. I will join you after she has prepared you for the ceremony. Is that okay?"

"Yes."

"Good, until then."

Afterwards I felt an inward glow. I always did when I met someone I was destined to work on. I knew someone needing help would come when I had the urge to sit at the café.

*****

Janan was already at the baths when I arrived. We embraced as old friends. I was very happy to see the permanent change in him, "Janan, you are glowing and I don't think it's from the heat of the water."

"Ah my son, its seems a long time since we met. I have some news: Romdev will arrive shortly to begin his work on the palace temple and my daughter Neelu will be returning in the next days. We want you to meet her, of course, why not come over for dinner when she arrives?"

"Okay, but I've been having it in my mind to invite you to my house. I want you to meet my housekeeper Regina and see the temple. It's complete enough to show you. Let's say on the new moon night. That should give enough time for your daughter to arrive. How does that sound?"

"Yes, fine but let me talk it over with Divea. I'm sure she will love to come to your house. Now tell me, you are becoming the talk of the town. What happened at the full moon celebration that has everyone so excited?"

I laughed and rolled my eyes. I rose, took a plunge in the cold water, and when I returned said, "It was not something I planned. Everyone was dancing just at the peak of the full moon. I joined in the celebration when the intensity of the moment overwhelmed me and I was swept away as with everyone else. I felt myself enter into the soul of every guest and merge with them."

" It was incredible to unite in such a collective way with so many. In a way it was similar to what happened with us but this was on a larger scale. I know I am a vehicle for the propagation of the new consciousness. Sometimes it happens through my own direction but as in this case, this was an occurrence beyond my awareness. It was like riding a stallion at full power, you can only surrender with the flow. I loved it, I must say."

"Yes, I can sense it as you are talking. Thank you for being so forthcoming."

"Of course, we are one now."

Janan rose and kissed me on the forehead. "Yes," he whispered.

"I must go now. If there is any problem about dinner, I will send a message."

"Until then"

*****

Torent arrived back in the palace a changed man. He met Kosa, his distinguished looking father with beginning gray hair, several days later in his private quarters. The robust and well-built King saw there was an air of something different about him. During breakfast Torent shared his amazing story and interaction with Kareae.

"Hmm, I see he has had a profound effect upon you, and it is not the first time I hear about this man. I heard he is the son of the high priest and priestess of Kanparu and has exceptional powers. Perhaps I will arrange a meeting with him to see for myself."

"You will not be disappointed, father."

They both looked up to the sound of footsteps to watch Anu, the wife and queen enter. She embraced both of them before sitting at the table. Glancing over Torent she gave an approving look as well and he ended up repeating his story.

Anu was perfect for the role of queen. She loved the pomp and ceremony and was still young and shapely enough to wear flowing gowns and attire that befitted a queen. Kosa still was attracted to her prominent aquiline beauty and regal grace. Indeed, he felt even now an inner stirring to embrace her. Devoted to her husband and wanting the best for her family, Anu was not power hungry. She came from a family linage familiar with money, power and governing.

"Yes," Anu said, "we must meet this Kareae; let us invite him soon."

"Okay, I will arrange it," Kosa said. "I will send my advisor Korpa to meet and invite him to the palace. I plan to see Korpa this afternoon to discuss our situation with Sol over their water problem. Torent, why not join me? It will be a good experience. Are you free this afternoon?"

"Yes sir, I am available for you."

"Very good. Now I must leave to take care of a few other matters."

"My son," Anu began, "I'm glad we finally have some time together. I thought about you every day and had to force myself from writing. If it weren't for the custom not to communicate to you on your travels, I would have. I am happy to see you have become a man in such a short time but I will miss my boy."

"Thank you, Mother."

"Your father has high hopes for you, you know, and I'm sure you will meet them easily, you have the same nature as Kosa. Your brothers, unfortunately have not passed his tests. Now it is up to you."

"I know I am my father's man and there is no problem

about it. I am ready to take the responsibility. Indeed, I look forward to it so don't worry about me."

"Yes, I feel you are right and I don't worry. My concern is to find a suitable wife for you. Now this is not an easy task."

"Mother, please rest assured that I am capable of finding a suitable woman. I appreciate your concern and you know I would never pick someone you didn't approve of," he said standing to give her a hug and a peck on the cheek.

"Torent, don't sweet-talk me," she said brushing a hair away from his forehead.

"Now I must take your leave as well, mother, to prepare for my meeting with the King." But as he was leaving, he let out, "By the way, I did meet someone at Prince Zolade's estate, his sister Sabna."

"Hmm, Princess Sabna," Anu reflected, walking up to Torent, "I have not seen her for some years. Yes, she must be a young woman by now. Why did I not think of her? Well, perhaps?

"I can see your wheels turning. But please, allow it to happen, as it will, Mother."

"Yes, of course" she said watching Torent run off.

*****

On the south side of the palace grounds, facing the Signa was the official government building where the King conducted the business of state. The administrative offices were located in another building just outside the palace area. The official building was relatively small and practical, containing a main reception area with several rooms attached to it. Here, the King could meet guests and have an office to do his private work. In addition, there was a living area with two bedrooms and a small hall for small official ceremonies.

That afternoon the King and Torent were in his office catching up, making small talk. With Torent away on his travels they had not spent much time together. Korpa was waiting in the reception area to be called in. Kosa was impressed with his son, listening to his travel stories. He's turning into a fine young man, he thought. _I like his ideas and the way he sees life and his new self-confidence. Not really confidence but a sense of acceptance, of being more relaxed with himself.

Korpa entered followed by the housekeeper with a tray of teas and sweets.

"I am happy to see both of you together." Korpa said after making the formal greeting and personally serving them.

The King agreed and said, "See my old friend and advisor, how time marches on especially when there is the responsibility of a whole Kingdom to consider. Now my son is grown and ready to join us."

"Yes, my King, time does march on. Since forty years I've been advising the Kings of Rai, starting with your father when he was about the same age as Torent. Now begins the third generation. I don't think there is any other place I want to be."

After a moment of reflection, the King said, "I will always be indebted to you, Korpa. But, let's get down to business. What is the latest news about the water situation with Sol? Hmm, might as well fill in the whole story for Torent."

"In a nutshell, it has not rained in Sol for three years; they are having a severe drought. We on other hand, are inundated with lakes and rivers. The Solians are basically a peaceful people but they are desperate to avoid widespread famine. There is talk about invading us even though they know how difficult it is to come down the ghats. However, their despair is bringing up certain elements that are screaming for invasion. The situation is not getting better. I am sure we can repel an invasion but still the Solians are distressed and our best policy would be to help them."

"Yes, I agree, but how shall we solve this?" The King turned to Torent, "Do you have any ideas?

Torent pondered, "Let me think for a minute." Then after some moments, "By Rai, I have it. It's simple, we need to give them what they want and need and that is, water. But how to do that? It's almost impossible to bring water up the sheer drop of the ghats?"

Both the King and Korpa smiled and nodded their heads and look at each other in approval. "Very good Torent, we have made the same conclusion. How to give them water? Now, I want to give you this very difficult assignment, to find a method of transporting water to the Solians. But I must warn you, we have talked to most of our engineers, and they have not been able to come up with a practical way to deliver the water."

"During my travels, I met some very intelligent men and some engineers I can contact. I will send out messages to them immediately. I did come across some ingenious methods of water irrigation in Sa. I want to travel to Sol and see how they are utilizing the water they still have. Maybe some improvements can happen in that area."

"Excellent, excellent. I'm sure Korpa agrees with your assessment and ideas for a solution."

"Yes, it is an auspicious day this meeting. I look forward to advise Torent when the time comes." Korpa replied.

"Now", the King said, standing and giving Torent a Raian hug, "Please excuse us as there are a few affairs I need to speak with Korpa about. When do you suppose to travel to Sol?"

"I would say within two weeks, I will be ready."

"Good, that will give you some time to spend with your mother."

Yes, and someone else for that matter, Torent thought.

Later the King and Korpa both expressed confidence in Torent that he would be more than capable of taking of over the reins of government. They had met with the King's other sons but they did not fare so well in the established tests. In Rai, the custom was that the next in line to rule was determined by ability not age. Even though the other sons were older, Torent would take over when the time came.

"Now there is one little matter I want you to take care of Korpa. I've been hearing from several people, including Torent, about a man called Kareae, who is making quite an impression. He is the son of Ashara, the high priest of Kanparu. I want you to meet with him and determine first his credibility and then if he passes, to invite him to meet me. Can you do this for me?"

"Yes of course, my King, I am always in your service. I heard also some stories about him. It seems he has become good friends with Janan. They have been seen in the baths several times together."

"Oh, that is interesting. Being friends with Janan is a good sign. In any case, I value your judgment and want you to meet with him first."

"Very good; now if you allow me I will take your leave."

"Yes, thank you Korpa." The King rose and walked over to the window to look out into the garden. "It is a beautiful day; let us enjoy some of it. Take care, my friend."

Korpa smiled as he rose, "My King, I love that you remain so down to earth, it is my pleasure to serve you. May peace be with you."

Chapter 18

DESTINY CALLS

For most of the morning I poured over my temple designs and calculations deciding on a plan of action. This was the first time I would be directly involved with the complete process of building. I felt great joy from personally choosing the materials and lumber to the actual construction work like carpentry and tiling.

Later that day I traveled to the commercial area by the river to initiate my search for exactly the right marble. Conveniently, all the building supply shops were close together on the same street.

After being in several shops, I got lucky in the last one to find some very special white marble having an excellent vibration. Surprisingly, just when I was making the final transaction, my intuitive sense picked up the scent of a pure heart. I looked up to see a young well-dressed woman with long pleasantly light brown hair walk into a cloth shop several stores away.

After completing my transaction, I stepped into the fabric store pretending to look for some curtains for the house. The young woman, when she saw me stopped speaking in the middle of a sentence, unable to continue until the shopkeeper started coughing.

I gave her a warmhearted polite smile as she was leaving but then pretended to return to my task of choosing cloth for the house. I watched until I saw her enter Thor Shipping just down the street. Oh, I thought fondly, she must be Neelu, their daughter. _

*****

Neelu just returned from her year of internship at a facility for physically and mentally impaired children close to Rosea's village, Do in Western Rai. She just completed her requirements to become a physician. Neelu looked happily forward to relax and spend time with her parents and friends before beginning her practice. Neelu was trained to employ different medical modalities, but she discovered early on, even as a child that if she focused her love onto the patient, often enough it had more of a healing effect than the treatment. With mentally impaired children she found that long hugs in which she totally embraced the child would often enable them to think clearer and be quieter.

From an early age Neelu showed a desire to help others without a real concern for her own needs. There was always some animal with a broken foot or bird with a broken wing she was taking care of. Where she found them nobody knew. Once she bought home a snake that had just given birth and was anxiously worried about how to feed the little babies. She tried everything, but unfortunately they all died. Instead of crying, she bought them to a spot near the lake, made a fire, chanted some simple prayers and bid them farewell. It was surprising for everyone because no one ever taught her about death and its rituals. When she was asked how she knew how to make a fire, she answered that she didn't know, it just came to her to do it. "But don't worry," she said, "they will live again." This was even more of a surprise because she was never taught about reincarnation. When asked again she replied, "I just know that's all." It was then that Janan and Divea realized what a special child she was.

Other than that, though, her teachers found her to be normal in intelligence and social skills with other children. She loved swimming and could be found at the lake or in some canal with friends whenever she could.

When she was older, Neelu met a boy with mental and physical disabilities named Marcin, who was amazingly sweet and open hearted. They became close friends and for a while she spent most of her time with Marcin until his family sent him, when his condition deteriorated, to the same facility where she did her internship. When Marcin died early, Neelu was happy for him that he could drop his body and was sure he would be born again somewhere else. Ever since that time, she had a soft spot for people with disabilities. She loved to be with them. It felt so natural and she never felt superior. During this time she decided to become a physician and help others like Marcin.

Raians were aware of reincarnation but rarely spoke about it because of their down to earth nature. For someone like Neelu to be so open about it then, was rare

Eventually Neelu became known as the pure hearted, and in truth she was. In her studies she was never driven but pursued them in her own soft way, very much as a female. Janan became more and more protective of her, not wanting her pure heart to be touched in the wrong way. He always had that concern but nothing ever happened.

*****

Neelu entered the office softly like a beam of light that touched everywhere. Janan was not expecting her so he gladly came out of his office to welcome her.

"Father, I was in the neighborhood shopping and I thought it would be a shame not to visit you. The store down the road has some lovely materials. But with all this shopping, I'm starving. Do you have time to have a bite with me?"

"Of course," he beamed, "I will have the kitchen prepare something and I know exactly what you like. That is, if you have not changed?"

"No father, my eating preferences are still the same and I can say my ability to eat has not become less," she giggled.

Neelu was tall like most Raians but differed from having the normal slender figure by being robust, having more of a full figure. Instead of distracting from her beauty, her uniqueness made her more alluring.

"Come, let's go into my office, I want you to try one of the sweets a client presented to me. They are unusually different but the taste is very pleasant."

"Father," she said with big eyes, "you really know how to keep me on your good side."

Once in the office Janan said, "Since you arrived I have not had a chance to see you. Now let me take a good look at you. Hmm, you have put on some weight but on you it's perfect."

"Thank you, you are kind and would not say anything else," taking a bite of one of the sweets, "Wow, these are really delicious. I've never tasted anything like it."

"Yes, they come from Mi. It is something we don't see here often. Here have another."

"You're so bad. It's a good thing mother is not here. But now that I look at you, there is definitely something different about you, you seem even a little younger. What have you been doing?

"Oh, I don't know," studying himself in a mirror for a second, "but I do feel great."

Just then there was a knock on the door. "Oh good, here's the food. Let's eat."

"Father," Neelu began after eating, "now that we are together here in the office, there is some business I want to discuss with you. I know I am just out of school and it might be a little premature, but I feel a calling to open a small clinic here in Rai to begin my work. What do you say?"

"My dear, of course you have my support and help. I think is very worthwhile to have such a clinic here in Rai. Just give me the particulars and we will fulfill your wishes. I imagine you have some idea from the time you spent at the clinic of what you need as far as equipment and space. If not, I can send someone knowledgeable about these matters to the clinic to make a report."

"That is an excellent idea. I have an idea of what I need but something might be missing. Let me communicate with the director first and let him know our plans."

"Yes, you are right."

"I do know where I want to build the clinic. There is a spot I found during my last visit. The alignment of the land there is perfect for healing? I want to inquire soon if it is still available. If so, can we purchase it immediately?"

"I don't see why not."

"Good," but then looking at Janan, she said, "Oh father I'm sorry, it must be being in the office that makes me so businesslike and not thinking of you. Please tell me, what you have been up to these days?"

"My daughter, I would love to chat with you, but I'm afraid it must be at some other time. I still have work to do and people are waiting to see me. Let us talk later tonight."

"Okay, of course you are right, I'm just so happy to be here with you." She said standing up and walking to the door.

"And I with you, my daughter. Now go and we see each other later."

"Until then."

*****

I returned directly home with a marble sample to show Regina. While I was explaining where I wanted to place the marble, I causally mentioned that I saw a lovely young woman today on the quay. "I was like a schoolboy," I said, "I followed her into a cloth shop but we didn't speak. I realized soon she was Neelu, the daughter of Janan and Divea when I saw her enter Thor Shipping. Regina, her heart is very pure. I now truly understand Janan's concerns about her."

"You will meet her soon when they come for dinner on the new moon."

"Dinner? Oh dear, I must go back to the kitchen, please excuse me. If I don't finish preparing, there will be nothing to eat." Saying that, Regina took her leave, and I returned my attention to the marble and the temple completely focused on my work.

Just being inside the shell of the temple, I felt the uplifting effect it already had. It will be very useful for my work, I thought, like with Rea.

******

The previous day Rea was greeted by Regina at the door. She bought her to the guestroom arranged with an altar containing the stones from Kanparu. Rea was instructed to shower, put on a flowing soft white robe and lie down on the mat to wait for Kareae. Curtains were drawn, candles were lit, and sweet burning incense gave the room an serene feeling. Rea was a little anxious but after a few minutes in that atmosphere she relaxed and fell into a light trance state.

Kareae entered wearing a similar white robe and his hair tied back tightly.

What happened next was a blur for Rea. She felt Kareae touch her head and then different parts of her body. When he touched her head, she felt herself expanding unable to tell where her body began or ended. It was an immensely pleasurable sensation and she experienced several releases of feelings that were orgasmic in nature but in a way as never before. When finally she could open her eyes, Kareae was gone. Rea had the sense of being absolutely cleansed and purified as if she was a newborn child. She looked for her pain but could not find it.

Rea was instructed to stay in silence, not to disturb

the healing process for the rest of the day. However, when she was leaving, Kareae came over and hugged her saying softly she should return in three days. She gratefully nodded and left.

******

Regina's call for lunch brought me out of my thoughts. I invited Patai, the contractor, to eat with me and then after lunch, with a cool drink, we discussed the building plans for the next days. Patai was not sure how to construct the apex part of the roof so it would be sturdy and still be in symmetry with the other corners. Finally, together we worked it out, coming up with an ingenious simple design.

Chapter 19

KORPA

Days later, I looked up from my work to find Regina standing with a letter bearing the official seal of the King. "There is a messenger waiting for a reply outside."

"Oh, then lets see it."

After reading the letter, I said, "It's a request from the King's advisor, a man named Korpa. He wants to arrange a meeting with me to discuss some business for the King. I would like to invite him for lunch tomorrow. Does that suit you?"

Regina just nodded in affirmation.

"I know, Regina, you will be busy these next days with tomorrow the King's advisor coming for lunch and then tomorrow night at the new moon, Janan and his family for dinner. Shall we get additional help for you?"

"Tomorrow will be fine but I will need help for the dinner on the new moon. I know someone quiet and efficient whom I can call."

"Very good."

*****

Korpa arrived the next day dressed in his official

advisor facade, formally introducing himself and sending greetings from the King.

"I am honored Sir, please thank the King and it gives me great pleasure to receive you in my home."

Inside, I could hear him thinking, Why he is so young, nearly a boy. But, I must admit, he carries himself and pays me respect like someone much older.

"Allow me to give you a tour of my house," as I took his arm.

Afterwards Korpa said, "I am impressed by your house and the temple is magnificent." We sat for lunch on the terrace to have a delicious meal. The main meal was eaten in silence, but the rest of the time was filled with superficial small talk and gossip about palace life. I enjoyed and found it interesting but towards the end of lunch I turned and looked directly at Korpa and made a statement that sent Korpa into a state of shock. His facade fell apart and left him in tears.

After moments of silence and tears, as if time was stopped and the stillness of the breeze could be heard, Korpa said, "How can you know that? I've kept hidden all these years the tragic sorrow of losing in death the only woman I've ever cared about, and was never able to express my feelings, as she was betrothed to some else."

I rose and placed my hand on his right shoulder and said, "Are you ready to finally let go of this suffering? It has been with you long enough but now you must prepare yourself for the final journey of life. Do you say yes?"

When Korpa looked up, wiping his wet eyes and nodded his head in affirmation, he felt like a weight being lifted off him and his head became crystal clear and light.

Even his face seemed to become younger. Again the tears came, but these were ones of joy.

I lifted my hands to the sky totally exhilarated in this happening. I telepathically called Regina to take Korpa into her bosom. When she did this, Korpa looked in love at Regina like a newborn looks at the mother the first time. For Regina, returning the motherly love was an inspiring experience. They lay in this circle of love motionless for some time. Finally, I directed Regina to take Korpa inside the guestroom to rest and reflect. "Please stay with him for some time."

"Yes, I want to very much."

I remained the rest of the afternoon in this exalted exhilarated state. The mind, I thought, always wants to give the impression there is nothing else to have, that life is limited - but it just goes on and on, deeper and deeper.

In the evening Korpa came and swore his loyalty to me. "Kosa is my physical king to whom I am still loyal, but you are my spiritual King and my loyalty goes deeper. And it surprises me to make such a statement I never thought possible."

"Korpa, nothing has changed, we are just friends. I might need your help someday in the future and I know you will be there for me. And don't worry, the King will be with us as well."

"Please stay for dinner. All your responsibilities can wait until tomorrow."

"Yes, yes," Korpa laughed.

The rest of the night I personally laid the marble tiles in the temple along with the stones and crystals from Kanparu. With each tile and crystal, I chanted and invoked a prayer and blessing. I finished as the sun was rising. I greeted the new day totally refreshed as if I had a full nights sleep. Breakfast was waiting for me on the terrace. Regina, this morning, had a glow of beauty that would make any man ready to move mountains.

I admiringly said, "Please, my most beautiful housekeeper, servant of the gods, I think my future wife would get very jealous if she saw you now."

"Yes," she said feeling a warm inner glow, "I feel like a virgin bride. I wonder if it should be me that is jealous? But I look and do not see this jealousy, only oneness with you."

"I am not surprised to hear this, Regina. We know there is no doubt between us."

"I feel to take a walk in the forest today, then go to the baths to get ready for the great meeting tonight. Is everything prepared?

"Yes, I'll go personally to the market and then I will also visit the baths to refresh myself before they come. I will send the workmen home early, they are in fact finished with almost all of the work"

"Yes, I worked all night, take a look at it when you get a chance."

"I will, and I leave you now to enjoy your breakfast."

*****

Korpa woke up the next morning with a smile on his face and a warm glow in his heart. By Rai, he thought, I can't remember when I woke with a smile before; this is really a miracle. In the King's office, both Kosa and Torent were surprised with the change they saw. Torent laughed knowingly, and the King, well, he was very impressed.

"Indeed," he said, "I must see this man soon."

Korpa reported everything. Before yesterday he would have cut off his right hand not to let people know about his pain and now it seemed so unimportant.

The King said, "Next week is Jalititi. Let's invite this man to our private family celebration. He can meet with me on my boat. Can you take care of this my dear new old advisor?"

"Yes, I will personally go to his house and invite him."

The King looked up, as this was unusual for Korpa, "Really, you have changed."

Now lets us talk about the finance for the new temple. Are there enough funds not to tax the coffers and put a burden on the people? If so, I can arrange from my private funds to cover the costs.

"Sir, there is more than enough, in fact your coffers are too full, we need to allocate spending on more projects to keep the funds circulating."

"Excellent. Romdev will arrive here by the Jalititi festival with the designs so I want to have these funds in place this week.

"There is no problem."

"Torent, after you finish with the Sol issue, you can put your energy into suggesting ideas for public projects. How does that sound?

"Very much like fun."

"Good, now let us have tea. Talking about finances always makes me hungry."

*****

I was walking in part of a forest actually on Zolade's land but close to the extreme east side. Suddenly, in my mind's eye, I saw Romdev. He communicated that he would be arriving at my house in Rai at the most, in one week. We have much to discuss, I had an encounter with Kalo as well. The situation is ominous. Until then and as suddenly, Romdev's image disappeared. I didn't mention that several nights ago I felt Kalo reaching out probing my mind. I kept my mind closed but he didn't tried to penetrate it. But, I wondered, what about the next time?

Chapter 20

DESTINY ANSWERS

Neelu was the most unsuspecting and unassuming person today. Her parents were vague about whom they would have dinner with tonight, other than he recently arrived and was some sort of advisor for people. Probably some late middle-aged man with bad breath, she thought. I guess I will have to appease my parents. Now when I think about it, they are somehow different since I've returned. Well, maybe I am different as well?

Neelu was down by the boathouse enjoying a swim and the afternoon sun. Lying on the deck, she looked at her body. Hmm my figure, well, I am a bit overweight but it's still okay. My lips and my hair are my strong points, she thought. Neelu had full beautiful lips and her hair, light brown, long and very flowing. She had a thought about the man in the cloth shop and felt a tingling inside. I wonder if he noticed me? He certainly gave me an exquisite smile.

Her thoughts remained until she rose for a last swim. The dive into the water was refreshing. Hmm, too long in the sun, she thought as she vigorously swam to the other shore and back. Quickly she jumped out of the water, dried herself off and made her way back to the house. She asked one of the housekeepers to start her bath while she considered what to wear for the evening.

She was just about finish with the bath when her mother returned. A short time later Janan arrived from the office. She heard Divea greet her father and shortly afterwards there was a knock on her door. Divea entered looking rather beautiful. "Mother, I don't know what it is but there is something different about you, like you are more full, more alive. What is your secret?"

Handing a towel to Neelu she said, "Oh it must be because I've been swimming everyday."

"My dear, wear something beautiful tonight, Kareae is special."

"Okay, mother but I don't see what the big fuss is."

"Let's meet on the terrace for tea in one hour, your father wants to see you before we leave."

" Well... okay," Neelu replied.

Janan was by the pond gazing at the fish in their little universe. The sound of the small waterfall was pleasant to his ears. Neelu arrived with a hug and was again taken back by the change in her father. He returned her hug and she felt a love with him in a way like never before. She stared at her father but Janan just fell into a big smile. "I love you my daughter and want to hear myself say it to you."

"Father what has gotten into you, you never been like this before?"

"Let's say something wonderful happened that revealed how much love there is."

"That is beautiful, but please tell me what has happened?"

At that moment Divea appeared and before he could answer, Divea hurriedly said, "We must leave now or we will be late. Whatever it is you are talking about must wait.

"Okay, but later, you promise, I'm dying to know," Neelu implored her father."

"Yes, I promise, soon you will know."

*****

Festive lamps of various colors decorated the house of Kareae, spreading out a colorful celebrative and warm atmosphere. The night was filled with many stars and the new moon was smiling. Venus could be seen hugging close to the moon.

"An auspicious night." I commented to Regina.

The Janan family entered in a cloudburst of energy. The love the parents felt sparkled bright in the moonlight. Neelu stood shock, unable to speak and once again stumbled from the tingling inside. Finally she stuttered out, "You are the man from the store."

"Yes," I answered, as I gave her the formal greeting and the same smile as before.

On the terrace Regina served drinks and tiny salt biscuits she baked earlier. I introduced her and remarked how fortunate I was that Regina allowed me to take care of her. Regina replied, "My master is very kind, I am only here to serve him," and left gracefully.

Janan said watching her leave, "I didn't realize Regina has so much beauty; she is certainly a evolved being. I guess so advanced that she can devote herself totally to serve you."

I nodded in agreement.

"Now let me show the temple; it is almost ready. On the full moon I am planning an opening ceremony so make sure to come."

The Janan family was in silent awe standing within the exquisiteness of the temple. Immediately upon entering they all felt a beautiful divine sense of never wanting to leave. I explained how I laid each tile, stone and crystal from the Kanparu temple.

Outside, Neelu whispered to her father, grasping onto his arm, "Now I know why you didn't tell me. My mind, how to say it without screaming, I feel has opened with a new sense of freedom, breaking all boundaries of doubt and separation. I feel totally this love as well."

"My sweet daughter, your heart is the most sensitive of all of us, if already you have arrived and have not even spoken to him yet."

"Father, does the flower have to speak to the sun to feel its power?"

"Yes, you are so right and so wise."

Divea and I were on the terrace waiting to welcome Neelu and Janan. I took the hand of Neelu and said, "Please, lets us eat." I sat Neelu to one side; Divea on the other and Janan sat across. Neelu's surrender was like a glorious sunset emblazed in pastels long after disappearing in the horizon. All eyes looked to her. Even Regina and her helper came for the view.

The dinner was light with much laughter. They listened to me telling how I spotted Neelu on the street and followed her into the cloth shop giving her one of his best smiles. Neelu reenacted acting cool when she first saw Kareae even though she was almost fainting. Then standing facing everyone, she declared her love for me. "That is," as almost a second thought, she looked at Kareae with the question, "If he will have me?"

I rose, took her hand and said, "I open my heart and soul to you, dear pure Neelu."

With that I kneeled and placed my head in her lap. Neelu lowered her head placing her hands on my head.

"So beautiful," Janan suddenly said, "that this happens so quickly with such love. Your mother and I have could only hope for this for some time and now here it is."

"My parents, what can I say?" Then looking at the platter of fruit and cheese that Regina bought she added, " Come, let's eat this divinely delicious looking food."

The rest of the evening continued in loving harmony.

Before leaving Neelu came and hugged me, "Let's meet soon."

"Yes, I'll come to see you in a few days ."

"Until then I wait," she said, joining her waiting parents.

Chapter 21

COMING TOGETHER

Next morning early Regina was surprised to see Princess Sabna at the door. "Please come in Princess Sabna and join Kareae, he is just sitting for breakfast. You can find him on the terrace."

"Thank you, Regina but don't bother about me; my visit will be short, and I've already eaten."

Hearing her voice, I stood to greet Sabna, soothing her with a warm embrace.

"It has been some time since we met, I miss your wonderful presence," she said.

"Please join me for breakfast. What a delightful way to begin my day with you my dear princess. You look radiant and I always love the way you dress."

"Okay," she readily complied, "I will join you briefly."

Sitting down together Sabna said, "What a beautiful table Regina lays out for you. Those muffins look too good to miss; I guess I can have one."

Sabna continued, "I didn't think you noticed how I dress. Anyhow I must confess I dressed especially nice for you," sighed Sabna unknowingly.

"Oh, before I forget, I do have a purpose in coming here unannounced. Zolade is in town and wants to meet us. His townhouse is not far from mine, so why not come first to my house in the afternoon and then we can go together?"

"Sounds fine. I see a client in the afternoon but it will not take long."

I rose as Sabna did to give her a hug. Sabna was lost in eternity when I separated to say, "Sabna, don't fall in love with me, your destiny awaits with someone else. I love you but it is not as lover. I met my future wife last night, you must know of her, Neelu, the daughter of Janan and Divea."

"Kareae, you always know everything about me, more than I know of myself." But looking with imploring eyes she said, "How could one not fall in love with you?"

"Yes, I know Neelu. We met when we were kids, but now I am very interested to meet her. Why not bring her along today?"

"Today is not possible. We need first to spend time together alone before socializing. Some other time we can be together, I promise."

"Now I must take your leave as I still have finishing work in the temple to do. I will send out invitations in the next days, but I want to request you keep your winter full moon night free for the opening of the temple."

"Yes, your temple looks magnificent Kareae. I eagerly await for the opening."

I said, "Yes, that will be a very important night for you."

Sabna's eyes opened wide stepping back from me

about to say something but no words passed her lips.

I gently touched her and whispered, "Until then."

*****

Rea arrived for her second appointment a new person.

She explained, "It's so unbelievable. I keep searching for the guilt and pain, but I can't find it no matter how hard I try. It's almost like losing an old friend. What did you do with it?"

"I sent it away to where it can never return," I said pointing upward with a wave and smile. "Have you noticed any other changes?"

"Why yes. I found I've become very detached. I watch things happen around me, but it's like there is a distance between the world and me. Even with my body and feelings, I feel unaffected. Never in my life have I felt this way continuously. Sometimes it does feel a little uncomfortable, like I don't how to sit with it all the time."

"Yes, that is why I wanted to see you again, to assure you. It is normal to feel some discomfort from a realignment because many old patterns have been released, which as you say, are like old friends. Please try to stay in this void as it is, without trying to fill it up immediately. In time, you will become rooted in the new you."

"Please give me your hands."

We sat together quietly until I gently let go of her.

"I think you will be fine now. If anytime you need my help, please contact me."

"Thank you. But how can I pay you for your work?"

"Your transformation is my payment and for you to

honor your new self. I want nothing else."

"You are very kind, dear sir. I know some friends that would like to see you. May I refer them to you?"

"Please. Perhaps you can arrange the appointments for me. I will give you the times when I am available. How does that sound?"

"I would love to perform this service for you."

"Good, now I must leave you as I still have much to do today. If I am not here, Regina is always available to take your appointment list."

"Yes, that would be fine, I say goodbye. I can find my way out"'

I bowed in farewell.

*****

A slight breeze blew in from the west during our walk to Zolade's house. We both wore light shawls and walked close together, mostly in silence. Occasionally a carriage approached; the sounds and smells resonating louder until it passed and faded into the distance. At this time of night most Raians were at home for the evening meal but still some strolled pass welcoming us for a good evening.

Being with Kareae always stops my mind. I cannot converse with myself in the normal way, Sabna reflected. If only I could have this for myself permanently.

I turned to her. "You will, Sabna. Just be patient and trust me."

"By Rai, Kareae, I always forget you can read my mind."

"Yes my princess, you can't hide from me," I teased.

"My dear Kareae, hiding is the last thing I want to

do with you. I appreciate and take to my heart every and any insight you give me."

"Yes, I know Sabna, that is why I can be the way I am with you. And I am grateful to you for our friendship. I also learn from your wisdom."

"Ah, just ahead, that house on the left is Zolade's," Sabna said running and laughing ahead of me. "You do make me feel like a school girl again."

I ran after and caught her, both laughing just as Zolade came out: our joy catching him like a sudden rainstorm. Zolade and I were pleased to see each other. We exchanged the Raian embrace.

"Come inside, I took the liberty of inviting another guest; he is in the garden waiting for us."

In the garden, Torent stood admiring a rare rose flower with a magnificent fragrance. When he saw Sabna his face nearly turned a bright red. I noticed but Sabna seemed to be oblivious.

After gentle greetings, we settled at the outdoor dining table to eat a pleasant meal with fresh vegetables and salad coming directly from Zolade's garden. The conversation was playful, but all felt Torent's restlessness.

"I am leaving shortly after the full moon to Sol to study their water problem." Torent said with a suddenness in his gestures.

"Ah," I said, "I have some knowledge of irrigation. Perhaps we should meet before you leave? My teacher and friend, the architect Romdev, might also be of help. He is arriving soon. I advise you to wait for him. I don't think it would a good idea to leave without his consultation."

"Yes, you are right. I will take your advice. I eagerly

wait to meet with the both of you. Now, I apologize, but I must be rude. I want to have some words with Princess Sabna alone... if she agrees?"

Sabna looked up with a slight surprised jerky movement but then answered, "Yes, of course."

"Come," Zolade called to me, "let me show you around the house and garden while they speak."

Zolade's A-frame house was not huge but well built in good taste. A porch ran entirely around the house with several different areas created for sitting. Kareae particularly liked how the kitchen took up the entire back of the house, being constructed with glass and wood that afforded a panoramic view of the gardens and the hills beyond. The garden was surprisingly extensive, containing orchards, flowers and vegetable gardens. The barn area for the horses and other animals was placed well to the side so the smell and flies of the animals did not reach the house.

At the stable, amongst the roaming chickens, the extensive woodpiles, sniffing dogs and barnyard smells Zolade commented, "I cannot be without my animals, Kareae, I feel so at home with them. But I must tell you, Torent is here by his own request when he found out Sabna was coming. He is quite smitten with her, but so far she doesn't seem to really see him."

"Don't worry Zolade, it is all happening as it should. I predict by the full moon they will both know more about each other. Listen, will you still be here on the winter full moon? I am having a little gathering to celebrate the completion of a small temple I built."

"I leave tomorrow, but I will return for your

celebration. I would not miss it for the world. Now, I have a small gift for you. Come into the barn with me. Remember the mare you rode last month? Well, there she is, and I want to present her to you. You can keep her here. She will be taken care of and will be available for your pleasure whenever you have time."

"I am most happy to have this horse; we had a wonderful merging if you remember," I said while petting and saying hello to her. "Thank you, my friend and brother. Hmm, you arouse my interest for a ride; let's saddle up these horses and leave our future couple to work it out by themselves."

"Excellent."

We enjoyed a vigorous ride even though the terrain was not as rugged as in the forest. Towards the end, galloping at full speed, neck and neck through a long flat, we were the most at one with each other. While resting and walking the horses, Zolade said, " I want to share with you how trouble-free my life has become. I now really enjoyed my life and who I am."

I listened in silence, and then we embraced in brotherly love. "It's amazing how quickly you understand. I have such a fantastic work to give people what they already have. This is a very important point in time when this trouble free life can be for all. And you, Zolade, are a part of this happening."

"By Rai, please tell me more, this is exciting."

"I will be able to tell you more in some months when I will be calling upon many people to help me"

"Ah, my mystery man, tangling the carrot; okay I will wait. Let's return and see what my sister and Torent are up to."

Returning, they found Sabna sitting alone.

"Torent had to leave for some important engagement at the palace but will be calling at my house tomorrow for dinner

He told me how much he cares for me. I guess being the King's son blinded me, but then I thought why not, he is a fine man. So, I invited him for dinner."

Zolade gave Kareae a "you were right look" and a quick hug to his sister. I remained silent. Sabna looked at both of us and called out, "What are you two up to? Do you know something I don't? Him coming for dinner is just so I can get to know him better."

"Yes, Sabna" Zolade laughed.

"Listen," I said, "I will leave you both now in peace; there are still a few things I want to do with the temple tonight. I want to say how much I love the both of you - what a great thing to have met you on the road."

The three of them embraced in a long hug before I gently pulled away and took my leave.

Chapter 22

ROMDEV

"Regina, I expect Romdev to arrive any day now, please have the guestroom ready for him. His tastes are simple and he likes flowers and mats on the floor to sit on."

"Yes Kareae, I've already taken care of it." Regina replied, having sensed it in my mind the night before.

"Hmm, of course," I knowingly answered.

I was in the kitchen watching Regina putting bread in the oven the next morning when we heard the sounds of an approaching carriage and the ringing of the gate bell. Regina opened the door to find an enormous man with very short hair and a two day old beard wrapped in a blanket standing there.

"Ah, dear lady, you must be Regina. Kareae has told me about you. I'm Romdev."

"Yes, I am sir. Kareae informed me of your imminent arrival. Please come in. I will direct the driver of your wagon where to bring your luggage."

Right behind Regina, I gave Romdev a Raian hug,

then we embraced patting each other's back.

I said, "After you get settled and have some food and drink, there is something special I want to show you."

"Oh." Romdev replied, opening his eyes wide with curiosity.

Later in the temple we remained silent while Romdev checked the integrity of the design, the construction and the vibrational power of the temple. Finally, he looked at me with a very serious face but after a few moments his face softened into a great laugh. We embraced again getting lost in his huge frame.

"My son, you have learnt well. This temple is sound and has a wonderful vibration. How did it come about?

"The impulse came spontaneously when I bought the house. I was very much inspired by the forest temple. What a magnificent work. Did you pay a visit there?"

"Oh, yes, Siktu is exquisitely divine. The evolution of the forest temple is beyond even my expectations. By the way, your parents send their most loving greetings."

"I'm expected to arrive at the palace in five days, so we have some time to spend together and talk more about our task. As you know, the King commissioned the building of a huge temple on the palace grounds. I have been given full freedom to create as I choose. I'm planning to use the temple to help finalize our plans. Let's spend the next days together. Cancel any appointments and devote your time to me for this period. Is there any problem about this?"

"No, of course not, there is nothing pressing except I was planning to spend some time with Neelu," I said giving Romdev a sly look.

"Oh, hmm, you met Neelu? And?"

"Yes, we met, and we will be getting married as is your wish."

Romdev beamed. "Yes, it is meant to be. Your union with Neelu will bring very good results, as did the union of your parents. I worked very hard to create someone like you and now you will continue the lineage, for your children will be instruments to bring humanity to an even deeper level than we can."

"I was surprised and had to laugh when Janan mentioned your interest in Neelu. It was then I knew your intentions and surrendered to them."

Romdev tenderly put his hand around Kareae. "Your parents gave me a necklace to give to you but now I see it's for Neelu. I have here in my bag, let me get it. See," when he took it out, "it is made from the same stones and crystals you placed in the temple here. Tell her to wear it all of the time; it will keep her pure even though, as I can see, she is very pure already.

"Thank you," I said, "Come, Regina has prepared a special meal for us on the terrace. We can sit and eat under the stars."

"Excellent, let us have something, and then I want to rest as I have been traveling much today. Tomorrow you will tell me what you have accomplished so far.

*****

The age of Romdev was a mystery. One of the many rumors was he was hundreds of years old but indeed he was much older than that. Some of the elder monks at Kanparu said he looked exactly as he he did fifty years ago. The truth was Romdev possessed most of the known powers and some obscure ones. He could bifurcate and astral travel by projecting his mind outside the body. Some stories existed that reported Romdev being recognized in two separate places at the same time. He possessed telepathy but this was common with Raians: Many were open to this vibration.

Through certain breathing exercises and the chanting of sacred sounds, he was able to slow down the aging of his body. Not that he was attached to living. He had a mission to complete, which required he remained in the body for an extended period.

As a young man his adventures were numerous but now his work required more privacy. Romdev lived on the Kanparu temple grounds in a small house hidden away from the main temple. His calling to raise the consciousness of man required many hours, days, months and years of intense inner energy work. Romdev utilized many intricate sequences of physical postures, chanting and breathing exercises that supported the union of the spirit, mind and body.

His greatest achievement was Kareae. Romdev coordinated the union of the high priest Ashara with the high priestess Leila at exactly the right astrological moment with the gathering of the maximum level of energy. No easy task but the result was Kareae, the herald of the new man.

The new man no longer had a need for the ego, that sense of being identified with the mind and body. When it is declared, "I am someone," then ego is present. In Kareae, the spirit could naturally live in the body without the middleman of ego. He was not identified as Kareae, the man with its personality and body. He was naturally aware that even though he was coexisting with the mind and body, he was a separate pure spirit. This brought the fruit of freedom to live and be in truth.

Romdev's love was architecture. He was trained to design buildings and other forms, utilizing the principles of sacred geometry during his many years as a monk in different Mystery Schools of Knowledge. He became a Master able to align his buildings to coincide with the pathways and lay-lines of natural forces and planetary movements. The resulting forms exhibited a perfect mathematically alignment where the entire structure was a perfect complete whole with each part aligning to the whole and to each part exactly. The upshot was that anyone who entered or even went near the harmonious vibration of the building felt oneness and peacefulness.

Chapter 23

THE PLAN

The morning quickly stole the darkness of the night, reaching without shame to drink the dewdrops hovering since dawn.

Within the small temple the still form of Romdev had not stirred for hours, engrossed perhaps, in some mysterious dimension of truth. I waited for him to eat breakfast. How many times have we lived together and sat in perfect understanding? I thought. Forever it seems but still it is fresh.

Finally Romdev joined me on the terrace for a simple breakfast of chopped nuts and fruits. In the temple later, I opened my mind and allowed Romdev to assess my activities since I left Kanparu.

"You have been busy, Kareae. Such phenomenal people you have met and all very useful for the work." He lifted his eyebrows and swayed his head. "When the time comes, we will call upon all of them, to gather with us in the completed temple. This is a change of plans, I know. Since the commission to build the palace temple, I feel the best time to initiate the final step would be at the inaugural. What do you say?"

"Yes, I agree, and perhaps we can throw Kalo off. Lets send out thoughts that we are afraid of him and have given up our plans and console ourselves to building the temple."

"That might bide us some time, but Kalo will see through it at some point," Romdev replied."

"Good," Romdev continued, "I have a list of persons that still need to be worked on individually. We should be able to complete the list in the two years it will take to build the temple. I am confident we will have the minimum number so that the rest of the population will be able to crossover into the next level of higher awareness. Lets keep our minds tightly closed and let Kalo see what we want him to see. It's a long shot but our only hope."

"Kareae, enough of this, let's go to your office. I want to show you the design plans for the temple. It will be magnificent. The vibrational power of the temple alone will almost be enough for the entire Raian population to crossover. Instead of a pentagon as you chose, I prefer a nine-sided enneagon figure for the main form. This will create symmetry not only in the four directions of the earth but also in the five additional directions of time and space. Contained in the inner sanctum will be a stone idol transported from the northern area close to where you attended the festival. Each side of the enneagon will lead to an upper floor and in some areas there will be even a third floor. This design will create a flow of perpetual motion. As you can see from the plan, I will construct nine additional small temples for daily use by the normal population. Once the perpetual motion is initiated, only those advanced enough will be able to tolerate the energy field. This is why it is important for most of the King's court to be ready. A person with negative emotions will only fall asleep inside the main building."

Romdev and I spent the next days sitting together in pristine formlessness. It was pure joy for us to be together in this way, in emptiness, without time and most of all without separation.

*****

On the following morning just as I about to join Romdev for breakfast, I saw Kalo in my mind's eye and heard him communicate. Come meet me at the river at the big bend with your great teacher and behold what you are powerless to prevent. Then, he closed his mind.

Romdev and I immediately met and looked into each other's eyes in silent surprise.

"Okay," Romdev finally said, "let's go but remember to keep your mind tightly closed about the temple empowerment. Let him have perhaps some useless information that will throw him of temporary."

The Sigma at the big bend was in an isolated area on the east side of the palace. Occasionally, ceremonies with large crowds were held there. We found Kalo sitting on a bench facing the gentle river on a perfect sunny day with a slight easterly wind. He was completely covered wearing his cloak and an unusual oval hat with two rare feathers of the albino eagle found only near the Kanparu temple.

"Ah," he said when he sensed we were present, "I was wondering if you would have the courage to meet me." He stood when we approached and faced us. Immediately,

I felt his power probing me, pushing me backwards, causing me to stumble backwards. Romdev and I both tried to counter-probe but he easily defected us laughing, "This is child's play. You are no match for me. I can enter you at will."

With that he directed another probe, much greater in force that knocked me unconscious for a few seconds. Within that time, I could feel something inside me splitting, wanting to break apart. After a minute it stopped but left me completely disorientated and dizzy.

"Now you know what I can do, you fools. This is my last warning. The next time I will scatter you in a million pieces among the universe."

This time his probe was like a lightening bolt hitting my gut that exploded, it seemed, into every pore of my being. My body convulsed and Romdev had to use all his attention to keep me from biting off my tongue. When I recovered somewhat and sat up, Kalo was gone.

Within an hour I was recovered enough to return home.

In the afternoon, in the temple, we opened our minds together.

"I am deathly afraid for you Kareae, I have no doubt that Kalo will carry out his threat. What I don't understand is why he even bothers to warn us. Perhaps he still has not gathered enough power to completely scatter you and change the matrix."

"Yes, I think that's it. I'm ready to go on no matter the cost. When he was probing me, I could feel his evil intent. If only we can find a way to stop him. I shutter to think if he is able to change the matrix for his own purposes."

"Kareae, you need to rest. I will let Kanparu know what has happened.

Chapter 24

JANAN FAMILY

Neelu just returned from visiting with friends. She was just about to go for a long swim when a messenger arrived with flowers and a love note from Kareae.

He said:

> *My beloved Neelu,*
> *Our love fills me with the passion of life. Our hearts beat together as one. I eagerly wait to see you again but my teacher Romdev has arrived and requested me to stay with him for the next days. I humbly apologize and pray forgiveness for my delay, but I must obey my teacher. Please accept these flowers and place them near to you that I may remain close to your heart.*
> *Your servant,*
> *Kareae*

"Mother, look, flowers from Kareae. Isn't he sweet? Unfortunately he will not be able to visit in the next days because he is with Romdev."

"Romdev has arrived? That is good news. Your

father will happy to hear it. I have not spoken to him today; how did everything go yesterday?

"Yes... the land," she said thoughtfully. "All went well in the end. We found out the property is owned by three separate parties. At first this was complicated but finally with generous offers, we were able to get the landowners to agree to sell. Probably we can take the titles within a week. Then the work begins. A bore well needs to be sunk, and the canal walls need to be reinforced or changed. Standing on the land yesterday, I was so happy my dream is coming true."

"My daughter, that is marvelous."

" Yes, but now I leave you for a swim before dinner," Neelu said kissing Divea's cheek and running off.

As the days went by, Neelu noticed with surprise, how much she anticipated Kareae's arrival, jumping up whenever someone was at the door. Even when out and about, she found herself looking around, hoping to meet or at least see him on the street.

Neelu together with Janan were inspecting the integrity of the canal walls attached to the proposed properties. She saw a rider coming down the road, approaching quite fast. He was dressed in one of the typical Raian overcoats and hats men wore when they were riding. The rider jumped off his horse as he came near and ran up to them. The man took hold of Neelu and she was just about to scream when he lifted his hat and she saw it was Kareae. A wave of happiness overwhelmed her, and they embraced as if already lovers, except without the physical longing.

Janan stood speechless but with smiling admiration.

"I was exercising this beautiful horse Zolade presented to me when I had a hunch you were here," Kareae explained breathlessly. "Please forgive me if I shocked you?

"Yes, you did, but I forgive you this time," she purred.

"So, is this the land you are purchasing for your practice?"

"Yes, do you like it?" Neelu replied not questioning how Kareae would know that.

"Yes, very much. Why not, when you have time, make a list of your requirements and ideas for your practice, and Romdev and I will design something for you. How does that sound?

"That sounds from heaven."

"Well, kids, let's go home," said Janan. "Kareae why not have dinner with us? We can feed your horse at the estate."

"I can think of nothing better. May I have your permission to take your daughter with me?"

"Only if you promise to go riding with me with this evening. It has been so long since I've been on a horse but you make feel like a young man again."

"Okay, it's a deal."

*****

I was careful to spend the next days courting Neelu without being physical. I knew that our physical union in oneness needed preparation. Neelu possessed a pure heart but her nervous system needed strengthening to fully embrace my energy. Even though Neelu was raised in a worldly way with proper education and exposure, she remained sensitive as she lived a sheltered life. I was concerned not to overload her system.

At the lake one day, Neelu inquired why I was so shy. I explained my concerns and suggested a certain diet and breathing exercises to strengthen her circuits.

I took out the necklace and placed it in both of their hands. I said, "My beloved, I've been waiting to give you this present from my parents and Romdev. It's a necklace made of stones and crystals from Kanparu that has been placed in the main sanctum to be charged and blessed. Wearing it especially when you sleep will help to strengthen your body."

"Oh, Kareae, and it is beautiful as well," she said as I placed the necklace around her neck. "I will cherish this gift and certainly follow your instructions. I don't want restrictions between us."

In this way, slowly merging more deeply as she became stronger, our love expanded into exquisite loveliness, a lightness and joy that everyone seemed to notice. In just a short time, many of the locals and shopkeepers came to know of us with our unique love. We became a familiar popular sight shopping or strolling along the river.

*****

Janan, Divea, Neelu, Romdev and myself sat for dinner at the boathouse terrace on a delightfully clear evening. A slight westerly breeze was afoot, almost as a caress to the skin. Romdev had everyone's attention with the story of meeting the King and presenting his plans for the new temple. He was a great storyteller but in the middle of his story, he suddenly paused almost in mid-sentence to say, "I cannot help it. Seeing Neelu and

Kareae in love in this way brings so much happiness to my heart." Looking to Janan and Divea, "I'm sure I can say to our hearts." They both nodded.

"Let us set a date for the wedding. I've been looking into this and have found that six moons from exactly this night will be the most auspicious time for the marriage. If it doesn't happen, then we would have to wait another year for another appropriate time. What do you say?"

I answered, "Six moons from now is perfect."

"What about you, Neelu?"

"Yes, yes, yes," she delightfully replied.

"I've also thought about this," I continued. "I would like to have a small ritual private ceremony at my house in the temple and then a more public ceremony and celebration here by the lakeside with the King and the court and all our friends present. How does that sound to everyone?"

"Excellent, I've been looking forward to this for a long time," Janan said. "What better place to have a wedding then on the estate that Romdev designed and built?"

"Yes, yes, yes," Neelu agreed.

Divea, who has been quiet for most of the evening, confessed that setting a date affected her. "I need some time to get used to the idea even though I want it as much as everyone." She paused as tears came to her eyes. "I'm sorry, I am getting so emotional, it's not usual for me. I guess everything is happening so quickly."

Janan looked to me indicating that I should come close to Divea. Together we encircled her. After a moment, Divea let out a loud sigh and began crying with her whole body. Romdev took Neelu's hand, and the four of us formed a circle around her.

In the circle Divea became more and more quiet until finally she opened her eyes with a sigh. "Oh my god" she said with a laugh and beaming with love. In turn, everyone else started laughing, and finally we separated and started dancing around the boathouse terrace in wild abandonment.

When order was returned and we were sitting once again, Divea said to everyone, "How could I have felt so separate? And where is it now? I can't find it."

"That is because it never really existed," I commented.

The rest of the evening was spent in quiet joyful celebration.

I walked with Divea back to the house but lingered to invite her for lunch tomorrow. She agreed and smiled into my eyes.

I noticed that this didn't escape Neelu, but she remained quiet.

With loving farewells, Romdev and I walked away in silence until we reached the palace gates. There we said our farewells as Romdev now had an apartment on the palace grounds.

Until we meet again, we both thought together.

*****

Divea was greeted at the door by Regina the next day who then had the good sense to become invisible.

Divea and I embraced once more, sharing oneness with the same intensity of love as our first encounter. "Last night," Divea said afterwards, "I found myself in such a deep hole I would never be able to share oneness with you again. Thank God everyone was there to help and heal me. I know this will be the last time we meet. I accept it is your destiny to merge with Neelu. And thanks to the healing I don't feel separate from this love, I feel really blessed to know you and learn from you on all levels."

"Divea, my love for you even surprises me. You will always be in my heart. For me, I could love the both of you equally but this would be awkward for Neelu and you. For that matter, I could leave for the forest and still be in this love and be happy. There might come a day when the both of you are more rooted in your own truth and we can be more open."

"Yes, you are right, sweet one, but please let me be the one to tell Neelu about us."

"As you wish."

Lunch was set on the terrace as if by magic. We shared in lovely blissful quietness that was like music upon our hearts.

*****

I met Romdev and Janan at the baths in the afternoon. Romdev was a huge powerful man whose presence not many wanted to disturb so we had the pools to ourselves.

"Tomorrow, why not the both of you come to the palace to look at the plans and see the site for the temple? I think I covered everything, but there might be something I missed."

We both agreed.

Suddenly I said, "Janan, Divea spent the morning with me."

Janan put a hand on my shoulder, "Yes, I know. Divea

told me beforehand, and I saw her afterwards as well. I understand totally your decisions."

"Your understanding, Janan, still impresses me."

"It is easy when there is no internal struggle and anguish," he replied.

Romdev interjected, "It was something none of us expected, that there would be so much love between Divea and Kareae. And yes, Janan, I agree with Kareae and bow my head to you."

"But now, let's find a quiet space in the lounge area. I want to tell you our plans. You will be the first in Rai to know."

Chapter 25

KAREAE'S TEMPLE OPENING

The power of the winter full moon could be felt already at the dawn. In the morning sky, grey clouds were present as the first entrée, but by the evening, the sun served a farewell sunset array of glorious light rainbow colors. Throughout the day, the effect of the moon was felt by many as a quickening in activity and a deepening sense of emotions.

In the course of serving Kareae's guests, Regina floated around them while they engaged in light conversation and enjoyed the colorful sunset. A slight collective "Ooh" was heard when the moon began its rise above the horizon. In the distance, the sound of fireworks and the howling of dogs charged the air. Regina marveled how the relaxed atmosphere of the house seemed to take hold of everyone. Almost everyone joined to dance when three musicians started playing light music with an alluring beat.

The Raians all learned the traditional folk dances when they were children. Some of the dances were complicated tribal group dances, but within it, couples could pair and dance together. Their long slender bodies coupled their natural grace and the precise synchronicity of movement was mesmerizing for Regina to see.

She watched Torent and Sabna dancing, obviously enjoying each other. This was their first time in public together and she heard people talking about them. However, Torent seemed oblivious to his surrounding, he was so focused on her. Sabna, in contrast looked a bit reserved with constant eyes on Kareae.

Korpa made a rare appearance as the representative of the King. Regina overheard the many surprised remarks of those who knew him of how much he had changed. One woman was heard saying, "I can't get over how open and soft his face has become and actually he is smiling." Korpa spent most of his time near Kareae almost like a protégé engaged in trivia conversation with Romdev, Janan, and Zolade. Nevertheless, the power emanating between them was astounding.

Just before the full moon was at its height, Kareae called everyone to take a place in the temple. The ceremony began with a simple lighting of candles and incense, followed by prayers and invoked incantations. Towards the end, though, when the group was circumventing the idol, Regina felt Kareae disappear and merge with everyone present. Even Romdev was taken to new heights.

If a late arriving guest entered the temple now, he would see a mass of bodies sprawled about nearly on top of each other. Considering there were a fairly good number of very powerful and influential persons present, it made it quite something to behold.

Slowly people recovered and made their way out into the moonlight. Kareae gave instructions for the music begin again and had the helpers moving around offering food and drink; in fact, insisting they eat to ground themselves. After midnight, the dancing went into full swing and continued until the sun began to rise. Very few guests left that night. All were so much enjoying the collective sense of freedom and oneness.

During the festive dancing, Regina was standing with Kareae when Romdev came over. "Tell me what was that you did," he said, "it was beyond anything I've experienced. You are really the new man and I bow to you."

"Romdev, please, I am as much in awe of what happened as you. It's something beyond me. This is now the second time it has occurred, the first time was on a full moon celebration as well. Ever since I met Rusai, I ..."

"You met Rusai?

"Yes, unsuspectingly I visited him at his house. I'm surprised you didn't see it in my mind."

"No, I didn't, but it makes sense. I am humbled. I have not been able to find him and you have. What a good reminder we are just a part of something greater than us."

"Kareae," called Sabna appearing out of the night, "come dance with me."

"Yes, coming."

Kareae moved away and disappeared into the flow of bodies swaying in the moonlight. Romdev sighed then dropped his seriousness, and jumped onto the dance floor in one big swoosh, moving gracefully for such a huge man. For a moment, Regina had a vision of a dancing fairy princess. Everyone seemed to let go in gaiety and love.

Afterwards, Sabna came to Kareae while Regina was serving refreshment and confessed her love to Kareae. Completely unaware that she was listening, Sabna said, "I know now that my destiny is with Torent, but my love is with you."

Kareae looked gently into her eyes. "I know, but you will soon see me in Torent as well.

*****

Unknown to anybody, a solitary man stood in the shadows outside absorbing the gaiety of the festival, wrapped in his long cape. Silent with his mind closed, he left just as the faintest of light came to warn him of the approaching dawn.

Chapter 26

WATER FOR SOL
TEMPLE FOR RAI

Torent was the only one of the King's sons who lived on the palace grounds. His two elder brothers preferred to live on their extensive country estates, not at all interested in government other than for maintaining their own properties. Torent resided in a large suite of rooms on the east side of the palace having its own private entrance and gardens. He converted one of the spacious rooms into an office after he returned from his travels.

Romdev and Kareae had an early morning appointment to meet with Torent in his office to discuss the Sol water situation. Their presence instantly filled the space as soon as they made their entrance. Torent soon noticed his mind had stopped thinking.

After warm welcomes, Torent directed them to an elegant sitting area with a beautiful view out to my garden.

"This is such a lovely space, my prince," Romdev

began. "elegant but with a simplicity of design."

"Coming from you, esteemed Sir, I take it in the highest manner. Thank you." I appreciate you could come by today and discuss the Sol water predicament."

Torent went on to explain in detail the Sol crisis including the possible threat of invasion.

"The biggest hurdle is how to transport the water up the ghats. Have you any ideas?"

Romdev answered, "I've been thinking about this problem ever since Kareae explained it to me. I have a solution utilizing existing technology. First, and I know you are planning this, it is very important to travel to Sol to inspect their irrigation systems. I have irrigation plans for that as well if you need."

"My solution to transport the water is to use a combination of solar, wind, and water power. We can utilize solar and wind power to initialize the water flow. Once the water begins to run, self-perpetuating pumps can take over. These pumps can generate power in the same manner as the steam engines."

"We will transverse the pipes, zigzag them so that there is a gentle angle to pump against. At each level there will be holding tanks and reinforcing pumps in action, all acting on the same self-perpetuating principle. We will utilize pipes, which are constructed with inner valves that allow water to flow upwards but not backwards."

"I think the steam engines can be easily converted to run with water. I drew up some preliminary designs for the engines and for the aqueduct that will be useful. I will leave them with you. Notice where I placed the support beams for the aqueduct. Please follow that plan exactly even if it doesn't seem correct initially."

"By Rai, I think this is it," Torent said after looking over the plans. "We have ample funds to build a prototype water pump and in the end we can lease them to the Solans to recover our costs. I will contact the company in Mi with your designs immediately. I plan to leave for Sol in a few days. I should return within one moon."

"Good Torent, do you see Sabna before you leave?" asked Kareae.

"No, but do you think I should?"

"I think she will like to be surprised. Go to her before you leave."

"Yes, yes, I will."

"Hmm, you will miss Jalititi; can you not go afterwards?"

"No," Torent said standing up in seriousness, coming closer to both men. "The situation is critical, I have to go now. My sources tell me the dissident elements in Sol are becoming more influential. Unfortunately there is no time to lose. The festival of lights will come again next year."

"Torent, your wisdom is great; you have the makings of a great King," Romdev said.

"It is natural for me, I am my father's son."

Kareae stood touching Torent on his shoulder. "You have our blessings and support. Feel free to come to us at anytime."

"Now, we will take your leave as Romdev wants to show me the site of the new temple. Go in peace but be strong with the Solans; make it clear the Raians will not tolerate any aggression but are willing to help fully as brothers. Don't underestimate the dissident forces."

"Thank you."

With that, Romdev gave the both of them a bear hug and for some moments time disappeared and love took its place. In that love, they left.

*****

The site of the new temple was on the north side of palace grounds comprising a hillock and level areas. There was also a natural water basin Romdev was planning to expand into a small lake. The location was perfect for alignment with the lay lines of the earth. Romdev's plans were impressive and complex utilizing the naturally rising levels to have different floors in his enneagon shaped temple.

Romdev and I took the time to walk completely around the site checking every spot in relation to the whole. We stopped at the nearly dry water basin to envision the intended expansion even both lying supine on the ground to understand the alignment.

"I can't see rushing the construction, " Romdev reflected, "it needs to go at its own pace."

"Yes, exactly my feelings. This temple must be built solidly as it will be the cornerstone of the new consciousness it will help to provoke. When will you begin?"

"The King is tentative planning a groundbreaking ceremony sometime after the festival of lights.

"Hmm, a good time I agree."

"He is looking forward to meeting you. Kosa inquired about you and mentioned how much fun Korpa has become. He joked on how he is missing his old serious face."

I smiled. "Korpa was easy, a very ripe fruit to pick. Let's go back to my home; Regina has just about lunch ready.

Romdev laughed. "Yes, I can feel her thought waves also. What a divine beauty and so sensitive."

"Ah, perhaps Regina would be someone for you."

"My son, I admire such a woman, but those interests left many, many years ago. In fact you wouldn't believe me if I told how old I really am. Being with Siktu at the forest temple almost rekindled my interest. It was wonderful to merge with her but we did stay non physical."

I said, "I remember the rumors about you when I was a child and you have not aged that much since then. I guess I've always felt you are eternal and will always be there. And yes, Siktu could melt a stone. Just now I see it. I will make one trip to the forest temple before I am married. Would you like to join me?"

"I would love to but my heart is now committed to the building of this temple. But I will visit Regina while you are gone, how is that?"

"Okay, that would be remarkable."

*****

Princess Sabna was already in bed when she heard a knock on her door. In her rush to answer, as it was very unusual for someone to come at such a late hour, she forgot to put on a robe but came to the entrance with only her nightgown. When Torent saw her with her hair down and her breasts almost revealed, he was so overwhelmed, he embraced her without thinking with the fullness of his passion and love. Sabna was so taken back by his action, but also entered into a state of no-mind and watched as she responded equally to Torent with the same love she was associating with Kareae.

Never before had someone approached her with such a passion that her passions were also set on fire. They fell onto the courtyard in deep ecstasy, kissing and exploring each other fully. Sabna was in total surprise this was happening with this man and she felt such a yes. She led him into her bed, undressing him and took off her nightgown. Their bodies met in a fire of excitement that consumed them.

When the daylight started to drip across the horizon, they were still rolled up into each other unable to separate from the plunge into the nectar of such bliss. Not a word has been spoken until Torent looked up and realized that he was leaving for Sol today.

"My darling, as much as it pains my heart, I must go as responsibility calls me to Sol. I will return in two weeks."

For once, Sabna's mind remained quiet. She could only look at him with loving eyes in a state of passivity accepting his leaving as his coming. "Come to me when you return," she said sitting up and kissing him.

Torent was wild, his passion rising when he saw her perfect body in the morning light. He brought her down on him once more, their fervor screams of eagerness singing with the songs of the morning birds. When Torent finally left, Sabna laid in bed in the nectar of the afterglow unable to rise all day. Her housekeeper was quite surprised by this rare event but glad, as it was obvious she is in love.

Chapter 27

JALITITI

The most colorful and festive springtime celebration in Rai was Jalititi, the festival of lights. Its origin was steep in mystery because it did not coincide with any natural occurrence, such as a harvest or change in seasons. Most Raians liked to imagine it just evolved because they loved to dance and celebrate for no reason. Those who knew, considered Jalititi to be one the oldest organized celebration, besides the full moon empowerment, in the surrounding Kingdoms if not the world.

Every house, wagon, boat and street in Rai would for two nights be lit with colorful lights and lanterns, in addition to many fireworks and big bonfires. The palace organized a magnificent display of incredible fireworks and maintained a big cauldron with burning oil for seven days. All Raians visited the cauldron at least once during Jalititi to add their own supply of sacred oil.

The custom of the royal family members was to spend Jalititi aboard the King's ship moored on the Signa. The King occasionally used this huge pleasant ceremonial boat to travel to the outlying areas although it was very slow and inefficient. Kosa especially enjoyed watching the Jalititi fireworks from the luxury of the vessel.

Loud explosions of shooting streaks and patterns of red, yellow and orange light commanded the star filled and cloudless skies when Korpa welcomed me. After exchanging a Raian embrace, Korpa escorted me to the open lower deck where the King and company were watching the fabulous displays. Although I didn't plan it, I had the time to observe the King and the family unobstructed.

Present beside the King, was the Queen, their two other sons with their wives, many kids and a bunch of friends and distant relatives. Zolade and Sabna were not present as they organized a big festival at Zolade's estate each year for the benefit of the locals.

The fireworks finished with a grand finale that had everyone standing and shouting with delight. In the excitement that followed, Korpa discreetly informed the King of my arrival. Kosa's face brightened, and he signaled for me to approach. Formal greetings were made to him and the Queen, and then the King invited me to sit next to him.

"I have been hearing incredible stories that you are a magician enlightening all that comes in contact with you," he said lightly, then turning to Korpa. "And here is the great miracle of Korpa. If I didn't see it, I would not believe it."

"Yes, my King, all of this is true and more so, I have only begun."

"Oh", said the King losing his smile and standing,

"then we must talk. Let us go to my salon on the upper deck where we can speak."

The salon was exquisitely laid out with many carpets and cushions. The most impressive feature was the big bay windows covering almost the length of the space. The view of the distance fires and lanterns throughout the city gave the atmosphere a surrealistic effect of floating in the air.

Kosa invited me to sit, and after cool drinks were served we remained together in silence until the King said frankly, "Yes, it is all true about you. I might be the King of Rai, but you are the King of the Higher Realms, that is very apparent."

"My King –"

"No, please call me Kosa," the King interrupted.

"Kosa, that you recognize me shows you are ready to become a King of the higher realms. I see your work is almost finished. With your permission I would love to arrange the retreat you long for. There is a temple in the forest built by Romdev that would be perfect. Torent will quickly become capable to handle the government and your absence would give him good hands on experience --"

"Ah, so, you can read my mind as Korpa says," the King interrupted, his eyes wide. "Nobody but my wife knows about my desire to retreat. But yes, you are correct. I am hoping Torent can take over while I am gone. Please continue."

"I would be honored to offer you my services to make all the arrangements and until the retreat happens, we can do some work together here. I would like to see you perhaps once a moon if possible. The temple at my house is geared to optimize my work. I can come to the palace but if is possible, if you can arrange to visit me, the work will go deeper."

"I don't see why not. Of course I can come. Let me arrange with Korpa a good time."

"Very good. Kosa, if you don't mind, I would like to tell you a little about the plans Romdev and I have for Rai."

" Oh? Kosa said, becoming instantly alert. Yes, please do."

"We are planning a major empowerment that will increase permanently the level of awareness of all Raians. Romdev has the idea to use the opening of the palace temple to initiate this uplifting, if this meets with your approval."

The King stood obviously excited. "I am startled by your words. By Rai, the implications are so far reaching, something I've always dreamed of but had no idea how to make real. Now young man, you come with the ability to do what was only a dream before."

"Certainly I will spend my nights reflecting upon this. We should meet together with Romdev for further discussions, but yes, Romdev has the full authority to use the temple for whatever purpose he teems fit. I wholeheartedly support your plans. So, lets see, we have two years to prepare, is that so?"

"Yes," I said, spontaneously embracing the King.

In my arms, I could feel Kosa melting. Afterwards he sat dazed but in a dreamy blissful space.

"Kareae, never has something like this happened to

me before other than with my wife. I am a man's man, and you turned me into a fainting female almost instantly. By Rai, if you can do this to me, I have a special request for you," Kosa said with a "Eureka!" look in his eyes.

"Yes?"

"I know four very influential but stubborn men from the provinces who still try to advise me to expand the Kingdom and create more wealth. I'm afraid they are more interested in hoarding additional wealth for themselves than helping their communities. Basically they are good men but their resistance to drop their personal desires and competitive natures, I feel, have become a hindrance. I suspect they may even offer resistance to the empowerment."

I placed a hand on the Kosa's shoulder, "Do not be concerned. I have a way to heal them totally and... all at exactly the same time."

The King also put his hand on me, creating a physical bond between us, "Excellent, I trust you implicitly, now let us join the others; I'm sure my wife wants to talk to you."

When Kosa and I entered the lower deck, Anu said, "Good thing you returned. We are eager to begin the Jalititi dances."

"Oh yes, I almost forgot. Then let us take our places immediately."

Raians all loved to perform the special Jalititi dances. After the lights and fireworks, the dances were essential. No Jalititi could end properly without performing them. Every Raian believed the Jalititi dances brought good luck for the year and will only miss it if they were very sick.

Children were taught gradually from an early age the complicated dance movements. In some sequences the hand went one way, the head looked the other way and the feet went in another direction, and all to an unusual rhythm. This could only be performed without thinking. Once proficiency was achieved, higher levels of awareness were elicited naturally during the dance. These states beyond the mind were very blissful and were most revered by Raians.

When everyone was in place, the music started and the dances began. There were four dances, each one lasting approximately thirty minutes. Every dance had a different rhythm emphasizing a different movement in relation to the group and movements within themselves.

Afterwards, with everyone at peace, the rest of day was spent in joyous celebration.

The King and his family could not remember a Jalititi celebration they enjoyed as much as today. Only upon reflection in the next days did they associate my presence with their feelings of oneness.

*****

Romdev was chopping vegetables when I arrived home in the evening. I joined him and afterwards at dinner with Regina, we discussed my meeting with the King.

"The King is a fine man, I always knew he is ready," Romdev said, "and he hit it right on the point to suggest those men. We will need to win them over. Let me think about a good plan to ensnare them all together before they know what hits them."

Regina, such a wonderful meal, thank you. But now

I will take your leave, my work is never ending."

"So?" I said when Romdev left.

Regina giggled, "Nothing is going on, Romdev is just a sweet old man."

"That sweet old man Regina, is a powerful spiritual warrior."

Regina gathered the plates and leftovers from dinner and as she was walking to the kitchen said, "And who do you think I am, just a housemaid?"

Following her into the kitchen, watching her work, "Never for a moment. I've always known who you are."

" I know Kareae. Now go, go see your future wife, she is waiting for you."

I bowed my head, "Yes, you're right, the evening is not over. I will bathe and change - and I'm sure my bath is ready, is that correct?'

"Of course, am I not here to serve you?"

*****

"Just in time for dessert," Janan cried when I arrived on the terrace. "A perfect ending to a perfect meal."

"My same sentiments to all of you," I replied. I sat next to Neelu after a round of hugs. "I see you had a big celebration here."

"Yes, it was a marvelous happening; I just love the Jalititi dances," Neelu said. "But come on, tell us about your meeting with the King?"

"I simply love the King. He is wise and compassionate and willing to learn. Being together with the royal family on their ship was something special. We also performed the dances. Everyone danced so perfectly."

They spent the rest of the evening listening to the

gossip until Janan and Divea left and we decided to take a walk by the lake.

"Kareae, I so much enjoy being with you."

"Yes, it is the same for me, I thought, how is it possible when I am totally with myself complete and yet I take pleasure in her so much?

Still, in the distance the lights of Jalititi were flickering and every so often, fireworks could be heard. The boathouse remained alight with festive colors and by the estate temple a big oil cauldron was burning for the entire seven days. Several of the groundskeepers were still cleaning from the celebration.

We sat on a rock by the lake and merged together in love.

"Oh, I wish this moment never ends, it is so perfect," Neelu sighed. "I never knew such love could exist."

I caressed her with our first scorching kiss, kindling our passion. We became consumed with touching and feeling as if we were young school children. I was able to stop myself only with great control from entering into oneness with her right then and there.

But, Neelu looked at me pleadingly, not understanding why, and then lying down with her arms around me, she pulled me to the ground on top of her. My passion took over and I entered her not as a tantric master but as a wild lover in heat. The pleasure was indescribable. Afterwards we retreated to her bedroom with the wild abandonment of young lovers.

The morning came like luminous golden ray drops splashing like waves on the surf, kissing the sand with its divine wetness. I lifted Neelu and took her out to the balcony. Later, when Divea found us cuddled together, her heart melted completely.

"Please come and join us for breakfast?" Divea said. We could only smile in love.

Janan's concern that our union was premature dropped as soon he saw us. "My daughter is now a woman," he said to Divea, "and is very radiant."

*****

Regina was all smiles when I returned home to prepare for my clients, my young passionate love singing for all to hear.

The word had spread so fast about my healing abilities that many people were requesting healings. I decided to continue to employ Rea to organize the appointments. An office was rented near the commercial area for this purpose although I continued to work with clients at home, the temple being an intricate part of my practice.

The demand became so great that I devoted my efforts in the next moons to initiate group healings, renting additional space near Rea's office. I was pleased to achieve the same results with a group as with individual sessions.

Lastly, to further assist me, I organized a training program for individuals with the gift of healing and sensitivity so that they could work as channels.

Chapter 28

KAREAE SPEAKS

Sabna and I were walking in the botanical gardens attached to one of the loveliest temples in Rai just outside the city. We had not met for quite some time. The early summer day was timelessly clear and fresh as a newborn with just a trace of breeze.

"You always knew about Torent, didn't you?" Sabna said.

"Yes, I did," I answered with a soft voice. "Now your heart and head both know as well, isn't it?"

With eyes deeply closed she replied, "Yes."

We sat at a pond full with different colored lotus flowers enjoying the rapture with nature. At last I said, "I will be going away, perhaps for two to three weeks to retreat in the forest. When I return, there will be much happening." Then he added, "And for both of us."

"Kareae, you can really see the future, can't you?"

"Yes, if I focus on a person or an object or even a location, I will receive information."

"How is that possible? Does that mean that the

future already exists?"

I took a moment to reply. "There are many futures that exist but some have more probability occurring than others. The truth is that time actually doesn't exist. There is no past, present or future, only oneness. Time seems real but it is created by the mind. In the dimension of mind, then the past, present and future exist together. So, seeing the future is like climbing up a tree to get bigger view. We all have this inherent ability, but it is more developed in some. Except for a very select few, we all see this world as solid; that only what we know is real. We don't realize that reality is bigger than our perceptions. For the man standing at the foot of the tree, the view is less than the person on top of the tree.

"We are always looking out the peephole; we never get to see the whole picture but only a part of it. The man on the top of the tree maybe has a slightly bigger peephole to look out of, maybe he can stick his head out and look around but still it's the peephole."

"Kareae, why are you so different than us?"

"For one I am standing higher in the tree and my vision is clear. My mind is not split nor does it linger thinking about the past or future. I remain in the present moment for more of the time, so I see more. My heart is one, not split, and I am not limited by any concept to be a certain way - nor am I identified being the personality of Kareae. I am born this way; it is totally natural for me without effort. My birth was not an accident but was conceived in higher consciousness by higher consciousness. Even the moment of conception was carefully thought out and executed. Still, that I exist is a miracle of grace. Humanity is ready to jump into a deeper understanding of who we are, and I am the first of the new humanity. My marriage to Neelu is not only our decision but also the result of the intervention of higher consciousness."

"It is truly amazing what you say, almost unbelievable; I admire you so much."

"Sabna, you are not far away; soon you will reside in what I am describing. You are very important in our plans."

"Our plans?"

"Yes, Romdev, my parents, Janan and others are involved. When the time comes, you along with everyone else will be informed and we will initiate the final step."

"Final step?"

"Yes, the entering of higher consciousness to all the humanity of Rai."

"But how could I help?"

"I'm sorry, Sabna, but it would not serve you to know as yet."

"Oh, Karcac, you are always so tough, but okay I can wait."

"Come," I said, "let us in tune in the temple and then return; the weather is going to change soon."

Sabna thought, Has it been eight moons since we met on the road? It seems almost like yesterday but so much has happened and my life is so different. Here I am in love with two men and one I will most likely marry. Torent is really a good man; I am ready to be with him. Ah, Kareae, my god in the flesh, what a miracle you are.

She stopped and gave me a kiss and I just laughed and laughed and she, well, could not stop herself but also started laughing. When some Raians passed by they also started laughing, as it was infectious. Kareae, she thought, you are such a magician.

*****

The sky finally darkened in the afternoon with a cloudburst that brought the first heavy summer rains to Rai. The rain was much needed after two months of dry weather. Neelu was down by the boathouse when the downpour started with some of her cousins and friends, passing the time gossiping and such, but in the back of her mind she was waiting for her beloved to make his appearance. She could think of nothing else. Her cousins teased her about it but they were also in awe of the change in Neelu from little more than a schoolgirl to a woman.

Sudden Neelu stood, pulled off her clothes and ran out into the heavy rainfall. "Come!" she said, "Join me." The other girls giggled but then followed her. They started dancing in a circle holding hands, laughing and celebrating.

Divea had a half a mind to join them and would have if Janan had not just walked through the door. He was about say something when he saw the girls dancing. "My, oh my, how beautiful - am I in heaven now?" he laughed.

"My dear, the sight of all these maiden fills me with passion. Let us go to our bedroom quarters," Janan cooed as he took Divea in his arms.

"Yes, my man, take me," she sighed.

A short time later, I made my entrance to see the women standing together in a sacred circle with the storm gushing over them. What a breathtaking moment to see these divine angels. I entered the patio, took off my clothes, and spread my arms upward to the sky surrendering to the rain in deep acceptance. When the girls looked up they saw not me but a ray of white light surrounded by beams of rainbow colors. They all let out a collective gasp. Slowly my figure was discerned, I opened my eyes then gave a smile that was impossible to describe other than to say it was something so totally otherworldly. We Raians are fairly unpretentious of nudity, but our nakedness was completely forgotten when I came and joined the circle.

Within the circle the orgasmic ecstasy flowed through each of us like an electrical current, waking and shocking us collectively into a state of happiness. For most of the girls, it was the first time to experience real happiness, its depth of feeling and tingling pulse of life -- a blissfulness beyond the reach of the mind that gave the real fullness and knowledge of being.

The circle of love continued even after the rain stopped. Divea came with towels and gently suggested for them to dry themselves and return indoors because soon the night would have a chill.

Everyone was in unity. There was not even a thought of jealousy or possessiveness or any separateness or self-consciousness, just a deep gentle acceptance of each other without tension. On the whole, the girls were in silent shock of the experience, unable to think.

A meal was served that seemed to revive everyone into gaiety and laughter. I was especially funny spinning some amusing stories about the monks in Kanparu, which everyone lapped up like milk to a kitten.

"My favorite friend," I was saying, "as a child was

Hanu: a monk, a warrior and the chief of the guards. We had and have still a great friendship. I used to spend as much of my free time as I could with him on his rounds or guarding at the grand front gate. Sometimes we would sit for days hardly saying a word and then Hanu would begin one of his stories of his youth and adventure that would have me spellbound for days. I loved to be with him in his free time when we would swim in the Goma, the river that flowed on the eastern border of Kanparu or sit for long periods inside the main temple. Because of him, I was allowed to enter areas that only very advanced monks were allowed."

"One of the greatest mysteries of Kanparu is the Great Arch. Its origin is ancient but unknown; it was standing before the building of Kanparu. Many of the monks believe it is a remnant from an ancient civilization before us. Engraved in the stone are many strange symbols whose meanings are unknown. In the center of the arch is a massive relief in the shape of a dragon. Nobody has a clue as to its meaning and significance; however, once when Hanu was undressing to go swimming with me at the Goma, I noticed a small tattoo cleverly hidden, on the backside of his shoulder blade, of the same dragon. When I asked Hanu about it, he was surprised that I could see it. His answer was vague about receiving it when he was young."

"I always suspected Hanu knew about the dragon, but I was convinced when I saw the tattoo. Hanu was unapproachable, though, even when I was old enough to probe his mind."

Reflecting for a moment, I continued. "Ah, that great

stone dragon arch with its huge metal doors is a power object on a power spot. There is nobody that passes through it that doesn't feel it."

I can tell you a little more. One night I followed Hanu, at first by accident but then when I watched him leave the front gate, by intent. I saw him enter into the stone arch and disappear. I became very excited and could not sleep the whole night. The next day at the break of dawn, I rushed out to the arch to try to discover how he entered it. I combed entirely the arch several times but was unable to discover how he entered inside. I tried to follow Hanu but it was impossible. Some days later, thinking I was doing a good job of stalking him, he taps me on the shoulder with a big benevolent smile as if I was a small boy, which I guess I was but I never felt like one."

"Do you think young man, I will let you discover all our secrets? I am surprised you have found out as much as you have. How you could see my dragon tattoo is beyond me. But come with me now."

Under the cloak of darkness we made our way to the great arch and lo and behold, to my great astonishment a door was there that I could not understand how I could not have seen it before. Hanu opened it with a key, we entered together, and I watched the door close behind me. And that's it."

After a few minutes of silence a series of collective oohs and ahs and pleas to continue drowned me. Finally I said, Okay, I've been sworn to secrecy but since it's so long ago, I guess I can tell you.

When the door closed, it was pitch black until Hanu lit a torch and I saw we were on the top of a circular wooden stairway. I followed him down to the next level where we encountered another door. Hanu again took out a key and opened it. I walked into a room that seemed huge but it was hard to tell. To my great shock, the lights went on and my parents and many of my friends started singing happy birthday. It was my tenth year. Never before had my parents celebrated my birthday in such a way. How they all arrived to this room I will never know. And till this day, the mystery of the dragon is unsolved."

Again the girls burst out with collective oohs and ahs greatly amused about the story.

"Oh Kareae, then please tell us more about Kanparu," Neelu implored gently putting her arms around me.

"Yes, now let me see." I took a drink then continued. "The great and wondrous Kanparu is not just a temple but almost a city with several small temples beside the main one and many buildings for the resident monks and the schools. Orchards, farming and some very elaborate gardens with mazes and power walks comprise much of the huge land the temple possesses. From the King's Road there is a very beautiful winding entrance road for about two leagues with some wonderful and rare trees not grown anywhere else. Just traveling on this road gives the pilgrims a sense of relaxation. Arriving at the dragon gate is always an awesome experience. By the time someone is on the temple grounds, he or she is already affected. Still, the guards are present, besides directing traffic, to screen the visitors and the ones with dark energy are keep under constant surveillance although they would never know it.

"The surrounding countryside is beautiful with

rolling hills. In fact, the main temple is built on the top of one. Among the orchards, my favorite is the olive orchard."

"Have you ever sat under an olive tree? For me they have such a pristine vibration. She is the mother giving all her fruits to her children. I experience such a sense of goodness whenever I sit under one. An olive orchard is truly a divine place. There are trees in the olive grove over five hundred years old, which gives some indication of how old Kanparu is. The evidence is that the temple was first built somewhere around a thousand years ago during the golden period of the Reichian civilization. This was destroyed as you all learnt in school by foreign invaders coming from Mi."

"The dragon gate is even older than this."

"Along the eastern side of the temple grounds runs the river Goma where sacred rituals and bathing take place. The bathing areas are situated in such a way that it is very difficult for outsiders to see in. I spent much time at the Goma just having fun when I could get away from my vigorous studies. During full moons, the bathing area is totally magical.

"I would say that at any one time there are 300 to 500 monks, devotees and students living and working in Kanparu. It is the major center for the achievement of Higher Consciousness through the practice of Tantrism. In tantra, we utilized all the natural forces to achieve higher consciousness. One of the reasons for the guards is to protect the very sensitive learning and processes that are happening constantly. Kanparu is very alive and vibrant, and I feel very fortunate to be born and raised there."

"One of the most astonishing aspects of the Kanparu is the architecture. Almost all the buildings are built utilizing the principles of sacred geometry, as is this wonderful estate of Janan and Divea. Sacred geometry is intelligent building not coming from the ego but arises from a deeper source where the alignment of natural forces, the use of appropriate building materials are merged together to form a building that has a organic whole. Because of this, anywhere in the building or its surroundings, someone will feel at ease and at home and have a sense of completeness. There are no dead spaces and there is never a sense that furniture is needed to fill up the space. Beside Tantrism, Sacred Architecture is taught as well. Romdev, who designed and built this lovely place, is the head of this school."

"I cannot end without a mention of the high priest and priestess, my parents. They are totally dedicated to Kanparu and its ideals. In fact Kanparu cannot be separated from them, they are Kanparu and Kanparu is they. I hope someday that all of you can experience their presence."

"Normally, I would succeed my father as high priest, but my destiny brings me to Rai to do a different extension of the work of Kanparu. Everyone experienced something tonight. For some of you, the change is permanent, and for the rest, slowly you will return to your usual state. My work is to bring as many people into this oneness as possible within the next two years. My fiancé, Neelu, and her parents, Janan and Divea, are helping me with this work."

"You must excuse me now but I will take your leave," I said, standing up, "Neelu, please come and walk with me?'

Neelu nodded and came to my side. The others all thanked me and bid me good night. Janan and Divea hugged me and all the girls came and embraced me.

"I love you Kareae," Neelu said as they as they walked away. "I love you, Kareae, and I can say it again and again. My heart is so full, and so silent is my mind. Is this the Self?

I stopped and took Neelu in my arms. "Yes, my love." We fell silent embracing in deep understanding.

Afterwards, as if I almost forgot, I said, "Neelu, I meant to tell you earlier, but I am planning to visit a retreat temple Romdev built in the forest. I want to leave in a few days, and I will most likely return within one moon."

Neelu looked at me with wide eyes and about to protest when something of acceptance rose in her heart. She said, "Please come my dear, and spend as much time with me as you can before you leave." She gave me another hug and afterwards I silently left into the night.

Ah, if they only knew the truth, the man of the shadows thought. Kareae, you don't fool me. Soon you will find out.

Chapter 29

JOURNEY IN RETREAT

In the last moment, I decided to take the mare Zolade gave me. I named her Spirit, for the essence that she was. Being on the road again was a resplendent experience. I enjoyed the possibility of having more freedom of movement and to provide Spirit with all her needs to run and wander. I had no purpose other than to be out and wandering. Although I encountered a few travelers on the way, it was a time to be alone, to assimilate all the new energies and forces surrounding me. My happiness was such that it flowed into all that was around me. Even the simplest of tasks of washing my hands in a stream, taking care of Spirit or watching a insect crawl on my arm, became a divine occasion.

When I reached Fritaye's inn, after a very welcome reunion, I left Spirit and continued on foot knowing it would be dangerous to take her into the deep forest.

Entering the external silence of the forest was always extraordinary. I connected uniquely with the wind, the earth elements, the trees and the animal spirits.

The wolves that came to my fireside the previous time appeared again almost by magic and we traveled together to the forest temple.

Siktu met me halfway in the forest. Her beauty was dazzling: such a serenity and purity woven together with her natural loveliness. For Siktu, she sensed my new power. Spontaneously without a thought, we came together in oneness. Afterwards, in complete understanding, we made our way to the forest temple.

Siktu mentioned, "There are now several people residing at the temple. Nearly all are on silent retreats, so we will not see much of them. There is one young boy who stumbled upon the temple in his wanderings; his name is Olai. He is very quiet and keeps his mind mysteriously closed. He is very useful for the needed work, and I like having his silent presence around."

"It's interesting he knows how to keep his mind closed," I said after probing Olai. His heart is good though, as you know."

"I want to spend several days or longer in complete isolation inside the cave and totally open my mind to the higher forces," I shared.

In the inner sanctum of the temple, we sat together and opened our minds. Each now had the experiences and memories of the other since we last met. There were only a few people whose minds were strong enough to merge with me in this manner. Perhaps Romdev and my parents were capable but not more.

To open the mind like this was exhausting and we both were happy to see that a silent Olai had already laid out a meal for us. Afterwards we both fell into a deep sleep and did not wake until the sun rose.

I savored in the quiet and simplicity of the forest and the sacredness of the temple. I spent a relaxing morning listening to the forest birds and sounds of the forest while enjoying simple physical tasks as chopping wood and carrying water from the well. The vegetable gardens were flourishing and needed much caring. I spent many days working in the garden, planting and harvesting the vegetables.

Janeac was mentioned only several evenings later. We were by the cave around a small campfire, watching the forest night sky. Even in the summer, the night air was brisk and we both were wrapped with light blankets.

"Janeac is the most powerful and alive person I've ever met," Siktu began. His time here was an absolute gift. The understanding that became part of him as a result of your work, aided him tremendously." Siktu face became softer. "We fit like a lock and key. I know when the time comes we will remain together. Twice he has been here but only for a short visit. Mi is not that far from here, shorter than to Rai."

Siktu rose to add a log and stir the fire, and then stood watching the rekindled flames.

"Janeac is a warrior with a new understanding. He is overcoming many old beliefs in Mi, but it's hard work. He comes here to recharge. He could certainly use your help."

I stood up beside Siktu placing my hands over the fire for warmth.

"I will go to Mi to meet Janeac and assist with the work but not for some time. It all depends on when the temple is finished and what occurs with Kalo. Janeac has to prepare the soil more; the Mians are not as advanced as Raians."

"Yes, it is so difficult for them to drop the old warrior's way that strength decides the issues. And, there is so much fear that if they drop fighting, then who are they, and how would they retain their dominance? Janeac is showing them how to retain their status using the strength of wisdom but it is painstaking slow. He meets resistance wherever he turns. It is fortunate he now has the authority to convince the others but he can use assistance. Thankfully, the inventor Patri understands him. They have secretly joined forces because they are concerned their association would be misunderstood and cause setbacks."

"Yes Patri, I would like to meet that man."

Siktu turned to the sound of an animal somewhere close by, then while adjusting the fire again said, "Kareae, I will come to the wedding. I want to be close by on your marriage night and your union into oneness with Neelu."

I took her in his arms. "Thank you," as I placed my head on her heart for a moment. "I am very happy you will be part of the energy circle during our union."

"Listen, is it possible to get a message to Janeac about the wedding? I tried to reach him by telepathy, but I guess the Mians are not as sensitive as Raians."

"Yes," she knowingly laughed, "that's true," and then dreamily said, "I would also love it if he attends the wedding."

*****

I entered the cave two weeks after my arrival. Once

I was settled into the second smaller room, where the altar and idols were placed, the entrance cover was closed, creating complete and utter darkness. There was no need to shut my eyes.

After a few moments the sound of Aum, the primal sound of existence, seemed to rise and became as loud as the roar of a raging river. My senses withdrew into myself and I watched as I left my body and, as well, this dimension of time that was considered reality. I found myself in a dimension of no time where nothing existed. Dissolved in nothingness, I remained for almost three days. Finally, the awareness of the body returned, and slowly I regained the normal dimensions of time. I spent another three days absorbed in the non-experience. Finally, I began to drink water and a thin vegetable broth left for me. On the seventh day, Siktu slowly let light enter into the cave, allowing almost a day for my eyes to adjust and recover. The first pinpoints of light were like an electric current shooting into my eyes exploding in vivid colors and patterns.

The next day with the help of Siktu and Olai, I left the cave and returned to the living quarters. I completely recovered in another five days. The understanding I received was beyond my mind and intelligence. However, I returned with a deep primordial understanding that eventually would be resolved into concepts. Siktu could only get a sense of my journey when we opened our minds but not more.

For the reminder of the time, I was quiet, light and carefree. In Siktu's eyes, I had become almost translucent. Luckily by the end of seven days of physical work, my connection with the body was sufficient enough to make the return journey.

On our last night, we shared in oneness. We lay together in softness so complete that even oneness seemed inadequate to describe it. Outside we could hear the wolves in the forest and the very faint coursing of the river in the distance. The moment was rich.

Morning came as a friend bearing gifts of light and form. This time Siktu accompanied me to the inn where we had a very festive evening eating rich food and enjoying a glass of the local wine. The entire inn seemed immersed in rich light colors of gaiety even though on the outer appearance nothing much was happening. The fortunate guests all left that evening with the sense of having a wonderful special time, as occurred in the other inn. Fritaye was ecstatic that I finally spent an evening at his inn.

In the early morning Fritaye and his family came to our room, and together, we had a joyful sharing of breakfast and love. The atmosphere was such that the family would have spent the whole day with us if duties weren't calling. Fritaye's wife Clarae was particularly grateful saying, "Now I have a husband and not an innkeeper."

The inn was so relaxing and comfortable we decided to spend another day.

When the sun rose over the trees the following morning, we made our farewells. Siktu watched me mount Spirit and ride off onto King's Road. She spent a little while longer talking with Clarae and her daughter, but then made her way back into the forest. Surprisingly, the wolves were waiting for Siktu, and they returned together to the temple.

Chapter 30

THE WEDDING PLANS

Janan's study was a comfortable, pleasant room with deep carpets and many uniquely carved wooden shelves filled with books. Interspersed between the shelves, were diverse wall hangings coming from different areas of Rai and beyond. The large bay windows were open so the music of the night floated in the air. Neelu, Divea, Janan and Romdev sat together discussing the arrangements for the upcoming wedding. Everyone would have preferred a simple ceremony, but it was not feasible because the King and many of his court would be attending. Plus, there were so many who wanted to go that loved both Kareae and the Janan family. The wedding had quickly become the event of the season.

Romdev was leading the discussion presenting his arrangement plans.

"See, I have the tables and the wedding platform arranged so that they are properly aligned. The guests will enter from the left and leave the ceremony from the right. The musicians will be placed behind the altar area."

Romdev was concerned about every detail - even

inquiring into Neelu's wedding dress and the ornaments she would be wearing.

Only those participating in the energy circle would attend the secret ceremony planned at Kareae's house. This would be the real marriage night. Romdev was hoping Neelu would become pregnant immediately because it would be a very auspicious moment, plus the force of the energy gathering would facilitate a good birth. Neelu still had not been informed about the intentions of the secret ceremony; he left that for Kareae to explain. He suggested meeting again when Kareae returns sometime tomorrow afternoon. Everyone brightened up with the news, taking as natural the telepathic connections between Romdev and Kareae.

After Romdev left and Neelu was attending to some other activities, Janan asked Divea when she planned to tell Neelu about her involvement with Kareae. With a sigh she replied, "I am not sure. I had requested to be the one to tell her, but now I have doubts. Maybe it is better if he tells her. I want to talk to him before he sees Neelu."

"Yes, this is a delicate matter. I feel that Neelu is strong and mature, but we don't want to jeopardize the wedding. So far, though, our worries have been pointless. Lets hope that is the case now."

"My husband, you are right. That is why I love you."

Janan smiled and relaxed, "Ah my wife, I feel these days like a young stallion." He embraced Divea and then slowly removed her clothes; they fell together on the floor in love and oneness. Neelu happened to walk by and heard their sounds of love. By Rai, she thought, who would ever think my parents would do things like this?

Feeling her own nature stirring, she dreamily longed for Kareae's arrival.

*****

Several days before, Romdev met with Neelu at the site for her new practice to discuss the design plans. As they walked along the grounds, Romdev pointed out the different aspects. Neelu's hair was tied back and she was wearing a white dress that gave her a very professional look. Romdev, meanwhile, wrapped in his blanket and now bald head with a mustache, looked like his usual massive self.

"The building is simple in design with an emphasis on functionality. Our plans include a reception area, treatment rooms, an office, overnight rooms and several small gyms that can open up into to one large gym when required. Outside will be a playground and a sitting area overlooking the canal. The building will be horseshoe shape with the playground in the center for privacy. Each room will have a view to the playground with its gardens and views to the canals."

They walked back to the road and stood facing each other.

"This is incredible. I am most lucky and honored to have such a place designed by you to do my work. May I ask how long will it take to build?

"Not long, I would guess probably in three moons it will be ready. I have my work crews and sources of materials already arranged, we can begin almost immediately. I've kept the design simple so we can build quickly."

Then, some time right after the wedding it will be

ready?

"Yes, after your honeymoon you can move in."

"Great. Already my temporary office is becoming inadequate. I don't how people are finding out about me but I even have patients coming from distant areas of Rai."

"It's understandable, your work with the Fotaea child is considered quite miraculous by many. The word spreads quickly."

"Yes, I cried the day she began to walk. It was such a mystery why she was paralyzed; there was nothing physically wrong with her. It seemed that just some pathways in her brain were mixed up at birth that were short-circuiting, causing the paralysis. Once I figured that out, I simply reset her neuronal circuits and the rest is history. Some of the treatments I gave her were unorthodox but not unheard of.

"Whatever it was, young lady, you have the gift and my full support. Now, my child, I must return to the palace to my other project."

"Before I forget Romdev, please come for dinner on the new moon. We want to discuss the wedding plans and enjoy your company."

"Very good. Until then princess."

"Until then, I think I will walk back home. There is so much to think about."

*****

Regina rose from Romdev's bed pausing for a moment at the window to observe the beautiful gardens of the palace. The thought of their love making the previous night made her tingle inside. To be in oneness with him, she reflected, is like entering a cyclone only to find myself in the center, silent and still. She inwardly said to him, "I sense Kareae arrives today, and there is much to do. He will arrive at the house to bath and then go immediately to Neelu." Romdev silently nodded in agreement and inwardly told her he would stop by in the evening.

From the outer appearance it seemed as if they were always silent, but inwardly they were having intense debates and lively discussions. In all his years, Romdev had never experienced and enjoyed a woman as sensitive and beautiful as Regina - so much so he dropped his vows to be a recluse without a thought. Regina in no way interfered with the work; indeed, she brought it to a higher plane. I'm an old dog, but I am always ready to learn new tricks, he giggled to himself.

*****

I arrived softly. Leaving my pack in the entranceway, I tiptoed to Regina on the terrace and embraced her. She stood there breathless in face of the changes in me. She was well aware of my time in the cave, but she was astonished at the results.

After my bath and change of clothes, she did mention that I appeared more like my old self.

"Regina, I'm off to see Neelu now, and will spend the night there."

"Don't worry, I am content to see you even for only a few minutes."

I bowed my head but then looked to Regina and said inwardly, Ah, yes, Romdev. Fantastic. I then left quickly.

I found everyone in the garden hothouse, each in their own space tending to the exotic flowers and seedlings. After copious greetings, Janan and Divea excused themselves quickly.

We walked to our favorite spot by the lake. Only then did Neelu mention the changes she saw in me. "Your body, it seems so... translucence. You appear to be floating when you walk."

We melted in our embrace, the passion rising like a lion's roar. I removed her clothes and she offered her nakedness to the moonlight. Timelessness and centuries of time passed before us, hurdling us to the beginning primal source of it all. In this beyond we lay bonded in eternity.

We woke to the welcoming song of the morning birds. A jump into the lake refreshed and shook off the rest of our sleepiness. Robes were found in the boathouse and as by magic, one of the housekeepers arrived with breakfast. Afterwards, in the lake for a longer more vigorous swim, we enjoyed the feeling of aliveness the water always imparted.

We lay on the deck with our heads to the sky. I said, "Neelu my love, there is so much to tell you about my wandering and time at the forest temple. I spent seven days in a special cave immersed in total darkness. I opened my mind totally to the higher forces of existence. I almost did not return. It took me nearly two weeks to recover my sense of body and still, as you see, I am not completely back. I am unable in words to explain my purpose; I do not completely understand it myself yet but it was necessary for me to do."

"Yes Kareae, I believe so."

I turned to face Neelu. "Siktu, the priestess of

the temple, took care of me during this time. She is a beautiful, evolved soul completely dedicated to truth. I met her in the forest on my journey to Rai and at our first meeting it was apparent she would become the priestess of the forest temple. I must tell you I shared oneness with her then and now as well. I love her not as our love is but as two consciousness in love merging together."

Neelu instantly sat up, her face turning white. Unable to speak, she collapsed into my arms. I gently picked up her and carried her to her room. Divea came to check on Neelu and afterwards, signaled for me to come out with her. In her drawing room I shared what happened.

"Go home now, Kareae, I will take care of her. She needs a mother's advice now; I will stay by her bedside. Come later in the evening if possible."

"Yes, of course," I acquiescenced, "I will return in the evening."

*****

Unknown to Divea, Neelu plunged into a trance state rather than a shock state when she heard Kareae's powerful words. The force of his truth vanquished her and although she remained conscious, she could not speak. She could see the world as if looking down from some great height. Within her, she felt as if the neurons in her brain were being unwound and rearranged. When finally she returned to the world, she felt curiously detached and clear. "Mother," she said when she could talk, "I love you. Don't worry about me; I'm fine. Please come and give me a hug."

With tears in her eyes Divea embraced her, seeing the serenity that had entered and changed her.

"Listen Mother, please don't worry. Do you think I cannot see that you are in love with Kareae and that he loves you as well? It is so obvious that you shared in oneness with him. I no longer see love as a possession, there is no I or you or he. I know you have this freedom with Janan and you can feel free to have it with me as well, I am no longer a child, and I'm no longer even Neelu.

"And here I've been worrying about you, not trusting your strength and the wisdom of Kareae. I feel so humbled. Kareae was wise to leave and let me receive this teaching."

"My dear, are you hungry, shall I send for something?"

"Perhaps something light, then I want to be quiet for some time."

"Yes, of course my child. I will send in Janan, he wants to see you and then we will leave you be."

"Yes, Mother."

*****

The moon was laughing, rejoicing its moment in the sky when I returned to join Divea and Janan on the terrace for dinner, happy to see the acceptance in Divea's eyes. I inquired about Neelu.

"She is fine and resting now," Divea replied.

Janan asked him, "How do you do it, my son? Do you sit at night planning your actions?

"Sometimes, but mostly it's a force that directs me, and I am only the instrument to deliver it. When I was leaving the forest earlier today, the feeling to see Neelu tonight and explain everything arose and I just surrendered to it."

"When Neelu went into the trance state, I was not

expecting it, but I understood it immediately and knew what to do." I contemplated for a moment. "I am naturally not in the way of life working through this form we call Kareae."

We remained silent for the rest of the dinner, quietly sharing and eating.

A slight wind picked up rustling the leaves while the moon put on a mask of clouds to hide when in the distance lightning was silently struck.

I excused myself to join Neelu. I lay down next to her gentle beautiful form, and she turned into my arms.

When the rain finally came, we were fast asleep.

Chapter 31

MI

Siktu woke up suddenly in the night wondering if Janeac would receive the wedding invitation in time. She decided to travel to Mi, leaving the forest temple in the care of Olai. Traveling swiftly, sleeping where she could, Siktu arrived four days later at the capital fortress city, Milopia.

Mians differed from Raians in many aspects. For one, their bodies were more physically orientated. In contrast to the long slender Raian type, Mians were tall and wide, solidly built with strong muscles. Their center of gravity clearly bestowed them with a firm sense of being grounded. In terms of physical strength, the average Mian was far superior to the Raian. One the reasons why Mians loved fighting was because their temperaments tended to be expressed through movement. Mians were intelligent, but their intelligence was focused on their practical physical nature rather than seeking higher knowledge as Rains do. They excelled in technology, such as designing engines and building aerodynamic vehicles.

The locals were surprised to see a Raian woman traveling by herself. Everywhere Siktu went, hundreds of eyes spied upon her, watching her every step. But, once within the fortress walls, on the narrow cobblestone streets of the old city, Siktu was less noticeable and could relax. She had little trouble to find Janeac's house. It was the largest house and also the center of government.

Siktu walked through a great arch entranceway to find Janeac in his courtyard practicing what seemed to be a fighting technique with several young men who appeared to be students. Janeac performed a movement in that moment, so precise and so quick, using his strength and power that was awesome to behold. Even his students seemed stunned.

One of them saw Siktu and quickly pointed her out. He turned and after a moment of shock, Janeac ran and buried her in one of his famous bear hugs.

"By Mi, I have been feeling all day something unusual was going to happen and here you are."

He turned to his very surprised students. "Let us quit for today. As you see, I have a very special guest coming all the way from Rai."

When alone, they embraced with great affection between them.

"I've come to invite you to Kareae's wedding," Siktu said formally but then beamed. "Oh and yes, I guess I wanted to see you as well. It's so good behold you again."

"Golden priestess, seeing you is a dream come true. To have you in my arms is like being in the bosom of the goddess." He took her arm, "Come, let me show you where you can bathe and refresh yourself. Then we can have food together."

Janeac's house consisted of four buildings together forming a square, with a courtyard and gardens in the center of it. The rest of the grounds were covered with cobblestones. An arched walkway connected all four buildings. Janeac and Siktu sat in one of the corner archways looking out to his garden and a beautiful fountain.

"This house is my ancestral home, one of the founding homes of Milopia and the seat of power."

"Yes, it is an incredible place; I feel all the ancient energies stirring here. Tell me, what were you doing with your students?"

"Since my awakening, I've had dreams about a fighting form that utilizes intelligence and awareness as well as strength. The knowledge just came to me over a period of one moon. It symbolizes the change I'm working for. The students you saw are all coming from the most influential families. If I train them now, later they will assimilate the new ways. I tried to change the minds of their parents, but that generation is very set in their viewpoints. Then, the idea arose to concentrate on the young ones while I can still mold them. The work is slow and the harvest is far away but to shape and train these young boys is very satisfying. Their parents think they are just here to learn fighting."

"I caused too much unrest when I first returned. In my excitement I wanted everything to happen at once. Those in power were very resistance to change and it would have led to violence and civil war if I continued. I realized a different approach was needed that would not cause too much initial upheaval. Then, one day while practicing in the courtyard, visions of the new form started to appear in my mind with my body automatically going into the different movements. I couldn't sleep for days in my excitement and realization of the implications of teaching and incorporating the form into Mian life."

"I'm sure Kareae will love to hear this but you can tell him yourself. Are you able to come to the wedding?"

"Of course, actually we heard about it even here in Mi. There's no way I will not attend."

"Well, it was a good excuse to visit you."

"Yes, such a great thing you came. You must stay long enough for me to show you Milopia and meet the family. How long can you stay?"

"As long as we need, sweetheart," she cooed.

Janeac lifted her up and took her into the house, closing the doors not to be disturbed.

Chapter 32

THE GUESTS ARRIVE

The date of the wedding was rapidly approaching in a whirlwind of arrangements and invitations. Two ceremonies, the King's attendance, the arrival of Kanparu and all of Janan's business friends and associates from Mi and Sol, kept the family busy. Every wedding invitation responded affirmatively. Nobody wanted to miss the talk of the town and the event of the year.

With the fall weather approaching, the nights were chilly, but the days were still clear, sunny and warm. There was some concern about rain, but it was not likely as the rainy season was at his end. Even so, everyone affirmed for the weather to remain clear.

*****

Meanwhile, I clearly divided my work between the two basic different levels of development in Raians. The first group comprised of those who were ready for awakening whereas the second group still needed healing and clearing beforehand. While the work with first group proceeded spontaneously, I was busy and focused more with the second group.

Neelu, when she had time from her own practice,

often joined me to create a circle of healing power around our clients.

Her vital energy circuits were becoming so much stronger that I decided to experiment opening my mind to her. Before sleep, I made more and more of my mind available to Neelu. By the end of seven days, I was convinced she was strong enough.

That night I opened fully my mind. At first, Neelu fell into a trance state again but then quickly recovered. In the ensuing days before the wedding, I taught Neelu how to unlock her mind and shortly afterwards, we were able to be completely open.

Siktu quietly arrived at my house one night several days before the wedding. After a welcoming warm embrace, Neelu said, "I've been wondering how I would react after Kareae spoke of the love for you. But all I feel is love for you as well and ... trust. I see your immense beauty and recognize there is not a Siktu to be jealous of. You are always welcome in my heart, dear one."

"Thank you," Siktu gracefully replied, "And the same to you."

In the temple later, we opened our minds. The vibrational power was so strong Romdev and Regina came to join, forming a circle. All throughout Rai that night, a quickening was felt by many, like a spark of enthusiasm or a deepening of commitment.

To everyone's great surprise, Janeac arrived the next day with two of his students. Siktu kept her mind closed about it because she wanted to keep his arrival as a surprise.

"So you did you receive our invitation?" Neelu asked.

"We were concerned."

"You would be interested to know, but the news of the wedding was even being talked about in Mi - there is no way I would have missed it." Janeac exclaimed, his immense power, aliveness and purity captivating everyone. "But yes, a very nice messenger came to deliver the news." He winked at Siktu, but then everyone laughed. They could read Janeac's mind, receiving the news of his affair with her. Even Romdev turned his head in wonder.

My parents with their entourage of monks were the next to arrive.

The high priest and priestess would have preferred to keep their arrival low keyed, but it had been over ten years since their last visit, and it would be difficult to avoid such a celebrated event. Indeed, thousands of Raians lined King's Road to welcome and receive blessings from them and the procession of monks, the highest authority of Rai. The monks dressed in ceremonial yellow and red marched and chanted as one, blowing the sacred horns and ringing the sacred bells that seemed to stretch for leagues.

*****

Patai, Kareae's contractor, had been waiting on the road for hours for the procession. He came early to make sure of having a good spot. As the hours moved on, the noise and festive excitement of the crowds increased until it reached its peak with the sight of the parade in the distance. At last, the head of the procession arrived with the lead monks carrying the sacred idols from Kanparu. Next a group of thirty monks blowing horns passed followed by an equal number striking bells. The high priest and priestess came after, sitting in a open carriage bestowing blessings to all they passed. Patai was overcome such a strong wave of bliss when Ashara and Leila were near that he almost fainted. After a few minutes, though, he recovered and was left with tears of joy. Patai could swear Leila smiled at him directly. With the passing of the rest of the monks, peace and silence gripped Patai like a vise, dissolving him into a glorious unity. Patai stood on the road as like many others transfixed for hours after the procession passed.

Luckily, Janan's estate was large enough to accommodate the gathering crowds. As the monks entered the grounds they created a circle with the high priest and priestess in the center. When all the monks had arrived, the horns and bells were sounded again followed by a short period of silence and then the final sounding of the bells. Ashara and Leila stood to bestow more blessings and then departed their carriage, followed by several senior monks and entered Janan's house.

Unknown to all, the man in the shadow, wrapped in his cloak, standing far from the center with his mind deeply closed, thought, Yes, my time is coming near. Soon you will all feel my wrath.

*****

The Janan family, Romdev and myself were present to greet Ashara and Leila.

Neelu and I were the first to formally welcome my parents but Leila raised her hand as she entered with a benevolent smile and said, "Please do not be formal, Neelu, you are already a daughter to us."

In her spontaneity of feeling Neelu bowed before Leila who placed her hand on her head.

"Yes," Ashara said turning to me, "You are blessed to have found someone as beautiful and evolved as Neelu." To Janan and Divea, he added, "Your daughter is a reflection of your own purity. I bow my head to you both."

Janan and Divea bowed in the formal way silently accepting their blessings.

Accommodating the senior monks with a separate guesthouse and settling my parents in another one, we all met later on the terrace for lunch.

Afterwards, the conversations were light and lively until the men eventually strolled off for a walk by the lake and the women returned to the guesthouse where Leila invoked special blessings for them. The resemblance of Leila and Divea was remarkable. They tried to trace their family lineage to see if there actually was a family connection, but did not come up with anything. They humorously concluded they were connected on a soul level - and this no one could deny.

I walked in silence with Ashara and Romdev, each one of us opening our minds. Nothing needed to be said, only a Raian hug given by Ashara to Romdev and me. Ashara opened his mind to me at a much deeper level then ever before. I was surprised to learn how much more depth there was to my father. I looked at the high priest with different eyes. "I didn't realize you did all that, Father!"

"I am happy for this day to allow you into my mind, as you have certainly earned it," Ashara said with some solemnity.

Romdev chuckled inside, and both Ashara and myself

turned to him with open eyes. "Well my boys," he said, "someday when you are old enough I will open the depths of my mind to both of you," he teased.

Ashara laughed. "Old ancient one, I don't know if we will ever get that old. By the way, I notice that you have been letting your body age; you look slightly older."

"That is correct, I am now allowing my body to age slowly. With my work finished soon, I can age and leave my body close to the time span of everyone else."

Romdev continued, "I am happy to announce that all the plans are in place, proceeding better than expected. I do not foresee any problem to fulfill our requirements. Then, with a heavier expression said, But, I am extremely concerned about Kalo. We were powerless to stop him at the river.

Ashara asked, "Do you think he is aware of our plans?"

"I am afraid so, although maybe not completely. I feel it is now up to the great mystery where it takes us."

*****

In the grand formal dinning room the men and women met for dinner; Regina was the only non-family member. The women were wearing matching flowing robes with one shoulder and the back exposed, differing only in color. Neelu wore white; Leila a light lilac, and Divea wore a soft red. They all had on a crystal pendent from Kanparu given as gifts by Leila and Ashara. They looked stunning together. Regina was dressed more simply in a white robe with a colored red scarf.

The men wore the formal Raian attire of long shirt, loose pants and vest.

It was the first time the families were together, but already it was like they were old friends. The food and drink were thoroughly enjoyed; everyone was at ease and relaxed eating in silence, as was the Raian custom. If it were not for the Janan family, there would not even be a need for any outward conversation.

During the desert of fresh fruit and cheese when conversation was more appropriate, Neelu looked up and asked Ashara if he could tell the story of how he met Leila. Ashara's eyes brightened. He glanced affectionately at Leila and then knowingly at Romdev. "Well, let's see, my meeting with Leila was kept secret for a long time, but I see no reason now why we can't tell the story if there is no objection from Romdev." He looked to him.

"None whatsoever," replied Romdev, "I love to hear the story."

"Of course I was a young man somewhere around the age of Kareae in training to become the high priest. My father was quite old when I was born, so he wanted me to take over the responsibilities of running Kanparu at a young age. It was something I was very well suited for coming from a long lineage of priests and saints. My training began very early, one could say even before I was born, as was the same with Kareae. I was reaching the age when every one in training goes a on a journey of discovery in the world alone without the protection of the temple. The Kingdom of Rai has a very similar custom with the person next in line to be King. One day, Romdev instructed that when I go on my journey I should search for a wife who would also become the high priestess. It is not always the case that the high priest and priestess are married. I was in some doubt about how to go about it, but Romdev assured me when the right person appeared, there would be no doubt. He also told me not to return unless I found the right woman. You could imagine how it made me feel."

"Yes," Romdev explained, "I wanted to make sure Ashara understood the importance of finding someone. I knew it would take away from some of the enjoyment of his journey, but it was imperative to find Leila."

Ashara continued, "My journey was full of wonder and discovery; it was the first time to be out in the world. I found my training prepared me well to meet any situation. There were a few times I was in danger, once from some hostile tribes in Pa and again in the forest with some wild boars I stumbled across. In that instance I just managed to escape alive. There were times I had to go for days without water or live off the land. Again my training in breathing and using my intuitive senses to find food saved me. I discovered the immense benefits of sun gazing in the mornings just as the sun is rising.

"I stopped at many different places and searched, but I did not find anyone. I was beginning to give up hope when I arrived at a small village located in a very pleasant and rich valley in Fa.

"Almost immediately I sensed a subtle tingling in my head and ears but I wasn't sure what it meant. I spent several days in the village exploring the valley and hillsides without any luck. I wanted to leave but somehow I couldn't. The proprietor of the inn was beginning to become suspicious as no one without a purpose stayed long in the village.

"But as it goes, on the next day just walking out of the inn on my daily journey I saw Leila walking towards me. She had just returned from visiting her relatives in another village high in the forest. I felt my heart explode on the spot: there was thunder in my ears and lightning in my eyes. I couldn't understand why the whole village didn't hear the explosion. Of course Leila walked by without even looking at me. After recovering my shock, I set about to find out where she lived. I described her to the proprietor of the inn, who at first could not understand whom I could mean but then it finally dawned on him. "Ah,' he smiled, 'that must be Leila, the daughter of the village doctor Serius.'

I immediately rushed to the doctor's house and asked to see Serius. In his office after formal introductions, he inquired about my ailment. I replied, "I am suffering from a heart condition. Seeing your daughter in the village has given me a heart attack and I don't think there is a cure. I want to meet her and ask for her hand in marriage."

"Well, you could understand the shock of the doctor. At first he didn't know what to say. Then standing up, he went to his cabinet to retrieve a bottle and two glasses. "Here," he said, "Let's have some of our local liquor, I think we both need it."

"After a few glasses and sitting together for a time, the doctor stood up again pacing the room, then looking out at the wonderful vista from his window he began. "When Leila was born, the men who read the stars told me that she would marry a man from a foreign land who would come one day and take her away."

"'Leila has always been an exceptional child with

a pure heart who is also very strong willed. For her to live here in this small village married to some local man would be a great waste.' Then he turned and faced me, he continued with moisture in his eyes, 'I've been dreading this day forever, but now that it is here, I see it not as a loss but that I am gaining someone new. I see you are a good soul and coming from a high position in society. I welcome you into our life, into our souls and into our destiny." With that we embraced.

Ashara paused in his story to take a drink. Everyone at the dinner table was spellbound by his story. Neelu took that moment to ask Leila if she would say something.

"Yes," she said with a loving look to Ashara and after a sip of water she began, "I was just returning from a week in the forest near my relatives. I was making a silent retreat in a cave and basically had not spoken to anyone for days. Returning to my village, I passed this strange and foreign man, and I had the same heart attack. I was so shocked that I could do nothing but pass him by like I didn't see him. I ran to my room in great shock. When my father tried to call me to meet Ashara, I couldn't answer. Seeing my condition, my father understood and told Ashara to return in the evening for formal introductions."

"By the evening my wits had returned, but still I was experiencing an emotion I never thought possible before. I felt as the caterpillar must feel just before changing into a butterfly, caught in the urgency and power of unknown force and change."

"We met in the main room of the house. I entered after Ashara arrived and made his formal greetings to the family. When I glanced at him, the world simply disappeared. I'm sorry, but I am not able to tell you the sequence of events for the rest of the evening. Maybe Ashara can say something more?"

"It was the same for me that first evening. When Leila entered the room the entire world disappeared. We were meeting it seemed, on many different levels I never experienced before. What I was certain of that night was the love we felt for each other and this was experienced by everyone in the room and in the village for that matter.

"We spent the next few months together in the village. It was a totally magical and wonderful time for us before all the responsibility of Kanparu. We were married by the local priest following the customs of Fa, which meant spending days in a marriage hut in the forest and celebrating with all the surrounding villages for days on end. It seemed that visitors to our marriage hut was never ending.

"We took another three to four months to slowly meander back to Kanparu. Another marriage ceremony was performed with Romdev, and then shortly after we became the high priest and priestess."

Ashara paused then said, "Yes, I think that's it. Let's stop and leave the rest of the story for another time if that is okay?"

The journey back from the village in Fa took everyone some minutes as if they were actually transported there. The atmosphere at the table was so poignant, that to start another conversation seemed superfluous. Everyone said good night and went to their own quarters: I headed off with my parents, Romdev and Regina returned to my house, and the Janan family spent the rest of the evening together for what may be the last time. In the middle of the night, with the sound of distant barking and the wind in the trees, I entered Neelu's room, where we spent the night nesting in love.

*****

Romdev, Regina and myself stood before the temple in my house making sure all the arrangements were in place, then deciding where each person in the circle would sit. A special marriage tent was erected in the center of the temple. After the initial ceremony, Neelu and myself would lie within the tent on a specially arranged platform while the circle of energy gatherers rearranged themselves outside the tent.

When we were satisfied, we returned to the terrace to enjoy a full-course meal. Later that day, Janeac, Romdev and myself joined Janan and Ashara at the baths. Romdev opened his mind again to Ashara. He was pleased to find out about Regina, whom he teased Romdev about. For these great men to be so open and childlike was a merry moment.

*****

Later, at Janan's estate, everyone sat for a quiet evening meal by the boathouse, eating and listening to the sounds of the water lapping on the shore. In the distance, the lights of the city were flittering and dancing while the moonlight was kissing the lake with brilliant beams.

For Ashara and Leila, it was a rare time for them to do nothing but enjoy the leisure of no responsibility. Other than a comment to Romdev about the magnificent design and architecture of Janan's estate, they both remained silent for the evening.

Leila's presence: her light and depth was felt by anyone sitting near to bathe in her pure divinity; her years of being a high priestess had dissolved what little ego she still possessed.

For the housekeepers, it was an extraordinary evening, akin to serving the gods. At one point it seemed like everyone disappeared and only white light was present. The next day several people with a view to the lake commented to their friends the feeling of seeing a bright glow emanating from the Janan estate.

Although a normal dinner in a normal place and everyone talking normally, it was the first time that such giants in consciousness met together. The effect was felt by the entire city even though they didn't know why all of a sudden they felt happy or peaceful or forgiving to their friends and loved ones.

Chapter 33

THE WEDDING

The dawn woke in all its splendor, casting forth rays of hope and light, shaking the frost from earth's sleepy eyes to welcome this most auspicious day of love, of the supreme union of the male and female, to the creation of a new vision only imagined in the dreams of the gods. Such it seemed this day, this day of the wedding that all the celestial angels had floated down to surround and bestow their blessings with flowers of peace and fragrances of joy.

Neelu, in all purity, was attired in a simple white silk robe with the ceremonial Raian headdress, a string of pearls and the crystal pendent from Leila. Kareae, in youthful exuberance, had on an open silk vest with simple silk draw pants. He wore only the crystal pendent of Kanparu around his neck.

The sun stood proud in its mid-day height when Romdev called the participants to gather in the temple. The marriage tent walls were raised so Siktu, Regina, Ashara, Leila, Janan, Divea and Romdev could enter the temple and make a circle around Kareae and Neelu. In preparation for the ceremony, the wedding couple had been chanting and performing special breathing exercises given by Romdev. The temple was overflowing with an abundance of colorful flowers carried by Thor ships from faraway places. Placed in and around the temple were plants from Kanparu and the forest temple. Rich silk cloths hung majestically throughout the temple, giving a soft radiant elegant look.

At the head of the altar, Romdev was invoking prayers and blessings, lighting incense and burning sacred objects. Sometimes, strange and exotic sounds escaped from him and with each sound everyone felt drawn into the center of existence in a cascading vortex of now. The world disappeared in a vapor and a light enveloped and infused into even the molecules and atoms. They entered the primordial beginning and end of creation and then beyond it into a vast nothingness so full as to blind someone in its richness. A humming began that broke the separation of mind and soul and everyone's eyes opened. Romdev stood and faced the circle and the couple with raised hands, commanding the circle to join together. When the circle became a rotating flowing beam of light, Romdev entered the circle to join Kareae and Neelu as one by placing his hands on both of their heads.

The sun was blending into the horizon when Romdev slowly lifted his hands and moved away. He lowered the walls of the marriage tent and sat with the circle. Near each person he placed sacred water from Kanparu for them to drink and instructed the circle to sit or lie without holding hands. A bell was rung three times signaling the couple that now was time for union into oneness.

With the approaching night, candles and incense were lit. Inside the tent Kareae and Neelu were merged in spirit but not yet their bodies. As from a distance, they watched as their bodies became infused with current, his with the male principle and hers with the female principle. Naturally they merged in holy union. In this joining together, the spark of creation exploded with quantum leaps.

Far from being exhausted, everyone was fully energized and awake when the moon gave way for the sun to extend its embrace upon the earth once again. Kareae and Neelu stole away to their sleeping chamber while everyone but Janan and Divea lingered on the terrace, reluctant to leave.

*****

The estate was ablazed with activity when Janan and Divea returned. They were busy non-stop until the late afternoon when finally they retired to their quarters to bath and dress. Down by the lake, many relatives and friends were already making use of the facilities. Their laughter was heard even in the private quarters. There was a small three-piece band playing local Raian folk music to the delight of the children and the elders, and an army of helpers was stringing lights and colorful banners throughout the estate, plus there was a makeshift kitchen where hundreds were preparing food for the festivities and setting up eating areas.

In front of the estate temple where the ceremony would take place, special arrangements were made for the King and his court. They were informed that the King would arrive an hour before the ceremony. A complete guesthouse was made available for him to relax and have his privacy. Kosa, wanting to keep a low profile, had Korpa circulate a message that he wanted only to be guest like everyone else.

By the time the King arrived with his entourage, the wedding party was in full swing. Janan and Divea were present to welcome him personally and show him to his quarters. After formal introductions were made, the King sat only for a short time before saying with enthusiasm, "Let's go out to be with the guests, no need to stay inside."

With that he rose and joined the wedding party on the terrace to the delight and joy of everyone. Janan was relieved the King was provided for.

When the moon rose later that evening, a bell was rung to announce the beginning of the marriage ceremony. Everyone gathered around a most beautiful canopy of flowers erected for the wedding in front of the temple. For this wedding, the official high priest of the palace was conducting the ceremony.

With music playing, Kareae and Neelu walked down the aisle to enter the canopy and sat before the ceremonial fire with the high priest. A lone musician with a stringed instrument played a piece of such high vibration that everyone immediately fell into a bubble of stillness.

When a curtain was drawn around the canopy, the priest began chanting the sacred marriage prayers and performed the sacred rituals. Upon completion, the curtain was opened and the couple stood to circumvent the fire three times. Sitting once again, the couple embraced and final blessings were made.

The guests rose and circled around the canopy many

times, throwing flowers and good will onto the couple, as was the Raian custom. The laughter, joy and lightness seemed to increase with every thrown flower, almost burying the couple in a short time.

Fireworks were set off, and cheers were heard not only by the guests but also throughout the city. The sound of lively music called everyone to dance around and with the couple, the atmosphere becoming increasingly joyous and celebrative until everyone was dancing in abandoned beauty. The music gradually became quieter and progressed smoothly to begin playing the traditional Raian wedding dance. Everyone then, took their place and performed the dance together. Now the atmosphere became blissfully solemn and stately, and in the end, Kareae and Neelu bowed to their guests and retired to the marriage tent, where they would receive guests throughout the night.

The King was the first to congratulate the newlyweds, entering with Anu, Korpa, his sons with their wives and a whole bunch of kids.

Torent and Sabna entered a few minutes later.

The King and Queen presented to Kareae and Neelu as a wedding gift: twenty eagles of prime land just north of Zolade's estate containing forests and a lake.

"It is the least we could do for the selfless service both of you provide for Rai. May your family prosper there for many generations."

"Thank you my King for you most generous gift. I am sure we will be appreciating it for many years to come."

The gift created a great rush of excitement and conversation about its location, possible building sites for their home and what type of house to build.

Torent and Sabna were next to congratulate the newlyweds. In conjunction with the gift of land, Torent pledged horses and livestock that he purchased from Zolade.

"The animals will remain with Zolade until you are ready for them," Torent said.

"Really you are too kind," Kareae replied, "thank you."

In the spur of the moment, Korpa, who had substantial wealth, pledged the cost of building a house in addition to the two fine pieces of art he originally planned to give. To Kareae's protests he said, "Really, it is such a small amount compared to what you have given me."

Very quickly the room began to be filled with all the loved ones - Romdev, Ashara, Leila, Regina, Janan, Divea and Zolade. When Janeac entered with Siktu, everyone was taken back as usual by his sheer aura of strength and vitality. Kareae and Janeac embraced hardily, then Kareae introduced him to everyone. The King was especially interested to meet him and they quietly stole off to converse.

The ringing of bells announced dinner, and everyone slowly made their way back the festivities. A grand meal was served, toasts were made and everyone was having great fun. As the evening wore on, the musicians got going again, and the dancing took off with even the King and the Queen cutting loose as if they were newlyweds.

Outside beyond the estate many groups of Raians gathered to join in the celebration, as the magic spread out through the entire city. Fireworks and bonfires could be seen everywhere.

Kareae and Neelu were sitting with a few others when Torent returned to the marriage room. Again there were warm greetings.

"We have not spoken since you left Torent, were you successful in Sol?"

Torent answered, "Yes, very much so. With the guidance and suggestions of Romdev and yourself, we were able to convince the Solans of the soundness of the water project. But let us talk about this at some other time. We are planning a big celebration for the opening of the aqueduct. Kosa will start the pumps and Jeson, the King of Sol, will collect the first waters. It will be a great day for both kingdoms."

Sabna entered while Torent was speaking but remained quiet. Torent in his enthusiasm didn't hear her arrive. When he finished, she put her arms around him and said, "And what about us, have you told them, my dear?"

Torent blushed. "I am getting to that - you know I save the most important news for last, and I wanted you to be here."

"So what are your plans now? Neelu asked. "I'm dying to hear when the next wedding is."

"Well," they both said looking at each other with joy, but then Torent spoke. "After talking with our parents, it was decided not to have the wedding for at least another year. The wedding of a King's son is not so simple. Many agreements and contracts between families must be made and important guests need to be properly informed. We are officially living separate but we have been staying together ever since my return. By Rai, Kareae, if you didn't tell me to visit Sabna that night, I don't know if this would have ever happened. Thank you, thank you."

"I never had doubt although it might have taken a bit longer for Sabna to see the light. But don't think this is the end, there is a more in store for you both and it will happen sooner than you think."

"Kareae," Sabna said laughing, "you always leave us with mysteries. Why not be straight forward and tells us right off? Oh well, I surrender again, it will happen as it does." She gave Kareae a hug.

"Your mind is strong, Sabna, but your heart is stronger. It is a good combination that will serve you well."

Janeac and Siktu came to the entrance and Kareae seeing them, waved them over.

"Have you two been officially introduced?"

Kareae said, "Janeac, I want you to meet the future King of Rai. This is Prince Torent and his bride to be Princess Sabna. Torent, I want you to meet the chief of the Mian warrior clan, Janeac and this powerful being is Siktu, The high priestess of the temple where your father will undergo a retreat."

The six of them felt drawn into a natural circle of love after Kareae's amusing introductions.

Janeac took Neelu and Siktu into his big bear hug and lifted them to the sky, "Come, let's go dance," Janeac said, and they all merrily ran after him carrying the girls to the music like they were little children.

The rest of the evening was spent in wild joyous celebration. During one stage of the festivities, Kareae's antennae rose when he noticed a man, whom he never seen before sitting on the side near the dance floor. He could feel that he was a man of power, but then Kareae was pulled back into the dancing and did not think of him again.

*****

In the silence of the late night when most of the guests were gone, we were sitting by the boathouse watching the moonbeams bouncing off the lake.

"Neelu," I said, " There is something I must share with you now that we are married. Let's open our minds."

Afterwards Neelu implored, "My darling, you are in grave danger. What shall we do?

"Please don't be concerned about me. If something happens, it is my choice. I will need you to carry on the work."

"I will always be concerned but yes, I will accept it," Neelu said slipping her hand on his bare chest. "Come let us go to the marriage chamber while we are able to."

*****

We spent our honeymoon by invitation at the King's lake residence near the Solan border. Except for the ground and housekeepers, we were alone to enjoy the immense gardens, forests and the huge lake. Our days were spent in love without a thought of the world, losing all boundaries of separation. Walking in the forest was an explosion of communion with all the animals and wild plants. Indeed, we had difficulty to stop the animals from following us into the house.

Everyday we went on long swims to an island in the middle of the lake to rest and lay about in a mindless state like two children at the lakeshore.

On a particular clear blue sky day with perfect temperature, towards the end of our stay, Neelu suddenly said, "Kareae, I think I am pregnant."

I placed my hand on her belly. "Are you sure?"

"Pretty much so. I've been feeling nausea these last few days, and I feel something inside is happening."

"This is really wonderful news. I'm sure everyone, especially Romdev, will be excited."

"Come Kareae, let's race back to the house." She jumped up, ran to the water and dived in. I was quickly behind her as we dashed for the land.

The return to Rai after one moon was a pleasant drive through the countryside. Regina and Romdev were present to welcome us home. Regina served dinner but then she joined us. Romdev was particularly quiet but towards the end of the meal, he stood up with a smile on his face, "Neelu, I have been looking into you and I can happily give you the news before even you can feel it that you are pregnant. That you became pregnant from the marriage night is a great joy and blessing to not only us but also the world."

"My dear silly friend, do you think I cannot tell if I am with a child? However, I am happy for your confirmation. Yes, yes, I am with a child," Neelu beamed.

Regina came to Neelu to make a blessing holding her stomach. Then she bowed down and said, "I am here to serve you as fully as with Kareae. This moment is a great day for all of us."

Chapter 34

WHEELS IN MOTION

Every morning, no matter the weather, Korpa went out of his way to his office just so he could walk past the temple and observe the building progress. He noticed that no matter what mood he was in, afterwards he felt calmer. One sky crisp colder morning, the sounds of construction reached his ears. In the distance he saw Romdev giving instructions for the day's work. What a strong and powerful man he is, he thought, yet there is such a gentle grace about him. As if Romdev could sense his presence, he turned with a smile towards Korpa, then waved for him to come over.

"Korpa" Romdev said wholeheartedly after they embraced in the Raian fashion, "Today I called you over because I want to share with you that while you were checking our progress, I've been checking yours. I am always very pleased to see you and sense how sacred your inner temple is becoming."

"Thank you Romdev," Korpa replied with some emotion. "Coming from you I honor and appreciate your kind comments. My gratitude to Kareae cannot be measured. I wake up every day in awe of the fullness and lightness that appeared like a miracle. I never thought this could be possible. My biggest fan is Kosa. He never fails to make a remark about me to whomever he speaks." Then looking at the temple, he said, "Walking pass this marvelous temple everyday is such a joy. What is it that makes me feel so happy when I am near it?"

"This temple is built without stress. The placements of the forms and structures are such that they are in exact alignment with the natural earth forces. When this attunement is present, a synchronicity occurs upon entering the attunement field. The result is, one feels naturally happy and at peace.

"On an energetic vibrational level," Romdev continued with his voice expanded, "soon the whole Kingdom of Rai will be bought into this attunement. Then, Rai will become like this temple to help attune the rest of the neighboring kingdoms and eventually the world."

"Your vision is great and far reaching. I can see it is possible what you say. Especially if you are able to enlighten me then the rest of the kingdom should be easy."

They both laughed at this.

"Please send my greetings to Kosa. Soon I will make an appointment with you to meet with him."

"Yes, but Kosa has told me that he is available whenever you need to speak to him. He has given you free reins with regards to design, funds and materials. He has absolute and complete trust in you."

"Thank you, yes, but I want to see the King for a different reason - and I will need some time to be with him alone," he declared with emphasis.

"Oh, in that case, why not make the appointment with me now? Let's say, after the opening of the aqueduct in three days time, first thing in the morning."

"Yes, hmm, that is fine for me."

The two men quickly touched foreheads and took their leave. Romdev climbed to the top of the temple to check a particular alignment and Korpa went off to his morning briefing with the King.

Romdev remained engrossed in his work until he sensed someone watching him again. Looking down he saw Kareae smiling and waving up to him. Wiping the sweat off his brow, he signaled for Kareae to climb to the roof.

"My son, am I getting that old that I don't sense your presence? How long have you been watching me?"

Sweetly Kareae said, "You are not getting old, but my ability to keep the mind closed has greatly improved since your gift of empowerment."

The two men studied the vista for some moments in silence.

"The view from here is magnificent," Kareae said

From their viewpoint they could see most of the city from the Signa to the eastern and northern forests. On the western side the great old wall and gate was clearly visible. The mixture of greenery in combination with the white buildings among the roving hills made a scenic vista.

"Are you finished soon? Regina wants you to come for lunch, and I would love to spend some time with you."

"Yes, I can leave now with you. Let us take the long way along the river if we have time?"

*****

Kosa was at his window watching Romdev and Kareae climb down from the roof of the temple. I am the King, but they are the real kings, he reflected. Funny, I am not envious; I only feel gratitude there is a higher intelligence present to guide us. I feel so limited in what I can do. Yes, I can be a great King of the land, but the spiritual kingdom is the real frontier. Having more money or power or wealth seems so small compared to what can be obtained through increasing my awareness. He turned around again to face Torent and Korpa, and was hit with a wave of love and appreciation towards them. I am so lucky to have such a great advisor and a son that is able, capable and ready to take over my responsibilities.

Korpa was talking about the final arrangements for the opening of the aqueduct but stopped when he noticed Kosa seemed so far away. The silence brought Kosa back out of his thoughts. "Excuse me, what were you saying?"

"My King, I said that tomorrow the caravan to the opening is scheduled to leave as the sun rises."

"Oh yes, we will be ready. Torent, Sabna and you will travel with us in my carriage. Torent, why not come to dinner and have Sabna spend the night here in the palace?"

"Yes Father, that is a good idea. I will leave now to inform Sabna of the change of plans."

Torent took his leave deciding to walk along the river where he met Romdev and Kareae. They sat on a bench close to the shoreline in silence but actually were in the process of opening their minds to each other. After greetings Torent asked, "Are either of you coming to the opening?"

"No, we are not planning to," Kareae replied for the both of them, "but please Torent, if you have time, tell us about your adventure to Sol."

"Oh, yes, it was quite an journey. I arrived in Sol none too soon. As you said, there were loud elements wanting to invade Rai to take over the water supply.

"They had a foolish plan to transport the water by wagon that even the King was not convinced of. I easily persuaded the King to hold off until I could study their water situation. And it was as I expected, they were wasting most of the water irrigating their fields in the old ways, by unnecessarily flooding the fields to water the crops. I organized and sometimes conducted courses to teach key people how to irrigate in the new way. We offered interest free loans to help the farmers install the new piping systems but mainly the King subsidized most of the expenses saying it was cheaper than going to war. The Solans always were jealous of our wealth and there were some ancient feuds between us, but now I think we begin a new era between the two kingdoms. With these new techniques, Sol's farming production and wealth will increase tremendously.

"The water aqueduct is almost complete. I had the engineers come from Mi to examine the site and see the requirements. Fortunately, there is wind in this area almost every day. They modified their steam engines to also work as a water pump. It's an incredible engine. The littlest of water pressure begins turning the pump, which goes back on itself to generate more power to keep the pumps moving. Initially the water flows with solar power when there is no wind. The pipes carrying the water have special valves inside that allow upward flow but not downwards. We discovered with our models that it was best to pump the water a short distance upwards to a holding tank. Then the water from the holding tank is pumped to the next tank and so forth until it reaches the top of the ghats.

"Considering the sheer vertical drop of the ghats, this was not a simple feat. Without your design Romdev, I don't think we would have been able to construct it. I didn't see the complexity and the genius of it until we were actually building because it seemed so simple at first.

"Yes, excellent, that all went so smoothly." Romdev said

"Torent why not come now and join us for lunch?" Kareae asked.

Torent was taken back by their presence and experienced a movement of energy inside when Kareae looked directly at him. After a moment he regained himself and answered, "I must go home and arrange travel plans with Sabna but..."

"Please come and bring Sabna. We would love to see the both of you."

"Yes, okay then, let's say in one hour.

"Yes, till then."

*****

It was after lunch. They were sitting on the terrace enjoying the afternoon serenity. Neelu joined them already showing the first signs of pregnancy.

Kareae casually mentioned to Torent, "You know, in

the future, having a meeting with you will not be so easy."

Torent looked at Kareae, "What do you mean?"

"Well, one day you will become the King of Rai"

"Yes, but not for some time, my father is still young and very healthy. He has many years before him."

"Yes, that's correct, but it's good to meet the leaders of Sol with that knowledge.

All of a sudden there was a gasp from Sabna. "By Rai, that means I will eventually be Queen!"

Kareae exclaimed, "Yes, finally I can tell you. Welcome to your destiny I saw on the day we met. Do not worry, Princess Sabna, you will be a fine Queen, and you are perfect for the role."

Torent took Sabna in his arms and lovingly said, "My Queen." He bowed to her in the formal way. Everyone laughed.

"What a shock, but yes I know I will be a good Queen. So this is what you saw in me. It's a good thing you did not tell me before. Now I understand your wisdom. Ah, we must go. I need to take different clothes now that I am the future Queen."

Later that evening all was well and quiet at Kareae's house with all the wheels in motions.

*****

The opening of Neelu's clinic occurred without too much fanfare. Only a small ceremony was conducted with close friends and associates to dedicate "Marcin Clinic" in honor of her old friend that succumbed to his disabilities.

Since the opening day, Marcin Clinic has been busy. Even Neelu was not aware how many were suffering from physical and psychological disabilities. More than half of her clients came from the surrounding kingdoms of Mi, Sol and Fa. Inside Rai, there was one particularly distressed area in the northwest that was known to have unusual high amount of natural mercury in the water. Many from that area were showing up with mental disabilities. Neelu was able to help in the majority of cases with use of herbs that absorbed the mercury from the blood and tissues. The results were quite dramatic.

Very often, the clinic just provided a place for those with permanent disabilities to come and socialize with others and perhaps have ongoing physical therapy.

There was never a charge to anyone that came to the clinic. The vast fortunes of Janan family in addition to the many donations more than covered any expenses.

Within only a few months, Neelu was thinking they needed to expand the clinic already working towards its capacity.

Within this Neelu was calm. She spent as much time as she could at the clinic but still allowed herself free time to enjoy and be with Kareae. Since she met Kareae, she had so much energy that only a few hours of sleep was required. This did not prevent her from lying together with Kareae for longer time.

*****

One morning I left early before anyone else rose. I walked east along the river to a more isolated area. Even at this hour, ships could be seen traversing the river. In the distance I spotted a man sitting by a huge tree close to the river's edge. Ah, I thought, this is the man I'm seeking. As I came closer, it was obvious the man was upset and tense even though he was sitting in a meditation posture with eyes closed.

"Excuse me sir," I called several times. When the man finally opened his eyes I said, "I could not help but notice you sitting here. May I ask what is your purpose?"

The man looked at me with sad but desperate eyes and said, "I've been sitting here for the last ten days with only water and a small amount of food. I made a vow that if I don't achieve inner peace, if I don't find Truth within ten days, I would jump into the river and drown myself. Today is the eleventh day, and I am desperate for nothing has happened. I was just planning to get up and go to the river when you arrived."

"Yes, I see you are disturbed, but you must honor your vow. Can I help you to the river?"

"Thank you," he said even though surprised I was not trying to convince him otherwise. "You give me the courage to make the first step."

He rose with my help and we went to the bank of the river. The river was running quite fast and looked dangerous. The man hesitated, but I held him steady. We entered the river together, and soon we were up to our necks.

"I will let go of you now, and the force of the river will take you. Are you ready?"

"Yes, I am ready."

Just as I let go of him, I looked into his eyes and could sense that he was experiencing himself becoming detached from his body. He watched as I let go and watched as his body floated down the river very relaxed and without a concern whether he drowned or not. Often his head submerged under the water. At a sharp bend in the river, coming closer to the bank, he watched his body turn over and swim to the shore.

When I caught up with him, he was smiling and relaxed. I helped him off the bank, and we sat under another tree. The man looked at me with great wonder. "You did something to me, didn't you? You were the answer to my prayers. I have experienced the truth of myself when I let go of living and surrendered to death. Who are you and how did you find me?"

"My name is Kareae. Last night I heard your quest. Don't ask me how I can hear, I just do. Please come with me now to my house for a meal and refreshment. Then I want you to sit in my temple to deepen your experience."

"My name is Ji; I live not so far from here, but I will gladly come with you. In fact, I am indebted to you for your help and I'm ready to serve you."

"Let us discuss later how you may be of service. I think you can stand now; please try, I will help."

Ji rose on his own power albeit a little weak, and slowly they made their way back to my house.

Regina was at the door to receive us even saying his name, which surprised him.

"How do you know my name?" he questioned.

Regina grinned saying, "My dear boy, there are many things we know that would surprise you. I have a feeling you will be learning some of our tricks. But right now, please join us for lunch and then rest. In the afternoon, we will bring you to the temple."

I embraced Neelu and introduced her to Ji, who seemed to go into even more of a shock seeing her than dying in the river. Everyone was surprised until Ji said,

"You will not believe this, but your face was in my dreams some days ago. I was wondering where such an angel could exist, and here you are. What a miracle!"

Neelu bowed her head and gave Ji a kiss on the cheek. "Welcome Ji, we have been waiting for you."

*****

The opening of the aqueduct was a grand success. The spirit of cooperation between the two kingdoms had never been so high. Torent was especially admired for his organizational skills and the regal bearing of his person. Sabna, by his side, played the perfect fiancé. Kosa returned to Rai in very high spirits and declared a special holiday to commemorate this special event.

The King in the last moment before their appointment decided to meet with Romdev at the temple site. After formal greetings, Romdev gave Kosa a tour of the temple. At this stage, the shells of the buildings were in place and most of the work was focused now on the interior such as laying the marble floors and walls. Romdev estimated the temple would be completely ready in about six to nine months depending on the delivery of materials. Thor Shipping was working to capacity to bring the needed materials.

The King said, "It is so amazing there is already such a vibration and the temple isn't even complete. I am very impressed. It's beyond even my great expectations of you, Romdev.

Romdev bowed his head.

In the office sitting area, the King with Korpa sat with Romdev obviously waiting for Romdev to begin.

"Now," Romdev said, "I want to discuss with you the

reason I asked for an appointment."

"Yes, what is it? I am very curious."

"Both Kareae and myself feel it is time for you make your first retreat to the forest. We have made arrangements for you to stay three-months with Siktu at the forest temple. Whenever you can organize your affairs, she will be ready for you."

The relaxation and relief on the King's face could not be mistaken. For some moments the King didn't speak but then nodding said, "Yes, it is time." After another moment of reflection he said, "My son and Korpa, my beloved and trusted advisor, can run the kingdom while I'm gone. I have full trust in them. I guess my only concern is Anu; I don't think we have ever been apart that long. I wonder how she will react to my leaving?"

"It will be difficult at first for Anu, but we will help. See if you can get her interested in taking a more active role as Queen."

"Yes, that is a good suggestion." Then reflecting again, he stood saying, "I must immediately go and see her; I have not been paying enough attention to her lately."

Romdev stood as the King did. "When you are ready to travel, please inform me. I plan to travel with you to the forest. But let me warn you, once you are at the temple you are no longer a King, and will have to follow the same rules as everyone else. Perhaps you will long to be King again?"

Kosa allowed that to sink in but then said, "I am ready to take that risk my friend and teacher."

"Good, I am happy with your answer."

*****

Anu was in the garden with two maiden charges when Kosa arrived unexpectedly.

"My King, what brings you here this time of day?" She asked but noticed something had transpired in his face.

"Let us walk and I will tell you," Kosa said, aware of the two maidens. When they were out of earshot he began. "I wanted to come immediately and tell you the news. I just had a meeting with Romdev. He suggested the time is ripe for me to make the retreat I've been always longing for. I thought about it and agreed. Lately, I've hardly been able to keep my mind at work."

"My only concern is for you, my dear. Will you be okay without me for three months? We have never been apart that long."

"I don't know what to say Kosa. Of course it is shocking, although I always knew it would happen one day. My husband, if this brings inner peace for you, I welcome you to go. Of course I will miss you." Tears came and over-flooded when Kosa took her into his arms.

"Don't worry, my dear, our spirits will always be together."

"Yes, I know," she said, wiping her tears away. "I didn't realize I was so attached to you."

Before dinner that night, everyone agreed that Kosa would leave in one moon to the forest. This assured he would return well before the opening of the temple.

*****

Torent was so busy preparing to run the kingdom that Sabna rarely had a chance to spend time with him. Finally being quite emphatic, Sabna convinced Torent to spend a few days at Zolade's estate with Kareae and Neelu. In the end, Torent was glad to take a break before the King left.

The ride to Zolade's estate in the winter air was invigorating. With the sun shining, it was still warm enough to be without a coat. They stopped frequently to admire a beautiful area, take in the sun's rays or have a brief stroll. Finally they arrived at Sabna's cousin's house for the night and to pick up Tia.

They reached Zolade's estate in the early daylight.

Kareae and Tia played most of the morning together by the barn watching all the different animals and feeding the ducks. Her ego has yet to return. I must meet with her parents again, he thought, they are doing such a fine job with her.

With a crisp and clear winter sky, Zolade suggested a ride in the forest and everyone except Neelu saddled up and took off. Neelu was contented to take short walks around the estate with Tia who began to become attached to her.

The riders returned famished. Amidst a great amount of noise and gaiety, a great feast was prepared. Zolade was in especially good cheer preparing a salad with his new girlfriend, Floru, unable to stay away from her for very long.

Later that day, they all piled into wagons to visit Kareae and Neelu's new land.

"This is a fine piece of land Kareae." Zolade commented. "The soil is rich for growing and grazing and there are many perfect areas just right for building. I've always had my eye on this land. There are some very interesting varieties of trees that I have not seen in other areas."

"Hmm, Now that I am here, I see us building and living here for the first time. It will become the estate and home especially for my children." Kareae said.

Chapter 35

THE WHEELS CONTINUE

TO SPIN

The winters in Rai rarely reached freezing temperatures. Snow was almost never experienced except for the few that made the long and hazardous journey to the northern kingdoms.

Romdev and Kareae were enjoying a steam bath after spending all day at the temple construction site. Work in the crisp cool dry weather proceeded quickly. Romdev was now setting his sights on opening the temple sometime in the summer after the birth of Neelu and Kareae's child.

In his mind Kareae said to Romdev, "I'm thinking about my first meeting with King Kosa and his concern about certain influential and powerful men."

"Yes, I remember. He was apprehensive of their

continued self interests and asked you if you could do something about it."

"That's right. I'm feeling now would be a good time to initiate a plan before the birth and opening of the temple. What do you say?"

"Yes, of course. Afterwards, they will be able contribute and participate with the empowerment.

"Have you any ideas how we should proceed?" Kareae said.

"Hmm. Who are these men and what do they have in common?"

"There are a total of four men in question. One of them I met on my journey to Rai. His name is Arjin from the south central. The others are Breen from the northwest, Warsea from the central west and Mogai from the northeast. All are large landholders and the heads of their local area even if they are not actually public officials. What they have in common is their power and their greed for more."

"I have an idea," Romdev flashed. "Let's have Janan arrange a meeting with them on the pretense of an investment of some kind. When they are all together, we can work on them."

"Excellent idea; let us go to Thor Shipping after we bathe."

*****

In the evening light, Rai shined with an enchanting glow. The sun, golden red, danced with the horizon safely behind the scattered clouds gave a spectrum of colors that impelled any person to stop and take a moment to marvel at its beauty.

Janan was pleasantly surprised to see Romdev and Kareae standing on the quay watching the Signa moving so quietly and lazily

He came out to welcome them saying, "Ah, the beautiful Signa, she is dreaming about the spring rains to dance again."

Both men smiled in amusement.

"By Rai, it is good to see you both again. Please come in and tell me the reason you are here, I feel you both have some mischief up your sleeves."

"Well, my astute friend, I didn't know you could read minds." Romdev chuckled. "But you are right, we are here for a purpose and we do want to include you in some little mischief we are proposing to do."

Once inside Kareae continued, "At the King's request, we want to encourage certain gentlemen to be more generous and would like your help. Are you available?"

"Of course, no need to ask. Who are they?

When Janan heard the story in more detail and found out who they were, his eyes went wide and said, "Oh, these are powerful men alright and they are not so readily available. I can tell you they are more interested in their coffers than in helping others. But of these men, Arjin I do not know."

"I know him", Kareae said. "He is the son of Jacki who you might have heard of. I was surprised to see his name on the list. I met him on the road with his sister and father going to the annual spring full moon empowerment festival. Actually I joined them for several days, traveling and attending the celebration. His sister is delightful, a pure being, one of the first I met on my travels to Rai."

"Yes, I know Jacki, a decent man, really," Janan replied reflectively. "All these men are powerful and a major force in their communities. It will not be easy to bring them all together at once; we need a really good excuse to get them here.

Ah, I've got it. Next month I will receive a delivery of a new type of ship. I can have an inaugural ceremony and invite them with an investment offer to have more of these ships built. This possibly might be enough of an enticement for them to come. I was anyhow planning some sort of ceremony."

"Brilliant," Romdev said standing to look out at the ships. "I knew you could help us. I want to have these men ready for the temple opening. Then afterwards, they can empower their own communities."

"Yes, we are close to the threshold of people needed for the final step, our work at this level is almost complete," Kareae said.

"Good, I will compose a letter tonight and send to these men plus a few others. Leave all the arrangements to me. Now, why not come for an evening meal? We would love to have you."

They readily agreed, and the three of them came together in a Raian embrace before leaving in deep brotherly love.

*****

The news of Kosa's leaving was unsetting at first, but after some days Anu accepted it. Now as the time approached, she was even looking forward for him to depart. I want him to fulfill this longing, she thought.

On the morning of the departure, Anu was together

with Kosa in their private quarters preparing to leave with Romdev after breakfast. The previous night they had a major discussion again expressing their hopes and fears but both went to bed feeling even more resolved about his decision.

Watching her husband, Anu felt only love for him. All the expectations and judgments were simply gone. For this reason alone, she thought, it is good he is leaving.

A knock on the door and Torent entered with Sabna. They sat on the terrace overlooking the palace garden for breakfast. Everyone was talking at once, excited about Kosa's imminent departure. The King joked, "Ah, my final breakfast. Afterwards it will be only bread and water." A little while later, Korpa joined them. After an Raian embrace Kosa said, "By Rai, It is so good to be here with my family and great friend. Torent, I've said this many times before but I trust you completely in any decision you make, and I'm sure Korpa will be there to guide you if he can get away from all his socializing." Everyone laughed and Korpa blushed a little and bowed his head. Kosa turned to Sabna, "Don't make yourself scarce around the palace."

"Yes" Anu added, "I would love to see you more often and I can show you some our customs."

"I am honored my Queen. I am always at your service in any way I can." Sabna bowed.

"Well, my future daughter in law let us not be so serious but friends."

"Very well," Sabna replied in relief, "I then most heartily look forward to visiting you soon."

An attendant came to announce Romdev's arrival.

The King instructed the attendant to have him come in. Romdev entered all set in his traveling clothes. After formal bows, Kosa invited him to breakfast, but Romdev refused politely, saying he had already eaten.

"Kareae and Neelu send their greetings and farewells to you," Romdev said "He asked me to tell you he most likely will come to the forest temple with Neelu for a short break but probably will not speak to you then as you will be in silence."

"Yes," Kosa said, "I understand."

"My King, and it will be the last time I will say that for awhile, the horses are ready and waiting. Once we leave the palace grounds, you are no longer a King but my student, is that clear?"

"Yes, I am ready," Kosa said with a sigh. "I've been waiting for this for a long time."

Everyone stood to go outside. After checking the horses, Kosa made his farewells and they left quietly by a rarely used side gate.

There goes my father, and now I am the acting King, thought Torent. I wonder how it will be?

Korpa, feeling his concern, came over to reassure him. "Don't worry, there is no pressing court business for at least a moon."

"Thanks Korpa, I appreciate your reassurance even though I know this." They had been working so hard to clear the King's agenda.

Sabna took Anu's hand whose eyes were moist. Korpa excused himself and the rest returned to Anu's private chambers.

*****

Kareae was everyday at the temple site supervising during Romdev's absence. The workers could hardly tell a difference between them because they seemed to act exactly in the same manner. Some even mistakenly called him Romdev although they looked completely different. Little did they know of the internal connection between Kareae and Romdev existing as one, their minds so merged even telepathic communication was not required.

Kareae loved to be on the site, sometimes physically working with the crews, getting up a good sweat. The workers all admired the way he moved around like a dancer. They found themselves imitating him without thinking.

A grassy area with a good view to the site became a popular place for the administrative workers to have lunch and take a break. Lately, since Kareae presence, more and more of the female workers were joining in. The completion of each new section or difficult maneuver was now met with applause and cheers. Nothing like this had ever happened in Rai before. Korpa had to organize a special section for the outside visitors wanting to see the building site as the news spread throughout Rai. Everyone who saw the temple was touched and felt reluctant to leave. Some of the office managers complained to Korpa that many of the workers were arriving late after lunch. Korpa just smiled and told them it was okay to allow it.

Romdev returned from the forest beaming. He felt great joy to see the crowds watching the construction.

"What a change in only one moon. The temple isn't even finished and already many are feeling the pull of the uplifting. I wished Kosa could see this, but he is entrenched in a different atmosphere in the moment and not all of it easy."

"Our journey to the forest was exhilarating, the King loved the freedom of traveling anonymously. We both felt very free. The only person that recognized him was Fritaye. I must say that man has a wonderful heart, so perfect to run an inn."

"The King was impressed with the forest temple complex. He felt immediately at home and was able to adjust very easily to the simple lifestyle. Indeed, I felt he relished in it. What I discovered to my surprise was Siktu can be quite a stern teacher. Kosa is learning to be humble. I can understand. Being a King for so long, the arrogance is deeply rooted. Siktu has her work laid out for her."

*****

Spring tiptoed quietly at first into Rai. The weather became more gentle and warmer, the flowers heard the call to blossom again and the songs of the birds could be listened to everywhere. The four of them - Kareae, Neelu, Regina and Romdev - were sitting on Kareae's terrace enjoying the warmth of the morning sun. Neelu's pregnancy was well advanced: her stomach was big, laden with the new life growing inside, now only two moons until she would give birth.

Every morning Kareae laid near Neelu placing his hand on her belly to connect and give strength to the body and soul of the new-to-be child. Since Kareae felt the soul enter the womb, he had been sending the fetus telepathic communications, knowing the child was aware of not only what the mother was experiencing but also of the external environment.

This morning Kareae sensed for the first time the child communicating with him in a simple way. Everyone turned to Neelu when this happened as they all sensed it.

Romdev immediately said, "This is very unusual, even Kareae was not able to communicate before birth."

Neelu smiled, "The baby has been communicating with me for at least a month but I was thinking it was normal."

At that moment Janan unexpectedly arrived and joined the circle around Neelu. The level of communication from the baby increased and they all felt the happiness of the child. They sat in silence union with the child until Neelu rose.

"Janan, please come with us to the palace, we can speak on the way," Romdev whispered once Neelu was away.

On the walk to the temple Janan announced that an investors meeting had been organized and invitations sent. All of the four men accepted and would be attending the meeting. "I offered such good terms it would have been foolish on their part not to attend," Janan confided. "The meeting is now set for two weeks from now at my estate. I don't think they will be able to escape our hospitality. And indeed, building more ships with their money is an excellent idea, which I will follow through with. It will give them all a greater sense of community and service along with greater profits."

"Divea and I were discussing the other night that now that Neelu was living with Kareae, that you, Romdev might like to build a home on the estate or take over one of the guesthouses. We would be more than happy to have you."

"Thank you, my dear friend, it's good to bring this up. As you know I am together with Regina and she is insistent we stay with Kareae and Neelu to serve them. I always have my apartment in the palace, but to tell you the truth, I don't need much. I am happy as it is, but of course when the baby comes more space is needed.

"I like your idea, Janan," Kareae joined in. "We could all move to your estate and keep my house as a center for my practice. Let us see what Neelu says. Eventually we want to build on the land the King gave us but that is still some years from now. When we come next week, we can look over the estate with the eye to create something."

Janan was visibly moved by Kareae's statement. "My son, it would be the fulfillment of our great desires if we all lived together on the estate. I can't tell you how touched I am by this."

Kareae and Romdev stopped and each both put an arm on Janan's shoulder.

"Of course, it so clear we will do this, I don't know why I didn't see it before," Romdev said. "Your estate is so huge, I think just by modifying what's already there will be more than sufficient. I even have plans of improvements in design, which came to me years later."

"Come, Janan, let's move on, I am very excited to show you the temple."

Kareae continued to join Romdev at the building site almost everyday. The temple was becoming more and more magnificent as the marble floors were laid and many other aspects were completed. The walls were a particular elegant mixture of marble and stone overlaid with wood beams interspaced with crystals coming from Kanparu.

The work site was buzzing with enthusiasm when they arrived. Nobody wanted to leave, some even working double shifts just to continue to be at the site. Worker attendance was incredibly high, each one felt the love, beauty and power of being part of the project.

The three spent the morning there together. Janan, seeing how the work force was organized, offered some good suggestions to increase efficiency without increasing effort.

From his window, Torent watched the three men moving about, looking like children happily playing on the sand pile.

"Korpa come, look at the children playing."

He came to the window and started smiling. "Yes, they are like children without a care in the world."

"Hmm, by Rai, enough of this serious King's work. Let's go and have fun." They both ran out to the temple.

Kareae greeted them with great affection. This started a chain reaction with most of the work force coming to see Torent and in a short time everyone was laughing and clapping hands. Torent and Korpa had joined into a lively discussion with some of the workers when Torent raised his hands and yelled out, "We are one! We are the same! We are together!" This precipitated a huge cheer from the workers that brought most of the palace workers and administrators out of their offices to see what was happening.

Kareae and Romdev look at each with an affirming

nod that said, 'See what effect the temple is having, we will watch this with the whole kingdom.'

In a spontaneous gesture, Torent grabbed Korpa and started dancing one of the traditional Raian celebration dances. Kareae and Romdev joined their circle and this started, first the workers, and then all the administrative staff to start dancing with their own circles. As if by magic, someone started singing, whose pure sounds captured the entire gathering into a joyous merging.

To everyone's delight, Torent instructed Korpa to have the palace kitchen bring refreshments and food, adding to the feeling of ease as if being in their own homes. Afterwards, although they had the option to go home, practically everyone in gratitude and love returned to work all with smiles.

On the grassy area Kareae noticed one man not celebrating and saw it was Kalo standing wearing the same cape. He bowed his head and Kareae heard his message inside his head. "Stop this foolish nonsense! Do you think this temple will protect you and your loved ones? Stop before it is too late!'

When Kareae tried to reply he felt his thoughts being blocked. Then he just waved and touched his heart to him.

Kareae returned with Torent to his office for a short visit. Torent had made a few, slight changes to the décor of the office to give it that elegant look similar in Torent's suite.

He shared with Kareae that ever since their meeting in the forest, there existed always a separation between the roles he was playing and him. "I no longer identify with my role. I can be the King fully, and I can let go of it and be me again. No longer am I troubled by this."

"Rai is very fortunate to have Kosa and now you as their leader," Kareae said. "What happened today was facilitated by your openness and this is only the beginning, wait until the opening. By late summer the temple will most definitely be finished. Janan gave us suggestions today that will shorten the completion time almost three months."

"Perhaps I should invite Janan to look at our work organization. I'm sure he can help us be more efficient. I will ask Korpa to contact him."

"Yes, now if you don't mind, I take your leave and join Romdev and Janan; we are headed for the baths. How about if Sabna and yourself come over for a quiet dinner with us, let's say on the quarter moon."

"We will like that, I'm sure. Until then."

When Kareae left, Torent returned to his desk. "Korpa, where are the reports from Sol? I like to go over them."

"I have them here." While Torent was reading Korpa said, "They were having some problems with the pipes bursting from the water pressure, but the pumps have now been adjusted."

Torent reflected, "The real test will come with the spring rains."

Hmm, have them check the foundations of the aqueduct to make sure they are solid and secure. We don't want it collapsing on us. In any case, make a note to inform the engineers to formulate ideas for a back-up system in case of some mishap. Perhaps it would be wise to increase the storage capacity at the top of the ghats? I would like to see a report in one moon if possible."

"Yes, it will be done, my Prince."

"I've been wondering if you have given any thought to suggesting new public projects as your father asked."

"I've thought about that but to tell the truth I've been so busy with Sol and my new responsibilities, not to mention a fiancé that wants love and attention. Actually nothing comes to the top of my head. All the public projects seem to have been taken care of. I mean, we could build some new parks or expand our waterway system. Our school systems and road systems are already marked for expansion and improvement. Why, do you have something in mind, Korpa?"

"Not really sir, other than we need to keep more of our surplus in circulation, not that our economy needs it but more as a safeguard. I guess we could lower some of the taxes without jeopardizing our foundation."

"Now that's a great idea to keep money in circulation. Let me see some figures when you got a chance."

Torent continued, "Still a positive public project would be more beneficial. Raians are well off already, and nobody is complaining about taxes or wealth. Hmm, I will ask Kareae and Romdev if they have any ideas how we can throw our money around. I will see them in a few days for dinner."

Chapter 36

THE PIECES ARE IN PLACE

Janan's A-frame conference hall was located on east side of the estate surrounded by a small tree grove having lovely views to the lake and boathouse. The gardens between were full with distinctively colorful rare flowers like orchids and exotic plants that kept a visitor enthralled for many a hour.

The days were warmer now although the slight increase in the humidity signaled the coming of the seasonal rains. By mid-morning all the invited guests had arrived and were enjoying a buffet brunch served by the lake. The atmosphere here was filled with anticipation and awe of the magnificence of the estate and the power it represented.

After a short introduction Janan thanked the guests for their participation, then gave a brief explanation about the ship. In conclusion he said, "Our first agenda in the afternoon will be a trip to the quays to tour the new boat. Until that time, please free to relax and enjoy our facilities as you like. Let's us meet here again at two pm."

*****

The new vessel was splendidly designed, sleek and aerodynamic, looking very impressive when the expedition arrived. On deck, after a tour of the boat, the captain gave a vivid description of the ship and its functions and threw in a few sailing stories to entertain the investors. The fact that a loaded ship had the same buoyancy of unloaded ship at first seemed almost unbelievable to the listeners until the captain explained the mechanisms involved. All of the investors left soundly convinced of the new ship's merits.

After dinner, the group gathered in the conference hall for the next meeting. Janan answered their intelligent questions and discussed the nuts and bolts of his investment scheme. Romdev and Kareae entered quietly and remained silent, sitting at the back of the hall until they finished late in night.

Kareae approached Arjin, but at first Arjin didn't recognize him. After a few moments his eyes lit up and he said, "Is that you Kareae, the man from the festival? By Rai, you have changed, I hardly recognize you."

"Yes, it's me," Kareae said with a warm smile. "How are you? And Susea and Jacki?"

"Good," but with a frown he said, "Jacki has been having some heart trouble since we returned from the festival, and I've practically taken over all his responsibilities. But life is good, and we are prospering more and more. As far as Susea, well, you can ask her yourself as she is here with me."

"That is marvelous. Perhaps tomorrow we should meet for breakfast?"

"Yes, I'm sure Susea will be very happy to see you. I think actually the real reason she came was to meet you. So Kareae, tell me, are you here for investing? It seems a very good opportunity, but it's a huge investment that would tie up a substantial amount of funds. What do you think?"

"Come Arjin, let us walk towards the lake, it is such a beautiful evening."

In the night air, the chorus of cicadas and a slight warm moist breeze from the east welcomed them.

"Arjin, I am married to Janan's daughter, but in any case I feel it is a very good investment. Janan is one of the most successful businessman, almost as rich as the King. I don't think he would steer you wrong. His desire is to help only the community prosper and not for personal gain. The ships are needed and will help commerce between your rural community and Rai. Of course, the initial expense of creating shipping docks and roads to your villages will be high, but in the long run your community will prosper."

"Yes, I think you're right." He looked at Kareae with some hesitation. "I had some trouble accepting you at first at the festival. Susea was so taken with you, and then if you remember, some of your statements to me were not easy to listen to. I left with resentment towards you. However, during this year, the truth of what you said kept being thrown at me. You were right: I can be selfish, thinking only of my own gain. I saw that clearly when

I took over Jacki's responsibilities and in the course of business brokered a few deals that profited our estate at the expense of the community. And this was on a large scale I must say."

"Yes, I know, even the King was concerned about it."

"Oh really?"

"Yes, it is the King's business to know what is happening in his kingdom especially when it is on such a large scale."

"Kareae," Arjin pleaded, "I have seen the errors of my ways with no small due to Susea. She is such a constant reminder at times I wished she would marry and move away."

Kareae said softly. "My dear Arjin, I see Susea's effect on you, and it is a joy to see your progress. The world is changing and rapidly, so your growth is welcomed since you have such a responsible position in your community. I see just a small amount of fear is still residing inside of you. May I take it away?"

Arjin nodded.

Kareae quickly took his head in both of his hands before Arjin could react. When he covered his ears something like an explosion radiated from his head to his toes that Kareae had to hold Arjin up. Although not big, Arjin was very solidly built, but Kareae held him easily and even helped him to the lake to lie down.

When he was able to sit again Arjin said, "I'm okay, I feel totally normal like nothing has happen."

"Don't worry," Kareae explained, "in time you will understand what transpired. Now please go and rest and allow the healing to penetrate into deeper levels."

Kareae remained silently sitting in the warm glow he always experienced after working on someone. He looked up when he heard footsteps to see Susea coming towards him. Her heart is as pure as Neelu, he thought. They greeted each other as if it was only yesterday when they last met. They sat for a long time until Susea said, "Lovely mentor and friend, it is a joy to behold your presence once more. I've felt throughout this time completely connected with you. I heard you are married, and I would love to meet your wife when it is appropriate."

" Yes, and Neelu will welcome you as I do. Come, we can go meet her."

On the way Kareae added, "I am happy to see the changes in Arjin; you have been doing good work with him."

"Yes, my dear brother is headstrong and thought he was following the right course to increase our wealth and power at the expense of the community. Now he begins to see the community is not separate from him but part of him and him in the community. But I see that you in one action have completed the work with him - no longer is his fear present."

Kareae squeezed her hand, "Susea, I am impressed by your sensitivity."

They found Neelu in the living area sitting with her parents. Neelu was dazzled by the beauty and purity of Susea and the obvious oneness between her and Kareae. After the formal introductions, Neelu and Susea looked at each other directly and then both broke into smiles and embraced in love. Kareae explained to the family, he met Susea on the road and traveled together with her father and her brother Arjin to the full moon festival.

Janan invited Susea and Arjin to stay in one of the guesthouses here on the estate saying, "Please, you are one of the family. I can see you have been touched by Kareae like the rest of us."

Everyone agreed. Divea rose to hug Susea and said, "Your heart is very pure, you are welcome here to stay and live if you like, you are as a daughter."

"You are very kind," she replied. "I take your offer into my heart, and when the time comes I will be most happy to join you here in this most wonderful and exquisite house. It would be heaven to live in such surroundings."

"In any case, my dear, come when you can even for a short visit," Janan said rising. "It will always be a pleasure to have you here. Now I will grab my wife and retire to our sleeping quarters."

Divea laughed as Janan took her hand and lifted her off the divan and whished her away.

"My parents!" Neelu sung out in fun. "They seem to get younger everyday. I can't believe the way my father acts sometimes, it's Kareae's fault I know."

"Yes, I am honored to take all the blame, my lovely wife."

Susea sighed and said, "You are both so fortunate to find each other. I still have not met the right man although I am happy as it is with the work I'm doing at home. I would like to meet someone like Kareae, and I will not settle for less. I can say as well, my unmarried state is the fault of your husband."

"Ah, you have me, and again I'm ready to take full responsibility for the exalted state of your being." Kareae answered.

Kareae took the two of them in an embrace, meeting in the timeless ecstatic awareness of eternity. On an impulse, Susea in her purity asked if she could stay the night with them and the three of them retired to Neelu's sleeping quarters to share the night in love without boundaries.

*****

Janan was explaining in detail the entire concept of increasing the fleet of ships and building ports and roads throughout the entire region of Rai. From first presenting a simple investment in ships, which they all agreed to, Janan led them to the idea of a expanded shipping network throughout the kingdom in such a way, each man was not able to withdraw because first of honor, and second because it was an excellent way to increase their wealth and power. However, when the costs of the project were presented, each one was shocked by the amount of needed expenditure, which would effectively tie up most of their resources. Doubts arose in every man.

Janan called for a break, offering refreshments and food by the lake.

Kareae took his cue by going over to each of the three men, talking to them for a few minutes and then placing his hands on their shoulders as if saying goodbye. Each man was not quite sure what happened but somehow felt different from the brief meeting, somehow lighter, clearer and more available but not able to place it.

Back in the conference room they found themselves enthusiastically supporting the project, committing themselves and their resources. Each one was wondering why it did not seem so simple and clear before as it did now. Their enthusiasm and support convinced the other men also to join and by the end of the conference everyone had pledged their support.

On a stroll to the house together with Romdev later, Janan asked Kareae what he said to convince the men.

"I looked them in the eyes and asked them if they wanted to live without fear. When they answered 'yes,' I took away their fears. After working with Arjin, I saw it was all that was needed. Let's invite the four of them to the baths for a final bonding and give them invitations for the temple opening."

"Gentlemen," Romdev said with approval, "we are coming really to threshold needed for the final empowerment. With these four men dropping their fears and becoming more a pure vehicle for their communities, we will have covered the support needed for most of the kingdom. I cannot tell you how much I appreciate the work the both of you have done. I am very happy on this day."

"And we to you," Janan replied in gratitude.

On the terrace, the men found Regina, Divea, Neelu and Susea looking like visions of divine loveliness and were taken back by the golden light that was emanating from them. They entered into the light disappearing into the beauty and wonderfulness of the feminine spirit.

Dinner was served and the gaiety, love and lightness of non-possessiveness spread higher and higher.

*****

Far late into the night wandering through the temple site, Kareae told Romdev he saw Kalo again, this time by the quay.

"He was strong, able to send me telepathic messages even when I tried to block them. In contrast, he easily blocks anything I send. Is there anything we can do?

"Unless we can change his mind, I'm afraid not. He knows if he can block you then in most likelihood, the empowerment will fail. That's why he's concentrating all his strength on you. We can only continue to fortify our position and hope it can withstand his attack. You must be careful Kareae but how I don't know."

Chapter 37

A TURN OF EVENTS

The night was at its most vulnerable point, darkest just before the dawn when Kareae awoke to the sense of a presence in the room. Aroused by Kareae's movement, Neelu sat up reaching out for Kareae and whispered, "Kareae, what is it?"

However, before Kareae could answer, Kalo, who was standing by the window completely enmeshed in his dark cloak replied, "Neelu, my child, please excuse my unwelcomed incursion but I am here to take your husband away."

In that instant Kareae felt a force pulling and lifting him out of the bed, as if he was a feather, then crashing him against a wall landing in a fetal position. Kareae was completely immobilized, unable to speak. He was not even capable to use his telepathic powers to call for help.

Neelu screamed, instinctively pulling the covers around her while Kalo laughed loudly, "Ah, my pure one, this is so easy. Your beautiful husband, savior of the kingdom, is powerless against me. I will take him and return what is left of him when I am finished."

Romdev and Janan came running when they heard Neelu's screams but were powerless to stop Kalo from leaving with Kareae under his spell. They stood in shock as Kalo disappeared right before their eyes. In Romdev's mind he heard Kalo say, "You fool! Did you think I did not know about your plans? I will take your precious boy and scatter him to the ends of the universe. I warned you but you didn't listen, now you will suffer the consequences."

"Romdev, father what happened?" Neelu cried, her voice and body trembling, "How did this man get into our room and take Kareae without a fight? How is that possible?"

Romdev sat by the edge of the bed, staring at the floor with his head between his hands. He looked up with defeat in his eyes and faced Neelu, "I have failed. I underestimated Kalo's power and put Kareae at great risk. We are like little children playing in the sandbox compared to Kalo. He has mastered inter-dimensional travel and he is able to appear and disappear at will. I have no idea where he has taken Kareae and what he will do with him."

Janan approached Neelu and she rushed into his arms. They sat silently, heavy with the huge sense of loss. Finally Janan asked, "Romdev, what shall we do? Is all hope lost?"

"I must speak with the others but I'm sure we have to continue - there is no choice. I will complete building the temple and the empowerment will go on but I'm afraid that without Kareae we will not be able to achieve the threshold we are after."

"I am sorry Neelu. I discussed the risks with Kareae

only hours before and he was not afraid to take the risk. Come, we must wake the others and tell them what has happened. Let us be strong. I'm sure that's what Kareae would want us to do."

"Yes, you are right." Neelu replied, standing and walking with Romdev and her father out of the room into the night.

*****

Later that morning Romdev received a communication from Kalo, "Your boy or what is left of him is lying under a tree near the Sigma where we met before. Let this be a final warning not to interfere with the transformation of the energy matrix or else I will scatter the rest of you, starting with you, then the high priest and priestess and then all your love ones.

They took Kareae to his house and placed him inside the temple when they found him in a deep coma. No probing or energy influx healing could awaken him even with the help of the entire population of Kanparu.

Romdev organized a vigil so that there would be always someone present but for the first days, mostly everyone stayed present around his bed.

"Oh, my dear lovely one," Neelu said, "at least you are still alive and breathing and look so beautiful. Someday I wish to be held your arms again."

"Yes, the body is alive but nowhere when I probe do I even find a trace of Kareae," Romdev said with great frustration. "What has that rascal done with him?" I shutter to think what our lives will be about once Kalo controls the energy matrix. The funny thing is that we will not even know the difference but as sure as I am standing here we will be his slaves."

Come here Romdev, let me soothe you," Regina said, "all is as it is, we must be ready to accept every consequence. You know that, I don't have to tell you."

While Regina began to massage Romdev's shoulders he said, "Yes, you are right. It's just I've been working so long to create someone like Kareae and raise the consciousness of the Kingdom. But yes, I will accept these consequences and we should go on as joyously with our lives as we can. In my mind though, I can't help but think there is something I can do that I am not seeing."

"Hmm, by Rai, Regina, you certainly have the magic touch."

Chapter 38

THE RETREAT

Kosa quietly returned to Rai with Siktu on the new moon. All their conversations were exhausted on the return journey, leaving only an enveloping rapture between them. Siktu gently parked him inside the same side entrance and departed to Kareae's house when she saw he was safely inside.

The King was a changed man besides his simple robe and shaved head. Layers of personality had been shed like the skin of an onion fostering more purity, quietness and simplicity. Anu was humbled by his presence, not knowing how to react to her husband and King. Kosa's embrace brought soft emotions and tears to her eyes.

"I am still your husband," he whispered, "although I have less baggage."

"My dear husband, I don't know why I cry, but I feel as if I am seeing the real you for the first time."

"Yes, it has been very fruitful time although it was difficult and Siktu was a stern master. Sometimes I had to use all my willpower not to run away. But this story I will save for later. The ride into Rai tonight was a breathtaking and profound experience. I almost couldn't believe I am King of all this. What beauty! What a grand existence! I felt so small beside it and yet for whatever reason, I been chosen to govern and rule this kingdom almost it seems by divine decree, and not by my own choice."

"My dear, let's go to our quarters so I can bathe and put on more suitable clothes. And," as they hugged again, "it has been three months since I've been with you, and I'm longing to lay with you again."

Anu giggled. "My King, I'm happy that your manhood is still intact," she said feeling the hardness under his robe. "Let's go quickly."

In the serenity of their quarters, after a bath and making love, Kosa shared more of his experience.

"I thought I wanted more than anything to go deep within myself, but when the time came to let go of my attachments, I found myself fiercely fighting Siktu and myself. At one stage, I had even a physical encounter with her. She had to use all her powers to subdue me. Thank Rai, Siktu is such a powerful woman. Kosa paused, suddenly aware of his surroundings then said, "Hmm, yes, it is very nice to be back in the luxury of the palace and to be with you again my wife and long time friend and lover." But then the thought came to him, I wonder if Anu is ready to give up the palace life and return with me to the forest? Well, lets wait until I tell her my plans.

Continuing he said, "I think as a last resort Siktu finally placed me in a cave for three days with only a small amount of water and food. I was not allowed to leave. At first, in the complete darkness, I experienced a fear of being enclosed so vast I was totally in panic. I thought I would die. But then, after the raving and ranting, pounding on the door to let me out, I fell to the ground in despair. Finally, I began to hear a voice inside me, at first far away, but then clearer and clearer. Actually I felt it was Siktu's voice telling me to lie fully prone on the floor on my back. She told me to feel the earth and take in regular full breaths on the inhale to draw in the power of the earth. Then, on the exhale, give it to the sky. After some time, I felt the despair and fear leave me. I remained there in a void, but this void had a fullness and completion I never knew before. At that point, I could have stayed forever in the cave. I was surprised when I heard Siktu voice, but this time from outside the door, telling me very soon she will start letting light into the cave and slowly open the entrance to take me out."

"The first tiny rays of light were lightning bolts hitting my eyes. I thought I would never be able to see again. But slowly, I adjusted until finally Siktu opened the cave that night and bought me to my living quarters."

"Those first days were unbelievable, just like being reborn and seeing the world for the first time. Everything was fresh and interesting. By the fifth day, I was almost back to normal, able to perform most tasks but the amazement of each moment continued. Something changed in me that is permanent, I can't even describe it really, but I can say that I am touch with a deep vital force, which grounds me to the roots, to the core of the earth. I went to the edge of utter fear and despair and walked through it. That is the moment I became a real being, a real King for the first time."

Kosa embraced Anu, and for a fleeting moment, Anu felt Kosa's experience.

Rising from bed, attired in a robe, Kosa looked out to the crescent moon with a star nearby. A new moon and a new beginning, he reflected

Anu joined him, wrapped in a sheet. "My dear, what an experience you tell me, my skin has goosebumps and is shivering from your story. But come, let's get dressed and join Torent and Korpa for dinner; they are waiting for us. That is, if you are up for it."

"Yes, of course, I look forward to see them. Is not Sabna with them?"

"We were not sure what space you would be in, but if you like we can call her, she is not far away."

"Yes, I would like very much to see her as well."

Torent and Korpa waited at a little used dinning area with an expansive terrace used more for special guests and occasions. Kosa made a joke about being now a guest of the palace when they arrived. A few minutes later Sabna entered with warm greetings. They sat down to a rather elegant meal the head chef prepared himself. The King was enjoying the food and wine with so such gusto that Torent commented, "Father, I never seen you enjoy your food and drink like this before. Almost you are like a little child."

"Yes Torent, I discovered to enjoy life as a child full of wonder and delight. Give me a little time and I will slowly share my experience in the forest."

The King during the course of the dinner repeated his story to the awe of everyone. Korpa thought, Kosa is finished and will not really return again to be King.

Sabna looked to the King with amazement, noticing how he now looked more like Torent's brother than his father. And Torent, he was feeling warmth and compassion towards him. He saw Kosa had been through the fires of transformation and the price he paid for the return of his innocence. When saying goodnight, Torent embraced his father with love. Kosa responded with the same warmth and they looked into each other eyes in complete agreement. Torent thought, tomorrow I will tell him about Kareae.

*****

Siktu entered Kareae's house to be showered first with flowers from Neelu, Regina, Romdev, and then by dancing around her, laughing with divine merriment. The air was light and the night was bright with festive lanterns. In the temple with Kareae deep in a coma, they surrounded her in a circle with Romdev chanting special incantations. Siktu was overwhelmed with joy and love by this welcome. Afterwards Siktu spent a long time alone with Kareae their heads closely touching.

She returned to the others in the garden to celebrate picnic style with food and drink and in due course Siktu told her story.

"I enjoyed the King's retreat from the beginning to the end. He is an exceptional man. At first, he was reacting like a small child but he was easy to handle even when he made some advances toward me. He thought he was struggling and being difficult but he began shedding his cloak of ego very quickly. He was ready for the cave much sooner than I expected."

"I had my concerns about him the first day in the

cave, I didn't know if he would be able to go through his fears without losing his mind. I used all my telepathic powers to communicate to him. Finally I was able to break through to his mind to give instructions on how to dissipate his fears. Even so, it was a constant vigilance. I didn't sleep for the three days he was in the cave. Olai was there to bring food and drink for me but I did not eat much. With Olai's help, I was able to bring the King out and return him to his quarters. Watching him recover, watching him be like a newborn looking at the wonder of the world for the first time was so precious, I felt such a gratitude to be part of his awakening."

The deepness of Siktu story was felt, each one tasting its richness.

Towards the end of her story, the weather began to change. The temperature dropped, and the wind picked up and began to blow. Looking up, they saw a dark rain cloud coming from the west, an indication the spring rains were finally arriving. Immediately after Siktu finished her story, they quickly rose and ran back into the house just in time. The rain poured all night, but in every Raian house, thanks was given, for the rains had arrived once again.

*****

The month of spring rains created a special atmosphere in Rai with the Signa overflowing and the canals at a brim. The land became very green, and the weather was cool. Many rejoiced in the pleasure to sit before the fires needed to warm their houses. For half a moon, it rained incessantly. In older times, the many floods were troublesome, but with the extensive canal and irrigation systems built by Kosa, this was almost never a problem. The flooding was contained only onto the fields designated for crops.

Nowadays, the Raians used this time to be quiet and spent it in reflection.

In those first hours, when the sun showed his face again after weeks of rains, the local people opened their shutters and joyously rang the ceremonial bells that had been the custom for as long as they could remember.

As the days passed and the rain became less, the Raians took this time to renew their friendships with their families and their friends.

Finally, when the waters of the Signa started to recede and the over flooded fields became manageable; the Raian farmers began planting their summer crops. Many Raians came to help the farmers with the tedious work of sowing the seeds, as machinery was not used. The Signa was always such a good mother, depositing more than enough nutrients and minerals needed for the crops - one of the reasons why Rai was so rich.

On one of these days when the sun was smiling for most of the day, with the rains coming only for a few hours in the evening, after a slow walk along the full and active Signa, that Neelu went to Kareae and said to his sleeping form, "The time is soon, the baby will come any day now."

Chapter 39

BIRTH

There was much discussion about whether to have the birth at home, at the Janan estate or at the Marcin Clinic. All the possibilities had merit, but it was decided finally to make the delivery at home in the guestroom next to the temple close to Kareae.

At this late stage of pregnancy, Neelu could hardly walk, being very heavy with the baby. Feeling the time was imminent, a flurry of activity pursued to prepare the guestroom and the temple. Neelu along with Romdev and Siktu were busy sending pleasant and relaxing thoughts to the soon to be born child, preparing the baby as best they could for the dramatic event about to occur. Ashara and Leila, as well, were sending messages and energy to the baby from Kanparu.

When Neelu's water broke and the labor began, Janan and Divea were summoned, and arrived quickly to the house.

The guestroom was set up with a low standing bed, an area to perform exercises and a small pool of body temperature water to help in the final delivery. Except for a few mats to sit on, everything else had been removed from the room.

Neelu began by performing breathing exercises and had Regina and Siktu put her in different positions to help make it easier for the baby. Sometimes they assisted her to stand or have her squatting or sitting on her knees. When the contractions became more frequent, she laid down.

Finally the head appeared. Again she was held up in a squat position and the contractions seemed to become easier. Lying down again, Regina sat behind her touching her head lightly to help her relax and give her the strength to let go into the pain. More than a few times Neelu screamed.

The baby was a quarter of the way out when Neelu was placed in the warm water pool. For a while nothing happened but then the contractions started again and Neelu was encouraged to push strongly and finally the entire baby came out under the water revealing a girl.

For those taking part in the birth, the moment of birth was like a window opening into divine presence. Almost all had tears of joy and rejoiced in the oneness.

The whole labor took a little over four hours leaving Neelu happy and exhausted. The amazing occurrence was that the baby came out smiling and only began crying after she was taken out of the water to cut and tie umbilical cord. Quickly she was placed into the arms of the mother.

When it was appropriate, Romdev took the baby into the inner sanctum of the temple and performed various prayers and chants, giving Regina and Siktu time to clean and check Neelu for any afterbirth.

All the sensitive people present could already feel the presence and power of the baby. Romdev was the first to declare that today the new woman was born. "It's great the baby will be present at the opening of the temple and perhaps the birth of the new dawn," he declared.

*****

In the days that followed, many came to visit, congratulating Neelu and seeing the baby. The King with Anu, Torent, Sabna and Korpa came with many gifts and blessings for the newborn. Standing before the baby, Kosa asked, "Have you named her yet?"

Neelu replied, "Yes, we have decided to call her Elicea, which means the beauty of the dawn."

The King picked the baby up, lifted her to the sky declaring, "Elicea, the beauty of the dawn, may your life be as full and rich beyond our expectations. May you always know the deepness of soul and may your heart be a generous as your parents." With this, still lifting her to the sky, he turned in the four directions, and then finally kissed her forehead and returned her to Neelu.

Everyone applauded turning the visit into a festive occasion of gaiety.

Kosa said to Romdev before leaving, "Come soon to see me, I have a special announcement to make but I want to speak with you first."

"If is fine for you, I can come tomorrow at your convenience."

"With Torent at the helm, I am quite free. Come mid-morning after breakfast."

"Until then."

*****

The comfortably warm weather and slight soothing winds of early summer brought the Raians out of their houses after the rains, to meander through the green and lush countryside and in the evening to stroll around the canals and riversides. Various small gatherings and celebrations of music and dance were performed in many gardens throughout the city making this time a year a most pleasant one.

Walking around the temple with Janan, inspecting and directing the work, the temple took on now a whole new different perspective for Romdev. No longer did it look like a construction site but had almost a completed look to it. For one, the landscaping of the gardens and fountains was finished and in place, that gave an established look to the grounds. Only a few minor areas were in need of painting or adjustments. Several artists were busy painting murals each drawing a different theme on the nine different sides of the building according to the sketches of Romdev.

"We are ready," a smiling Romdev said after they returned to the open workspace, which overlooked the entire temple and palace. "It is so beautiful I can hardly tear myself away from being here. I will miss the joy of building and being here everyday." But after a few moments, Romdev perked up shaking off the thought and said, "This temple is my heart, and I can never leave it."

Janan silently agreed with him, "It has been so ... exhilarating to assist you in place of Kareae, on this greatest temple of Rai and the world for that matter. I will always cherish this time."

"Thank you Janan. I go now to meet with Kosa, but then afterwards I will send you a message to come and we can start making arrangements for the opening."

*****

Romdev found the King dressed in a simple robe in one of the private gardens attached to the palace, sitting with eyes closed and a newly found look of serene peace. After a while the King opened his eyes to see Romdev smiling, sitting across from him.

"Oh, how long have you been here?" Kosa asked. "I didn't hear you coming."

"Only some minutes my King; I did not want to disturb you, you looked so peaceful."

"Yes," then Kosa slowly said, "with the help of all my dear friends, my search has ended. In that cave, beyond my fears and despair, I found the real self that is eternally complete." Contemplating this for some minutes, the King looked to Romdev. "I asked you to come today because I want to discuss with you my desire to abdicate the throne to Torent. I could continue being King, there would be no problem; indeed I would enjoy it even more than before. My only regret is that Kareae is not here on this auspicious day."

"If Torent weren't so capable, there would be no question of returning. However, I am free, and I choose to pursue other areas in life or just like this morning, sit in contemplation. I plan to move to the lake estate where Kareae and Neelu had their honeymoon so I will not be completely unavailable if needed."

"What do you say to this, Romdev?"

"Kosa, I agree with you totally. I think it is wise not

to return to the forest and live like a recluse, as you have been contemplating. This solution will also be better for Anu; I don't think she would do well as a hermit."

They both laughed at this thought and the King said, "Good, it is settled. Let us go in and meet with Torent and Korpa, and please ask Janan to come as I can sense you want to tell me something. You know your lessons on silent communication has developed this sense in me."

"Ah, my King, you are becoming very sensitive. Then I shall send for Janan, as he is waiting."

After changing his clothes, Kosa and Romdev joined Torent and Korpa at the administrative offices. Torent and Korpa were surprised that Romdev was present with the King especially when Janan joined them a few minutes later.

Torent was about to speak but Kosa raised his hand saying, "My son and Korpa, I asked Janan and Romdev here because of their great wisdom. After discussing with Romdev, the final decision has been made; I will abdicate the throne to you. That is, if you want it?"

Seeing that Torent remained silent, Korpa said, "My King, I have served you and in these last months I've served Torent. I am very confident of his abilities to rule and I wholly support your decision to abdicate. The kingdom will not suffer with your absence. However, we must prepare the people for the transition, so that they remain confident and continue to trust us. I suggest you remain as a figurehead, for let's say one year, during which we can organize a proper crowning ceremony and the people can see in this year how Torent is governing Rai."

"Excellent, I agree. I plan now not to return to the forest as we spoke before but to move to the summer estate by the lake. I will become a country gentleman," he said amusingly. "But what about you Torent, you have been so quiet?"

"Well Father, although we have discussed it, that it is to become a reality sends me into shock. Oh by Rai, can I do this? I do love the job of King, and actually I know I am capable but still... the whole of it coming on my shoulders is daunting. Korpa's suggestion is a relief; thank you, Korpa. And I'm sure, Father, that Anu will be relieved you are not planning to return to the forest. Have you told her yet?"

The King nodded, explaining he spent the previous night discussing it with Anu.

Romdev was silent up to now but cleared his throat and everyone turned to give him attention. "To begin with, in due respect," he said, "the kingdom will not suffer but will benefit greatly from the rule of Torent. Kosa, you are wise to abdicate not only for your own sake but also for the changes that might happen in Rai. It is good a younger man takes over. He will implement many new long-term projects that will need his advice in the years to come."

"Yes, you are right Romdev, that is an aspect I had not considered before. It makes it even more the right action. Thank you, dear sir."

"Ah," Romdev exclaimed, "I have been checking the stars, and there will be a very good configuration in nine months for both the official abdication and the wedding of Torent and Sabna. We can have the marriage a day or so before the coronation of the new King and Queen."

The news of the coming marriage lightened the tone of the conversation, everyone breaking into smiles and easiness. Romdev gave Torent a pat on the back but then said, "I have also some more good news. The temple is very nearly complete. We are ready to send out announcements for the opening of the temple. We have compiled a list of guests we want present in the inner sanctum to inaugurate the temple. As you might know we will be performing an empowerment that I still hope will have very profound effects upon every person in the kingdom, but perhaps not completely the way I envisioned before we lost Kareae. The people on this list are exactly the people we need to achieve the threshold of the empowerment. The other guests will be seated in the outer sanctum and on the grounds. I will want to see the list of guests for the outer sanctum as well, just to make sure, although I am not concerned."

"What date would you like for the opening?" Torent asked.

"There was a choice between having it on the black moon or the full moon in two moons. Finally I decided the full moon. So, the full moon in two moons will be the best time for our empowerment."

"Let me have the list, Romdev, and I will have the invitations printed sent out." "Thank you Korpa. I will bring the list and the text of the invitation over later today."

"Now," Kosa invited, "let's go to the guest terrace for lunch and refreshments. Anu and Sabna will join us. And I think there will be a special celebration meal for us."

Chapter 40

THE UPLIFTING APPROACHES

"I've never seen anything like it," Fritaye declared to an arriving guest in the courtyard. "For weeks, King's Road has been full with caravans and travelers to Rai for the inaugural. We have been working non-stop ever since. Even our campgrounds are full beyond capacity. To tell you the truth, I'm looking forward to close the inn in three days and join the pilgrimage. I would not miss it for the world."

"By Rai, I agree," the guest replied. "In our village, the news seemed to spread faster than the flooding Signa, and I hear the same account from other villages. Almost our entire village is deserted except for those few unable to travel. I feel like a magnet is pulling me to Rai. It's almost as if I have no choice."

"Yes, I hear that from many people and I feel it myself," Fritaye said returning to his reception desk. "Now, my friend, let's see, what we can do for you? Ah, we do have an opening, but your family must share a room with others. I'm sorry, but I cannot offer you private quarters. Is that okay?

"Yes, of course, we are happy for any accommodation you can give us."

"Very good."

Just then Clarae called out from the kitchen, "Fritaye, please come, the delivery wagon is here."

"Yes, in one minute. Now, let me show your room, but then I must run."

*****

At first Korpa was a little skeptical of Romdev's suggestion to organize many large campgrounds to accommodate the pilgrims, but as the influx of wagons and people continued to grow, he was thankful for his foresight.

In his daily briefing to Torent he reported, "Many Raians have been opening their homes, either taking the pilgrims in or allowing them to camp on their grounds. But to be on the safe side, I think we need to organize several more campsites."

"Yes, I agree. More campsites and a few more communal kitchens are necessary. It's incredible isn't it." Torent said, "Everyday the air of anticipation seems to grower stronger. Let's make sure all our faculties and storerooms are open to have food available for everyone who comes."

"I'm concerned about the emergency medical areas? We need at least one in every campsite and let's see if we can get more volunteers at each site."

"Yes," Korpa replied, "there is a long list of people who want to offer their services, I don't think we will have a problem."

"Good," Torent nodded, "I noticed on my morning walk today that most of the pilgrims go directly to the palace grounds when they arrive. Let's have some volunteers direct the new arrivals to the other campgrounds on the outskirts of the city."

"Yes, that's a good idea."

"Korpa, I leave soon to meet with my father and mother. If anything comes up, feel free to use your own judgment."

"Thank you. Then I will not keep you further and take your leave."

*****

Ashara and Leila arrived a week before with almost the entire population of Kanparu and the other auxiliary temples. Only Hanu, the head guard, and a skeleton crew remained to guard the temple grounds.

Janan's estate was full and incredibly busy. Janan organized the feeding and housing for all the monks staying on the estate and for whomever came. The monks themselves were spreading themselves throughout the city, helping wherever they could, even directing traffic.

Interestingly enough, even with all the excitement, Raians were pretty down to earth, taking it in their stride. They all attended the full moon empowerments in the high desert since childhood, and thought this one would be similar.

The evening before the opening a meeting of the inner circle was called at the temple. Romdev gave specific instructions of where each person should sit. Romdev cautioned the group, "We will be entering into the great unknown and anything can happen. So, please look within and decide if you are ready to undergo a permanent change. If you are not ready, please speak up now. We are the main link and if this link breaks, we have no idea what effect this will have; we might all be lost not able to return properly to our bodies. You all know what happened to Kareae, so now is the time to back out if you have concerns for your safety."

"Surrounding us will be the monks of Kanparu. They will be a buffer for the rest of the population. If something goes haywire, they will absorb and protect so that the general population is not affected."

Romdev looked around but no one came forth to withdraw. "Excellent" he smiled, "I didn't think anyone would speak up. Once again I want to warn you that the possibility of something going wrong is high - we are entering into the extreme unknown. I know many of you have already made some of that journey in your own way; so I hope that you will be safe. This time, however, is going to be bigger and we anticipating everyone in Rai will feel its consequences. We made arrangements in the temple's private quarters for everyone to rest afterwards in case you have trouble to stand and walk."

"Please relax for the rest of the evening; eat as usual and let's say we meet here tomorrow two hours before sunset and the rising of the full moon. I want to thank you for your help; I bow my head to all of you."

To Neelu, Siktu, Regina and Kareae's parents Romdev instructed them to meet at Kareae's temple room at mid-morning. "I have something very important to tell you."

*****

The next morning they gathered around Kareae in a circle. He was sleeping peacefully as always. Romdev placed his hands on Kareae's forehead for some moments and then let go and looked around the room directly connecting with every person.

"I must tell you that two weeks ago I met with Rusai." After everyone's amazement quieted down Romdev continued, "Yes, I finally made it to his house after quite an effort. Funny enough, even the same man who helped Kareae cross the sigma before in a boat was mysteriously drawn to return to that part of the river again."

"Rusai and I spoke for a long time. He told me that after deep searching he discovered that Kalo had Kareae trapped inside a black hole, frozen as if stone. His spirit is whole; Kalo did not scatter him as he had threatened. This was very good news because if Kareae was scattered we would not have any hope."

"After conferring with the other keepers, they figured out that they could return Kareae to his body but at best it would be for one day. Then what Kalo does again to Kareae we will be powerless to prevent as before. I want it to be very clear what risk again we are subjecting Kareae. He in all likelihood will never return. I know this is difficult for all of us, but I'm afraid we must go ahead. Is there anyone here who objects to continuing?"

"As his wife and mother of his child, and I think I speak for everyone, we need go on with empowerment or else all is lost. Kareae would not want it to be any other way."

There were nods of agreement from everyone in the room.

"Good, then in fifteen minutes following Rusai's instructions, everyone is to put their hands on Kareae and allow whatever to occur. I'm sorry that I didn't tell anyone before but I had to make sure Kalo would not sniff it out. Even now for the rest of the day, keep your mind as closed as possible.

"Okay now," Romdev declared when the time came.

It began with a glow that became brighter and brighter until Rusai's face appeared. Everyone could hear him say, "Now concentrate and draw the energy into Kareae." Then the glow became even brighter, Rusai's face disappeared and the glow began spinning faster and faster until there was nothing left but white light. At this point there seemed to be an explosion and everyone collapsed.

At first Kareae appeared not to be affected but then after fifteen minutes, a slight movement could be discerned in his fingers and hands. After awhile his face began to twitch and finally Kareae opened his eyes to the relief and joy of everyone.

Kareae looked around in bewilderment. "Why are you all here and why am I lying in the temple?

Neelu jumped in bed with Kareae, "My darling, you have been in a coma for months. Kalo attacked you and imprisoned you in a black hole. I am so happy that you have no memory of this and by the way," with Neelu beaming, "you are the father to a beautiful girl."

"What, is this true? A girl? That's wonderful."

"Hmm, I remember waking up to a presence in the room but then everything is blank. So, what day is it? What about the temple and the empowerment?"

Romdev spoke now. "Kareae, you must get ready, today is the empowerment. Rusai has returned you to your body. We don't know how long it will last and what will happen once Kalo finds out. Please keep your mind closed as tight as you can. You still have the choice to back out. For sure Kalo will attack you again once he knows. What do you say?"

"I am ready as ever. Let us do it."

"Good Kareae, you stay here then and be as quiet as you can, keep your mind completely closed. When the time comes, several monks will bring you to the temple disguised as a monk. We will take no chances of somebody recognizing you and spreading it to the collective. Even at the temple you will sit among the monks to protect and hide you. Only when the empowerment begins will you let your mind become active. At this point you will be again vulnerable to Kalo. Do you understand?"

"Yes"

"Okay, good lets us all rest until then."

Chapter 41

THE TEMPLE OPENING

The sun innocently rose the next day as it usually did during early summer, with a thin layer of clouds that dissipated quickly, allowing the sun to shine uninterrupted. All the normal tasks of the morning, like getting ready for the day, went on as usual. But today there was a sense of change lingering in the horizon, like a flower bud just about to open in the warmth of the spring air. By the afternoon, huge crowds were gathered at the temple with many more arriving by the minute. In some places it was almost impossible to move. Several new sitting areas were quickly organized to accommodate the swelling crowds.

As far as Romdev could estimate, he figured around seventy to eighty percent of the Raian population was present.

Romdev, Neelu, Regina, Siktu, Janan, Divea, Ashara and Leila were in the temple since early morning sitting in silence, generating and gathering energy. When the King with Torent and Sabna arrived in the afternoon, there was a loud cheer from the crowds gathered outside.

They were placed in the second row. Korpa stayed behind to be available for any situations that might arise. He joined right before the start and sat near the monks. In the last section before the monks, were the ones Kareae and Romdev worked on including Zolade, Arjin, Susea and Fritaye.

Just as the sun was setting several monks entered and sat among the other monks. Everyone was quiet, focusing on the temple, feeling the power of oneness.

Softly at first and then louder and louder, a single drum started to beat in a slow syncopated rhythm. With eyes closed, the gathering fell into a deep space of relaxation, aware only of the sound of the drum. Thoughts of the past and future disappeared and then, even the awareness of the present. A slight swaying of bodies began. If someone had opened their eyes, they would be surprised to realize they were hearing the drum inside their heads, coming from an internal source rather than from someone physically sounding a drum.

The rhythm became slightly faster and the vibration rose higher becoming continuous, no longer a beat but one sound penetrating to the core. A sound never heard before. A sound that began to consume any ideas about being separate, or the holding on to any ideas of an 'I am" and ideas of attachment to the body.

A collective consciousness began to exist in an oneness as never before. The sound rose even higher while the new consciousness took hold of every Raian present. In the brain, neuronal circuits were being rearranged and the molecules themselves seemed to be changing. By the time the full moon reached the zenith, the entire metamorphosis was complete. Almost everyone fell into a deep sleep except for some of the inner circle.

*****

Romdev, Ashara and Kareae opened their minds to the universe allowing their consciousness to merge first with each one of the inner circles. When complete, they radiated outward as a single wave first through the monks, then the outer circles and finally to the far outer groups. For those who could stay awake during the metamorphosis, most could not; they felt their own consciousness merging in oneness with the consciousness of others forming a new intelligent entity.

Kalo immediately sensed Kareae's presence and sent all his power to scatter Kareae but he could stop the momentum of the empowerment.

At which point the threshold was reached was difficult to say, but by the next morning everyone in the kingdom of Rai was sitting in the new consciousness - the caterpillar had become the butterfly.

The first and foremost change was the realization of the collective mind. Mind always had existed as a collective mind but now all knew it as they knew they were a man or woman. No longer was there a illusionary belief of a separate individual mind, only the knowledge of oneness.

The result of truly knowing this brought the second result: the conscious knowledge of compassion and love, the glue that held the world together. Every person, although an individual, knew they were part of a greater whole, a greater intelligence and felt and knew this love.

It was similar to the billion of cells comprising the body. Every cell was an individual, had individual intelligence, yet knew it was part of the whole. The cell performed its work in full trust. A muscle cell performed its task knowing that the heart cell was doing its work. The thread was love and a great synchronicity. A heart cell or muscle cell could not go its own way. They had to work together or they could not exist. When a cell forgot who they were, forgot this trust in relation to the whole, it was called cancer.

For the first time, Raians were free; free to be who they are and be free from the prison of separation. Gone were the anguish, the suffering, the greed, the anger and the pride. All just naturally disappeared. Gone was the zombie like behavior of false belief, of sleep walking in a dream state of illusion.

From then on, the Raian society existed as collective consciousness, as one unit, each aware of each other through love, trust and intelligence.

It was simply not possible for a person be able to live in separation, in darkness, thinking only of his own benefit. Every action could only arise from the intelligence of the entire consciousness. What one Raian did was felt by the whole, and was indeed acting for the whole. Compassion, love of the other, was no longer a question or an ideal to be achieved because everyone knew it.

*****

As the butterfly flew from the cocoon, the Raians, once recovered from the metamorphoses, slowly began to return to their homes as the new consciousness. There was no confusion or chaos and not even much discussion. What they did feel was empowered, more intelligent and stronger. They felt different, like seeing from a different viewpoint, as something new had become part of them and something of them had become part of the whole. All in all, it felt good and non-threatening.

It was a welcoming change. Daily life became easier because there was no longer resistance due to the ego saying I am separate. There was no longer any need to fight. If a desire arose, it was the desire of the collective and the collective moved so that that desire would be fulfilled. If a person needed work on his house, for example, the collective would operate in such a way that materials and labor would manifest with the least resistance. It was the collective desire for the building of the temple and it manifested with almost no conflict. Kareae, Romdev and the others were already living with this knowledge.

Anger was never a prevalent issue for Raians, but now there was no reason for any anger to arise because there was no separate will to hurt or be hurt. Desires would not arise if they were not part of the whole. And if a desire did arise then there was the least resistance for that desire to be fulfilled. Nobody got frustrated, hurt and then angry blaming the other because there was no other.

Raians soon learnt they needed to spend less and less time being concerned about the needs of living because of this great synchronicity.

As future evolution progressed, these tasks would become automatic like the digestion of food. In the far future, even the need to remain in the body would disappear, as the Raians became light beings, shedding the ethereal bodies as well.

At first, life seemed to continue as normal in Rai. The sun rose and set and people went about their business. But as the days went by, the Raians became more aware of the changes that happened to them. They found they naturally felt complete within themselves - they felt self contained. No longer did the changes in the external world seem to affect them like they used to, or did it feel as important as it used to. What an incredible freedom this was, not to be a slave to ever changing external world.

When meeting another, there was a sensitivity that was not present before. It manifested as a higher understanding, tolerance and acceptance. No longer was the other someone to exploit or someone to be careful of. Nobody felt threatened; rather there was the intrinsic feeling of working together each knowing that they were part of the same whole. Almost immediately the increase of synchronicity was noticed in every aspect of the community life. A thread was connecting everyone one as never before. As a result of the collective consciousness, communication between people became more silent and more intuitive.

Now for the first time Raians were no longer like robots but were free to utilize their energies to be more creative, to learn new endeavors or to further increase the scope of their awareness. Their interests now were freed for a more vertical growth of their being, and this was never ending.

Kareae and Romdev were giants of men and they

remained giants even after the empowerment. The farmer remained a farmer; the storekeeper was still a storekeeper. This did not change. However, the farmer and the storekeeper were aware that they were part of the collective whole and saw others as part of this whole. This thread of love enabled the society to exist in a real way for the first time.

Raians discovered that ownership, private property and the creation of wealth were not an issue, for the other was not seen as separate. If someone had a desire for land or a house, this desire was part of the collective desire and the collective would help to fulfill that desire. And in love, someone was allowed to have land and property for their needs and enjoyment.

Chapter 42

COLLECTIVE

CONSCIOUSNESS

Korpa, wrapped in a long cloak, joined the empowerment only after safeguarding the palace and making sure all the participants, both the inner and outer groups, were accommodated as best as he could. There was a place allocated for him near the inner circle, just where the monks were sitting.

Walking from the office, it was so silent that Korpa began to wonder if anyone was there. Shortly, he heard the drum, which had a soft hypnotic effect upon him. He felt ready to sit down anywhere, but somehow he made it to his place.

The masses of people were already swaying together when he sat down. The sound of the drum didn't become louder but began to fill his head more and more until there was nothing else. It was as if the drumbeat became the heartbeat of all and all became one. He lost all sense of his body and felt like he was whirling on a cosmic wave being moved into unknown and undiscovered feelings and sensations. Through out this, it was not the normal Korpa that was aware of what was happening. On and on it went until at last Korpa let go of being Korpa, of being alive, and then of just being. There was no longer any reason to hold on to any form of identity. The dissolution into oneness was so exhilarating, in such a way, not to be understood with the normal perceptions of the normal mind. At this stage, the threshold had been passed and the wave had enough power to transform all. Not even Kareae could say what occurred during this time. The result though, was obvious: the change from a collective unconsciousness to a collective consciousness.

*****

As the sun began to pry open the dawn, Korpa was one of the first to wake and behold the masses of people still in deep sleep.

Korpa had the sense of traveling light years away, but now he felt almost normal returning to the body and functioning again. When he stood, though, a wave of bliss softly entered him and parked itself permanently. A knowingness of completion was only way he could describe it.

Among the inner circle, Regina was the only one to wake so far. She watched over the rest of the circle. When Korpa arrived, they embraced in love with hardly a touch.

Regina said, "Kareae is asleep again as well as Ashara and Romdev We will have to make arrangements to move them. The others, as far I can sense, will wake shortly within the hour."

Slowly the masses of people began to wake and experience their new awareness and knowingness. Intuitively, with the new synchronicity operating, they all sensed to rise quietly and return home to rest. Many of those not from Rai, gathered in small groups to silently spend the day. Nobody felt like talking much.

One by one the rest of the inner circle woke up to the new world. When they all were awake, they ceremoniously carried Kareae, Ashara and Romdev to the private quarters of the temple. The women stayed with the men while Korpa left to make sure the King and his party were securely back in the palace. Anu, who remained in the private quarters of the palace during the ceremony, was helpful to assist with Kosa, who still had not quite come fully out of it.

By the evening, it became widely known that the men had not awakened and might not return. A huge spontaneous assembly gathered within and around the temple to keep vigilance and show their support and love. Each person lit a candle that gave the temple and grounds a magnificent enchanting look. By the second day, the assembly became massive. Everybody in Rai was concerned and present to help the men return to their bodies. On the third day, Ashara and Romdev awoke both smiling. During the time they were not able to wake or to communicate, they were aware of what was happening and the crowds that had gathered outside. A loud cheer could be heard when the news of their awakening became known. Another three days passed, when Kareae in the middle of the night, stirred and opened his eyes. The first persons he saw were Neelu and Siktu sitting beside him. Kareae was still very weak and after a short time fell asleep again. But everyone was relieved that he had returned. Romdev explained later, "Kareae's consciousness was the most instrumental in dispersing within the collective. That he is returning after the coma is not a good sign. It means this time Kalo did scatter him. Even after he recovers he might not be the same. We will have to see how well he does; it might take some time."

The news of Kareae's return spread quickly, but still there was concern for his weakened condition. In a few days, he was strong enough to be taken to the Janan's estate to recuperate. There, he had the freedom to walk in private and sit by the lake.

Janan was taking a long time to recover as well. He awoke along with others but had not regained his full power.

Janan and Kareae spent long hours together sitting at different places but hardly talking. Janan was more present than Kareae, who remained distant with quite a faraway look in his eyes.

For the women, the metamorphous was a smooth process, perhaps because women were more suitable to give birth; it was hard to say.

Romdev and Ashara recovered more quickly. However, they felt the need to rest and be quiet as well.

Romdev spoke to the others, "I don't think Kareae will be able to return unless Karo directly releases him. This doesn't mean I will not try everything in my power to help him."

"I've been probing his mind, staying in constant

contact with his life force; this is helping him to stay somewhat in the body. We just have to wait and see how and if he progresses. The black moon in seven days will be the best time to perform a healing circle."

"Yes, we must do everything we can." Neelu said. When I placed my hands on him, I realized that now he was scattered and it wasn't temporary. I will not give up hope. At least his body is still alive and part of him is here even if it's a very small part."

Neelu noticed Romdev's pale face and saw he was struggling as well to recover.

"Come here you big man, let me give you a hug." Surprisingly she was able to pull him easily to her. Regina was close by and came to join, embracing Romdev.

Tears came to Romdev eyes, "Thank you both; your love could tame a lion." Then, almost as after thought he shared, "Let us not fret about Kareae and Janan. We will do what we can, but it is as it is. Again I say that they would not want us to be too worried about them. They acted in love, in surrender to something greater. I would regret not seeing Kareae again, but if he doesn't return at least I know he surrendered fully to his fate."

His statement visibly relieved Neelu, "Yes, you are right. How could it be any other way?. But...I do pray for their return."

Still in Romdev's arms, Regina gently touched Neelu with a knowing sympathy. "Stay with Kareae and Janan giving loving care, and they will return."

Neelu looked at them with a yes in her eyes and left.

*****

The majority of monks left almost immediately to

Kanparu. The consensus was that the recovery from the empowerment and further exploration into consciousness would be more easily facilitated at Kanparu. Only a few monks too deeply affected remained behind to recover. Janan's estate took on the appearance of a monastery, very quiet with monks in different areas sitting for hours in meditation.

Ashara and Leila, after their recovery, spent as much time as they could either sitting with Kareae or opening their minds in the temple in an attempt to bring him back. Not being successful, and after a discussion with Romdev, they decided to return to Kanparu, their beloved temple and school.

"Perhaps with the aid of all the monks, we can affect something from there," Ashara was saying to Romdev with some concern."

"I don't think it is in our hands," Romdev reflected, "if he didn't return from our healing circle, I feel it is not in our control. Kalo has him again locked in his grip and this time he scattered him."

"Maybe it is so. I want to look over all the files my father had on Kalo. Perhaps something will be revealed."

"Hmm, good idea."

"When are you planning to leave?"

"In a few days. We want to meet with the high priest here and then with Torent and Kosa. We don't plan to go straight back but will make a tour of the other temples. If there is any change with Kareae, please inform us immediately."

"Of course. You will know as I know."

Ashara remarked in the next days that passing the

threshold was not the end but just the beginning of many new areas of exploration into consciousness. Many new possibilities only now will become known. "We are excited to return to Kanparu to initiate new experiments."

*****

As the months flowed on, the effect of the empowerment became more apparent. The milieu of love, of trust, undiluted by the friction of separation, became the daily normal atmosphere. Everyone was swimming in it. Rai was an inspiring place to live, but now it had taken a quantum leap and existed on a different plane. From the outside all seemed the same. People were living, working, having children and dying. But now there was an inner contentment, an inner knowing of belonging. This made the outer worldly activities inconsequential to the immensity of their inner contentment. At first a visitor would think Rai was like everywhere else, until they interacted with the Raians or even just stayed for a day or so. They experienced that everyone was happy in a deeply grateful kind of way. Anyone who came into this new collective consciousness could not help but be infected with oneness. Its permanent effect on them then depended upon their spiritual development.

Thor Shipping underwent a radical reorganization without Janan at the helm. With his blessings, the company became the first collective consciousness enterprise. Janan still received compensation but no longer was there individual ownership. The managing director was chosen by the collective consensus of who best represented the collective will. There was no disagreement once the decision had been made. Everyone working for Thor Shipping accepted the direction of the leadership in trust and love and did their work with the same trust and love. None of the employees were concerned about exploitation nor were the directors worried about the efficiency of the employees or any sort of dishonesty. The reason this worked and past systems did not was because now this organization of commerce was based on love, not on greed, the need for power or the fear of survival.

Arjin became an instrumental force within the organization. He ordered more ships and directed the planning and building of the new shipping ports and roads. Under his direction, the other investors opened up all their funds to him. In addition, after meetings with Torent and Korpa, Torent pledged to match any amount he could raise with public funds. This enabled Thor Shipping to build a much more extensive network of shipping and distribution of goods. And all this occurred in a deep level of synchronicity.

When Jacki passed away, Arjin with Susea relocated to Rai and built a estate near Janan.

*****

Prince Zolade immediately left the temple upon awakening without speaking to anyone. His need to be in nature among the forest and animals was consuming him. He rode his horse for a day and night to return to his estate. Once home sitting at his favorite place near the horse barn, he felt his consciousness go out and become part of the land, the forest, the house and the animals. Only after this was complete could he relax and retire to his room for a much needed rest.

The next day to his amazement, he awoke feeling himself everywhere. He sensed the horses in the paddock, the cows grazing on the meadows and the breeze of the wind through the trees. Inside the house he felt its aliveness.

His days now were of total communion and synchronicity. If he focused on any area, such as his forestlands, he received information and an awareness of their condition. He could sense where in the forest thinning of the trees was needed to prevent disease and fires. The same applied with his animals. If an animal was sick, he would be aware of it and know what to do about it. Animals became easier to work with because he could understand them better and, it seemed that they became more intelligent in knowing how to perform their functions.

Zolade was not positive, but the plants seemed to grow healthier. Milk production definitely was up.

His horses always remained a source of pleasure for Zolade. He loved riding in oneness with them. He was always reminded of the vision of Kareae merged with his horse.

Paradoxically, instead of feeling tied down to his work and farm, Zolade felt free for the first time as worry and uncertainly disappeared. Information in the moment arose to tell Zolade what to do or not to do. Even he could get a good sense of the weather. Zolade pursued his interest in sculpture and still had lots of free time to spend with his girlfriend.

*****

At first Torent didn't notice a change, feeling his

dive into oneness had already happened. It came to him more slowly than Zolade, to encompass the knowledge of the whole kingdom like it was his own body. In the initial stages, any sense of lingering doership dissolved, leaving him an absolute channel for governing. Intuitively, he would know if there was some problem somewhere in the kingdom that needed to be addressed. He didn't have to spend time thinking about it; it would just appear to him. Decisions of state arrived this way as well. When he spoke, he spoke for the entire collective consciousness of Rai, never as a separate individual for a separate individual purpose.

Sabna felt her heart open in a way she could say for the first time. In comparison, her compassion and knowledge of the oneness was just intellectual before. Now she felt it is truly in her heart.

At a governmental summit meeting, after consultation with Kosa, Korpa and other influential persons, it was decided the title of King and the system of government would remain. There was no need to change, and relations with other kingdoms would be easier with the familiar old system.

Kosa publicly announced his retirement from the throne, and it was unanimously declared by the summit council that Torent would be the King. Sabna would become the Queen once they were married. Korpa was elected to be chief minister.

*****

To meet Kosa after the empowerment was like meeting translucent light full of playfulness. After the abdication and crowning of Torent, Kosa and Anu retired to his summer palace. There he lived a full life in love and grace helping and advising those that came to him. More frequently, government officials and private persons from other kingdoms came for advice - so much so that he had to build an additional guesthouse to accommodate the visitors.

Chapter 43

LIMBO

Zolade welcomed Neelu and family at the gate, then jumped onto their wagon and rode with them to the main house.

"Has it been two months since the empowerment?" Zolade commented after warm greetings. "I've hardly left the estate since that time."

Thoughtfully Neelu replied, "Yes, but for us it has been a long two months," referring to Kareae's condition. "I felt that perhaps the open fresh country air would help to invigorate Kareae, he has been so listless ever since. His body is present, he moves and acts but his spirit is only dim reflection of his former self."

Zolade looked with concern at Kareae. He seemed so far away as if in another world.

The wagon stopped by the main house. Zolade jumped down to help them and said, "Please, my home is yours. You are welcome to stay as long as want, even live here if you so desire."

"That is very kind of you, Prince Zolade."

"But come, let us have early lunch, it's all prepared."

"Ah, such a beautiful home, I forgot how homey it is," Neelu said when they were seated.

"Yes, I really love it here," Zolade said with an appreciatively look around.

Later, towards the end of the lunch, when conversation was appropriate Neelu said,

"We performed a healing circle for Kareae with almost everyone from the inner circle, but as you can see, he still has not returned, only a part of him is here. Romdev is not optimistic about his condition. He told me that only Kalo can release him. Kalo, however, can not be found even with all the powers of Kanparu coming together."

"Well," Zolade said, "let's see what some fresh air and some outdoor work and tending the animals will do. I've left instruction for the staff to keep a distance and I asked even my lady friend, Floru not to visit, at least for the first few days."

"Thank you, but please, we would be happy if Floru is around. Please allow her to come when she likes."

"Okay, I will; I do enjoy having her here."

The days passed pleasantly relaxed. Kareae was neither depressed nor unhappy. They even were able to share in oneness sometimes. Several weeks of performing simple tasks like splitting logs and horse riding, made Kareae's physical body more solid and grounded but still, he was far away, only slightly more responsive.

Neelu devoted much of her time taking care of Elicea, who seemed to be a perfect baby. She hardly ever cried and followed the routines that made nursing easier. The secret was Elicea and Neelu had been communicating since she was in the womb. Neelu knew almost instantly her needs. Because of this, Elicea seldom cried for attention or want. Sometimes she was frustrated because her mind was so much more advanced than her body. Neelu often sang to soothe her and sent her thoughts of patience. She relaxed almost instantly whenever Kareae had her in his arms. Indeed, they spent long hours sitting together. This gave her time to do healing work with the animals like she did as a child. She forgot how much she enjoyed working with the animals.

They returned to Rai on a glorious fall day, crisp, clean and clear. Neelu happily surprised everyone with the announcement she was with child again. At dinner with Romdev, Janan and Divea, Romdev said, "Perhaps it is right time to begin building on the land. Maybe working on the construction would be beneficial for Kareae."

"Yes, it is good for his body but after our visit to Zolade's estate, he has not changed. I don't feel very hopeful but lets begin for the day he might return." Neelu said.

"Good, then I will start to work on the designs immediately," Romdev answered.

"Yes, I think it cannot hurt to begin. In any case, we need both estates." Janan said.

"I agree, "Romdev said softly. "I will also draw up additional plans for here. I have not forgotten our original plans."

"Romdev," Janan said thoughtfully, "let's meet at the baths tomorrow and discuss this. Are you free?"

"Yes, in the afternoon is better."

"Okay."

*****

The fall winds from the east seemed their strongest the next afternoon when Janan and Romdev met at the baths. The deteriorating effect of the empowerment on Janan's body was obvious. Everyday he seemed a little weaker. During the course of soaking in the soothing hot waters, Janan said, "Ah, my friend and mentor, I must say my life has been blessed. I have no regrets and to live to see this day makes me very grateful and humble. But this old body was not prepared to handle the intensity of the empowerment. And as everyone can see, I have not much time left. I don't think I will make it to see the birth of my second grandchild. I called you here so we can make the necessary arrangements for when I leave the body. I don't want to burden my family. If you can take charge, I will be greatly relieved and thankful. I don't need anything special to be done for me; I wish my body to be cremated in the normal Raian way. I would like a quiet leaving but I know that many people will come to pay their respects. This is why I want to make sure you will be present, so that all is organized."

Romdev touched Janan gently with his hand, "Please cast aside any worries, I will take care of everything. And I will be there to help you leave the body through the proper channels."

"But tell me," Janan inquired, "is there any help for Kareae?"

Romdev sighed, "I'm afraid not. We tried everything in our power. Recently I heard from Ashara that the entire community of Kanparu participated in an attempt to bring Kareae back and were unsuccessful. Then they used their powers to search for Kalo sending their minds into other dimensions, but were also unsuccessful."

"My dear friend, there is nothing to do but wait and see."

Chapter 44

THE JOURNEY ENDS

Several moons later, on a cold but bright winter day, dressed in winter longcoats and woolen hats, Kareae and Neelu were by the lake with Elicea. Kareae played with the baby, sometimes raising her high up in the air to her giggling delight. Neelu was nearby sitting by the shore, throwing pebbles into the lake reflecting, I have two children now. Kareae is so simple like a child, I have to do everything for him but at least he's still beautiful and I can sleep with him every night.

But look, what a lovely smile he has, she thought when she walked over and took Elicea.

It happened while they were near the boathouse without any warning. Kareae lost his balance, fell to the ground and passed out. He began having mild tremors and then his eyes open wildly with rapid eye movement. After a few minutes he became still.

Neelu gasped at first, but holding the baby she was not free to help him. In her mind and physical voice she called out for help. Luckily Romdev was visiting the ailing Janan and came running after several minutes, along with some of the house helpers. They carried Kareae to

Neelu's old bedroom where he could lie down.

After examining and probing with his mind Romdev declared, "He is in a deep coma again, I can just barely reach him. I have no idea what this means."

Just then his body began having strong tremors, this time propelling him to almost fall off the bed. Romdev had to hold him down. Once more his eyes opened with wild chaotic eye movements. After a few minutes his body went still again.

"My beloved, what is happening to you?" Neelu cried, sitting down on the bed, taking his head into her lap and stroking it.

Divea arrived and sat next to Neelu, putting her arms around her.

Romdev explained the situation. "We must arrange someone to be with him constantly. Regina and Siktu will come soon with Ji and I will contact Susea to help. All we can do is protect him from hurting himself when he has a tremor attack. He is far away and I don't know if he will ever return. Perhaps Kalo has become stronger and can finally pull him totally away."

"My god." Divea murmured.

When Regina and Siktu arrived, Romdev instructed them to take special care of Neelu. "Make sure she gets some rest; her mind is very fragile right now. Between you and me, I think this is the finally blow. Make sure Ji or someone else is in the room with Neelu, she should not be alone with him. I leave now to inform King Torent and Sabna of Kareae's condition. I want them to hear it first hand. If anything occurs just contact me and I will return immediately."

Regina affirmed with a nod and both left to join Neelu.

The next day Kareae was constantly watched. Almost nobody could sleep. Kareae's tremor episodes became less and he appeared to be sleeping peacefully.

On the morning of the third day of the vigilance, Kareae's body suddenly went into a violent spasm that Ji had quite some difficulty to hold him down. Everyone rushed in the room to watch as Kareae's body collapsed and became dead still.

Neelu screamed, "He is not breathing," and broke down sobbing covering her eyes with her hands.

Finally, just when they were taking Neelu out of the room to soothe her, they heard a stirring and turned to see Kareae sitting up in the bed as if he just rose from normal sleep. He stood to everyone's amazement, stretched his body looked around and at his body, then asked, "How long have I been gone?"

Shouts of relief and gasps of glee arose from everyone.

With tears of hope in her eyes, Neelu ran to Kareae embracing him, "My precious, precious man, to see you again leaves me breathless. We all have been so concerned whether you would ever return. You have been gone well over five months. My love, I am already pregnant with our second child."

Kareae separated from her, and sat down on the bed still showing some confusion and disorientation, almost passing out again. But then he shook his head awake and said, "For me it has been an eternity. Only after a long and arduous journey am I able to return and only in last moments was I assured of my success."

Sitting silently with Neelu at his side, Kareae suddenly looked up and exclaimed, "Oh your father, I must go and see him. He is very weak and needs my assistance. Please help me go to him, there is no time to lose."

"Yes, father is on his deathbed, we are expecting him to leave any moment now. I think he has been waiting for you to return."

"Then let us go quickly."

Neelu and the others helped Kareae up but even as they were walking Kareae seemed to be getting stronger with every step. Shortly, they were sitting beside Janan's bed and when Kareae put a hand on his head, Janan opened his eyes with a soft smile. He nodded and whispered, "My son, I've been waiting for you, and now I can leave in peace knowing you are okay."

Kareae smiled for the first time. "Listen, I'm sorry to disappoint you but you still have a few years left." With that he got in the bed with Janan, lying by his side almost on top of him embracing his body. Kareae remained this way until he was satisfied then left Janan sleeping peacefully and looking already more alive and vibrant.

"No way you could go before we share a little more time together my dear man." Then Kareae whispered to Neelu. "Now, I want to eat but before I take my rest, let us all gather and I will tell my story."

"Are you sure you are up to it?" Neelu asked

"Yes, I want to share my journey while it's still clear in my mind. By tomorrow it might be gone. Tell everyone to meet in the garden room in one hour."

"Yes, my darling. I'm so happy you are back."

******

The garden room right off the terrace was a perfect place to sit and enjoy the view to the gardens on cold bright sunny days. Fill with lots of ferns and small palms and elegant cane furniture, it gave the room a tropical atmosphere. Completely enclosed with glass and drapery made it one of the favorite rooms in winter.

Kareae, Romdev, Kareae, Siktu and Ji were already sitting when Kareae entered with Neelu.

"My dear loved ones," Kareae began, "to be sitting here together with you, to look at your faces, was something I could only dream of for a very long time. It's still hard to believe I am back in this young body. Well, I might as well start at the beginning. True to his threats, Kalo was able to block my full return to the body. He scattered the rest of me in another dimension, on another planet and among strange but peaceful people. I was able to look into his mind just as the moment he attacked me. He was angry about not to be able to stop the empowerment and he wanted to scatter me in many fragments, but was only able to succeed in splitting me in two. Most of me landed on this strange planet where people had four arms and used the bottom two arms as legs to run like animals. They were incredibly fast. I was lucky to arrive on a special day when everyone was in the temple performing some sort of ritual ceremony. Indeed, I appeared right in the middle of their altar. Later, I realized it was their prayers that drew me to them, most likely it helped me to stay in one piece. I could not understand their spoken language at first but their minds were quite open so I knew their intent. Slowly I learned their language even though it was difficult to pronounce. I don't how I was able to have a body there but I had one with only two arms. This fact greatly disturbed them as they never seen anyone before like me. It was clear to them that I came from the gods so I was treated in a royal fashion. Considering the situation, I could not have been luckier. I was given the best of everything, becoming close friends with their emperor and advisors as I did here. Yes, there was a woman who took care of me but there was not a physical attraction. You must realize I was untouchable, a god so to speak. Nobody would dare to touch me.

Yes, it was a great life but... my being was split and the yearning to rejoin always pulled on me. I had no idea how to return. I sent my mind out to the universe but Kalo's hold on me prevented me from finding anything.

I searched the world over many years, visiting any healer, magician or person of power that could heal me. I spent over thirty years searching, my hair turning grey and my back starting to ache, when finally I met a man, a man of power that was able to aid me. He actually came to me because I appeared in one of his dreams asking for his help.

On an auspicious night after days of fasting and chanting, he performed a ceremony that didn't put me together but transported me to Rusai."

"By Rai, Rusai you say. That is amazing. Again he comes to our aid." Romdev commented.

"He told me he was not prepared for Kalo's actions. In truth, he thought it was not possible for Kalo to accomplish splitting me. At first he was not able to locate me but finally after a extensive search he found me but didn't know how I could return. He could not break through Kalo's web until he figured out that he might be able to transport me to his dimension, as it is not the earth. Again probing the planet, he found a man of high power, sending him additional power and by entering his dreams he was able to set up the conduit to transport me."

Kareae started to feel weak and sat down and took a hot drink Neelu had ready for him. Looking out at the gardens, he said, "So great to see this again."

Continuing, "And he was successful. I can't tell you the relief I felt to walk through his gate again and see his laughing face. I spent what seemed eons with him and his wife. It was a heavenly realm and if my being wasn't constantly yearning to be whole again, I could have stayed there forever."

"Rusai was not able to break the spell of Kalo even in unison with other creators. It was not that Kalo was that strong just his spell was unbreakable. The only possibility was to find him and to transport me to fight it out if necessary. Finally Rusai, while probing my mind when I had that brief access to his mind, figured out Kalo's simple camouflage that hid him so effectively. Ingenious really the way he did it."

"I am feeling tired so I will skip some of the story and take you to my meeting with Kalo. Rusai was able to transport me and after a long journey through very hostile and arid land, I finally came to his lair."

"He was waiting for me on his terrace and said when I approached, "I was wondering if ever the day would come when you would be standing here. I am the only one that can free you. I see that you don't come in anger and that is why I didn't destroy you leagues before you arrived. Well come in, you might as well refresh yourself before our battle begins."

Kalo's home was actually a huge series of caves set into a cliff. It was a unique spot that had an underground spring running to the surface. All around the caves were gardens growing vegetables and rice; so beautiful in contrast to the beak desert-like surroundings. Inside was quite comfortable and warm with many animal furs and woolen carpets. And on the far wall, there hung a massive relief of the dragon exactly as on the great arch of Kanparu.

"So, you found me after all these years. I failed to prevent the empowerment or prevent you from initiating it. I should be still vengeful but I'm not. It will not change anything. However, I will not give you your freedom easily. You have to take it from me. One thing I will give you is that you are stronger here in this dimension, I cannot easily take you as I did on earth."

We spent the next two days in battle. Not that we physically fought. I sent my mind into his and he would try to block me. Most of the time, he was successful but there were moments I would get through. We were both exhausted by the third morning but I gave it one last chance. I gathered all of myself, opened to Rusai's energy, and took a final plunge into his mind. I was able to break through for a minute and the image of the dragon came strong in my vision. From the surprised look in his eyes, I knew I had found the key."

"I ran to the dragon relief and placed my hands on

it. I could feel the energies moving inside it. My first attempts were clumsy and Kalo kept trying to prevent me. Finally, I took the dragon down and ran out onto the terrace and away from his house. I climbed up the cliff. Funny that Kalo did not attempt to follow me. Once on the top I leaned the dragon against a rock and with my last strength, I kept an image of the dragon of Kanparu, Hanu and the great arch in my mind. I picked up the dragon and hurled myself out over the cliff into space."

"The next moment I knew was waking up in Neelu's bed."

Everyone was speechless, stunned by the story. Nobody moved until Romdev stood and bowed to Kareae and gave him a Raian embrace. Everyone followed and soon Kareae was smothered in the center of the circle.

Finally he said, "Now that my story is told, I can sleep and I need lots of it. Please Neelu take me to your room.

Two days later he awoke with everyone by his side to welcome him.

Romdev had tears in his eyes and was speechless. Siktu immediately embraced him. Susea, Regina, Ji and Divea were also present; each hugged and sent him love. By this time, the whole city of Rai knew of his return and planned a big celebration. They were just waiting for the signal he was awake again. "Kareae do you know there are huge crowds outside on the grounds wanting to get a glimpse of you?"

"Really? Then help me to go to the window."

When Kareae showed his face, the crowds exploded in joy. In the evening, huge fireworks were lit and displayed, continuing for the whole night.

The next day after the crowds left, King Torent, Sabna and Korpa came to express their gratitude. They found Kareae sitting with Elicea in his arms. For a six-month-old baby, her eyes were totally opened wide and she looked as if she was aware of everything. The baby smiled when she saw Torent and he could swear he heard a tiny voice in his head say, "Hello Torent King."

"My dear sir," Kareae said with a big smile, "meet the herald of the new woman who will brings us even to the next level."

www.ingramcontent.com/pod-product-compliance
Lightning Source LLC
Chambersburg PA
CBHW021425240626
47153CB00001B/22